Advan[ce...]
DELIVER[...]

"Readers will have fun with this book. [Luber's] engaging characters are intricately connected, yet they stand distinct and clear like columns throughout the story. . . . A classy writer."
—JANE LANGTON
Author of *The Shortest Day*

"Overriding an intricately woven plot, guaranteed to keep the pages turning, Philip Luber has created richly drawn characters who reveal his intimate knowledge of human behavior. A captivating novel."
—GORDON RYAN
Author of *Dangerous Legacy*

Acclaim for the work of Philip Luber

"Philip Luber is a fine writer with a hell of a future."
—LAWRENCE BLOCK
Author of *A Walk Among the Tombstones*

"Absolutely thrilling."
—MICHAEL PALMER
Author of *Silent Treatment*

"One hope[s] Luber will keep on writing for years to come."
—*Philadelphia Daily News*

By Philip Luber:

DEADLY CONVICTIONS
FORGIVE US OUR SINS*
DELIVER US FROM EVIL*

*Published by Fawcett Books

Books published by The Ballantine Publishing Group
are available at quantity discounts on bulk purchases
for premium, educational, fund-raising, and special
sales use. For details, please call 1-800-733-3000.

DELIVER US FROM EVIL

Philip Luber

FAWCETT GOLD MEDAL • NEW YORK

This book contains an excerpt from the forthcoming paperback edition of *Pray for Us Sinners* by Philip Luber. This excerpt has been set for this edition only and may not reflect the final content of the forthcoming edition.

Sale of this book without a front cover may be unauthorized. If this book is coverless, it may have been reported to the publisher as "unsold or destroyed" and neither the author nor the publisher may have received payment for it.

A Fawcett Crest Book
Published by Ballantine Books
Copyright © 1996 by Philip Luber

Excerpt from *Pray for Us Sinners* copyright © 1997 by Philip Luber.

All rights reserved under International and Pan-American Copyright Conventions. Published in the United States by Ballantine Books, a division of Random House, Inc., New York, and simultaneously in Canada by Random House of Canada Limited, Toronto.

Grateful acknowledgment is made to Let's Have Lunch Music, ASCAP, for permission to reprint an excerpt from the lyrics of "Wandering Moon," written by Pierce Pettis. Copyright © 1988 Let's Have Lunch Music, ASCAP.

http://www.randomhouse.com

Library of Congress Catalog Card Number: 95-96174

ISBN 0-449-14940-4

Manufactured in the United States of America

First Edition: July 1997

10 9 8 7 6 5 4 3 2 1

For Cindy and Holly,
and for my parents,
with eternal and boundless love

I am a father, I am a son
I am no longer the only one
        —PIERCE PETTIS

ACKNOWLEDGMENTS

I am grateful to Paul O'Brien for his comments, suggestions, and friendship.

I thank my friends for their help: Tyler Carpenter, Nancy Connolly, Sara Eddy, Lenny Gibson, Peter Hickey, Marcie Kaplan, Karen Katz, Paul Lavoie, Larry Strasburger, Jonathan Strong, and Gary Taylor.

Once again I thank my editor, Susan Randol, and my agent, Alice Martell.

Special thanks go to Rachel Humphries.

No one who, like me, conjures up the most evil of those half-tamed demons that inhabit the human breast, and seeks to wrestle with them, can expect to come through the struggle unscathed.

—SIGMUND FREUD

1: Hit-and-Run

"He died instantly," said the medical examiner, though he knew he wasn't speaking the truth.

"His suffering was slight," said the police chief, though he knew what he said was false.

They were harmless lies, designed to shield the victim's daughter from needless additional grief.

This was the truth: The deceased crawled and scratched twenty excruciating yards after he was struck by a hit-and-run driver in an unidentified sedan. He spilled body waste and an enormous amount of blood along the way. Death was anything but instant, and his suffering was intense.

As they left the daughter's home after bringing the news of her father's death, the police chief said, "She seem odd to you, Doc?"

"In what way?"

"Not very broken up about it. Just a minor setback, like a run in her stocking."

"Delayed grief reaction," the medical examiner said. "The poor woman is in shock."

"Yeah," said the police chief. "I guess so."

2: Suffer Evil The Natural Way

JANET ROSE KLINE
August 3, 1954–February 4, 1987
Beloved Daughter, Wife, and Mother
"Even though we are apart
You will stay here in my heart"

When your wife lies buried just a mile from your home, you can spend a lot of time walking among tombstones. That's how it was with me for more than a year after Janet died. Once or twice each week I walked past North Bridge and the site of the first pitched battle of the Revolution, into Concord center and over to Sleepy Hollow Cemetery.

Janet's grave was on the side of a low hill, less than a hundred yards from Authors Ridge—the steep rise that holds the graves of Concord's nineteenth-century Transcendentalist masters. There I sat, sometimes for an hour or more, trying to fathom the unfathomable.

I learned to recognize the others by sight, even though we never spoke: the survivors, all of them much older than me, who came regularly for whatever combination of pain and solace such visits can bring. I took particular comfort from the presence of one old woman, gray and bent, who arrived at precisely two in the afternoon every Thursday. She placed a single flower on a fluted tombstone, made the sign of the cross, then slowly walked away. Her constancy

soothed me. I began timing my visits to match hers. Then
one Thursday she failed to show, and then he next, and the
next after that. A short while later I found a freshly dug
grave next to the fluted marker. And soon after that I began
to visit Janet's grave less and less often. Somehow the
death of that old woman I never knew helped me ride out
my grief.

I was down to three visits a year now: I brought my
daughter with me on Mother's Day and Janet's birthday,
and I came alone on our wedding anniversary. And so it
came to pass that I was sitting on a bench near her grave
on a mid-April Tuesday afternoon, six springs after her
death, on what would have been our sixteenth anniversary.

Lost in memories, I didn't notice the young woman approach. She said, "Sir, may I share your bench for a minute? I didn't realize how hilly it is here and I'm very tired."

I hate it when people call me "sir." It's something people
say to my father. I'm not that old, I thought as I moved
over to make room for her.

"Thank you." She leaned back and sighed. A gust of
wind blew a long red curl across her forehead. She brushed
it off and closed her eyes for a moment. "I never knew a
cemetery could be this lovely." She pointed to Authors
Ridge. "I can't believe Thoreau's grave is so simple. Just a
small stone marker with the name Henry."

"I don t think he wanted it to become a tourist attraction," I replied. "He really wasn't very sociable."

"Yes, I know. My mother had a favorite passage from
Walden. 'If I knew for a certainty that a man was coming
to my house with the conscious design of doing me good,
I should run for my life, for fear that I should get some of
his good done to me—' "

" '—some of its virus mingled with my blood,' " I continued. " 'No, in this case I would rather suffer evil the
natural way.' "

She smiled. "You know your Thoreau."

I shrugged. "I've lived in Concord a long time. It comes
with the territory."

She gestured once again toward the ridge. "It seems like half the things in town were named for one of them. Emerson Hospital. Hawthorne Inn. The Alcott School."

"Don't forget the Thoreau Club," I said. "They cut down six acres of trees to make room for swimming pools and tennis courts, then they named it after the godfather of environmental awareness."

"I wonder if they appreciated the irony."

"Probably not," I said, "but Thoreau would have."

She sat quietly for a while, then looked directly at me for several seconds. "I think I know you," she said. "Aren't you Harry Kline?"

Surprised to hear her call me by name, I studied her more closely and tried to place her face. She was no more than thirty, a dozen or more years younger than me. She was uncommonly attractive. Her long red curls were streaked with shades of brown and gold; they were offset by light green eyes and a fading tan. She carried her sweater over her arm, the afternoon having turned unusually warm. Her light cotton blouse revealed enough to be enticing, yet was demure enough to make you think the enticement was all in your own head.

Somehow she knew me. She was waiting to see if I knew her. I didn't, and I found it hard to believe we'd ever met, for I couldn't see myself forgetting her if we had.

"It's me—Marjorie." Again she brushed a dangling curl off of her forehead. I still didn't remember her. "Elizabeth Morris's daughter."

Professor Elizabeth Morris was my favorite teacher when I was an undergraduate at Tufts. I formed a mental image of a freckled tomboy with skinned knees who liked to tag along with me whenever Professor Morris brought her along to the campus. Then I glanced again at the beautiful young woman beside me.

"Marjorie Morris," I said. "If you're this grown up, then I must have gotten old and decrepit without realizing it."

"Not at all, Harry." She smiled. "I think you look wonderful."

I kept in touch with Professor Morris for a few years after I graduated, but I hadn't spoken with her in more than a decade. Now Marjorie told me her mother had passed away a few years earlier. "My parents divorced years ago. My mother went to teach at Florida Atlantic University. She used to call Boca Raton the home of the newly wed and nearly dead."

"That sounds like something she would say. During my junior year I was thinking about switching from prelaw to premed. I really wanted to be a doctor, but something was holding me back. Your mother cut right to the heart of the matter. She said, 'Just because your parents *want* you to become a doctor, that doesn't mean you have to become something else.' "

"And did you become a doctor?"

"I'm a psychiatrist."

"Uh-oh. Maybe I should watch what I say."

It's an occupational hazard for psychiatrists: Some people think we have a magical ability to detect their innermost secrets from just a few words. And so they withdraw as soon as they know what you do for a living, afraid of being found out.

She laughed. "I'm just kidding. God knows I've talked to more than my share of shrinks."

We sat silently for a minute or two. A caretaker's truck rumbled slowly past on the service road. Marjorie asked me why I was visiting the cemetery. I told her about Janet's death.

"Oh my," she said. "What a terrible thing to die so young. How old was she?"

"Thirty-two."

"I'm so sorry, Harry." Marjorie waved toward the newest section of the cemetery. "I came to visit my father's grave. We buried him early last month." She paused for a moment. "Did you know him? His name was Charles Morris."

"I don't think so. The name sounds familiar, though."

"You probably read about his death. He died in a hit-and-run accident while he was jogging near our house."

Something like that was big news in our quiet suburban town. Five or six weeks earlier it was the lead article in the weekly *Concord Journal* and a two-day story in the *Boston Globe*. No one had been charged yet with her father's homicide. I knew that he was a successful Boston attorney. That's all I remembered reading about him in the paper.

Marjorie said, "My father moved to Concord after my mother left him. He had a second wife for a couple of years, very young. Then she left him, too. And then he lived in the house by himself, until I moved back from California last summer."

We talked a little while longer, veering between past and present, catching up haphazardly on the turns our lives had taken in the twenty years since we last saw one another. I'd remained in Massachusetts the entire time, becoming a doctor, husband, father, and widower. Marjorie stayed in California after college. For a few years she tried to make a living as an actress. She did have a small role in one low-budget film, but her acting career ultimately proved to be a bust. She had a failed marriage and various other troubles that she didn't give any details about. And now she lived alone in a luxurious home overlooking the Sudbury River.

"Moving into my father's house was my final admission of defeat. When I was growing up, I told myself that I wanted my life to be different, that I didn't want to be just like everyone else. Unfortunately for me, I got exactly what I wished for." Her voice began to quiver. "I should never have come home. I bring trouble with me wherever I go. I'm not even thirty, and now I'm an orphan."

She sighed deeply, then continued. "My father and I used to run every morning. We always followed the same route. Sometimes we went together, sometimes we went separately. The morning he was struck, I had just come back from running the same roads." Tears welled in her eyes. "My therapist says I have survivor's guilt."

I offered her my hand and she grasped it tightly.

"Do you have children, Harry?"

"A daughter."

"How old is she?"

"Ten. Or as she would say, ten and two thirds."

Marjorie quickly did the simple subtraction. "She was only four when your wife died. Goodness, how sad."

"Yes, it was."

"Did you get married again?"

"No."

"Do you think you ever will?"

"I don't know. I've been seeing somebody for about a year."

"Does she live with you?"

"Not officially."

She smiled. " 'Not officially.' I'll have to check the rule books to see what that means. Is your friend a doctor, too?"

"Veronica? No, she's a lawyer. She works for the FBI in Boston."

"She's an FBI agent?"

"Special agent, actually. Then again, they're all called special agents. I guess sometimes there's nothing so special about being special."

She laughed politely at my weak joke, then stared into the distance at nothing in particular.

Marjorie Morris was a child when I last knew her. In her sadness now, she seemed like a child to me still. I wanted to stay longer, but I had to return home for an appointment in my office with a new patient. I said, "I'm tempted to say I know what you're going through, but how could I really know that? I know what *I* went through, though, after my wife died. And how important it is to have friends to talk to."

She sighed. "My friends are all in California, and I've burned most of those bridges."

I stood. "I need to get back to my office. Promise you'll call me if you need someone to talk to."

"I will, Harry." She stood and held my hand, then touched my fingertips to her face and kissed them. "Thank you. You know, I had a terrible crush on you when I was a little girl." She smiled. "I hope I'm not embarrassing you."

She walked off toward a grove of balsam firs. I returned to my wife's shaded gravesite. I kneeled and said a silent prayer, then headed toward Monument Street and the short walk home.

Michael Cafferty was a student at one of Concord's private prep schools, sent by wealthy parents to live and study with the sons and daughters of other wealthy parents. He did a quick visual survey of my office when he entered for the first time. "No couch?"

"No, no couch."

"I thought psychiatrists are supposed to have couches."

"Psychoanalysts have couches," I replied as I sat behind my desk.

The teenager sprawled his gawky frame across a chair, trying to look calm and nonchalant. He took a swig from a Coke can he'd carried into my office. He wore new blue jeans that were artfully tattered. His hair was tousled but otherwise well groomed. He asked, "What's the difference between a psychiatrist and a psychoanalyst?"

It sounded like the first line of a joke, but my new patient wasn't smiling. I said, "Psychoanalysis is a specialized form of psychiatry. It's a more intensive treatment, not practiced very much anymore."

"*In*tensive and *ex*pensive, I bet."

"I suppose you could say that."

He yawned. "So not all psychiatrists are psychoanalysts."

"No."

"Just the really good ones, I suppose. The ones who know what they're doing."

It was a hostile remark, but I let it pass. I tilted my head slightly without speaking: one of the pieces of body language and gesturing I'd developed unconsciously over the years. They were cataloged for me once by a hypervigilant patient—a young woman who studied every nuance of every movement I made, sensitive to the slightest sign of rejection, real or imagined. "First we have your basic head tilt," she said, "then your shoulder shrug, the one-eyebrow lift, the two-eyebrow lift, the palms-up-and-out subtle supplication, the permutations and combinations of all of the above. . . ."

Michael Cafferty asked, "Did you study that in school?"

"Study what?"

"That thing you just did with your eyebrows. They teach you how to do that in school, or what?"

I smiled. "It's not a formal part of the curriculum."

My new patient was a month shy of his seventeenth birthday. He was the slowest and clumsiest of three youths who tried unsuccessfully to break into a Concord residence a couple of months earlier, and the only one who was caught. Luckily for him, in Massachusetts you had to be seventeen to stand trial as an adult. His case was disposed of quickly in the juvenile court system. "Continued without a finding," the Concord Academy dean of students reported when she referred Michael to me, "on the condition that he get some therapy."

"You know how much I hate those situations," I told the dean, "trying to do therapy with a captive audience."

"Come on, Harry," she said, coaxing me. "He's a good kid who's fallen in with a not-so-good crowd. I allow myself one rescue fantasy per semester. Michael is my spring candidate."

"What happened to his partners in crime?"

"Michael wouldn't reveal their names. I think I know who they are, and they're both seventeen, so the adult court wouldn't be quite as easy on them. Michael thinks he's passing some rite of manhood by taking the fall himself and not turning them in."

Michael Cafferty was nervously twiddling something in his hand. I couldn't see what it was. He said, "What am I supposed to call you? Dr. Kline? Harold? Or what?"

I was going to turn the question back on him, ask him what he wanted to do. Then I noticed his left leg shaking, and the beads of sweat on his neck. "Most fellows your age feel comfortable with 'Dr. Kline,' " I told him.

"And what am I supposed to talk about? Confess my sins, or what?"

"We can talk about anything you want to talk about."

"Terrific," he said with obvious sarcasm. "And for that I'm supposed to pay you a hundred and twenty bucks a pop."

"Actually, your father will be paying me a hundred and twenty bucks a pop." I regretted the words before I'd completed the sentence. I'd taken unfair advantage of the power differential between us, putting him in his place by reminding him how little control he felt he had over his own life.

"I don't need this shit," he said, more to himself than to me. Then he looked at me. "This was all my lawyer's idea so I would look good in court. He said I should come here. Him and the stupid dean of students."

"Dean Maxwell sounded concerned about you when she spoke with me."

"Yeah, well, that's what they pay her to do—be concerned."

It was the second time that he'd commented sneeringly about people who earned money by providing services to others: first me, now Dean Roslyn Maxwell. I was tempted to point out the pattern, then thought better of it. He'd likely hear it as a challenge or a put-down.

He took a sip of Coke and gazed at the bookcase to his right. He scanned the shelves for several seconds until his eyes came to rest on two particular volumes. He said, "You wrote those?"

"Yes."

"What are they?"

"I used to work with war veterans. The first book is a series of case studies. The other one is a novel about a Vietnam veteran."

"Are you famous, or something?"

"No, I'm not."

He snickered. "Are they any good?"

"You're welcome to borrow them."

He hesitated. "Maybe some other time." Borrowing a book would imply a pledge to return, and he wasn't making any commitments just yet. "My father managed to avoid the service during the Vietnam War. He says the people who went were suckers."

"Some of the people who went feel the same way."

He pondered that for a moment, then asked, "What does my father get for his money? Do you call him with progress reports, or what?"

"No, nothing like that. He pays the bill, but you get to call the shots."

"Yeah, right." He snickered. "My father always calls the shots. He can buy and sell you a thousand times over. If you have something he wants, he'll find a way to get it."

"You make him sound formidable. What does he do for a living?"

"Kills rivers and streams. He's in the industrial polluters' hall of fame. But once a year he gives a big party for handicapped orphans, they put his picture in the paper, and everyone calls him a great humanitarian."

He could have been expressing genuine disdain for his father's values, or just reacting bitterly to the fear that he might not measure up to his father's accomplishments. I waited to hear more.

"So you don't talk to him about me?"

"Not without your permission."

He threw his hands up. "Ah, who am I kidding? He wouldn't be interested, anyway. And my mother won't be asking you any questions, either, because she'd be afraid of what she might find out." He paused. "So what I tell you is—what do you call it—confidential, right?"

"Yes."

"Suppose I told you I wanted to kill myself?"

"We'd talk about it, and if I thought you were in danger of hurting yourself, I'd hospitalize you."

"Even if I didn't want you to?"

"Yes."

Some patients back off after hearing that, fearful that I might overreact to a rash statement and sign an emergency commitment order. Others feel relieved to know that someone will take them seriously enough to help them stay safe, and this lets them open up about the anguish in their lives. I didn't know Michael Cafferty well enough to know which camp he was in, but I hoped it was the latter.

He said, "And suppose I wanted to talk to you about a murder?"

"That depends."

He arched his eyebrows. "Depends on what?"

"On whether it's a murder you're thinking about committing, or one you've already committed."

He looked confused. It wasn't the response he expected. He didn't say anything.

"If it's something you're thinking about doing, I'll try to protect your victim—and you—from what you're contemplating."

He yawned. Apparently his failure to shock me with his question had caused a profound lack of interest in anything I might say in response.

I continued anyway. "If it's a murder you already committed," I said, knowing full well we were really talking about confidentiality and trust, not homicide, "then I'm duty bound to keep your confidence."

"You'd want to do that?"

"It's not a question of 'want.' I'd be duty bound to keep your confidence, whether I wanted to or not."

"Just like a goddamn priest," he said. "Hey, maybe that's what I should call you—Father Harold. What do you think of that?"

"Perhaps there was more you wanted to say about *your* father," I said.

Michael Cafferty snickered.

Veronica laughed. "Look at your father's face," she said. "He looks like he's taking his life in his hands."

My daughter, Melissa, pointed at the bowl of beef stew

in front of me. "It won't kill you, Dad. Veronica did a good job."

My housekeeper had the evening off. Veronica had volunteered to make dinner. It was my first exposure to Veronica's uncertain culinary skills. We'd known each other for almost a year, but she'd never prepared anything more complicated than frozen waffles for me.

The broth was a bit too salty for my taste, but most of the ingredients were identifiable. "Not bad," I said. "Not bad at all."

"I'll take that as a compliment, I guess," Veronica replied.

"Well, *I* think it's *great*," Melissa said.

Melissa thought that everything Veronica did was great. When I began dating Veronica, my daughter was jealous of the time I spent with her. And I think Melissa was afraid that if she liked Veronica she would be betraying her own mother. But that was behind us now. Melissa had learned that love isn't a zero-sum game: You can add some in one part of your life without subtracting from another part.

"I tried calling you at work today," Melissa said to Veronica. "My teacher wants to know if you'll come talk to my class about the FBI." Melissa had probably been bragging about her at school, thus prompting her teacher's request.

"I know you called, honey," replied Veronica. "I was out of the office all afternoon. I didn't get the message until I was just getting ready to leave for, uh, here."

She'd almost said "home" instead of "here." But it wasn't her home, even though she'd spent almost every night of the previous six months sleeping there. She still kept her condominium in Watertown; it was a sore point between us.

"Speaking of phone calls," Veronica said, "I tried to reach you, Harry, around two o'clock."

"I was out," I said.

"I thought you were seeing patients this afternoon."

"I had some time free, so I ran an errand."

It wasn't really a lie, but it felt like one. I'd spent that time mourning one woman and renewing an old acquaintance with another. I didn't know which one was more responsible for my evasiveness with Veronica.

I checked my watch. "Speaking of your teacher," I said to Melissa, "I'd better get moving or I'll be late."

There was a parent-faculty conference at Melissa's school that evening about a proposed sex education curriculum. My daughter was only in the fourth grade; I really wasn't ready yet to contemplate the sexual aspect of her being. But if the school system was ready to so contemplate, then I damn well wanted to know what they had in mind.

Veronica said, "If you can wait a few minutes for me, I'd like to come, too."

I hesitated for just an instant, but it was long enough to betray my reluctance and create a chill in the room.

"That's okay," I said. "I don't mind going by myself."

She glanced at Melissa, who looked down at her dinner. Veronica turned to me. "It wasn't an offer of help. It was an appeal for inclusion. I didn't say 'Would you like me to come?' I said I wanted to go with you."

She's my daughter, I thought, Janet's and mine. Had it not been our wedding anniversary, I might not have had that particular thought, or waffled so obviously in the face of Veronica's request. "Sure," I said, in a tone that wasn't at all convincing. "That would be fine."

"Never mind," Veronica said as she rose to take dishes to the sink.

"No, really," I said, "I can wait for you."

"Never *mind*!" She turned her back toward me and began scrubbing the dishes ferociously.

My daughter pushed her chair back from the table. I thought I saw tears as she brushed past me. "Nice going, Dad," she muttered, then bolted from the room.

3: Blood Beach

Bobby Beck sloshed another french fry through the pool of catsup on his plate. "So, pal of mine. What exactly is our problem here? Are we talking the L-word?"

"The L-word?"

"The L-word," Bobby repeated, jabbing the air with his french fry like he was still in court, trying to hammer home a point with the jury. "Do you love Veronica?"

"Yes."

"Does she know that?"

"Yes."

"The word has passed through your lips and into her ears?"

"Yes, damn it, yes. What's your point, Bobby?"

"All right." He paused a moment to chew his food. "You love her. Does she love you?"

"Yes, she loves me. Yes, she's told me so. She knows I love her, I know she loves me. I know she knows I know. She knows I know she knows. We're both very knowledge-able."

"My, my. We're a little testy today, aren't we?" Our waitress brought refills on our soft drinks. "So. If we're not talking the L-word, we must be talking the C-word."

"The C-word?"

"The C-word, Harry. Commitment. And not the rubber-bumper-room, men-in-white-coats kind of commitment,

15

either. You know the sort of commitment I'm talking about.
If I'm not mistaken, she wants it, and you ... well, let's
just say you're ambivalent."

I thought about the previous evening. Veronica was already asleep when I returned from Melissa's school. Then
her alarm went off at five in the morning; she said she had
to stop at her place on her way to work. This kicked off another round in our ongoing argument about living arrangements. I said, "If you add up my empty closet space, it's
more room than you have in your entire condo. I wish you
would just move in with me, once and for all."

"Why don't you move in with me?"

"Not enough room."

"Somewhere else. We could move into a new place together, the three of us."

"That's ridiculous. This is a great house." The former
farmhouse was built around 1800, and it sat on two acres
of land that abutted a conservation area. Janet and I had
moved in years earlier, before Melissa was born.

"I know it's a great house, Harry. But you want me to
give up what I have, and you want to keep what you have.
That's ridiculous."

It was my house, and it was Melissa's house: Veronica
had reminded me of that a dozen times. But I knew what
she was really thinking, even if she never did more than
hint at it: *This is still Janet's house. And as long as you're
in it, you're still Janet's husband.*

Bobby Beck watched me as I thought about my conversation with Veronica. "It's Janet, isn't it?" he said.

"It's me," I replied, and then I changed the topic. I
pointed toward the garish surroundings of the fast-food
joint. "When you invited me to this magnificent lunch, you
said you had some business to discuss."

He paused for a moment, just long enough to let me
know he realized I was avoiding his question about Janet.
"I want your help on a civil suit. Do you know Frank
Porter?"

Porter was a psychologist in Lexington, the next town

over from Concord. "I've heard of him," I answered. "I don't know him."

"Funny, that's exactly what he said when I mentioned you to him. Well, his malpractice insurance company retains my firm. He's being sued by the parents of a former patient, and I'm handling the case."

"Sued by the parents, rather than the patient?"

"They're suing on behalf of their daughter's estate. A wrongful-death suit."

"Oh." I pondered that for a moment. "How did she die?"

"Her name was Celeste Oberlin. She was in therapy with Frank Porter for almost two years, on and off. She was a very troubled young woman. A couple of suicide attempts, psychiatric hospitalizations, drug abuse, an abortion. About a year ago she jumped out of a fifth-story apartment window, and now her parents are suing Frank Porter. They say he drove her to her death. They claim he screwed her."

"Literally, or figuratively?"

"Both," Bobby replied.

"Do you believe them?"

"I don't know if it's true. But *they* definitely believe it's true." He reached into his briefcase and produced a large manila envelope. "These are copies of letters, tapes, and other things they say their daughter received from Porter. In a *criminal* case, they'd have a hard time proving guilt beyond a reasonable doubt."

"But you think they might succeed in a civil suit," I said, "where the burden of proof is lower."

"They might."

"What sort of help do you want from me?"

"My firm will hire you to help me prepare the case." Bobby slid the envelope across the table. "Read the materials. Listen to the tapes. Then tell me what you think. But don't put anything in writing until I tell you differently."

"Why not?"

"I want to see how the judge rules on the plaintiff's discovery motions. Until then, I don't want to take a chance of a written report from you winding up in their hands—which is unlikely, but not impossible, depending on how the judge decides."

"When will it go to trial?"

Bobby shrugged. "The insurance company wants to settle. But we're getting some resistance to that from Porter. Frankly, I don't get it. It's the company's money, not his."

"But it's his reputation."

Bobby shook his head. "His reputation isn't on the line, at least not yet. The Oberlins haven't gone public with their charges. And we can make a settlement that's contingent on their continuing not to go public. Happens all the time in civil suits—Porter admits no wrongdoing, the insurance company coughs up more than it wants to but less than it might have to if it went to trial, and Celeste Oberlin's parents get a chunk of dough without having to wait years for the case to run its course."

"Provided they agree to keep their mouths shut."

Bobby smiled. "Provided they have decent legal advice. A good attorney would remind them that the object of a civil action is to collect concrete damages, not to produce abstract justice."

Our waitress came with the check. Bobby picked it up, checked the addition, then looked at me and spoke softly. "Getting back to the previous topic, before you so maladroitly changed the subject. I know that yesterday was your anniversary. Did you visit the cemetery?"

I nodded.

"Did Veronica go with you?"

"Are you crazy? She doesn't even know *I* went."

"Okay, okay," he said, surprised by my reaction. "Sorry I mentioned it."

I paused for a moment to let my feelings settle. "Say— you'll never guess who I ran into at the cemetery."

"Louisa May Alcott?"

"Marjorie Morris. Remember her?"

He pondered for a few seconds. "Not a clue," he said.

"Professor Morris's little girl. You know—the little kid

with bright red hair, sort of a tomboy, used to come to class sometimes with her mother."

He thought some more, and then a look of recognition flashed across his face. "Sure. She was, what—nine or ten? Marjorie Margarine."

"Marjorie Margarine?"

"Right. That was her nickname. Don't you remember?"

"No," I said.

"I never knew what it meant." He swallowed his last french fry, whole. "What was she doing in the cemetery?"

"She moved to Concord last year," I said as we walked toward the cash register. I briefed Bobby on our chance encounter.

He walked outside. "You say she was in a movie before she dropped out of acting?"

"Yes."

"Which one?" Bobby was the biggest movie buff I knew. Inside his head he carried a database of movie titles, cross-referenced with directors, actors, and God knows what else.

"I think she said it was called *Blood Beach*."

He considered that for a moment, then his eyes lit up and he broke into a wide grin. "Well, I'll be damned. So *that* was Marjorie Morris. Let's see if the video store has it."

The video store was right next to the restaurant. It took Bobby a few minutes to find what he was looking for. The store had one copy of the tape in a battered box. He studied it for a moment. "Sure, here it is. She even got her name in the credits on the back of the box." He looked at me and smiled. "It was a small part, but very—how shall I say this? Very memorable." He handed the box to me, still grinning.

I read the plot summary. Released six years earlier, *Blood Beach* was the story of a serial killer who murders pretty young women in Malibu.

Bobby said, "Sort of a combination—*Beach Blanket Bingo* meets *Halloween*."

"Never heard of it," I said. "Not my type of movie."

He took it from me and led me to the checkout counter.

"Well, you might find it interesting. Our friend Marjorie Margarine is certainly—how shall I say this? She's certainly physically fit. And quite limber, too." He paid for the rental and handed the tape back to me.

We walked outside. The sky had grown dark, and there was the sort of stillness in the air that comes just before a New England thundershower. Bobby looked at the gathering clouds. "I have tickets for the Red Sox tonight," he said. "Always an iffy proposition, weather-wise, during the first few weeks of the season." He turned to me and smiled. "There are two types of people in the world, Harry. People who pack as much as possible when they travel, and people who pack as little as possible. Which type are you?"

"That's easy. The less I have to deal with, the happier I am."

"And Veronica?"

"She's the same way."

"Aha! This is definitely a relationship worth saving."

As we parted ways, Bobby Beck—my oldest friend, the best man at my wedding, my daughter's godfather—looked steadily at me for several seconds. He placed a hand on my shoulder. "I know how much you miss her, pal of mine," he said. "I miss her, too."

"You're rushing Christmas, aren't you, Chief?"

Alfred Korvich, Concord's police chief, hesitated for a moment on the other end of the phone line. "I don't get you, Doc."

"You usually wait until the fall to ask me for a contribution to the Christmas fund."

He chuckled. "That's not why I called, Doc. I called to talk about one of your patients."

I leaned back in the chair behind my office desk and considered his statement. Chief Korvich was experienced enough to know it would be unethical for me to give him any information.

"Michael Cafferty," he continued. "You began treating him a day or two ago."

"I can't even tell you whether I know such a person, Chief. You realize that."

"C'mon, Doc," he said, with a trace of irritation in his voice. "The kid is required to seek therapy as a condition of probation. He gave your name to his probation officer, so I know he's seeing you. But, look—I didn't call to put you on the spot. I just called to give you some information about your patient."

"I never said he was my patient."

"Sure, sure. Anyway, we got him for that one break-in in February. But we think he was involved in some other burglaries over in West Concord. Maybe he'll talk to you about it."

"Now, just a minute—"

"Hold on, Doc. I'm not trying to get you to break that thing you have—you know, doctor-patient privacy."

"Confidentiality."

"Right. Like I said, I just want to *give* you some information."

"I'm listening," I replied.

"They tell me he's not a bad kid. And he's scared shitless his daddy's gonna take him out of Concord Academy because of the trouble he got into. I'm after Cafferty's buddy, the one I think is behind the burglaries." He paused. "Carter Ellington Junior."

"You're kidding me. You mean, his father is—"

"Carter Ellington Senior."

"Senator Carter Ellington?"

"Obviously. How many people do you think are walking around with a name like Carter Ellington?"

Ellington was a publicity-hound state senator from the western part of the state. Handsome and wealthy, with the telegenic charm of a Greek god, he had his eyes set on the governor's office.

I said, "I don't care very much for him. If I lived in his district, I'd consider moving."

Chief Korvich laughed, an irritating high-pitched cackle. "Yeah, well, the apple didn't fall far from the tree. The kid's smart, smooth, and rich, just like his old man. And he's the worst kind of bastard. He takes from other people not because he needs what he takes, or even wants it. Hell, he probably throws the shit away so he doesn't get caught with it. Carter Ellington Junior takes from other people just for the sake of taking. For the sheer joy of causing misery. I really want to grab that little motherfucker." He paused to calm himself down.

"I still don't understand what this has to do with me."

"With a little time and effort, maybe we'll tie Michael Cafferty to the break-ins in West Concord. But I'd rather use him to squeeze the senator's son."

Michael Cafferty tried to make himself look tough, but underneath he was just a frightened adolescent with bad taste in friends. That's what the dean of students told me when she referred him to me, and that was my impression after our first session. I said, "I think we should end this conversation."

Korvich sighed. "Sure, Doc, sure. Just remember—if the Cafferty kid talks to you about this stuff, you can do him a big favor by telling him to give me a call. And I'm completely sincere about that."

I glanced at the videotape box on my desk, the one Bobby Beck had rented for me a few hours earlier. "Wait a minute, Chief—before you hang up, what can you tell me about that hit-and-run accident over near Nashawtuc Hill?"

"Charles Morris? Can't say too much, Doc, because it's still under investigation."

"So there haven't been any arrests?"

"You'd have read it in the paper if there was."

"Any suspects?"

"Can't really say, Doc."

"Any leads?"

"Like I say—I can't say. You psychiatrists aren't the only ones who get to keep confidences." He cleared his throat, then asked, "What the hell do you care, anyway?"

"I'm a friend of his daughter."

"Are you, now? *That's* interesting."

I wondered what he found so interesting about that. "Is there anything you can say about the case?" I said, letting my irritation show.

He considered my question for a few seconds, then replied. "Sure. I can tell you he took one hell of a hit, judging from the damage done. Whoever rammed him must have been going at a damn good clip, much too fast for that little road. Nice talking to you, Doc."

I hung up and tried to figure out what to make of the phone call. Alfred Korvich was police chief in a small, prosperous town that hardly ever had serious crime. Concord had seen one murder in the dozen years I'd lived there, and neither the victim nor the perpetrator was local; they were tourists who got into a drunken fistfight in the woods behind Walden Pond. Recently one of the town's well-heeled residents had been charged in a high-profile case of securities fraud, but that was a federal matter; the local police dealt mostly with traffic accidents, drunk drivers, and acts of teenage vandalism. The police department log in the weekly *Concord Journal* listed calls about tree-bound pets, battered mailboxes, and motorists who locked their keys in their cars.

Like many of Concord's civil servants, Alfred Korvich couldn't afford to live in the town that employed him. Perhaps that caused him to envy us, even resent us. And if he was driven to such thoughts about town residents, he certainly would resent wealthy prep-school kids from out of town who caused problems for him.

I scribbled the name of Carter Ellington on a piece of scrap paper and tossed it inside my desk drawer.

Marjorie makes her first appearance just after the opening credits of *Blood Beach*. She is stuffed tightly into a two-piece swimsuit that leaves little to the imagination. She and two other well-developed young women are walking on a California beach at sunrise. All of them are stunning, especially Marjorie.

Seeing her that way unsettled me. I had a difficult time reconciling that scene and my memories of a pencil-thin preadolescent girl. And I felt ashamed, as if somehow I were lusting retroactively after that child I'd known twenty years earlier. I was glad that I'd waited to watch the film until after Veronica retired for the evening.

Less than a minute into the story, Marjorie and her pulchritudinous friends stumble upon another equally pulchritudinous young woman, lying on her back, whose attire leaves even less to the imagination.

She is naked.

She is beautiful.

She is very, very dead.

A thin stream of dried, clotted blood leads from her mouth to her neck. Her eyes are open wide in terror, as if images from the final moments of her recently snuffed life are still etched onto her brain.

Marjorie is the brave one: While her two friends shriek and avert their eyes, she leans over the body and searches vainly for a pulse. She tries CPR until her friends pull her away from the corpse.

The next shot is magnificent in its framing and composition. The camera apparently is placed between the dead woman's splayed legs, low to the ground, aiming over her body and down the beach. The tips of her breasts are visible on the sides of the screen. Between them, Marjorie and the others are running away, their scantily clad buttocks jiggling as they flee. A bright orange sun crowns the top of the screen.

The director had filmed that shot to run at a speed slightly slower than normal, highlighting the bouncing flesh of the three women. And somehow he'd arranged the lighting and the lens opening to keep everything in focus: the foreground breasts, the background sun, and the three figures racing into the distance.

The low-budget thriller had clever plotting and snappy

dialogue. Pretty young women were turning up dead on or
near the beach, knives stuck deep in their backs. A sinister
police detective was in charge of the investigation. He was
so unsympathetic a character that I was certain he was
actually the killer. The detective's prime suspect was a like-
able young man who was a lifeguard by day and a night-
club bouncer by night.

Incidental to the main plot, a young newspaper reporter
has his first major assignment covering the case. Two thirds
into the film, Marjorie appears for the second time when
the reporter befriends her in his effort to learn more about
one of the murder victims.

Marjorie brings the reporter back to her nearby apartment. In a scene shot from their waists up, they stand together in the middle of the room and trade flirtatious
innuendos and double entendres. Then she unfastens her bikini top. It stays suspended for a moment, held in place by
the broad jut of her breasts, then falls silently to the floor.
On the side of her left breast, nestled just below the tan
line, is a tattoo of a red butterfly.

The reporter's eyes open wide, and he gasps when she
pulls his hands to her breasts. As he awkwardly fondles her,
she slips off her bottom piece and flings it across the room.

She leads him toward the bed on the far side of the
room. She kisses him, hard and feverishly, then wraps her
arms around his hips and rubs against him. Then she leans
backward onto the bed, pulling him down and guiding his
lips to her breast. He lifts her nipple into his mouth. She
wraps her long red curls around his head. She sighs and
whispers something to him, and her hips begin to roll as he
bites down harder on her. Then, with his hands on her
breasts, he slides his head down her body until it moves out
of camera range. The expression on Marjorie's face leaves
little doubt where he is and what he's doing. When he
comes back into the frame, Marjorie pushes him onto his
back and lifts herself above his body.

Now the camera is looking up at her, as if we are viewing the scene from the vantage point of the reporter.

Marjorie slowly eases herself onto him, shuddering and closing her eyes as she moves. She lifts herself up, then pushes down again, a bit harder and faster than the first time. She continues this way, up and down, picking up the pace, until she is pounding against him like a rapid-firing piston. The red wings of her tattooed butterfly seem to open and close as she shifts up and down.

I was mesmerized by her: the jouncing of her flesh, the rhythm of her heavy breathing, the beads of perspiration on her nipples, the guttural groans each time she planted herself on him. It was an utterly convincing display of aroused abandon. I wasn't prepared for what happened next.

What happens next: At the climactic moment, when all of her energies are supremely focused, Marjorie's body suddenly turns rigid. Her eyes bulge open. There is a short intake of breath. At first it looks like a powerful orgasm: a short-circuiting of movement caused by sensory overload. But then there is a sickening gurgle. Frothing red blood fills her mouth, empties, and spills onto her breasts. She falls onto her side. Her body twitches—a final spasm of life— and then her eyes glaze over and all movement ceases.

A knife protrudes from her back. She is the latest victim of the Blood Beach killer.

I grabbed the remote control and turned the movie off. I was repulsed. I was excited. I was awash in the confused commingling of sexual and violent images.

I double-checked the locks on the doors and downstairs windows, something I rarely did. I shut the lights and walked upstairs.

I slipped into bed and nestled against Veronica from behind. She stirred slightly. "God, Harry—you're shivering. Your body is ice-cold." I rubbed against her for warmth. She responded with some gentle rubbing of her own. She turned to face me, then reached down and grabbed me. "And my, oh my—you've been thinking nasty thoughts." She held on to me, she kissed me, and we made love, quietly and completely.

Sleep began to envelop me while I was still holding on

to Veronica. She startled me with a good-natured poke in the ribs. "Hey, you," she said, laughing. "Didn't your mother ever tell you it's not polite to talk about food after having sex?"

"My mother has never officially acknowledged the existence of sex. Anyway, what are you talking about?"

"I'm talking about you, just a few seconds ago. You were yawning and drifting off to sleep. You're supposed to be completely satisfied and fulfilled, and instead you're talking about eating."

"Eating?"

"You mumbled something about margarine."

"Margarine?"

"Margarine," she repeated. "Of course, maybe you had something more exotic in mind than eating with it. Like in that scene from *Last Tango in Paris*. Or was that butter? Hey—relax. It was just a joke. No need to look so tense."

4: Battlefields

Heavy static made the transmission from Bobby Beck's car phone choppy. He said, "The Porter case spells trouble, doesn't it?"

"With a capital T and that rhymes with P and that stands for psychologist."

"Did you read the whole file?" he asked.

I propped the phone against my ear with my shoulder and slid two slices of raisin bread into the toaster. "Just some of it. Enough to realize that Frank Porter's therapeutic technique is—to put it as kindly as possible—idiosyncratic. The Oberlins' lawyer will eat Porter for lunch when he takes his deposition. And they'll have no trouble finding expert witnesses to discredit him. If you put me on the stand, I'd probably wind up hurting your case on cross-examination. Hell, I'd probably wind up hurting your case on direct examination if you put me on the stand."

"That's terrific," Bobby said, with no evident sarcasm.

"Maybe it's terrific for Celeste Oberlin's parents," I replied. I looked out my kitchen window and saw Veronica returning from her morning run, heading up the long drive-way with the *Boston Globe* tucked under her arm.

"It's terrific for me, too, pal of mine," Bobby said. "When I tell Porter what you said, maybe he'll start to think more sensibly about agreeing to a settlement." His voice began to fade and the static became more pronounced. "Heading into Sumner Tunnel, Harry. Talk to you later. Say—did you watch *Blood Beach*? What did you think of Marjorie Margarine?" There were several seconds of white noise, followed by a dead line and then a dial tone.

I placed the phone receiver in its cradle. I turned the kitchen television on and let it drone softly in the background. The toaster popped just as Veronica stepped into the house. "Want some raisin toast?" I asked. "Cream cheese and juice are already on the table."

"Thanks." She ran a hand towel under the cold water faucet, then folded it in half and draped it across her forehead. She dropped into her chair, took a sip of juice, and leaned back with her eyes closed. Rivulets of water from the drenched hand towel trickled down her cheeks and mixed with droplets of perspiration on her neck.

"How far did you run?"

"About four and a half miles, down Lexington Road to Old Bedford Road and back. There were a few dozen men with muskets in Colonial uniforms milling around at the intersection."

"That's Merriam's Corner. After the battle at North Bridge, the British headed back to Lexington A group of Minutemen fired on them at Merriam's Corner. The annual reenactment is on Sunday. The men you saw were probably rehearsing."

She spread cream cheese on her slice of toast. "Well, I think I'm in pretty good shape for Monday. I should be able to do thirteen miles in an hour and a half."

She was planning on running the first half of the Boston Marathon on Patriots' Day, four days later. Melissa and I were going to meet her at the thirteen-mile mark in Wellesley, then the three of us were going to her father's home nearby for a late lunch.

Veronica spread the newspaper open and reached for her toast. "Where's Melissa?"

"She's late, as usual." I went into the hallway and called upstairs for my daughter.

When I returned to the kitchen, Veronica looked up from

the newspaper and asked, "Have you ever been to
Pittsfield?"

"I passed through once on a drive to the Berkshires,
years ago. Why?"

She glanced at the kitchen clock. It was four minutes before eight o'clock. "Because in exactly four minutes my
beeper is going to sound. It'll be Martin Baines telling me
to go to Pittsfield."

Martin Baines was Veronica's boss, the special agent in
charge at the FBI office in Boston. He was only in his
midforties, just a few years older than me, but he'd been
with the Bureau since the days of J. Edgar Hoover. He was
on the cusp: forced by circumstances to be a New Age male,
yet a product of the days when female agents (and there
weren't many back then)—or male agents, for that matter—
would be sent packing to Upper Volta if they were known to
cohabit outside of marriage. Martin Baines knew me, and he
knew where Veronica was. Calling her by beeper was his
way of avoiding embarrassment on anyone's part. And waiting until eight to call was his way of respecting our privacy.

"Why Pittsfield?" I asked.

Suddenly we heard my daughter screeching from another
room. "I hate my hair!"

Veronica said, "She'll have to run if she expects to catch
her school bus."

"What else is new?" I said.

Melissa burst into the kitchen out of breath, a stack of
schoolbooks teetering precariously in her arms. "Gotta run.
Gotta run. 'Bye, Veronica. 'Bye, Dad."

Veronica said, "You look very pretty today, honey." They
kissed each other lightly on the cheek. It still seemed a little
odd to see that: my daughter embracing the woman whose
presence she initially resented so strongly. Hell, sometimes
I still felt strange when I was with Veronica: the only
woman in my life since my wife's death. We'd all come a
long way in a little less than a year.

Melissa ran out the kitchen door and down the driveway.
I said, "I think you've made a friend for life."

Veronica smiled. "I certainly hope so." Her beeper sounded inside the zipped pocket of her jogging suit. She reached for it and checked the phone number on its readout display. "Very good, Martin. Exactly eight o'clock."

Veronica went into the den to call her boss. I turned up the television sound and watched the local news broadcast. The lead story was about a twelve-year-old girl from a small town I'd never heard of in western Massachusetts. The previous afternoon a stranger with a gun tried to abduct her as she walked along a quiet road. She eluded his grasp and scurried into a nearby wooded area. The man started to run after her, but he was overweight and clumsy, and he quickly grew short of breath. He stumbled back to his car and sped away. The little girl was able to get the number of his license plate, and late that night he was placed under arrest in Pittsfield. His name was Louis Laggone.

Questions were raised about possible connections between this case and two unsolved cases of missing children from the previous few years. One of those cases involved a child on the other side of the border between New York and Massachusetts, so it was assumed that the FBI would be brought into the investigation.

I glanced at the *Boston Globe* lying on the kitchen table. It was folded open to a story about the foiled abduction; that was how Veronica knew her boss would be calling her and detailing her to Pittsfield.

Veronica returned a few minutes later. She nodded when she saw I was reading the paper. "You've heard the news, I gather," she said. "Martin likes to use me in cases like this. He figures that since I used to be a prosecutor, I'll know how to interrogate the suspect about the missing-children cases without jeopardizing the attempted-kidnapping case they're holding him on."

She'd once been an assistant district attorney who specialized in homicide prosecutions. Since joining the FBI, she'd had extensive training in the investigation of serial rapes and murders. "Sexual psychopaths," she said. "Where would my career be without them?"

She was smiling, but I could tell she felt ambivalent about her new assignment.

"Seriously, Harry—do you ever wonder what you've gotten yourself into—what sort of woman you're involved with, whose life revolves around such perversion?"

"I love you for your perversion."

"I'm serious, damn it."

I walked to her side and kissed her. "I do love you," I said. "With or without your peculiar interests."

"Speaking of peculiar interests, where did you get this?" She was holding the videocassette of *Blood Beach*.

"Oh, Bobby and I were in the video store yesterday. He's already seen it. He knows I like mysteries and said I should check it out. I watched some of it last night after you went to bed."

I was talking too much, with forced nonchalance, like a guilty child trying to talk his way out of a bad situation.

She said, "But you don't like mysteries."

"Sure I do, sometimes."

"Hmm," she said as she read the cassette box. "A movie about a serial killer. Maybe I'd like this."

"I don't think so." I said it reflexively, still trying to steer the conversation somewhere else. "I gave up on it in the middle."

"So I see. Tsk, tsk. You really should rewind, Harry. Be considerate of the next deviate." She laughed, then studied the credits on the box. "I never heard of any of these people." She looked at the clock on the wall. "I've got to shower and get moving. It'll probably take two hours to get to Pittsfield."

I took the cassette into the den after Veronica dashed upstairs. I put it in the VCR and began rewinding, then inadvertently pressed the play button and found myself watching Marjorie's undulating form once more: lifting and lowering, lifting and lowering, over and over again. What was it Bobby had said? *She's certainly physically fit. And quite limber, too.* After several seconds I resumed re-

winding: I knew it was only a movie, but I really didn't
want to watch her die a second time.

The phone rang, and it was Bobby again. He'd just spoken with Dr. Frank Porter. "Can you see him this afternoon? He said he can talk to you at four-thirty, after his last
appointment of the day. I figure you go to his office, so
he'll feel more at ease. You talk things over with him, try
to get him to see things the way you do. Maybe he'll listen
to a psychiatrist better than he listens to his lawyer."

"Did you tell him what I think of the materials I've reviewed so far?"

"I figured you'd want that pleasure for yourself."

"Thanks."

"Seriously, though—I didn't want him to get defensive
about you before he even meets you. So, tell me—how did
you like *Blood Beach*?"

"It's really not my kind of film," I replied, evading his
question.

"Did you watch it?"

"No," I said as the tape finished rewinding. "I didn't
watch any of it."

I had one patient that morning: a middle-aged man with a
successful plumbing business and a failing marriage. We'd
met only a half-dozen times, and on this morning, as always,
he focused his conversation on criticisms of his wife. Listening only to his side of the story, one might have believed the
woman was the pettiest shrew ever placed on earth.

"So I figure I'll help out a bit, and I start clearing the
dishes away after breakfast. And I pick up this goddamn
gourmet syrup she uses on her pancakes—she's the only
one in the goddamn house who uses it—and I say to her,
'Where does this go?' And you know what she says? She
says, 'It goes the same place I always keep it.' Can you believe that? It goes the same place she always keeps it. I
mean, if I knew where the hell she always keeps it, would
I be asking her to tell me where the hell it goes? I swear
to God, I don't know why I don't just leave her."

His anger was accessible to him, but I knew it would take us a while to dig through it. He would hold on to that anger for as long as he could—because once he got beyond it he would have to confront the hurt and sadness that lay behind it. I wanted to tell him what I was thinking, but I knew he wasn't ready yet to hear it.

After lunch I walked the short distance to North Bridge. Around that same time of year, more than two centuries earlier, the Minutemen from Concord and surrounding towns put up the first armed resistance to British troops at that wooden footbridge: the shot heard 'round the world. On the coming weekend tourist hordes would descend on this site for the annual Patriots' Day reenactment. But on this Thursday afternoon only a few other people were milling about.

I recognized one of those people from a distance. Cindy was one of Janet's closest friends. She lived a couple of miles down the road, near Merriam's Corner. She sat on a bench by the gravesite of the three British soldiers who died at that first pitched battle of the Revolution, and she waved as I walked toward her.

Her two-year-old daughter was running back and forth along the path. Cindy said, "I was just thinking about you a little while ago."

"Pigeons, Mommy," the girl shouted as she ran by us.

"Yes, sweetie, they are pigeons." Cindy turned to me. "We ate lunch at the Colonial Inn, and the waitress gave Holly a cookie without asking me first if it was all right. Pure sugar and saturated fat. I took the cookie away, and Holly started to cry, and the waitress looked at me like I was some sort of monster. And then I got flustered, and I was going to try to explain myself, and then I thought, Why should I have to justify my actions to this stranger? And that's when I thought about you and Janet, and the time you were investigated by social services."

One day when my daughter was just a toddler, she and Janet went grocery shopping. Janet opened the hatchback door to load the grocery bags into her car, and she let Melissa climb into the backseat through the hatchback entrance.

The following evening we received an unannounced visit from a Department of Social Services caseworker: a gum-popping young woman who had difficulty matching her nouns with verbs. "Your daughter," she said. "And your wife. Your car. Trunk. Shutting her in there. Someone saw her, called us."

It took a minute for me to figure out what she meant. When I did, I became indignant. But before I could say anything, Janet came to the door and politely invited the woman in. The woman interviewed us separately, then together. Then she insisted on talking to Melissa without either of us present. That must have satisfied her, because we never heard from her again.

Cindy said, "I don't think there's much chance the waitress will report me to social services. After all, it's not like I shut my daughter in my car trunk." She laughed, and so did I.

I said, "The thing I remember most about that visit is Janet's reaction. I was really angry, because if there was one person in the world who would never do anything to harm her child, it was Janet. But Janet thought it was wonderful. 'Someone was watching out for our daughter,' she told me. 'I wish there were more people in the world like that.' "

"That sounds like her," said Cindy. "Sometimes I miss her so much."

"Yes."

She paused. "I'm sorry. I didn't mean to bring you down."

"No, that's all right. I like talking about her."

Cindy watched her daughter running in circles around a bench. "How is Melissa?"

"She's having a bad hair day."

Cindy laughed. "Fortunately, Holly and I won't have to contend with that for a few years yet. And your friend— I'm sorry, I forget her name."

"Veronica Pace."

"Right, Veronica. Things are going well with the two of you, I hope."

"Sure."

"Well, I'm glad. You were so forlorn after Janet died, I thought I might have to sleep with you myself to bring you out of it. Don't look so alarmed, Harry. It's just a joke. I'd never really take a lover, because I couldn't bear having to tell the story of my life all over again to someone new."

Cindy gathered up Holly and headed for the parking lot. I continued my walk: over the wooden footbridge that crossed the narrow river, past the Minuteman statue, up the path to the top of the hill. There I sat on a bench in front of what was once the Buttrick mansion, now the National Park Service visitor center.

I thought about Janet and her incurable optimism— sometimes inspiring, sometimes exasperating. I'd never known anyone so motivated by a desire to see the good in others.

Veronica had an entirely different appeal: an intensity that sprang from her belief in evil and her desire to root it out and quash it. After law school she became an assistant district attorney in Rhode Island's Bristol County. Within a few years she was the prosecutor in charge of all homicide cases. "I took that job because I had a mission when I decided to study law," Veronica once told me. "I wanted to hurt people who hurt other people."

I leaned back and surveyed the scene before me: the sculptured garden, quaint brick walkways, and the gently sloping hill with the wooden footbridge at its base. It's ironic that battlegrounds are so often the sites of such great serenity. I considered myself fortunate to live so near this place. Janet and I bought the old farmhouse just before the explosion in real-estate prices that was brought on by the what-me-worry profligacy of the Reagan years. And if I wanted to, I could sell it now for nearly triple what we'd spent, and I could take all that money and . . .

What the hell was I thinking about? I was perfectly happy the way things were. Veronica was the one who had problems with our status quo, not me. I wasn't trying to change her, so why was she trying to change me? I felt irritable just thinking about it.

I recrossed North Bridge at the bottom of the hill and stopped again at the gravesite of the British soldiers. I read the inscription on the burial marker.

> *They came three thousand miles and died,*
> *To keep the past upon its throne:*
> *Unheard, beyond the ocean tide,*
> *Their English mother made her moan.*

I felt an odd affinity for the nameless men underneath that soil: yanked suddenly from their loved ones, stuck forever in an alien, distant place.

A young woman had turned to him for help, and now she was dead by her own troubled hand. The young woman's parents were suing him, alleging a variety of misfeasances and malfeasances, omissions and commissions. It was a serious matter, but you wouldn't know it from looking at him.

Frank Porter yawned and said, "I was surprised when Beck said he wanted you to consult. I didn't even want a lawyer, but the insurance carrier insisted. This case won't go anywhere. The Oberlins will change their minds about suing me once they get over their grief."

He was dressed with impeccable casualness in a knit shirt and unwrinkled jeans straight out of a J. Crew catalog. He sported a carefully sculpted beard, trimmed close to the skin. He had an unwavering vacuous smile, and when we spoke he gazed not directly at my eyes, but at a point an inch or two above them. And from the moment we shook hands in his Lexington office, he conveyed an attitude of casual lightheartedness that belied the grave nature of the circumstance that brought us together.

He said, "Someone once asked me if this office building was named for John Adams, the president, or Samuel

Adams, the beer. I told him it was named for Margo
Adams, the slut. Remember her, Harry?"

He apparently assumed I'd feel comfortable with his just-
us-guys informality. Or maybe he was trying to control the
interview by making me feel uneasy. Worse yet—considering
his profession—maybe he hadn't the slightest idea how he
was coming across.

He continued. "They say Wade Boggs is a great hitter
because he has such good eyes. I swear, you couldn't prove
that by looking at Margo."

Margo Adams had been Wade Boggs's wife-away-from-
home for two years when he played for the Red Sox. Then
he threatened to dump her, and she threatened to sue him,
and he threatened to threaten her in some vaguely threatening
way. So she turned him into an object of ridicule and herself
into a household name: holding press conferences to implicate other Red Sox players in Wade's dirty little secret and
to give anatomically correct descriptions of her coast-to-coast
genital and oral cavorting with the team's star third baseman.

Porter asked, "Do you remember that network interview
Wade did with Barbara Walters after the story broke? There
he was, with his wife at his side, publicly proclaiming himself to be a sex addict. And looking more than a little
pleased with himself, if you ask me." He chuckled. "I
swear, it was a glorious moment for support groups and
self-help organizations everywhere. And if Margo's testimony is true, old Wade could have been a founding member of a brand-new recovery movement—Cunnilingus
Anonymous."

It said something about Porter that he would talk that
way to someone he'd just met. It confirmed the doubts I already had about his professional abilities. A good psychotherapist eventually adopts a basic reserve in his approach
to new situations: a conservatism derived from respect for
others' sensibilities.

Porter's office was large and expensively furnished, well
soundproofed from the waiting room. His second-floor win-

dow faced a paved bicycle path that cut through Lexington center on its way from Bedford to Cambridge.

On his desk was a paperweight fashioned from a chunk of amber. Preserved whole inside the amber was a fossilized insect. He saw me looking at it and said, "A gift from a former client. It's supposed to represent the human mind. The bug is like a forgotten memory, frozen in time, waiting to be unearthed."

"It's very striking," I said.

"Thank you. I'm very fond of it."

"How long have you practiced here?"

"About four years. I opened this office right after I got licensed. I also share a smaller one in Cambridge with a couple of other psychologists."

"You must be busy."

"About forty-five hours a week, give or take. You have to take the work while it's there. The competition keeps getting stiffer, and then there's all this managed-care bullshit. But I guess you know all about that."

I've always thought that thirty hours per week is the most time someone should spend practicing psychotherapy. After that point—sometimes even before that point—patients' stories blend into one another, and you don't have time to recover from the cumulative mental strain that comes from working on so many problems with so many people. But I didn't mention any of that to Porter.

He said, "I've started branching out into other things. Stress-management workshops, consulting to personnel departments about their procedures for screening applicants, things like that. In case my practice dwindles—you know, with all these insurance companies making it harder for people to use their benefits. I swear, with all this managed care, it's a wonder that anyone manages to get any care."

I did some quick multiplication in my head. I figured his annual income as a psychotherapist to be between $175,000 and $200,000. Expenses probably took away $25,000. I didn't know how much he was making from his other endeavors.

He said, "You're in Concord, aren't you?"

"Yes."

"How's business there?"

"My practice is smaller than yours."

"Well, the new rules make the therapy game a rough one. You have to really hustle to stay ahead of it."

I could have told him that I preferred a small practice, and that the money I inherited from Janet, along with her life insurance policy, provided more than enough for a comfortable life. But I didn't see any purpose in revealing information about myself to him. I also could have said that I didn't like hearing him refer to psychotherapy as a game. But no good would be served by alienating him.

"Nice town, Concord," he said. "Very Thoreauvian, if there is such a word. I went walking there not too long ago. A very pretty place—Esther Brook Woods, or something like that."

"Estabrook Woods. I go there several times a week. I can walk there from my house. You're right—it is pretty. Thoreau wrote that it would make a princely estate in Europe."

Having established some minimal rapport, I was ready to begin asking questions about Celeste Oberlin and her parents' suit. But before I could start, he said, "My five o'clock client just arrived." He turned his desk clock around so I could see it. "I have an indicator wired in. This little light down here. I usually can't hear a client arrive, what with the soundproofing and everything. The light goes on when someone enters the waiting room. You look confused. Didn't you ever see one of these before?"

"It's not that. It's that your lawyer told me you'd be finished with patients at four-thirty. I thought we'd have more time to talk."

"I told him I'd be *free* at four-thirty, that I could squeeze you in for a half hour. He must have misunderstood."

I doubted that. "Bob Beck thinks the Oberlin suit could become a real problem for you."

"Yeah, well, you know what they say about the difference between a catfish and a lawyer. One is a scum-sucking, garbage-eating, bottom-dwelling scavenger. The other is a fish."

I leaned forward in my chair. "Listen to me, Frank."

"Hey—it's just a joke. No reason to get so upset."

"Listen to me really well. Let me tell you how I met Bobby Beck. My freshman year in college, there was an intramural baseball league. I was the catcher for my dorm's team. We made it to the championship game, and we were winning by one run in the bottom of the ninth inning. Then Bobby Beck—I'd never met him before—Bobby hits a double with two out, the potential tying run. The next batter hits a single to center, Bobby rounds third base at full speed, and he and the ball arrive at home plate at the same time. He slams into me and we both go sprawling. I put the tag on, and I think I get him, but it's really close and I know the call can go either way. Meanwhile the umpire is completely out of position. There's no way he could have seen whether Bobby was safe or out, and any call he makes is just going to be a guess. But before he can make the call, Bobby rolls over on his side, looks up at the umpire, and says, 'I'm out.' The umpire can't believe what he's hearing. I can't believe it. The umpire says, 'I think you were safe.' Bobby says, 'He tagged me before I touched home. If he didn't drop the ball, I'm out.' The ball was still in my glove, and the umpire called Bobby out."

Frank Porter drummed his fingers on his desktop. "What's your point?"

"My point is, if Bobby Beck tells you something, you can take it to the bank. If he says this case is trouble, then this case is trouble."

He didn't say anything for several seconds. Then he glanced at his desk clock. "I really need to see my client."

I stood and walked toward the door. "We need to talk more about this, Frank. It's not going to go away."

I passed Porter's next patient, a young woman in a bright yellow dress seated in the corner of the waiting room. Outside the building, I walked to the end of the block and sat on a bench on the town green. A work crew was readying the green for the weekend commemoration of the Battle of Lexington. They were constructing a reviewing stand at one end, where Pitcairn's British troops stood that fateful April morning. At the other end of the grass expanse, where colonists stood and then fell under British fire, flags were being attached to light posts.

I thought again about that college baseball game. After the umpire called Bobby out, I helped him to his feet and thanked him for what he'd done. He pushed me away, told me to do something to myself that was biologically impossible, then stalked off.

That evening I approached him in the dining hall. We'd never actually met before, so I introduced myself, and then I said, "I don't get it. Why did you tell the umpire you were out?"

"Because I thought he was getting ready to call me safe."

"So what? Maybe you *were* safe. It was close, and it's his play to call."

He slapped his silverware against his plate, betraying his impatience with me. "What would you have done if he called me safe? Would you have argued with him?"

"I don't know. Probably, I guess."

"Because you thought I was out?"

"Yes."

"Well, I thought I was out, too."

I said nothing, uncertain how to respond.

"Listen, Harvey—"

"It's Harry."

"Sorry. Listen, Harry—what I did has nothing to do with you. It's just a matter of keeping accounts straight."

"I don't get it."

"I don't care. Like I said, it has nothing to do with you."

I watched the activity on Lexington Green for a few minutes more, browsed in a couple of stores, then headed toward the parking lot near the bicycle path. Just before I got to my car I saw Frank Porter and the woman in the bright yellow dress, fifty yards away. They were heading away from his office building, smiling and walking close together in what appeared to be a friendly conversation. They ducked into the Yangtze River restaurant. I couldn't tell for certain, but I thought I saw Porter's hand brush against his patient's shoulder as he followed her inside.

"That does sound a little unusual," Bobby said.

"It's one thing to be warm and accepting toward your patients," I said as I balanced the telephone base in my lap. "It's another thing to conduct your therapy over egg rolls and moo goo gai pan."

"I'll call him again. Maybe the three of us should sit down together."

"You're not one of his favorite people," I said.

"Even after you told him the baseball story?"

"Even then."

"I'll tell you, pal of mine—if I'd known you'd be hung up on that game for so many years, I would have let the dumb son-of-a-bitch call me safe at home. Speaking of safe at home, did Veronica get back from Pittsfield yet? *That* sounds like one hell of an interesting case."

"Not yet," I replied. It was almost ten o'clock.

"Well, maybe she stopped to have a guy with the drinks after work."

"You mean, a drink with the guys."

"Either way."

I nodded off during Jay Leno's monologue. Just before midnight Veronica peeled back the blanket and slid into bed next to me. She reached for the remote control and clicked the television off.

"Loony Louie," she said.

I yawned. "That's one hell of a way to greet a guy."

"Not you. Louis Laggone."

"Your kidnapping suspect?"

"Uh-huh. The kids call him Loony Louie. He's an usher at a movie theater outside of Pittsfield. A funny-looking fat little guy, lives with his elderly mother, and I guess they gave him that nickname because kids like to have someone to make fun of."

"Did you talk to him?"

"Yes."

"What about the little girl he tried to kidnap? Is she okay?"

"I don't know. I didn't interview her. The district attorney asked me not to do anything that could jeopardize the case. Not to talk to the victim at all, and not to talk to Laggone about the incident."

"Then what did you talk to him about?"

She yawned. "Three years ago a young boy from the area disappeared. Last year a girl visiting from New York vanished. No trace found of either one. And on the day the boy disappeared, he told a friend he was going to a movie at the multiplex where Laggone works."

"I'm surprised Laggone's lawyer let you talk to him about those cases."

Veronica laughed. "His lawyer is in way over his head. A friend of the family who's handling the case for free. He's not even a criminal lawyer. He's a real-estate attorney, for crying out loud. Of course, he wouldn't let Laggone answer any direct questions about those two kids, whether he knew them, or ever saw them, or anything like that. But he didn't mind letting me show his client some maps."

"Maps?"

"Potential burial sites. Survivors always have this intense need to find the body. It's like those Greek dramas they made us read in high school, with spirits that are unable to enter the afterworld until there's been a proper burial. The lawyer probably thinks that if Laggone leads us to the bodies, then maybe the DA will go easy on this kidnapping charge."

"But if Laggone admits to knowing where the bodies are buried, won't he get charged with murder?"

"Not necessarily. Eventually the lawyer will let Laggone give just enough information to narrow down the search successfully, but not enough information to reveal an exact location. It's a balancing act, and the amazing thing is that the lawyer is almost right."

"What do you mean?"

"Just knowing an approximate burial location probably doesn't constitute enough evidence to bring a murder charge. But what my real-estate friend isn't counting on is transfer evidence."

"What's that?"

Veronica hocked her leg over mine and began rubbing slowly. "Whenever people make physical contact—sex, assault, even a simple handshake—there's a transfer of matter. Substances and marks taken and left behind. Not to mention fibers and other material. If we find the bodies, we may find some usable evidence. But first I have to do this dance with Loony Louie, get him to tell me more than he wants to tell me, which will still be less than I want to know." She draped an arm across my chest. "You psychiatrists have it easy. At least the people you interview want to tell you the truth."

"Sometimes. But a lot of people come to talk to me in order to avoid talking to me."

"You're babbling again," Veronica said, still rubbing her leg against mine.

"It's late," I replied. "What I mean is, patients keep secrets from me all the time. Sometimes what a person doesn't talk about is more important than what he does talk about."

"I'm going out there again tomorrow, before Laggone's lawyer gets smart and cuts off my access." Veronica set the alarm clock by her side of the bed. "I need to get an early start. I promised the district attorney I'd meet him for breakfast. You may have heard of him—Andrew Galloway."

"He sounds vaguely familiar."

"He was a running back for the University of Oklahoma about fifteen years ago. All-American in his junior year."

"I didn't know you followed college football."

"I don't. He told me. But I thought he might be bull-shitting me, so I checked it out. He was telling me the truth."

"Why did you think he was bullshitting you?"

"He wants to sleep with me. I thought the football story was just a pickup line."

"What makes you think he wants to sleep with you?"

"Please, Harry—these things aren't difficult for a woman to figure out. You men reveal your hormonal strivings in a hundred subtle ways, the little things you do and say."

"Like what?"

"In Andrew Galloway's case, I could tell from something he said."

"And what was that?"

"I think his exact words were, 'How about staying at my place tonight so we can fuck each other's brains out?' "

"Very subtle."

"Well, I guess it seemed perfectly natural in the conversational context at the time."

"Must have been one hell of a conversation."

She patted my chest. "You're cute when you get jealous."

"Who said anything about being jealous?"

"Don't worry. He has one of those achingly perfect bodies that I'm sure I would find terribly boring." She laughed, and then she yawned. "I need to swing by my place first thing in the morning. I have notes there from another case that might help me on this one. I wish I didn't have to get up so early."

"Well, it's like the billboard says. 'If you lived here, you'd be home now.' "

"Damn it, Harry. Let's not go through that again. Give it a rest." She pulled away and turned her back toward me.

"Sorry."

She sighed, then rolled back toward me and kissed me. "No, I'm sorry. I guess I'm just not in the mood for a billboard." Her hands began to roam underneath the covers, working their magic on me. "Another kind of board, perhaps. Maybe a two-by-four, or something like that."

5: The Doorknob Effect

"What kind of animal do you think Goofy is?" asked Michael Cafferty. "You know—in the Disney cartoons."

I shrugged. "He's a dog, isn't he?"

"Shit." He stood and began to walk back and forth across my office. "That's what Junie says. That's what *everyone* says. But it doesn't make sense. Goofy can't be a dog."

"Why not?"

"Because Pluto is a dog."

"So?"

"Pluto is the only one who doesn't talk. Mickey Mouse, Donald Duck, the others—they all talk. And Goofy talks, too." He paused. When I didn't respond, he said, "Don't you see?"

"What would you like me to see?"

He threw his hands into the air. "It's not consistent. Goofy talks, but Pluto doesn't. You can't have it both ways. Either dogs can talk, or they can't. That's why I say Goofy can't be a dog, because if he's supposed to be a dog, then why is he able to talk?"

I thought, Because it's only a cartoon. I said, "There's something else to consider."

"What?"

"Pluto is naked. Goofy and all of the other characters wear clothes."

His eyes lit up. "Exactly! That's my point. Goofy isn't a dog."

"Then what is he?"

Michael Cafferty frowned. "I don't know. What kind of animal do *you* think Goofy is?"

"Suppose we can't determine what sort of animal he is. Would that trouble you?"

"What troubles me is that everyone says Goofy's a dog, and no one cares that it makes no sense at all."

He was struggling under typical teenage pressures: the stress of carving out an identity, and the tides of his own hormones and endocrine glands. He needed to forge chaos into some sort of order. Inconsistencies bothered him.

Michael returned to his chair. He opened the can of Coke he'd brought with him and took a sip. Then he rested his chin against his chest and began to pout. "I still don't see why I have to come here two times a week. I saw you on Tuesday. I shouldn't have to come back three days later."

"It was just a recommendation. If you can manage it, coming twice a week often can help move the process along."

" 'Manage it.' You mean 'afford it,' don't you?"

Before I could respond, he said, "Junie says psychiatrists are really messed up, that they don't give a shit about other people, that the only reason they become psychiatrists is because they want to figure out how they got so messed up in the first place."

I said, "And no sensible person would want to put his trust in someone like that."

He was silent for several seconds; he was probably surprised that I wasn't getting into an argument with him. "Well, I guess I can manage it. And my father can certainly afford it. Shit, I once cost him three million dollars, so paying you is peanuts."

"How did you cost him three million dollars?"

He smiled. "I thought that would get your attention." Just as quickly, the smile vanished. He gazed out the window and said, "When I was eight, I had a brain tumor. Spent three months in Children's Hospital, half-paralyzed. They thought I was going to die. My father told our priest that he'd give half his fortune to the Church if God would let me live. He was worth about six million at the time. A month later I walked out of the hospital, and he was worth half that."

He continued to stare out the window for a minute or two, twiddling something—I couldn't tell what—in his hand. Then he looked directly at me and said, "I'm not sure my father has ever forgiven me for that. On the other hand, he learned that even God can be bought off, and that was probably worth something to him."

Agree with a teenager that his parents are monsters, and soon he'll hate you for hating them. Disagree, and you'll be dismissed as the parents' untrustworthy coconspirator. I said, "Your father kept his promise to the Church. Some people might find that honorable."

"Yeah, well, you don't want priests going around calling you a welsher. That would be a real public-relations problem. Anyway, I'm tired of talking about my father."

"Perhaps you'd like to talk about Junie."

His eyes widened slightly and he pulled back a few inches. "What do you mean?"

"You've dropped her name into the conversation twice, but I don't know who she is. Is she your girlfriend?"

He looked at me without expression for a few seconds, then started to laugh. "My girlfriend? Hey, that's a good one, Dr. Kline."

He continued laughing until he began to gasp for air. After he caught his breath he sat quietly for the last few minutes of the session, chuckling occasionally to himself. When I told him it was time to leave, he sighed and rose slowly. When he reached the door, he turned and said, "Is there some kind of test . . . you know . . . some way of telling for sure . . ." His voice trailed off.

"A way of telling what?"

"Whether a guy likes girls, or whether he likes other guys."

* * *

Psychiatrists call it the doorknob effect: On his way out
of your office, when there's no time left for discussion,
your patient finally tells you what's on his mind. It may be
his way of asking to stay longer: presenting you with a
bomb that must be defused immediately. Or it may be an
act of subtle aggression: challenging you to solve a problem, then giving you no time to work on it. But usually
he's just testing your response to something, gauging your
reaction to see if he might feel safe discussing it at length
some other time. I thought Michael Cafferty's tentative
revelation probably fell into that final category.

I scanned the *Boston Globe* at the lunch table. There was
a small article about Louis Laggone on the second page of
the regional news section. The article focused mostly on the
girl who eluded the kidnapping attempt, with testimonials
from the local police and school officials regarding the level-
headedness she'd shown. Laggone's attorney was quoted
near the end of the article: He said that his client was innocent, and that he was cooperating fully with investigators.
There was no mention of the FBI or Veronica.

Mrs. Winnicot, my housekeeper, set a sandwich in front
of me. She said, "You'll be driving Melissa to her counseling appointment this afternoon, won't you?"

"Yes." Usually that task fell to Mrs. Winnicot, but once
every couple of months I went with my daughter so I could
speak to her social worker in person.

Mrs. Winnicot stood by the table, a few feet away from
me. I glanced up, our eyes met, and she turned away as if
she'd been caught in a thought she'd rather not speak out
loud.

I turned to the sports page. The Celtics still had no hope
of making the basketball play-offs. The Red Sox still had
unrealistic expectations early in the baseball season. And
Mrs. Winnicot still hovered in the background. I glanced up
again.

She said, "That woman sure can get a person to talk."

"Melissa's social worker?"

"Yes. She can get you to say things you didn't even know you were thinking."

"She's a good therapist," I said, uncertain where this conversation was headed.

Mrs. Winnicot sighed. "She might mention it when you see her this afternoon. Something I told her when she asked me how I was doing. I'd rather that you hear it first from me."

I put my newspaper away. Mrs. Winnicot sat down across the table from me. She said, "I'm visiting my son and his family next week, school vacation week."

"I know."

We had agreed that on her way to New Jersey she would drop Melissa off at the Connecticut home of her grandparents—Janet's parents. Veronica and I would have the house to ourselves for five nights: something she and I had never had before.

Mrs. Winnicot continued. "I miss my grandchildren."

"They're sweet kids." Mrs. Winnicot's son and his family had moved from nearby Arlington to New Jersey a few months earlier. Her grandchildren used to come with us on picnics.

She paused, then blurted everything out in one breath. "My son and his wife are looking for someone to provide day care, they have an extra room in the new house they built, and they've asked me to come live with them. We're going to discuss it when I visit them next week."

"Are you interested?"

"Yes."

"Oh."

She had been working for me more than a decade, living in the converted barn a few dozen yards from the house. After Janet died, her importance in Melissa's life—and mine—increased exponentially. Though a widow, she was only in her fifties, and I'd assumed she'd be with us until Melissa was old enough to leave home.

She said, "It isn't a final decision yet, of course."

"Of course."

"I was thinking, maybe when Melissa's school year ends, two months from now. Would that give you enough notice?"

"Yes," I said. "That's very fair."

"It was one of those conversations where the social worker talks to you privately to see how things are going with Melissa from your point of view, and then before you know it you're telling her your life story. Melissa didn't hear me say I might leave. She doesn't know about this yet. And like I said, Dr. Kline, nothing is certain yet."

"I understand, Mrs. Winnicot."

After all the years we were still on a last-name basis with one another. I'd never discussed it with her, never made a unilateral or consensual decision for it to stay that way. I remembered an episode from Mary Tyler Moore's old show, where her character experimented by calling her boss "Lou" instead of "Mr. Grant." The experiment failed. Old habits die hard.

Mrs. Winnicot began to say something, then changed her mind and remained silent. A moment later she said, "I'll come back later to clean the dishes."

"That's all right. I'll take care of it."

She headed out of the room, then paused in the doorway. "It would be very hard for me to leave her. And you." She walked away before I could respond.

Melissa's therapist had an office in Belmont, a twenty-minute drive from our home. My daughter had been seeing Anna Santiago for almost a year, but the problems had been brewing for much longer than that. I guess that's usually the case.

Janet had died more than six years earlier. Her struggle with pancreatic cancer had been mercifully brief: Just a few months passed between the first signs of illness and her death in the early hours of a cold winter morning. Afterward I came home from the hospital and sat in Melissa's room, waiting for her to awaken so I could tell her the news. When she finally opened her eyes, I tried to say the lines I'd rehearsed—about God loving Janet too much to see her suffer any longer, and Janet going to heaven where she would watch over us forever. But I couldn't get the words out.

Without expression Melissa said, "Mommy's dead, isn't she?"

"Yes, sweetheart. Mommy's dead."

She responded with motionless silence: no tears, no wailing, no reaching out to me in anger or pain. I tried to hug her, but she pulled away. I tried to get her to talk, but she kept her thoughts buried inside. Then, and for five years afterward, her pain remained mostly hidden from view.

But then a mentally ill man I knew attacked me. Melissa witnessed it. That incident was probably the trigger for what occurred a short time later: At the end of a school day, Melissa broke down just before she would have boarded the bus for the trip home. She ran inside and locked herself in the bathroom. When I arrived on the scene, summoned by her frightened teacher, Melissa pressed her face against me and screamed, the sound muffled by my chest. Then she sobbed for several minutes, until the tension in her body dissipated and she collapsed against me. It had been a long time coming.

A colleague directed me to Anna Santiago, and my daughter and the social worker had been meeting ever since. Every two or three months Anna asked to talk with me and with Mrs. Winnicot. She did so with my daughter's permission. She wanted to know us better—the better to understand Melissa's world and its impact on her. She asked questions. She listened. But she was always careful not to reveal any information Melissa had told her in confidence.

And so on that Friday afternoon in April, she invited me into her consultation room after her session with Melissa. She was a large woman with long hair, prematurely gray, pulled back tightly into a ponytail. Her dark complexion contrasted with piercing blue eyes that seemed to bear down on me with unwavering intensity.

She began our brief meeting with her usual opening remark. "I asked Melissa if she wanted to be present while we talk, but she preferred to wait in the reception area."

Dolls and children's toys were piled high in one corner of the room. In another was a computer that displayed a Snow White screen saver. "My daughter never talks about her therapy."

"Do you ask?"

"I try not to push."

"Why is that?"

"She's been pushed enough."

"By whom?"

"By events."

"I see." She paused. "What do you think would happen if you asked her about her meetings with me?"

I shrugged. "It might harm her therapy."

"How so?"

"If she thought I was going to ask her about it, she might not talk openly with you. That way she wouldn't have to lie to me when she answered, 'Nothing much.' "

She laughed, though I hadn't intended it as a joke. "That does seem to be one of her stock phrases. But tell me—is it possible that by not asking, you make her think you don't care about her?"

"Did she say that?"

She didn't answer. She knew that I knew she wouldn't respond directly to a question about her private conversations with Melissa.

I said, "She knows I care. There's no way she could doubt that."

"Are you sure?"

"I'm sure."

"I see."

"Listen," I said, a little irritated. "We have problems sometimes. Who doesn't? But we have a good life together."

"We?"

"Melissa and me."

"What about Mrs. Winnicot?"

"What about her?" I asked.

"She's part of your household, too, isn't she?"

"She's not family. She's an employee."

Anna Santiago cocked her head to one side and raised one eyebrow. I guess every therapist has a grab bag of gestures to choose from.

"All right," I said. "She's more than an employee. A lot more. And yes, I know she's thinking about leaving us. She just told me a few hours ago."

"Does Melissa know?"

"Not unless you told her."

"I wouldn't do that. It's not my prerogative."

In the silence that followed I became acutely aware of the distant buzz of the white-noise machine in the reception area. It was there to muffle any sound that might come through the office's thick door and soundproofed walls.

"What about your friend Veronica?"

"What about her?"

"You didn't include her in your 'we,' either. And I think Melissa would consider her to be a part of your household." When I offered no reply, she continued. "When we spoke the last time, I mentioned that it might be useful for me to meet her."

"Yes."

"I haven't heard from her. Perhaps she feels uncomfortable with the idea."

"I think she'd feel pretty damn comfortable with it."

"Oh." She paused. "That would mean . . ."

"That I didn't tell her you wanted to talk with her."

"May I ask why?"

I sighed. "You probably won't believe this, but I forgot to tell her. Didn't even think about it until you mentioned it again just now."

I recalled my reluctance earlier in the week to let Veronica come with me to the parent-faculty conference at Melissa's school. I thought I wanted the two of them to be close. Maybe I wasn't as certain of that as I believed I was.

I said, "People do forget things sometimes."

"And often with reason." She smiled. No further interpretation was necessary. "Perhaps you'll consider asking her to call me."

"Would you like to call her? I'm sure she wouldn't mind."

"That's really not my prerogative, either," she replied.

Anna Santiago stood and nodded, her way of letting me know our meeting was over. I walked toward the door, then turned back to face her. I said, "An old love song from some 1930s or 1940s movie. My parents used to have it on an old seventy-eight record. 'I'm Putting All My Eggs in One Basket.' Ever hear of it?"

"I don't believe so."

"I heard it on the radio as we were driving here. Melissa hates it when I play that station. Anyway, it made me think—I'm my daughter's only basket. Mrs. Winnicot and Veronica are very important to her, sure. But I'm the only parent she has left, and that puts a lot of pressure on both of us, especially since she's a girl. I mean, what do I know about being a little girl? I can't begin to count how many times she's asked me something, and I've wished I could say, 'I don't know. That's a girls' question. Go ask your mother.' "

Anna Santiago smiled softly. "I'm sure you're familiar with the doorknob effect," she said.

On our way home from Belmont to Concord, we made a deal. Melissa agreed that it would be all right to take a detour past the Tufts campus, and I let her put one of her cassettes into the dashboard tape deck. The sound came blaring out: a heavily syncopated, barely decipherable ode to the pleasures of teenage lust.

"What *is* that stuff?"

"It's Megadeth."

"How apt."

"Huh?"

"Nothing. Please—turn it down, will you?"

"*Dad-dee!* you said I could listen."

"You can listen, and I'll have to listen, but since we can't put it to a vote of everyone within a five-mile radius, let's be more considerate of them."

She turned the sound down from nerve-damage range to mere earsplitting. "It's better than that stuff you were playing earlier," she joked.

Tufts was just a few miles out of our way, set on a hill that straddled the town line between Medford and Somerville. With its ivy-lined brick buildings, and its large trees that weren't yet in full spring bloom, the campus stood in sharp contrast to the stores and triple-decker homes of the working-class neighborhood that surrounded it. Its founder was reputed to have said, "I shall set a light upon the hill." Latter-day college officials referred to it as "a small school of high quality." In my day we referred to it as a blight upon the hill, and a high school of small quality. I mentioned that to Melissa and watched her suppress a chuckle.

I could drive there from Concord in less than half an hour, but I hadn't visited Tufts in years. There were several buildings I'd never seen before, wedged into previously open corners of a campus that had no room to expand beyond its perimeter. It was a curious blend of the familiar and the new, like running into an old friend who had lost weight or changed her hairstyle since the last meeting.

We drove past the ball field where Bobby Beck called himself out at home more than twenty years earlier. I parked near the student center and we walked up the hill toward the administration building. "Your mom and I used to bring you here in a stroller when you were very little," I said. "Do you remember?"

"I don't think so."

We came to the classroom building where Marjorie Morris's mother used to teach. Then we passed the chapel, with the tiny sheltered antechamber where Janet and I sometimes went late at night. One winter evening a resourceful campus cop followed our footsteps in the snow

and surprised us as we huddled in the small alcove. He
checked our ID cards, wished us well, and went on his way.

The library was next to the chapel. It was artfully designed to inhabit the hill, rather than to sit upon it. Thus its
two aboveground stories seemed to grow sideways out of
the embankment. And you could walk directly onto the
roof, which was dotted by rectangular plots of grass to
heighten the overall effect. From the roof, we had a pano-
ramic view of the Boston skyline, stretching left to right
from Government Center to the Back Bay.

"This is where your mom and I first met. I was a senior
and she was a freshman. One night there was a power
blackout on campus. You couldn't study or watch TV or do
much of anything else, so your uncle Bobby and I took a
walk up here to the library roof. She was here with a
couple of her friends. Uncle Bobby introduced himself and
me to them."

"He was pretty cool, huh?"

I laughed. "Yeah, I guess so. But then he did something
stupid, and your mom got angry and walked away. I went
after her to apologize, and that's how we got to know each
other."

"What did he do that was stupid?"

I shrugged. "It was a long time ago. I don't remember."

What Bobby did was pull a six-pack out from his trench
coat and offer beer to three underage freshman girls, but I
didn't see any reason to tell Melissa about that. The first
girl giggled. The second girl reached for one of the cans.
Janet knocked the can out of Bobby's hand, glared at him,
and lambasted him for doing something that could put them
on disciplinary probation. She stormed off down the hill
toward the women's dorms.

"Nice going, Bobby," I said. "She knows our names,
thanks to you. I'll try to calm her down so she doesn't report us." I ran after her and fed her some nonsense story
about Bobby being under a lot of pressure because he'd just
learned his grandmother had died, and I promised I'd make
sure he got some professional help. She kept walking

toward her dorm. She didn't tell me to leave, so I walked with her.

She turned to me when we reached the dorm. "Is your friend going to his grandmother's funeral?"

"Well, she died in Arizona, and we Jews bury our dead before the body gets cold, so he missed it. That's why he's so upset."

She sneered at me. "I'm Jewish, too. And your whole story is horse hockey, isn't it?"

"Horse hockey?"

"You're probably more at home with the term 'bull-shit.' "

I grinned. "Well, some of it might be 'horse hockey,' but he really does need professional help."

Her sneer turned into a smile. "Just the same, it was sweet of you to walk with me. Good night, Gary." She stood on her toes, kissed my forehead lightly, and ducked into the building.

I snapped out of my reverie when Melissa said, "Did you know right away that you would fall in love with her and get married?"

"Well, I knew right away that she was someone special, and that I wanted to see her again."

The truth was, I was smitten by her—so much so that only on the third or fourth casual meeting on campus over the next couple of weeks did I work up the courage to correct her after she called me "Gary."

Melissa said, "You've been talking about her more."

"What do you mean?"

"You used to talk about Mommy a lot. Then for a long time you hardly talked about her at all. And now, for a little while, you've been doing it again."

"Oh." I hadn't noticed a change, but I didn't doubt Melissa's observation. "How do you feel about that?"

"Ugh. Now you sound like Ms. Santiago. She always wants to know how I *feel* about things. Yech. Barf city."

I laughed. We began retracing our steps to the car. "You

know that what you and Ms. Santiago talk about stays private, don't you?"

"I know."

"But if there's ever anything you want to tell me, you can."

"Are you asking me something?"

"No," I said. "That's not my 'prerogative.' "

"Your what?"

"Never mind," I said. "It was just a joke."

When we reached the bottom of the hill I pointed out the dorm Janet used to live in. A young couple walked out of the building and strode arm in arm toward the student center. Melissa studied them closely for a minute or two, and then we got into the car.

She said, "It makes me nervous."

"What's that, sweetheart?"

"When you talk about Mommy, it makes me feel nervous."

6: The Scene of the Crime

Listen, my children, and you shall hear
Of the midnight ride of Paul Revere,
On the eighteenth of April, in 'Seventy-five;
Hardly a man is now alive
Who remembers that famous day and year.

Longfellow got it wrong. Writing eighty-six years after the fact, he mentioned neither William Dawes nor Dr. Samuel Prescott, the other two riders; and he elevated Paul Revere to a prominence that was not truly deserved.

It was two by the village clock,
When he came to the bridge in Concord town.

Actually, at two o'clock in the morning, Revere was standing with his thumb up his rear in a Lexington field, captured and taken prisoner by the British. William Dawes eluded the soldiers, reversed direction, and hightailed it back to Lexington center. Dr. Prescott guided his horse over a stone wall and through the underbrush to spread the alarm that the British were coming: the only one of the three riders to make it safely to Concord.

These things matter, at least to the citizens of Concord. There are other New England towns just as tranquil, with upscale gift shops just as quaint, homes just as stately, woods and open meadows just as flush with natural beauty. But Concord's heritage sets it apart: battlefields and historic homes, lifelong residents who trace their lineage back to the Revolution and beyond, townsfolk who speak fondly of Thoreau—always placing the accent on the first syllable—with such familiarity that you'd think he was still living in a room at Ralph Waldo Emerson's house.

Concord's heritage: At daybreak on April 19, 1775, British soldiers fired at a band of Minutemen on Lexington Green. A few hours later, at North Bridge in Concord, the colonials fired for the first time at the British. Those two battles, and the skirmishes at Merriam's Corner and other points in between, marked the beginning of the armed American insurrection. Nearly two and one quarter centuries later, that beginning is still celebrated on the third Monday in April, known in Massachusetts as Patriots' Day.

As I walked through town on Saturday afternoon preparations were well under way for the Patriot's Day celebration two days later. Small flags were attached to the parking meters, tricolor bunting adorned the storefronts, and a work crew was piecing together the final slats of the reviewing stand for Monday's parade. When I reached the town square, I walked around the grassy ellipse toward the Colonial Inn. Bobby and I had planned to meet there to talk about the suit Celeste Oberlin's parents were filing against Dr. Frank Porter.

A few tourists were sipping beverages on the front patio of the old hotel. Tea and scones were being served in the lobby. I passed through to the small taproom in the rear of the inn.

Bobby wasn't there yet. I sat at one of the small tables, ordered sparkling water, and watched the basketball game on the television above the bar. The Celtics were playing the Bulls. Scottie Pippen was yelling and gesturing at a referee who'd just called a foul on the Chicago forward.

"Christ, I hate that crap! Don't you, Doc?" Alfred Korvich, the town's police chief, sat down next to me, uninvited.

"Have a seat, Chief," I said, but the sarcasm was too subtle for him to appreciate.

He was watching Pippen argue. "I really *hate* it. Play ball, damn it. Whatsa matter—aren't you getting paid enough? Ah!" He waved his hands in disgust.

"Pippen's got a good argument, Chief. He had his position established. It should've been called an offensive foul against Boston."

"It doesn't matter. Once the ref calls the play, that's what it is. You ever see a referee or umpire change his mind just because a player bitched about it?" Without waiting for a reply, he said, "Of course not."

I glanced at the beer in his hand. He noticed, and said, "Off duty, Doc. No hurry to get home, though—I'm married, after all." He laughed at his own poor joke, then pointed at the television screen. "I played forward in high school. All-state my senior year. I learned when the ref calls you for a foul, you keep your mouth shut and you raise your hand."

"Raise your hand?"

He nodded. "That makes it easy for the scorer to tell which player to charge the foul against. You accept the responsibility, and you respect the ref's authority."

I was surprised to learn he'd starred at basketball. I'd never thought of Alfred Korvich as the athletic type, probably because of the impressive mass of flab around his middle. Bobby referred to him as Lower Case *b* because of his shape: a prodigious potbelly hanging off an otherwise skinny frame.

"You play any sports when you were in school, Doc?"

"Baseball."

"What position?"

"In high school, catcher. In college, left bench."

"You don't look like a catcher."

"I guess my college coach had the same opinion."

He downed a gulp of beer, made a lip-smacking sound, and turned his eyes toward the television again. "Too much money. That's what's ruining the sport. Just like baseball. Don't you think so?"

"It's a complicated issue, Chief."

He snorted. "You must be one of those people, sees everything in shades of gray. Well, some things are gray, I guess. But most things are black-and-white if you cut through the crap. Black-and-white, right and wrong. Like with my youngest boy, twelve years old. You know what he did the other day?"

"What's that?"

"He tells me he made up this poem. 'Listen my children and you shall hear of the midnight ride of diarrhea. Over the pillow, over the sheet, the fifty-yard dash for the toilet seat.' He lost half his allowance for that."

"You punished him for making fun of 'Paul Revere's Ride'?"

"I punished him for telling me he made the poem up. It's been around for years. I heard it the first time when I was in grade school."

"He was trying to impress you. Sons do that with their fathers."

"Well, lying doesn't impress me." He watched some more of the basketball action. "The game has changed too much. You grow up around here?"

I nodded. "Newton."

"Then you know what I mean. You're old enough to remember how it used to be. The Celtics against Philadelphia, Russell against Chamberlain."

"Sure."

"Back then, the middle of April meant the championship series. Now the season drags out until June. I swear, being in the basketball play-offs is like being in the phone book. You practically have to make a special effort to stay out."

It was the longest face-to-face conversation I'd ever had with Alfred Korvich, and he was the one who began it and kept it going. I wondered what he wanted from me. Then, just as I was getting ready to conclude that I was being needlessly suspicious, he said, "You give any thought to what we talked about the other day on the phone?"

"What do you mean?"

"That new patient of yours, Michael Cafferty. You saw him again yesterday. He say anything about his friend, Senator Ellington's son?"

"And what makes you think I saw this Michael Cafferty yesterday?"

He slapped his free palm—the one that wasn't wrapped around his beer mug—against the table with moderate force. "The kid damn well *better* have seen you yesterday. He told his probation officer he'd be getting two sessions a week, and the probation officer wrote it right into the supervision plan." He paused, then smiled slyly. "Hey, maybe we should require the kid to bring something in writing. A note from you every few weeks to verify that he's keeping his appointments. I'd hate to see him get in trouble for violating the terms of his probation."

I thought of a half-dozen wiseass replies, but the man was obviously goading me, and I didn't want to give him the satisfaction of succeeding. I glanced at my watch, wondered where the hell Bobby was, and tried to focus on the basketball game.

"You don't like me, do you, Doc?"

"I don't like the way you try to get me to reveal information about my patients."

"Okay, okay," Korvich said. "No more pressure. Of course, you realize you just admitted he's your patient. But don't worry, Doc—your secret is safe with me. And I'm completely sincere about that." He laughed.

"Didn't you say you were on your way home, Chief?"

He stopped laughing. "All right, no hard feelings. Look, I'll tell you what I'll do. That hit-and-run case. The other day on the phone, I gave you the brush-off when you asked me about it. You still want to know about it?"

"What can you tell me?"

"Well, the victim, Charles Morris—I guess you knew him pretty well."

"I knew his ex-wife, who's deceased. She taught me when I was in college. I never met him."

"You know his daughter, though. That's what you said over the phone."

"Barely. I met her when she was a little kid. She saw me the other day and recognized me. I didn't know who she was until she told me."

"The other day on the phone, you told me you and she were friends."

" 'Acquaintances' would be more accurate."

He considered that for a few moments, then said, "We don't have much. Seventh of March, Sunday, a little after five in the morning, about an hour before sunrise. Charles Morris went out alone for his morning jog. Sometimes his daughter goes with him, but today she doesn't. He's running along Musketaquid Road, down at the base of Nashawtuc Hill, less than half a mile from his house. Then, wham!" He smacked the table for emphasis. "Checkout time. Do not pass 'Go,' do not collect two hundred dollars. Proceed directly to meet your Maker. Or then again, maybe not—he was a lawyer, after all."

"I see you're all broken up about it."

"Didn't know the guy." He sighed. "Still, I guess it's a lousy way to go."

"The *Journal* said he died instantly."

"The *Journal* was wrong," Korvich said. "Morris crawled a good fifty, sixty feet. We could tell from the trail of blood—of which there was a hell of a lot, let me tell you. We gave the *Journal* the 'quick death' story because that's what people like to hear, and no harm done."

"So you lied," I said. "Like father, like son."

"It's not the same thing," he snarled. "You want to hear about this, or not?"

I nodded. "Any idea who did it?"

"Let's see how smart you are. It was dark, but it was clear, and the road was completely dry. The stretch Charles Morris was running on is straight with pretty good sight lines. His jogging suit had reflector stripes. No skid marks near the point of impact. And no alcohol or drugs in the victim's blood. What does all that tell you?"

I shrugged. "I don't know. That whoever hit him was driving recklessly?"

"You got it. Drunk, probably. If the driver's sober, he's more likely to stop, because he usually realizes he's doubly fucked if we get him for leaving the scene of an accident, too. But if he's drunk, he figures he's doubly fucked if he stays around. Better to let the alcohol wash out of his system, which only takes a few hours."

"You're assuming he knew he hit Morris."

"He knew. He or she."

"What makes you so certain?"

Korvich reached for the beer nuts on the table. "Like I said, there weren't any skid marks near the point of impact. But there were skid marks about eighty feet *past* the impact, leading away from the victim. And tire impressions right near the skids, on both sides of the road—like you'd make if you were doing a three-point U-turn. I figure the driver jammed on his brakes after he made contact, then turned around and drove back to see what had happened. Then he made like a bat out of hell to get away."

"How do you know that?"

"The live-in maid for one of the Musketaquid Road residents was out walking the dog, says a dark sedan whipped by and almost hit her. Scared the shit out of her. She tried to get the license number, but the car was going so fast she could only get the first two digits, and she wasn't even sure of that."

"Can you tell what kind of car it was from the tire impressions?"

Chief Korvich shook his head. "Tires don't tell you very much. We got the tread size, a Goodyear model pretty common on midsized cars. If we come up with a suspect vehicle, we'll be able to match them up. Until then, not much good it does us."

I glanced at the television screen mounted above the bar. The Celtics were down by twenty points midway through the third quarter. The bartender asked us if we minded letting him switch to a golf match. Neither of us cared.

Korvich continued. "Paint chips, they're a different matter. With a good spectrographic analysis, you can get a fix on the make and year of the vehicle, sometimes even the model. But we didn't find any chips."

"Did you have any luck with the partial license number?"

"Two numbers don't narrow things down very much, and the maid who gave them to us wasn't very sure of even that. I played one hunch, but it didn't pan out."

"What was that?"

"You familiar with Musketaquid Road?"

It was a narrow rural road, little more than half a mile long, running behind a bend in the Sudbury River. "I know where it is. I can't remember the last time I drove on it."

"There's no reason you'd use it, unless you lived nearby or you were visiting someone who lived there. Especially at that time of morning. And that was my hunch—that whoever killed Morris lived in the area. So I got the registry to send me the license-plate numbers of all the cars registered to people in the neighborhood. But none of them matched the two digits the maid gave us. Then I did record checks on all the residents, came up with two people who've had arrests for driving under the influence. Checked their cars for damage, looked for a tire match. Didn't find anything."

"It doesn't sound very promising."

"Nope. Of course, that's not what I'd say publicly. A case like this, sometimes the best you can hope for is the driver turns himself in, because he thinks things will go better for him. For that to happen, he has to think there's a good chance of getting caught. That's why the official line is, 'We have a witness and we're working on some promising leads.' But the truth is, we've got zilch. Nada. Bupkis."

"So why are you telling me this?"

He stared directly at me for several seconds, and his facial expression seemed to soften a bit. I thought it was just the effect of his beer, but then he said, "I was in the National Guard. I appreciate what you tried to do about the statue."

He was referring to the statue of the Minuteman that stood near North Bridge. It was sculpted by Daniel Chester French, a Concord resident better known for his statue of Lincoln at the Lincoln Memorial. A few years earlier the National Guard asked the town for permission to make a copy of the statue; they wanted to place it outside their national headquarters. At a raucous town meeting, a few residents—myself among them—argued in favor of the proposal. But most townsfolk were loath to share the statue. They spoke piously about preserving the town's history by ensuring its uniqueness, but I thought it was just Yankee parochialism at its most base. In any event, their point of view prevailed.

Alfred Korvich raised his half-empty beer mug, as if offering a toast, and recited the words found on the base of the statue: " 'By the rude bridge that arched the flood, their flag to April's breeze unfurled. Here once the embattled farmers stood, and fired the shot heard 'round the world.' "

Korvich set his mug on the table. "There are a lot of selfish, tight-ass dickheads in this town," he said, breaking the poetic mood he'd created. "On that particular occasion—and I'm completely sincere about this—you weren't one of them." He glanced beyond me and gestured toward someone. "Unlike that asshole over there."

I turned in the direction of Korvich's gaze. Bobby Beck waved to me from the doorway. As Bobby made his way toward us, Korvich stood.

"Hey, pal—sorry I'm late. Glad to see you found yourself some company while you were waiting. How are you, Chief?"

Bobby extended his hand. Korvich glanced at it for a moment, then gave it a perfunctory shake. He turned to leave.

Bobby said, "A pleasure talking with you, Chief."

"Don't push it, counselor," Korvich replied, and then he walked briskly from the taproom.

"There he goes," Bobby said. "Lower Case *d*."

"I thought you always called him Lower Case *b*."

"When he's walking left to right, he's Lower Case *b*. At the moment he's walking right to left. What were the two of you talking about before I came in?"

"Nothing much. Basketball, Paul Revere's ride, the epistemological ramifications of the big bang theory and quantum mechanics. Do you want to order something to drink?"

"No thanks." He pushed Korvich's mug to the far end of the table. "Charming guy. I guess he doesn't like lawyers."

I shook my head. "He doesn't like you. He didn't like your efforts to keep the National Guard from making a copy of the Minuteman statue. Words like 'asshole' and 'dickhead' rolled trippingly off his tongue."

"Eloquence is such an important quality in a public official."

"Indeed. And he's completely sincere about that."

"I don't get it."

I said, "It's just an expression he likes to use." I dropped a few dollars on the table, then we walked outside.

We got into Bobby's station wagon in front of the inn. "Just move Kenny's baseball glove out of your way," he said. "You can throw it in the back."

Bobby's younger son was in his first year of Little League. I examined the boy's glove for a few seconds. It was one of those unusually pigmented Japanese creations. When I tossed it onto the backseat, it landed on two aluminum bats. The bats clanged together.

Bobby said, "Blue gloves, metal bats—things have really changed." He pulled away from the curb. "It saves money on broken bats. But it's sad to think of kids growing up and never hearing the sound of wood making contact with the ball when they hit it."

"Korvich would probably agree with you. He's a sports purist."

"Another fine quality." He glanced in my direction when we reached the corner, looking past me for cars approaching from our right. He must have noticed me yawning, slouching back into my seat, because he said, "You look tired, pal of mine."

"I didn't get much sleep last night. I dreamed that Lamb Chop died—"

"The hand puppet?"

I nodded. "I dreamed that Lamp Chop died, and I was the one who had to break the news to Shari Lewis.".

"Funny."

"It didn't seem funny in the dream. When I told her, she just stood there with a blank expression on her face and her lips tightly sealed. But her other two puppets started screaming and crying."

"Ah, the mark of true artistry in a ventriloquist. Did she drink a glass of water at the same time?"

"Finally Shari Lewis screamed, and I woke up and couldn't get back to sleep."

"What did you have for dinner last night?"

"We went to Sol Azteca. I had the enchiladas rojas. Why?"

He turned right and cruised slowly down Main Street. "Maybe you should stay away from there for a while."

"I don't get nightmares from Mexican food."

"Then what was it?"

The sidewalks were teeming with tourists and Saturday shoppers. We passed the reviewing stand, now fully constructed for Monday's parade. I said, "Helen Winnicot is thinking of retiring, and—"

"And you don't know how you'll break the news to Melissa."

"Very good. I should put you in charge of interpreting my patients' dreams."

"You actually do that stuff?"

"Only when they insist."

"Yours is certainly a very strange profession." Bobby continued along Main Street, past the town library and Concord Academy. "Speaking of which, tell me what you think of the Frank Porter situation."

Bobby had first mentioned the case and given me the

materials to review three days earlier. I'd met with Porter the following afternoon and spoken briefly with Bobby afterward. But this was our first conversation since I'd reviewed all of the materials. I said, "From what you told me about Celeste Oberlin, she was probably so unstable for such a long time that any therapist would have a hard time treating her."

"So I gather."

"It's one of the paradoxes of psychotherapy that the sicker a patient is, the easier it is to make an immediate impact, but the easier it is to blunder into making things worse."

"And you think Porter blundered?"

"I think we're way beyond blundering here, Bobby. You're definitely in the realm of malpractice. The Oberlins' attorney is probably salivating."

"Now that you mention it, some of his written correspondence has felt a little moist. How would you summarize Porter's malpractice? Harry? Are you listening?"

"Huh? Oh—sorry. I just realized where we were. Make a right turn at the corner coming up."

Bobby turned onto Nashawtuc Road, a country lane leading across the narrow Sudbury River and up to Nashawtuc Hill. After we crossed over the river, I told Bobby to turn left.

Musketaquid Road had the bumpy feel of a New England road that had seen its share of winter freezes, but wasn't so buckled yet as to require repaving. Its narrowness forced drivers to slow down for cars moving in the opposite direction.

Bobby said, "Lose something?"

"What do you mean?"

"The way you're looking out the front window, scanning both sides back and forth. What are you looking for?"

"Marjorie Morris's father was killed somewhere on this road. I was wondering exactly where."

"Ah yes—Marjorie Morris. She of the supple torso." He

paused. "But since you didn't watch the movie, you don't know what I'm talking about."

"I think I can guess," I said.

Bobby turned around when we reached the end of the road. As we drove back along the short stretch, I found myself trying to visualize the fatal accident. But then I realized I had no idea which direction Charles Morris had been running, or whether he was struck by a car from behind or heading toward him.

Bobby said, "We met him once. Do you remember? Professor Morris had both of us over to dinner one night."

"I remember going to her house, but I don't remember anything about her husband."

"Me neither. I just remember not liking him." Bobby gestured toward the side of the road. "Hell of a way to go. Lucky for him, the paper said he never knew what hit him."

"Korvich says the paper got it wrong."

"Why were you and old Lower Case talking about Charles Morris?"

"We'd already said all there was to say about the big bang theory and quantum mechanics."

"Are the police making any headway on the case?"

"He's almost certain that he can rule you out as a suspect."

"Well, the locals aren't very experienced dealing with this sort of thing. And I don't think Korvich could find his ass in the dark without a flashlight." Bobby turned back toward the center of town. "You were about to tell me what you thought of Frank Porter's therapy with Celeste Oberlin."

It was the photographs that first caught my attention in the packet of materials Bobby gave me—materials the Oberlins said had been given to their daughter by Frank Porter. There were four pictures of Porter sitting on a couch in his office. He was smiling at the camera in three of them and gazing forlornly in the fourth snapshot. Each picture had a handwritten message on the back side. *This is me when I think about you. . . . When you're lonely, remember how much I love you. . . . Smile right back at the sun.* The fourth picture carried this caption: *Baby Girl, I'm sad when you're sad.*

All four captions were signed, *Love, Dad.*

There was an audiocassette of Porter singing lullabies and reading children's bedtime stories like *Goodnight, Moon* and *Runaway Bunny.*

There were dozens of notes addressed to Baby Girl, with messages of encouragement and exhortation. *Just remember, I'm still your Dad. . . . Don't forget to take your cold medicine. . . . Your Dad will always love you.* Some of the notes hinted at something darker. *I miss you, all of you. . . . I wish I could be there to hold you and stroke you until the pain goes away.*

"I've never seen anything like it," I said. "It looks like Porter was involved in some bizarre effort to reparent Celeste Oberlin. It's not unusual for a patient to respond like a child to her therapist. But I've never heard of a therapist who urged it on so directly."

"Could it have contributed to her final depression?"

"Well, you said she was unstable. You mentioned drug abuse, previous suicide attempts, psychiatric hospitalizations. Did any of it predate her therapy with Frank Porter?"

"Yes," Bobby replied. "She started seeing him right after she was released from the psychiatric ward at Mount Auburn Hospital. It was her fourth psychiatric admission in two years, and three of them resulted from intentional overdoses or cutting herself. How is that related to the question of his liability for her suicide?"

"Dermatologists have a saying that's supposed to summarize everything there is to know about treating skin problems. 'If it's wet, dry it; if it's dry, wet it.' "

"Cute. But what's your point?"

"Psychiatry can be summed up neatly, too. If a patient is too stiff, loosen him up. If he's too loose, tighten him up."

"Keep going."

"The more unstable your patient is, the more important

it is to stick with what's real. You don't encourage someone to explore their fantasies—you sure as hell don't guide them into creating new fantasies—when they're having a hard time distinguishing fantasy from fact. Celeste Oberlin was too loose. Porter needed to tighten her up. Instead he just made her more loose, until she must have felt like her insides were spilling out of her."

"Do you think he was screwing her?"

"I don't know. But he was definitely playing into any fantasies she may have had about that sort of thing."

Bobby sighed and shook his head sadly. 'I can't imagine anything worse than outliving your own child. Especially when the child is the instrument of her own death."

"How much are the Oberlins asking for in their suit?"

"You're not permitted to specify an amount when you sue in Massachusetts. But if they could, my guess is they'd be asking for five million, maybe more."

"Have you met them?"

"No. But if Porter insists on letting the suit go forward, it's inevitable that I will. I'll have to depose them, and I'll have to try to get them to reveal themselves as the sort of parents who would make any kid crazy enough to try to kill herself."

"Nice guy."

"Believe me, I don't want it to come to that. That's why I'm adopting my fifty-fifty strategy for this case."

"Fifty-fifty?"

Bobby slowed down to let some pedestrians use a crosswalk. "If this thing goes to trial, the Oberlins stand at least an outside chance of getting their five million. I want to end this fast, without pissing the insurance company off. If I can persuade Porter to let me make a settlement, I'll offer the Oberlins six hundred thousand dollars. Normally my first offer would be much less. But I think there's a fifty-fifty chance they'll take the six hundred without dragging things out."

"Their lawyer would take one third of that, right?"

Bobby nodded. "Not a bad return for investing twenty or thirty hours of time so far."

"Do you know your upper lip sweats whenever you talk about large sums of money?"

"It's an allergic reaction," he said.

"What sort of allergy?"

"I'm allergic to poverty."

"I hear they're developing shots for that."

"It's about time."

We drove through the center of town, then a mile up Monument Street to my house. We sat for a few minutes in the driveway. I glanced at Mrs. Winnicot's quarters: the old barn that had been converted into a garage and an apartment. Bobby asked, "Is she definitely leaving?"

"She's going to decide in a week or two. I haven't told Melissa yet. No need to alarm her unless it's certain. She's known Mrs. Winnicot her entire life."

"How do you think she'll take the news?"

"I don't know."

I recalled a patient I treated briefly, seven or eight years earlier. The middle-aged CEO was referred to me by his internist. At our first meeting the man told me he couldn't concentrate on his work and was afraid of being fired by his board of directors. He wasn't depressed. He wasn't anxious. He just couldn't concentrate on his work, and he didn't have a clue why.

When I took his history, I learned that many years earlier he had witnessed a boating accident that claimed his young son's life. But he didn't want to talk about that. "I'm here for a tune-up," he said, "not an engine overhaul."

"But you've kept everything inside," I said, "like a dam blocking a river."

"So?"

"Dams overflow. Sometimes they burst. Your problems at work are a warning sign. You have to let some of the water run off while you're still in control of it."

He stopped meeting with me after three or four sessions. He accepted a generous severance package and resigned from his job. Several months later he came upon a dog that had been struck by another driver. The animal, barely alive, lay whimpering and shivering in the road. As a small crowd gathered, the man watched helplessly while the dog expired in his arms. And then the dam broke. He cried uncontrollably, screamed his son's name, raved until he was restrained by bystanders. He was rushed to a hospital emergency room. That evening, while awaiting transfer to a private psychiatric hospital, he hurled himself through a window and fell to his death.

Bobby shook my shoulder. "Wake up, pal of mine. What are you thinking about?"

I sighed. "My daughter. This would be a bad time to have to deal with another loss."

"I didn't realize there was such a thing as a good time."

7: Drawing First Blood

Early Sunday afternoon, playacting Minutemen lined up against playacting Redcoats and performed a modern-day rendition of the skirmish at Merriam's Corner. There was no blood, no screaming, no battered bodies or tattered flags strewn upon the ground: only the playful whoops of the participants, the spectators' applause, and the anachronistic jingling of an ice-cream truck on the shoulder of Old Bedford Road.

Veronica cheered as loudly as anyone there. "Aren't you glad I talked you into coming?" she said.

"Not really. It's not my idea of a good time."

"But it's history. And you're always telling me how much you enjoy the town because of its history."

"I like the parades. I like the memorial ceremonies. I like the historic homes and the old gravestones. But I can do without the mock battles. I've treated too many victims of the real thing." Years earlier I ran a psychiatric ward at a Veterans Administration hospital. The patients there didn't whoop when they talked about war.

"Geez, Harry. Lighten up."

"Yeah, Dad," echoed Melissa. "Lighten up." She and Veronica looked at one another and shared a conspirators' grin.

A Minuteman with poor judgment blundered alone into a

line of British soldiers. Three rubber-tipped bayonets dispatched him to a bloodless death.

Janet had always shared my disdain for sanitized replications of combat. "What an odd ritual," she said shortly after we moved to Concord. "It's like recreating a car accident or a plane crash."

"It reminds me of cartoon violence," I replied. "Like the coyote who was always chasing the Road Runner. He used to fall off a cliff, land in a puff of desert sand, and then reappear in the next scene. Those cartoons made me anxious when I was a little kid. I couldn't figure out whether I was supposed to feel frightened by them, or amused. Pretty dumb, huh?"

"Of course not," Janet said, placing her hand in mine. "I think it's sweet."

Janet thought my aversion to simulated warfare was a mark of my sensitive nature. Veronica apparently thought I was an idiot.

Pungent smoke from the firing of muskets wafted over the three of us. The battle was proceeding at a leisurely pace, with long pauses between volleys. I asked Veronica, "Have you ever seen any of those old Road Runner cartoons?"

"Sure. With Wile E. Coyote."

"Who?"

"That's the coyote's name," she said. "Wile E. Coyote."

"How do you know that?"

"I'm an avid reader of film credits. You know, 'Wile E. Coyote appearing as—himself.' " She looked at the blank expression on my face. "You're not very observant, Harry. Those contraptions he used to order from the Acme Corporation to trap the Road Runner—they were always addressed to Wile E. Coyote."

"Oh, right. What do you suppose it means?"

"What do I suppose what means?"

"The symbolism of the whole thing," I said. "What do you suppose the coyote represents? Is he some sort of classical fallen hero, like King Lear? Is he being punished for some tragic flaw? Is that why the laws of gravity and the impermeability of objects are suspended for the Road Runner, but not for him?"

"You've devoted quite a bit of thought to this, haven't you?"

I ignored her sarcasm. "Maybe it's a metaphor for man's attempt to impose meaning onto a chaotic and meaningless universe. Like the characters in a play by Pinter or Ionesco. Or maybe it's an existentialist depiction of hell, with the two of them condemned to plague one another into eternity. What do you think?"

"I think it's very interesting," Veronica replied. "Very interesting that this would become the end product of so many years of higher education. Your parents must be very proud, with their money so obviously well spent."

Melissa chuckled. She likely had no idea what Veronica and I were bantering about, but she recognized a put-down when she heard one. She was getting to the age where a child enjoys seeing a parent taken down a rung or two.

"Dad, I see Cindy and Holly over there. I'm going to say hello, okay?"

Thirty or so yards down the road Janet's old friend was holding her two-year-old daughter. "Sure, sweetheart."

There was a final volley of muskets. The Redcoats withdrew unhurriedly, heading east on Lexington Road. Their slain comrades rose up and merged into the retreating line. The fallen Minutemen stood and regrouped with their compatriots, and they all gave a rousing shout.

Just then I felt a hand touch me lightly on my back, and I heard a woman's voice call my name. When I turned around, Marjorie Morris was smiling at me. She was wearing a pale green designer jogging suit that matched her eyes and contrasted nicely with her dark red curls.

I was suddenly mindful that the last time I'd seen her—in the video of her movie—she hadn't been wearing any clothes at all. That's probably why I reflexively did a quick head-to-toe scan—actually, more like a neck-to-knee scan—as if I were trying to correlate the pixels of that video image with the points of the person standing before me. When I realized what I was doing, I felt myself turning red in the face. But if Marjorie noticed what I was doing, I couldn't tell from her expression.

I sensed Veronica's presence behind me, like a faint undertow pulling me back from another direction. I turned to her. "This is Marjorie Morris," I said, "an old friend. And Marjorie, this is—"

"Veronica," said Marjorie, completing my sentence for me. "I'm happy to meet you. Harry told me all about you."

Just then Veronica hooked her hand inside the crook of my elbow, escort style, subtly communicating a sense of proprietary interest. "Yes," she said, "and he told me all about you. Didn't you, Harry?" She dug her nails into my arm and smiled coldly at me. We both knew I'd never mentioned Marjorie to her, and she was driving the point home privately to me in her own inimitable style.

"I was so impressed when Harry told me you're with the FBI. When I was a little girl, I wanted to grow up to become a G-man. I guess I should say G-woman. I was quite a tomboy back then."

"Really now," Veronica said. "I never would have guessed. That's very interesting. Isn't that interesting, Harry?"

Marjorie pulled a small paperback book from the pouch around her waist. "Now that the house is mine, and it looks like I'll be living here for a while, I thought I should become more familiar with the local traditions. I've driven past this place dozens of times, but I never realized how important it was until I glanced at this guidebook last night. In Lexington, the British opened fire on the Minutemen for the first time. Then at North Bridge, the Minutemen returned British fire for the first time. But later that day this was the first place the Americans took the initiative and opened fire. If they hadn't done that, the Revolution might never have happened. We'd all still be Her Majesty's loyal subjects."

Veronica shrugged. "It would have spared us the Reagan–Bush years."

Melissa came galloping toward me. Cindy walked slowly in our direction, carrying her young child. "Dad! Cindy wants to know if I can go home with her and Holly!"

"Oh, Harry. Is this your daughter? She's beautiful. What's your name, darling?"

"Melissa," she answered, out of breath from running.

"Melissa, my name is Marjorie. I've known your daddy since I was a little girl, even younger than you are now."

"How old are you?"

I said, "That's not polite, Melissa."

"It's all right, Harry. I don't mind answering her question. I'm twenty-nine."

The crowd was beginning to thin out. A police officer removed the barricade that had been blocking vehicle access to Old Bedford Road. The musket smoke began to dissipate, but the acrid smell of gunpowder still hung in the air.

Marjorie asked, "Do you like to go swimming, Melissa?"

"Sometimes."

"Well, I have a very nice heated pool. Perhaps your daddy can bring you for a swim when the weather gets a bit warmer. You, too, Veronica, of course."

"Of course," Veronica replied.

Marjorie smiled at me and our eyes locked for a moment. "It was good seeing you again, Harry. Battlefields and cemeteries—I seem to run into you in the most unlikely places." She looked at Melissa and Veronica. "And it was good to meet the two of you. I think it would be nice . . ." Her voice trailed off for a moment. "I think it would be nice if we could all be friends." She patted Melissa lightly on the shoulder, then walked off toward the center of town.

Just then Cindy reached us, still holding her little girl. "We're going to the playground for a little while, Harry. If Melissa can come with us, I'll bring her home in time for dinner."

"Can I go with them, Dad? Please?"

"Sure, sweetheart. Just be good, and listen to what Cindy says."

"Dad-dee!" she whined, with an exasperation universal to all preteenage girls who think their fathers are treating them like little kids. "I'll be *okay.*" She walked off with Janet's old friend.

Veronica and I got into her car and headed home. She said, "Did she recently get a divorce settlement?"

"Cindy? No, she's happily married."

"Not Cindy. Your friend Marjorie. She said something about the house being hers now."

"Oh. Her father died recently, and Marjorie was his only survivor. She inherited his house near Nashawtuc Hill. I'm sure you read about it—the hit-and-run accident last month."

"I remember. They never caught the person responsible?"

"Not yet. Alfred Korvich thinks it was a drunk driver."

"How do you know that?"

"He told me."

"When did you talk to him about it?"

"Yesterday. I saw him in town."

"And he just happened to mention it?"

I shrugged. "We don't get many homicides out here. I was interested in the case."

"Is that all you're interested in?"

"Is that all I'm . . . For chrissake, Veronica—she's just a kid."

"She's less than two years younger than I am." Veronica guided her car around the ellipse in the center of town, then headed toward my house. "How come you never mentioned her to me?"

"I barely know her. I met her a few times when I was in college, twenty years ago. Her mother was one of my professors. Then we just happened to cross paths last week. I didn't even remember her until she told me who she was."

"You ran into her last week?"

"Yes."

"When?"

I hesitated. "I think it was Tuesday."

"I don't recall you saying anything about it."

"I guess it didn't seem worth mentioning at the time. Like I said, I hardly know the girl."

"Woman."

"Well, pardon my political incorrectness. She was just a girl when I met her, so maybe I still think of her that way."

"I'm just saying she's not a girl anymore." She paused. "And she's obviously interested in you."

"What are you talking about?"

"She's interested is all that I'm saying. Any woman can tell when another woman is interested in someone she cares about."

"For chrissake. She just lost her father, she's new in town, and she's just looking for someone to talk to."

"And I'm just a jealous, insecure female who doesn't know what she's talking about. Is that it?"

"I didn't say that."

Veronica turned off the road and drove slowly up the long gravel driveway to the side of the house. "Your friend said she saw you at the cemetery," she noted.

"I went for a walk there."

Veronica slipped the car into park and turned the motor off. Looking directly at me, she said, "That's an unusual place to go for a walk."

I didn't know if she realized Tuesday had been my wedding anniversary. I certainly hadn't told her. But even if she didn't know that, she probably assumed I would have visited Janet's grave while I was at the cemetery, whether or not that had been my purpose in going there. She sat quietly, waiting for me to make the next move.

I glanced over at my housekeeper's apartment. "Mrs. Winnicot is thinking about leaving," I said.

"I know."

"You know?"

"She told me a couple of weeks ago," Veronica said. "She said she wanted to be the one to tell you, so she asked me not to mention anything to you."

"And yet you're accusing *me* of keeping secrets."

"When someone asks me to keep a confidence, I keep a confidence," she said. "Don't try to change the subject."

I didn't know what to say. We sat there for several seconds, neither one of us speaking. Then I opened the passenger door, ready to get out of the car.

She asked, "What did you say Marjorie's last name is?"

"Morris. Why?"

"I just find it unusual that you didn't mention her before." She sat for a few more seconds. Suddenly her eyes widened as if she'd just recalled something she almost forgot. "I'll be back in a little while. There's something I want to pick up in town."

"I'll come with you." I started to shut my door.

"No, that's not necessary."

"I don't mind."

"Take a hint, Harry. I want to go by myself."

Veronica returned about a half hour later. I was stretched out on a lounge chair on the enclosed sunporch in the rear of the house, sipping a soft drink and watching the baseball game. I heard Veronica drive up, turn off her motor, and walk into the house. She didn't come out to the sunporch, and I didn't go looking for her.

I wasn't the only one having a bad day. Roger Clemens was pitching for the Red Sox, struggling against the weak-hitting California Angels.

I dozed off for a while, then I was awakened by a loud beer commercial. When the advertisement ended and the live action resumed, a relief pitcher was taking his warm-up tosses on the mound for Boston.

I walked inside the house and into the den. Veronica was curled up on the sofa, her legs tucked under her. She was watching something on television. She glanced at me for a moment when I walked in the room, then turned her attention back to the screen. She said, "She's very pretty."

"Who?"

"Your friend."

I stepped toward her so I could see what she was watching. It was *Blood Beach*. She'd just reached the part where the newspaper reporter strikes up a conversation with Marjorie's character on the beach.

"How did you know about this?" I asked.

"Like I said, I'm an avid reader of film credits." She gestured toward the empty videocassette box on the coffee table. "I read the box the other day, and then I made the connection a little while ago when we were sitting in the car."

She had an eye for detail and a memory like a bank vault. These talents served her well in law school—memorizing statutes and cases—and in her work as a prosecutor and with the FBI. Now it seemed as though she was using them against me.

On the television screen, Marjorie was inviting the reporter back to her apartment. Veronica said, "He's going to kill her."

"How do you know that?"

"I figure these things out for a living, remember?"

Marjorie unfastened her bikini top. As it fell to the floor I reached for the power switch on the television set.

"Get your fingers away from there," Veronica commanded.

I pulled my hand back and let it drop to my side. I turned to walk out of the room.

"Stay where you are." She patted the sofa next to her. With a false saccharine sweetness, she said, "Come, my love. Watch the movie with me. We have no secrets from one another, do we?" I hesitated. "Sit down," she said, the artificial congeniality gone from her voice. Looking at Marjorie, she said, "The butterfly tattoo on her breast is a nice touch. I wonder if it's real."

Together we watched as Marjorie heaved and groaned through her persuasive performance of sexual abandon. Then once again I saw her eyes bulge and her body tense. Suddenly her rhythmic writhing gave way to spasmodic twitching; there was a gurgling sound, blood spilling out of

her mouth, and a final convulsion as the knife cut through
her from behind.

"I knew he was going to kill her." Veronica turned the
television off with the remote control. "Sometimes I wish I
could forget some of the things I know."

I asked her to explain, but she didn't reply. She slowly
twirled the remote control in her hand, over and over again,
as she stared out the window at the long field next to the
house. "Where are we going, Harry?"

"What do you mean?"

Her voice took on a distant, wistful quality. "Where are
we going?" she repeated, more to herself than to me.

"Why do we have to be going somewhere? What's
wrong with where we are?"

Still looking out the window, she said, "One day last
week, I was sitting on the commuter train in North Station,
waiting for it to start the trip out to Concord. Another train
was on the next track, getting ready to pull out of the station. All of a sudden I could've sworn that I was moving
backward. But it was an optical illusion. The other train
was moving forward, while I was just sitting in place." She
turned to face me. "That's my life, Harry. Everybody's
moving on, and I'm just sitting still. Moving backward,
compared to them."

"You're not moving backward," I said, unable to think of
anything more intelligent to say.

She put the remote control on the coffee table. "You
bumped into someone you hadn't seen for twenty years.
How come you didn't mention that to me?"

I shrugged. "I guess it didn't seem that important to me."

"The other night, when you were talking about your
work, you said that the things someone doesn't talk about
can be more important than what he does talk about." She
paused. "But it's more than that. You lied about the movie."

"I lied?"

She nodded toward the videocassette box. "I saw that in
the den Thursday morning. When I asked you about it, you
made up some story about Bobby recommending the movie

because he knows how much you like mysteries. It would've been a lot easier to tell me you rented it because an old friend was in it. Why did you lie?"

"I don't know."

"You don't know?"

"I don't know, damn it. I don't know why I do half the things I do."

"Well, you're right about that." She inhaled deeply. "Is there anything else?"

"What do you mean?"

"Is there anything else you think I should know? Maybe I should say, is there anything else you *don't* think I should know?"

"No."

She looked directly at me for several seconds. "Why did you go to the cemetery on Tuesday?"

I thought about lying, but it seemed futile. "It was my wedding anniversary," I said.

Veronica winced. "Great. That's really great." She stood and walked toward the kitchen.

"Wait. I can explain," I said, even though I had no idea what explanation I could give her.

"You don't have to explain," she said as she headed out of the room. "I already understand too much."

I followed her into the kitchen. Veronica stood in front of the sink with an empty glass in her left hand. She turned the faucet on and held the glass under the running water.

I reached for her right hand. "Can we talk about this?"

"Leave me *alone*!" She pulled away. Her left hand slammed against the sink, shattering the glass. One of the jagged shards sliced her finger. She started to bleed. "Damn! I can't believe this is happening."

She offered a little resistance as I grabbed her hand and ran it under cold water. There were no slivers embedded in her skin. I found a gauze pad in the cabinet underneath the sink and pressed it against the wound.

"I'll do that," she said.

I released my hold on her hand. I got some adhesive tape; she let me wind it around the gauze.

"Give me a few minutes," she said, then she walked upstairs.

A short while later she returned to the kitchen with a small suitcase. "I think I should spend the night at my place."

"How will you get to Hopkinton in the morning?" The Boston Marathon began at noon in that small village. I was supposed to drop her off there, then drive to the midpoint in Wellesley to wait for her.

"I know how to get there," she replied.

"All right. I'll take you back to Hopkinton to pick up your car after I meet you in Wellesley."

"I guess so."

"What do you mean, you guess so? Why are you making such a big deal out of this?"

Just then there was a knock at the screen door. A bearded fellow a few years older than me stood there. He looked familiar, but I couldn't place the face. I yelled, "What *is* it?"

He moved back a half step, startled by my gruff greeting. He said, "I brought Melissa home," and then I recognized him as Cindy's husband. "She's in the field over there, said to tell you she'd be right in." He glanced at Veronica through the screen. "Hi. I'm Phil." He noticed the bloodied gauze taped to her finger. "Hey, are you okay?"

"I'm all right."

"Uh-huh."

I opened the door and stepped outside. "Thanks for bringing my daughter home. I hope she wasn't a problem."

"Nah, hey—she's a great kid." He glanced back through the door. "She okay?"

"Yes."

He looked at me. "You okay?"

"Yes."

He paused. "Then I guess everything's okay."

"Couldn't be better."

"Uh-huh." He paused again. "Well, I guess I'll be seeing you."

"Right."

"Uh-huh." He glanced once more at the screen door, then ducked into his car and drove down the gravel incline toward Monument Street.

I turned to walk back into the house. Melissa reached the door a step ahead of me. "Hi, Dad."

"Hi, sweetheart. Did you have a good time?"

"I had a *great* time. It was almost like having a little sister, pushing Holly on the swings and stuff like that. I can't wait till I can have my own kid."

In an instant I saw my daughter's entire adolescence unfold in my mind's eye: boys, cars, stolen kisses; experimental hair colors, experiments with recreational substances, white and not-so-white lies.

"Then I helped Cindy plant grass in some bare spots on her lawn."

"I was a golf caddy one summer in high school," I said. "I learned about this experimental grass a scientist was working on, something that would stop growing forever once it reached just the right height."

"That's silly. You can't stop things from growing."

I sighed. "I guess not," I replied. "It was just a thought."

We walked together into the kitchen. Veronica was still standing there, one hand wrapped in gauze, the other gripping her small suitcase.

Melissa stared at the valise and began biting a fingernail.

"I'm getting a head start on tomorrow, honey," Veronica said to Melissa. "My place is a lot closer to the starting line than your house is."

"Can I come with you?"

"I don't think so. I wouldn't be able to leave you alone when the race starts."

"We could all go," Melissa said.

"My place is pretty small, honey. You remember—you were there once."

"I could sleep on the sofa, or I could even bring my sleeping bag. It would be like an adventure, wouldn't it, Dad?" Her voice and facial expression seemed to alternate between mild panic and forced gaiety.

Veronica leaned toward her. "Honey, you need to stay with your father."

"Oh, God! You're bleeding!"

"It's nothing, honey. Really. Your dad can explain it to you. I really have to leave now."

"Why are you bleeding?" she yelled as Veronica walked out of the house. Then she turned to me, her jaw set and her eyes wide with anger. "Did you do that to her?"

"Melissa! Of course not. How can you even ask such a thing?"

She stared at me for a moment, saying nothing. Then she walked briskly past me and toward the doorway.

I thought I heard her mutter a word I never expected to hear from her. "What was that?" I asked.

"What was *what*?"

"You said something."

"I didn't say anything."

"You said *something*."

"I didn't say *anything*!"

She stormed out of the room, down the hall, and up the stairs. The pieces of Veronica's broken glass rattled in the sink when Melissa slammed her bedroom door.

8: The Fathers

Monday morning broke, chilly and bleak: a mediocre day for Patriots' Day parades and ceremonies, but a good day for runners in the Boston Marathon.

Mrs. Winnicot served French toast to Melissa and me. It was a quiet breakfast: My daughter was giving me the cold shoulder, and I didn't feel much like talking, anyway. If Mrs. Winnicot took special note of our silence, or of Veronica's absence, she kept her thoughts to herself.

I went into the den and dialed Veronica's number. I wanted to apologize if that seemed necessary, or accept an apology if one was offered. Most of all I wanted to forget the previous afternoon had happened, to slip back into the comfortable pattern we had established for ourselves. After four rings, Veronica's answering machine clicked on. I wished her luck in the marathon and told her we would meet her at the halfway mark in Wellesley.

Melissa and I walked into town for the parade. We passed the parking lot for North Bridge; it was filled with tourists' chartered buses. The area had been busy all morning, starting with the dawn musket salute that had awakened me from a restless sleep.

"You and Mommy didn't used to fight," Melissa said, her first nongrunting utterance of the morning. No doubt she was wondering what had transpired between Veronica and me the day before while she was away from home.

92

"The word is 'argue,' " I replied, "and yes, we did. You were just too young to remember now. Besides, we tried not to argue in front of you if we could help it."

"Why?"

"Because little kids sometimes overreact to arguments between grown-ups. Your mother and I didn't think it would be fair to fight in front of you."

"I thought you said the word was 'argue.' "

"Right," I said. "Argue."

"But that's not being honest."

"What do you mean?"

"Pretending everything is okay when it's really not. That's dishonest."

I said, "Being honest doesn't always mean saying whatever is on your mind to anyone you happen to meet. Sometimes saying that you're being honest is really just an excuse to hurt someone. Do you remember that old rhyme about sticks and stones can break your bones, but words will never hurt you?"

"Uh-huh."

"Well, it's not true. Words can hurt, and you can't pull them back after you've spoken them." I reached my arm around her shoulder. "I hope you'll remember that when you grow up."

She pulled away from me. "I *hate* it when you do that."

"Do what?"

"Lecture me like I'm a little kid."

But you are a little kid, I thought. And then I remembered something my father once told me.

"Why are you *laughing* at me?" she shrieked.

"I'm not laughing at you. I was just thinking about a lecture Grandpop gave me when he and Grandma dropped me off at college for the first time."

"What did he say?"

In my mind I could see my father looming over me, tall and strong—the way he was before age and illness began to take their toll. My mother had just gone through her third compulsive description of the scheme she used for organizing the clothing she insisted on unpacking into my dresser and closet. She told me how certain she was that I would do well, then betrayed her uncertainty by preaching anxiously about the importance of building a solid record so I could get into a good medical school. She kissed me good-bye with her trademark display of muted hysteria, then left my father alone with me in my dorm room.

"All right," I said to him. "Do you have a lecture for me, too?"

"Not really." He shrugged. "Just try not to think with your pecker. But make sure you wear a rubber if you do."

I guess I expected something more along the lines of Polonius's classic advice to Laertes: an exhortation to be true to my own self; to be familiar, but by no means vulgar; to give every man my ear, but few my voice; to neither a borrower nor a lender be. But the truth of the matter was this: My father's blunt remark—an understated metaphor for all his worries and concerns about leaving me there—stayed with me longer than any platitude would have.

Melissa said, "Well? Are you going to tell me what Grandpop said to you?"

"It wasn't very important," I replied.

Again she said, "I *hate* it when you do that."

We walked past the Colonial Inn and found a curbside space in the town square, in front of the rectory of the Catholic church. Melissa saw a classmate standing on the opposite side of the street; she crossed over to join her, pleased to have an excuse not to stand with me.

From around the corner I could hear the sounds of drums, piccolos, and horses' hooves coming up Main Street. The horse-drawn carriage carrying that year's Honored Citizen passed by. Every year the town singled out one of its longtime residents for recognition. Sometimes the honor was based on good works; other times, on longevity. This year's honoree fit both categories: an elderly widow who was spending her twilight years redistributing the family fortune for the benefit of others.

The man to my right said, "Top of this extremely dreary morning to you, Harry Kline. It is Harry, isn't it?"

Father John Fitzpatrick had become the town's Catholic priest about a year earlier. I'd met him once before, at a town committee meeting. "Good morning, Father."

He was probably about ten years older than me, but he looked twice that. He had the barrel-chested look of a long-shoreman, and the ragged, gravelly voice of an inveterate or recovering tobacco addict. He had a bulbous nose, a bit crooked, with tiny red lines formed by broken capillaries. I surmised that his road had not been an easy one.

He glanced around me. "You seem to be alone."

"That's my daughter," I said, pointing out Melissa where she was standing across the street.

He looked at her, then said, "Ah. No doubt her mother must be quite beautiful."

"She was. She's deceased."

"Ah, yes. I see. I'm very sorry for that."

A delegation of Minutemen from the town of Acton paraded in front of us. Behind them was a marching band from the air-force base that straddled the far eastern sliver of Concord and portions of two other towns.

Father John Fitzpatrick said, "If I remember correctly, it's *Doctor* Kline. You're a psychiatrist."

"Yes."

"You know, one of my favorite sayings comes from another psychiatrist named Harry. I'm sure you must have studied Harry Stack Sullivan."

"Yes."

" 'We are all more simply human than otherwise.' It's one of the wisest things I ever read. I had it engraved on my desk set so that I would see it every day. I find it wholly consistent with everything the Church teaches." The priest smiled. "That's 'wholly' with a 'w.' Not 'holy' with an 'h.' "

A group of women and children in Colonial-era costumes marched by.

He continued. "I think our professions have much in

common. They both deal with people's most exalted aspirations and darkest secrets."

I said, "I don't believe I've ever thought of my work as exalted."

"But you must hear many secrets."

"Yes and no."

"Oh?"

"Very few of the things my patients say are really secrets, from their point of view. On the other hand, they all become secrets once I hear them—because *I* have to keep them confidential."

He smiled. "Ah, yes. I see. Tell me—who does the keeper of secrets tell his secrets to?"

"Usually, he doesn't."

"Then perhaps we have more in common than either of us realizes."

Melissa's friend and her parents walked away from the town square area. My daughter crossed the street and rejoined me. I introduced her to Father John. She'd never met a priest before, and she seemed both shy and curious at the prospect now.

Suddenly my beeper sounded. I felt myself become tense, a reflex action: No one ever beeps you just to pass the time of day. On the beeper's digital display I saw the Wellesley phone number of Veronica's father.

Father John said, "You can use the rectory phone to call the person who paged you." He pointed to the front door of the rectory. "It's on the table, just inside on the left." He handed me his keys. "If Melissa would like, I'll be happy to wait here with her so she doesn't have to miss any of the parade."

I dialed the Wellesley number from the rectory phone. Veronica answered. I recognized her voice, of course, but I hadn't expected to hear it. My confusion quieted me for a few seconds, creating an awkward silence.

"I slept at my father's house last night," Veronica said. "It's a few miles closer to Hopkinton than my place is." She hesitated for a moment. "My boss paged me a little while ago. He needs me to be in Pittsfield. I'll have to miss the race and my father's party."

"Damn!"

"It's not my fault!"

"No—I'm not angry at you. I'm upset because you trained so hard, and I know how much you wanted to run."

"Oh." Her voice became softer, more sorrowful. "Things keep going wrong. We're on a bad roll here."

"Things aren't that bad. We can talk when you get back."

"How is Melissa?"

"Angry at me because you left."

"I'm sorry. Tell her I sent my love."

"I will. And tell your father I'm sorry we won't be seeing him today."

"You should still come, Harry. I know he really wants you to."

"I'll talk it over with Melissa."

I rejoined my daughter and Father John Fitzpatrick. We watched the rest of the half-hour parade: Minutemen from several nearby towns, various civic clubs, and two small marching bands. As we were parting, the priest said, "Come by sometime to see me, Harry. I'm sure there are many things we'd enjoy talking about."

"He was nice," Melissa said when Father John was out of earshot. "Have you ever been to services at a Catholic church?"

"No."

We headed toward Monument Street for the short walk home. I said, "Are we friends again?"

"I guess so." She placed her hand in mine. We walked for a while without talking. As we passed Nathanial Hawthorne's old homestead, Melissa asked, "Is the only difference between Catholics and Jews that the Catholics believe in Jesus Christ?"

"I think that's the biggest one."

"But Christ was Jewish, wasn't he?"

"Yes."

"Then I don't get it."

I wanted to help her comprehend, but I felt like I was walking in the valley of my deepest ignorance. As I struggled to come up with an answer, she said, "Dad, how come we never go to temple? Didn't we used to, when I was little?"

"Yes, we did." Beginning when Melissa was three years old, Janet and I used to take her to services at the nearest synagogue, in Lexington, about once a month. I lost interest after Janet died a year later. Now there was a synagogue in Concord, but I'd never set foot in it. I said, "If you want to go again sometime, we can."

"Would Veronica go with us?"

"I'm sure she would if we asked her to."

"Even though she's Episcopalian?"

"I'm sure she'd come anyway."

"Episcopalians are Christians, aren't they?"

"Yes."

"And Catholics are Christians, too, aren't they?"

"Yes."

"Then how is being Episcopalian different than being Catholic? What does Veronica believe?"

I thought, I don't know what the hell Veronica believes. "I'm really not sure, sweetheart."

As a child in Hebrew school, I learned that there were three types of people: Jewish, Christian, and Other. I knew that Catholics and Episcopalians were lumped together in the second category, along with many other denominations. That remained the limit of my understanding.

Melissa said, "I think I'll ask her when we see her later. She's good at explaining things."

She meant no harm, but the words pained me. I remembered what I'd said to her therapist a few days earlier. *I can't begin to count how many times she's asked me something, and I've wished I could say, "I don't know—go ask your mother."*

Melissa sulked for a few minutes when I told her about my telephone conversation with Veronica. Then she decided she wanted to proceed with our plans: viewing the Boston Marathon from the halfway point in Wellesley, then eating lunch at the home of Veronica's father. She was probably hoping that Veronica would change her mind about going to Pittsfield. I knew better.

The starter's gun goes off in Hopkinton at midday for the runners; they fire it a bit earlier for the wheelchair entrants. Melissa and I reached Wellesley at around half-past noon, just in time to see the lead wheelchair zip past us on Route 16. The young man had thickly muscled arms and broad shoulders; he had no legs. I once assumed that the legless entrants had an advantage over the others, since they were carrying less weight. But when I worked at the Veterans Administration hospital, one of my paraplegic patients informed me that this was not necessarily so. It had something to do with one's center of gravity and the stabilizing effect of the weight of one's legs.

"These guys always amaze me," I said. "I don't think I could do it if I were disabled."

"I don't think you could do it now." Veronica's influence, I thought. "And my teacher says we're supposed to call them physically challenged."

I hated those politically correct euphemisms, and the movement to cloak the world's harshness with sanitizing and misleading terms. The state's Department of Mental Health had recently begun referring to its hospitalized patients as "consumers," even though many of them were actively psychotic and committed against their will, and thus not in a very good position to choose whether—or what—to consume. I'd recently seen a hospital report that read, "This consumer has command auditory hallucinations. He reports that his voices are telling him to disembowel and drink the fresh blood of other consumers." If the trend continued, the Department of Consumer Affairs would need to get a new name in order to avoid confusion.

I said, "Pretending that someone doesn't have a problem is just a way of excusing yourself from lending him a hand.

And if your teacher gives you a hard time about that, tell her to talk with me."

"Geez, Dad—lighten up." Veronica's influence again.

A knot of six male runners, the leaders, came through a little after one o'clock. All were Asian or African; when the marathon planners bucked the amateur tradition a few years earlier and began awarding serious prize money, the cast of participants took on a distinctly international character. The lead female runners ran past us about ten minutes later. We watched for another twenty minutes, then drove the short distance to Veronica's father's home.

Donald Pace's estate was set on the Charles River near the mansion reserved for the president of Wellesley College. The Georgian home had a square main body, with latter-day additions spreading out from its sides like bookends. A tennis court, horse barn, and riding corral dotted the property.

Donald was a senior attorney in the corporate-law division of Putnam & Blaine, one of Boston's most prestigious old-line firms. He made a fortune representing companies bidding for business in China after Nixon opened relations there. Eventually he was mentioned as a candidate for appointment as U.S. Trade Representative, but that speculation ended when Nixon was forced to resign.

There were already a dozen cars in the circular macadam driveway when we arrived. Three were chauffeur-driven, and the rest were luxury items that made my Camry stand out like a pustule. Inside the house, buffet tables stretched across the vast party room, crammed with serving dishes of catered delicacies. Well-groomed men and women in expensive casual dress milled about. In the middle of the room, effortlessly commanding center stage, was Shana Pace, Donald's second wife and Veronica's stepmother. She smiled when she saw us enter the room, excused herself from the fawning circle of people gathered around her, and walked over to Melissa and me.

"Donald will be so glad the two of you decided to come," she said in her distinctive Eurasian accent. "He is in the sitting room. Melissa, perhaps your father will let you come with me so I can show you off."

I nodded to Melissa to let her know that she should go with Shana, then walked into the sitting room. Donald was holding a drink and sharing a laugh with two other men in their late fifties. He beckoned me to join them and made introductions all around.

"Glad you could make it, Harry. We were just talking about the new administration. Oliver is certain that we're going to hell in a handbasket with a Democratic president and the proposed North American Trade Agreement. And Parker over here, who has grave concerns about the same issue, goes even further, speaking of the Antichrist and making statements that would earn him a visit from the Secret Service if he had a less discreet group of listeners. Perhaps you can provide a more moderate perspective."

I said, "I'm smart enough to know when I'm totally ignorant about something."

Donald laughed. "Well, that's certainly a commodity in rare supply around here."

The one called Oliver looked at me with a stiff smile that seemed stapled to an otherwise dour face. He repeated my name quietly, as if he were trying to remember where he might have heard it before. Then he said, "Of course. You're the Jewish fellow that Donald's daughter has been seeing." His handshake was limp: the kind that feels like air and gives you no clue regarding the substance of the man offering it. "Ask the wives here, and half will tell you that Jewish men make wonderful husbands. Of course, none of them have firsthand experience in that regard, which makes you wonder why they perpetuate the story."

It was, I thought, one of those subtle anti-Semitic put-downs: one so laced with droll humor that you risk stamping yourself as provocative or even paranoid if you confront the person uttering it. I smiled politely and didn't take the bait.

Donald asked, "Is Melissa here with you?"

"Yes."

"Harry's daughter is ten years old, going on twenty-five."

Oliver said, "I didn't realize children were welcome here today."

Donald smiled at me as he answered the other man. "Melissa is *always* welcome here."

I said, "You're right about her being precocious. Just this morning she asked me what the differences are between being Catholic and being Episcopalian."

"What did you tell her?" asked Donald.

I looked at Oliver. "I told her I didn't know."

Oliver smiled, moving only the corners of his mouth, uncertain how to interpret my response. The other guest, Parker, cleared his throat.

Donald said, "If you gentlemen would be good enough to leave us, I have a private matter to discuss with Harry."

"Certainly," said Parker. He turned to me and said, "Many of us at Putnam & Blaine have been trying for years to get Donald to meet privately with a psychiatrist."

The two men left Donald and me in the sitting room. Donald said, "Oliver often makes a poor first impression. I'm sorry if he made you feel uncomfortable."

"You don't have to apologize for your friend."

"I'm not apologizing *for* a friend. I'm apologizing *to* a friend."

"Thanks."

He offered me a drink. I declined, and he walked to the bar in the corner of the room to refresh his glass. "Where is Melissa?"

"I left her with Shana."

"Then she's in good hands." He swirled the liquid in his glass. "One of my greatest regrets is never having a child with Shana."

"I know. You've mentioned that before."

Like me, Donald Pace had become a widower in his thirties, and had been left with one daughter to raise. We both knew something of what the other had endured, and this had always made it easy for us to feel comfortable with one another.

He sat down, gesturing for me to follow suit. He said, "When I look at Melissa, I'm often reminded of Veronica at that age. The same intelligence, the same intensity. And underneath it all, the same vulnerability. You know, I can barely imagine what it must be like to lose your mother when you're so young. I've seen it, I've lived with it, but I don't think I can ever really understand it."

"Nor I."

"Does Melissa ever visit her mother's grave?"

I nodded. "We go together around Mother's Day and Janet's birthday. I know of at least one time she walked there by herself. The cemetery is only a mile from our house."

"Did you know Veronica has never visited her mother's grave?"

"No, I didn't know that."

"She hasn't been there since the funeral, more than twenty years ago. And she just shuts down if you try to talk with her about it." He paused for several seconds. "I know it's pointless to measure one person's sorrow against another's to see which is greater. But I think Veronica had a much harder time than Melissa."

"How so?"

"Well, there's the very nature of the tragedy, of course. So sudden and so terrible." He drummed his fingers on the side of his chair. "You know about that, I assume."

"I do."

"I thought so." He continued. "But more than that—Melissa's father wasn't gone half the time on business. He didn't immerse himself in his work as a way of avoiding his own grief. And he was strong enough to be there for his daughter when she needed him most." He sighed deeply. "Veronica was not as fortunate in that regard."

"Perhaps you're misjudging your daughter's father," I said.

"Perhaps, although I think not. Anyway, someone else

will do the final judging." He smiled. "Episcopalians do believe in God."

"So I gather."

He sipped his drink. "When your child suffers such great pain so early in her life, you want to shield her from anything else that could ever hurt her. Even though you know that's not possible, or even advisable. I'm sure you've had such feelings concerning Melissa."

"Of course."

"Well, that feeling will always remain, no matter how old she is. You'll always want to make things right for her, whether she wants your help or not."

Donald set his drink down. He leaned forward and spoke quietly. "Veronica was crying when she came here yesterday."

"I really didn't, uh, it wasn't like—"

He held his hand up, stopping me in midsentence. "Please. I'm not trying to intrude. And you certainly don't need to give me any explanation. I just want to know if I can help in any way."

"I think Veronica and I have to work it out for ourselves. But thank you. Really."

"Well, at least that's better than what Veronica said when I asked her the same thing. She told me to butt out, or words to that effect."

I smiled. "That sounds like her."

"It does. I have such a stubborn child. But she has seemed more at ease this past year, since you and she have been together. I'm sorry she didn't stay today."

"I am, too. I wish her boss hadn't paged her this morning."

He furrowed his brow and looked away, as if he were debating whether to say what was on his mind. Finally, he said, "Her boss didn't page her."

"But when I spoke to her before, she said—"

"Her boss didn't page her," Donald repeated. "No one did."

He leaned back in his chair and gazed out the window.

Shana and Melissa were walking across the carefully mani-
cured back lawn toward the marble bench that faced the
Charles River. He said, "We've both become very fond of
Melissa. We would miss her very much if we couldn't see
her anymore."

"So would she."

And I would miss you, I said to myself. Donald was
probably thinking the same thing, but neither of us gave
voice to the thought.

He said, "Your parents are retired, aren't they? In Florida, if memory serves."

"Yes."

"Healthy?"

"Pretty much."

"Secure?"

"Very."

"What sort of work did your father do?"

"He was trained as a pharmacist. Then he started a phar-
maceutical distribution company, eventually sold it for
enough money to live off the interest. He was a man ahead
of his time—a drug dealer who retired to Miami."

Donald chuckled. "I'm sure they're good people. And
your wife—I'm sorry, I don't recall her name."

"Janet."

"Yes. Are Janet's parents still living?"

I nodded. "Melissa is going to spend the rest of school
vacation week with them in Connecticut."

"I'm sure they're good people, too."

I hesitated. "We've never been close. Even less so since
Janet died."

"Yet you allow Melissa to visit with them. I respect
that."

"She should know her grandparents."

"And they should know their grandchild," he replied. He
looked out the window again to watch his wife and my
daughter. "Such a sweet girl. I would be very pleased to
have her in my family someday." He turned toward me.
"I'm sorry. I have no right to say that."

"No offense taken."

Melissa and Shana were walking back toward the house. We watched them without speaking until they walked around the side of the building, out of sight.

Donald said, "I'm a very wealthy man."

"I know."

"Shana is wealthy, too."

"Of course."

"I mean, she's wealthy in her own right. Wealthier than me." He laughed. "I even suggested we sign a prenuptial agreement, for her protection. She wouldn't hear of it. What I'm trying to say is— Shana won't need anything from me when I'm gone. Veronica will inherit everything. And all of that will eventually go to my grandchild."

Veronica—Donald's only child—was destined by her biology never to bear children of her own. I knew Donald understood that, and he probably assumed I knew. And so he likely would never have a grandchild unless Veronica adopted, or married someone who was already a father.

He said, "I hope I'm not making a fool of myself."

"Of course not."

"But if you or Melissa ever need help . . . whether or not . . ." His voice trailed off.

"I understand. Thank you."

The door swung open. "Dad! Did you know that Aunt Shana's mother was a real, actual princess?"

The four of us returned to the party room. Donald and Shana got caught up in separate conversations with small groups of guests.

"Dad, that man over there is staring at us."

I looked in the direction of her gaze. She was speaking of the man called Oliver. I didn't know whether that was his first or last name. "He's probably looking for horns."

"Huh?"

"Nothing, sweetheart. I'm just joking."

We avoided Route 128 and took the back roads home, through Weston and Lincoln. Somewhere near Walden

Pond, as we crossed over the town line into Concord, Melissa said, "How did Veronica's real mother die?"

"In an accident, like she told you."

"I know. But I mean, like what kind of accident? I asked her once, but she said she didn't like talking about it."

"She doesn't. She's only talked about it once with me."

When Veronica was nine years old, her mother surprised a burglar in their home and was beaten to death for her trouble. Veronica witnessed her mother's final moments. "They never caught him," Veronica told me on the one occasion she discussed the murder with me. "A few years later, when I was in junior high, I read a Greek tragedy where the spirit of a murder victim was condemned to wander in limbo until the person who killed him was brought to justice. I can't tell you how much that has haunted me."

Veronica graduated with honors from Harvard Law School. Her classmates took high-status or well-paying jobs: corporate counsel positions, clerkships for federal judges, associate positions at big-name firms like the one where her father practiced. But Veronica became a prosecutor because, as she had explained to me, "I had a mission when I decided to study law. I wanted to hurt people who hurt other people." That unfulfilled passion for vengeance, triggered by her mother's death, fueled her tenacity at rooting out evil—first as a prosecutor, then as an FBI special agent. It was also responsible for the brooding moroseness that was so much a part of her character.

"Since you know," Melissa said, "you can tell me. I really want to know how Veronica's mother died."

"If Veronica didn't want to tell you, then it wouldn't be right for me to talk about it."

"I *hate* it when you keep secrets."

I remembered Father John's question: *Who does the keeper of secrets tell his secrets to?*

When we arrived home, Melissa went upstairs to gather books and toys to take along on her trip to Connecticut.

In the den, the message counter on my telephone answering machine indicated that two people had called. I pressed the playback button. First came Veronica's voice, more tentative and halting than I'd ever heard it. "Harry . . . I may be here longer than I realized. Maybe a week . . . I'm not even sure where I'll be. I'm sorry. . . . I'll call tomorrow. If you want to talk to me, just page my beeper. . . . If you want to." She stayed on the line for a few seconds more, then hung up.

The machine's synthesized voice announced the time of Veronica's call, then there was a beep, and then I heard another voice, equally tentative and halting. "Hello, Harry? This is Marjorie . . . Marjorie Morris. I was wondering if— hoping, actually . . . Would you like to come for dinner some evening this week? And Veronica, of course . . . Melissa, too, if you'd like. They'd both certainly be welcome. . . . Well, please call me."

The empty box from the tape of *Blood Beach* was still on the coffee table. The tape was in the VCR where Veronica had left it, just before she walked out on me. *Walked out on me.* I hadn't thought of it quite like that until just then. Maybe I was reacting to the evasiveness I sensed in her phone message, or the lie she told earlier about getting paged by her boss.

I leaned back on the couch and closed my eyes. All I could think of was the argument, Veronica's bleeding hand, and her apparent desire to have some time away from me. I didn't want to think about it anymore.

I turned the television and the VCR on and pressed the button that engaged the videotape. I rewound, looking for Marjorie.

9: Running from My Feet

"I hate my stupid hair," Melissa shouted from the up-stairs bathroom. "I hate it, I hate it, I *hate* it!"

Mrs. Winnicot was standing by the door, ready for their trip. "There's nothing wrong with that child's hair," she said.

"I know."

I'd already loaded all of their luggage into Mrs. Winnicot's car. It was Tuesday morning, and they wouldn't be back home until Sunday. I said, "This will be the longest I've ever been apart from her."

"I'm sure she'll be fine."

Melissa skulked downstairs. Mrs. Winnicot said, "That's a very nice outfit you're wearing. I'm sure your grandparents will think you look beautiful."

Melissa said nothing in reply.

"I'll wait in the car while you say good-bye to your father."

After Mrs. Winnicot left, I said, "I'll miss you."

"Why aren't you coming?" she asked, still pouting.

"I thought it would be nice to let you have some private time with your grandparents." I also had no desire to spend five days in their company, but there was no reason to burden Melissa with that knowledge. "I'm sure you'll have lots of fun."

She grunted.

We kissed each other good-bye and she started to leave. When she reached the door, she turned to me and asked, "How much am I allowed to tell them about Veronica?"

"You can say anything you want to say."

"Can I tell them the two of you sleep in the same room?"

"Do you really think that's likely to come up in conversation?"

She shrugged. "They might ask."

"I don't think they will."

She shuffled her feet and looked at the floor without speaking.

"What is it, sweetheart?"

"Do you think they miss Mommy?"

"I'm sure they miss her very, very much."

"Then how come they never talk about her?"

I thought, Because their grief is too profound for words. I said, "Sometimes people keep things that hurt them deep inside."

"I do that sometimes."

"Yes, I know," I said. "And maybe they're afraid it would make you sad if they talked about your mom."

"It makes me more sad when they don't talk about her, because it makes me afraid to talk about her."

"You're the bravest person I know," I said. "You don't have to be afraid of that."

She dashed back to where I was standing and threw her arms around me. Before I could say anything, she was out the door, in Mrs. Winnicot's car, and on her way to Connecticut.

"Pal of mine, I think you should eat breakfast in the raw."

"In the raw?"

"In the raw," Bobby repeated through the static on his car phone. "Your birthday suit. Naked. Nude. Bare."

"I know what it means. But why should I do that?"

"It's what I do on the rare occasions when I know I have

the house to myself without any likely intrusion. It's how I
express dominion over my kingdom. And it's why I got rid
of my vinyl kitchen chairs."

"You are a lunatic."

"The hell I am—you try sitting in a vinyl chair with a
bare ass. It's not a very pleasant experience."

"You realize that I have the legal power to sign an emergency order of commitment to a psychiatric hospital."

"No problem. I know a good lawyer. He'd get me out of
there in no time."

"Anyway, it's too late. I've already eaten breakfast, and
I'm already dressed."

"Hold on—I'm going through a tollbooth." A few seconds later he said, "When is she coming back?"

"Sunday. Mrs. Winnicot is picking her up on her way
back from her daughter's place in New Jersey."

"No, not Melissa. Veronica—when is *she* coming back?"

I hesitated. "I'm not sure. We were having a disagreement the day before yesterday, and she sort of walked out
suddenly."

"What kind of disagreement?"

"She found out about my visit to the cemetery on my
wedding anniversary."

"How did *that* happen?"

I didn't feel like going through the whole thing again:
Marjorie, the videotape, Veronica's bloodied hand. "It came
up accidentally in conversation."

"I thought you psychiatrists believe there's no such thing
as an accident. Everything has some sort of deeper meaning."

"Well, it's like the man said. 'Sometimes a cigar is just
a cigar.' "

"Sure. Anyway, I gotta get off the phone. I'll try to set
the conference up for tomorrow. I like your idea about
doing it in your office."

He'd called to sound me out about meeting with him and
Frank Porter to discuss the suit. I suggested that we use my

office as neutral ground: more familiar to Porter than a lawyer's office, but not as comfortable as his own place.

Bobby said, "Gotta go now. Think about what I said. Eat
your next meal naked. Just be careful with the onion dip."

I had an uneventful morning. I went for a walk in
Estabrook Woods, saw two patients, and ate lunch. I did all
of these things fully clothed.

Michael Cafferty was my only patient that Tuesday afternoon. During our two previous meetings, typical adolescent
pouting alternated with typical adolescent sarcasm. This
time, however, there was a sense of forlornness so palpable
that I could almost touch it. As soon as he settled in a chair,
he said in quiet, empty tones, "I don't like coming here. It
makes me feel sick. Like, how could I lead a normal life if
I'm seeing a psychiatrist? If I keep coming here, it means
there's something wrong with me."

I thought about the old joke: Anybody who goes to see
a psychiatrist ought to have his head examined.

He looked at me and said, "What would happen if I
stopped coming?"

"I suppose your probation officer would call eventually
to see if you've been coming here."

"And what would you say?"

"I wouldn't say anything. I wouldn't even acknowledge
that I know you."

He winced. "Is that supposed to make me feel better?"

"Without your permission to reveal information, even
telling him that I know you would be a violation of confidentiality," I said. "When I said I wouldn't even acknowledge that I know you, I didn't mean it as a put-down. It
was a poor choice of words. I'm sorry."

"You're sorry?"

"Yes."

"I thought when you join the grown-ups' union, they
make you sign a pledge to never apologize to a kid." He
paused. "Anyway, I don't care about my probation officer.
What I meant was, what would happen to *me* if I stop?"

"Well, I once heard someone say that you can't run away from your feet."

"What's *that* supposed to mean?"

"You can rid yourself of me, but you'll still be stuck with you. If you're already feeling badly about yourself, bailing out of therapy probably won't make you feel any better. It may just make you feel more like a failure."

He snickered. "Terrific," he said, and then he lapsed into silence. He said nothing regarding the girl named Junie, or his inquiry about a test for determining someone's sexual orientation. He just sat quietly, looking out the window.

Finally, he looked directly at me and said, "I'm fucked either way. I'm fucked if I tell you, and I'm fucked if I don't."

"In that case, you might as well talk to me about what's bothering you."

"Easy for you to say."

"Does it have anything to do with Junie?"

He glared at me. "That is a closed subject."

Obviously, I had struck a nerve. Under those circumstances, it's usually better to back off, especially when your patient is young, and when you haven't known him that long. He was talking about dropping out of therapy; pressuring him into revealing something he wasn't ready to talk about would just push him further away.

I knew a psychiatrist whose office was in a medical building that had its own parking garage. The doctors had rubber stamps in their offices to validate parking tickets, which entitled their patients to reduced rates in the garage. He once told me, "Some days, that's probably the only useful service I provide to them." Sitting there with Michael Cafferty, I felt pretty damn useless. Something was eating away at him, but I couldn't get him to let me help.

When it was time for his session to end, he stood and walked slowly to the door. With his hand on the doorknob, he turned back and said, "Junie's right. I'd probably be better off not coming here anymore."

* * *

Veronica hadn't given me a phone number where I could reach her. I thought about paging her, then decided to wait for her to call me. When my phone rang at nine-thirty that night, I answered with an enthusiasm that no doubt confused my caller—who was not, it turned out, Veronica.

"Harry?"

"Yes?"

After a few seconds I heard, "It's Marjorie."

"Oh, Marjorie. I'm sorry I haven't gotten back to you. I got your message last night, too late to call back. And this has been a very busy day for me."

"I forgive you, so long as you're going to accept my invitation. What evening would be good for you?"

"Well . . ."

"Harry! You have to come. Or I shall hound you mercilessly until you accept."

I explained that Melissa and Veronica were away for several days.

"That's all the more reason for you to come," Marjorie said. "Why should we both have to eat alone?"

The prospect of going to her home for an intimate dinner for two appealed to me, but the sense of intrigue was immediately replaced by guilt. "I'd have an easier time meeting you for lunch," I said.

She hesitated. "Of course. Would you like to come here tomorrow?"

"How about the day after?"

"Well, I'll be at work on Thursday, but we can meet in town."

"You're working?"

She laughed. "You needn't sound *quite* so surprised, Harry. I'm a drama coach at Concord Academy. I don't have faculty rank, and I don't actually teach any classes. I just help the drama students rehearse. It's not a full-time position, but I didn't take it for the money. I just wanted to feel like I was doing something useful." She paused for a moment. "We can meet at the school, then walk to the pizza shop on Thoreau Street."

We agreed on the details, and she ended the conversation by saying, "Wonderful. It's a date. Good night."

My guilt impelled me to explain that it wasn't actually a date, but she had already hung up.

I waited until well after ten o'clock for Veronica to call, and then I went for a ride.

I had no particular destination, at least not one that I was conscious of. I drove down Lexington Road, past the Merriam's Corner battle site, and continued across Route 128. After a few random turns, taken with no purpose in mind, I found myself near the border between Lexington and Waltham. I drove past the darkened buildings of what once had been a state hospital for the mentally ill. Metropolitan State Hospital was one of several facilities closed by our Republican governor—a man who, when asked where his family had gotten the millions of dollars he pumped into his own campaign effort, said, "We don't *get* money. We *have* money." And now he was bent on balancing the state's budget on the backs of those people least likely to object in person over a squash game or lunch at the Harvard Club.

A couple of miles down the road I drove past McLean Hospital, where I did my residency training in psychiatry. The world-renowned private institution sat atop a lush hillside in Belmont. Every old-line Boston Brahmin family probably had sent at least five members there for a multimonth stretch. In nearly a century of service to the rich and famous, it had welcomed so many notables that it was a wonder the cafeteria didn't have a gallery of autographed pictures. One of McLean's buildings was originally erected by a wealthy patient as a private home for himself, with residential quarters for his psychiatrist. If our Republican governor ever needed psychiatric hospitalization, McLean would probably be his first choice.

Farther along, I crossed from Belmont into Watertown, and I realized I was only a block or two from Veronica's condominium. She occupied the second story of what once was a single-family home. The building had been divided

into two units. It sat near the crest of a hill between Trapelo
Road and Mount Auburn Street, in the shadow of the Oak-
ley Country Club.

I drove past her building. Her driveway was empty, but
a lamp was on in one of the windows. Was she there? Had
she carelessly left a light on before going out of town? Perhaps she left it on intentionally while she was gone to make
it look like someone was home; maybe she even had it set
on a timer.

I didn't know what her habit was in that regard. Hell,
when I compared our relationship with my marriage, I realized how much I didn't know about her. I didn't know the
name of her best friend from childhood. I didn't know who
her favorite Beatle was. I couldn't identify her favorite
high-school teacher, her college major, or the names of any
of her previous lovers.

I didn't know why she left. I didn't know where she was.
I didn't know if she was coming back.

10: The Murder Weapon

"You got a minute, Doc?" asked Alfred Korvich. "Friend of yours is here at the police station, wants to talk with you." He lowered his voice to a whisper so the other party in the room with him couldn't hear what he was saying into the phone. "She needs a ride home and she won't accept one from us. I think she's pissed off, but she's too fucking polite to say so outright. Here—I'll put her on."

After a brief pause I heard a familiar voice. "Hello, Harold, dear. I have a bit of a problem."

Only one person outside my family called me by my full given name. I said, "Mrs. Peterson—I thought you were still in Florida."

"I came home the day before yesterday. I must be getting old, Harold, because the winter season never seemed as boring to me as it did this year."

"Why are you at the police station?"

"Oh, dear, this is terrible. The police have seized my automobile. They say it was used to kill someone in an accident."

"Are you hurt?"

"Am I—oh, heavens, no. The accident occurred while I was in Palm Beach. A hit-and-run, so they tell me."

"Charles Morris?"

"I believe that was the gentleman's name. Did you know him?"

117

"No," I said. "Let me talk to the police chief." When Korvich came back on the line, I exploded. "Damn it, Chief, are you insane? If Lorraine Peterson had anything to do with Charles Morris's death, then I'm the next pope."

"Calm down, Doc. Nobody is saying she was involved in it. Her Buick was involved, is all we're saying."

"Are you sure it's the car that hit Charles Morris?"

"I'm sure. I'll tell you all about it when you get here." He hung up.

Even with no patients that Wednesday morning—and with no daughter, lover, or housekeeper around to keep me honest—I'd risen as early as usual, eaten, showered, and dressed. I had no plans until the afternoon, when I was to meet with Frank Porter and Bobby in my office. I was sitting on the sunporch, idly scanning the sports page, when Chief Korvich had called to shatter my plan for doing absolutely nothing all morning.

I met Lorraine Peterson through her late husband, a neurologist who taught me in medical school. After I moved to Concord, Dr. Peterson and I developed a close working relationship. When I left the Veterans Hospital to concentrate on building a private practice, he referred many patients to me. And when he began to falter, I often visited to chop wood, do yard work, or handle one or another chore. Since Dr. Peterson's death two years earlier Mrs. Peterson had lived alone in their mansion on the crest of Nashawtuc Hill. She was tended by a live-in maid who also accompanied her to Palm Beach for the five-month winter season.

The midmorning traffic was light as I drove through the center of town and turned left onto Walden Street. The police and fire departments occupied a brick building a half mile down the road. Alfred Korvich had left word with the officer at the reception desk to show me immediately to his office.

Mrs. Peterson was seated at a slight angle on a lumpy imitation leather chair. Her thin, small-boned body looked frail against Korvich's fluorescent-light-and-Naugahyde motif. Her hands were clasped tightly together as if in prayer. Her eyes were cast downward.

Korvich was yawning without covering his mouth as he poured a cup of coffee for the old woman. "Here's the doc now, Mrs. Peterson, just like I told you. He'll take you home, and I'll see if I can get a loaner for you this afternoon."

She looked at me with a puzzled expression. "A loaner?"

I said, "A temporary replacement for your Buick, until the police are through with it."

"Which unfortunately may be quite a while," Korvich said, "depending on what the DA wants to do."

Lorraine Peterson looked at Korvich, willing herself to be measured and calm. "I own a Mercedes and a Lincoln, thank you," she said, dismissing the offer of a car with the implication that it wasn't worth the effort to her to accept it. Turning to me, she said, "This is such an extraordinary thing, as I've been telling Mr. Korvich—"

"You've been talking to him? Shouldn't you talk to your lawyer first?" I glared at the police chief.

He smiled. "I just got off the phone with some people in Florida. On the night of March sixth, Mrs. Peterson here was a guest of honor at a dinner at some famous woman's home. Esther Lauder, the perfume lady."

"Estée Lauder," I said.

"Whatever. Anyway, I talked with Mrs. Lauder personally." Korvich seemed quite pleased with himself for that. "Until almost midnight Mrs. Peterson was in a room full of people, and very important people at that. And the next morning she teed off at eight-thirty at a place called the Breakers. There's no way she could have been in Concord at five o'clock that morning when Charles Morris was killed. And I'm completely sincere about that."

"But you did think you had to check it out," I said, with obvious disdain.

"Well, sure. I wouldn't want Mrs. Peterson here to even have to consider talking to me without a lawyer present unless I could assure her I knew she was completely uninvolved with this matter."

It was likely the longest complete sentence he'd ever uttered. He probably had no idea what he'd just said.

I said, "Tell me what happened, Mrs. Peterson."

"I returned to Massachusetts on Monday. I'm sorry I didn't let you know I was home, Harold. I was planning to call you later today."

"Don't worry about that. Tell me about the Buick."

"The Buick—oh, my. This morning I used it for the first time since returning home. I was on my way to visit a friend in Lexington. You know, I didn't think very much about this at the time, but when I switched on the automobile radio it was turned extremely loud, with music that was quite irritating. Surely nothing I would ever choose for my own enjoyment."

Korvich said, "So Mrs. Peterson here takes the car for some gas at the Mobil station at the corner of Thoreau Street and Sudbury Road. And that's where Stan—you know Stan?"

"No," I replied.

"Fine young fella. I think he'd like to be a police officer himself someday. So that's where Stan notices a dent near the front right fender, and the right headlight bent back like it had hit something. He looked close, and that's when he sees the yellow fibers stuck between the headlight and the side grillwork." Now he was beaming. "I guess I don't have to tell you whose jogging suit the fibers matched up with."

"Charles Morris, obviously."

"Obviously," he repeated. "Mrs. Peterson was just getting ready to tell me who had access to the car." Turning to her, he said, "Do you keep it locked in your garage?"

"No. I only have enough garage room for my two other cars. The Buick is eight years old. I let it sit outside."

"Who has car keys, besides yourself?"

"My maid, naturally."

"And she was with you in Florida?"

"Yes."

"Anyone else?"

"Surely you don't think this was done by someone I know."

"Maybe, maybe not," Korvich replied. "No obvious

signs of tampering with the ignition, no indication of forced entry. Someone still could have stolen it, of course. But someone steals a car, they're not so likely to be as careful about getting it back to its owner. Who else had a key?"

Mrs. Peterson wrung her hands nervously. "George Foley. I hire him for odd jobs now and then." She gave Korvich the man's address and phone number in Maynard.

"Anyone else?"

She thought for a moment. "Just a high-school boy I hired to start the engine once a week while I was in Florida."

"What's his name?"

"Teddy Richardson. But I'm certain he wouldn't take the car for a drive without my permission. He's a nice boy, very . . . delicate."

If Korvich realized she was using "delicate" as a euphemism for a nontraditional sexual orientation, he didn't let on.

"Does that mean you think George Foley *is* the sort of person who would take the car without telling you?"

"Certainly not. Why are you putting words into my mouth?"

"You volunteered the belief that the student wouldn't do it. You didn't volunteer any such belief about the handyman. I just wondered what that meant."

She glared at him. "It meant nothing."

"Of course. Anyone else?"

"No." She turned toward me. "I would appreciate that ride home now, Harold."

Korvich spoke up. "Sure, sure—just another couple of questions, ma'am. Do you ever have a passenger in the back of the Buick when you drive it?"

She pondered for a moment. "No. I hardly ever drive the Buick. And if I were going to drive someone else around, I would use one of my nicer automobiles. I only keep the Buick for sentimental reasons. It meant something to my husband. Why do you ask?"

"The car was spic and span inside, except we found a ring tab on the floor in the backseat area."

"A ring tab?" asked Mrs. Peterson.

"You know—the thing on top of a beer can. You flip it up to open the can."

"I don't drink beer, Mr. Korvich," she said, her voice ice-cold.

"Well, I guess it could also be from a soda can."

"I don't drink from cans."

"Okay." He rubbed his chin. "Do you keep a spare key to the Buick somewhere in your house?"

She nodded. "On a pegboard in the pantry."

"Well, then—who has keys to the house? Besides you and the maid."

They stared at each other for several seconds. Finally, she sighed and said, "My sister, Virginia Whitney."

"On Lowell Road? The Widow Whitney?"

"What a lovely thing to call someone. Won't my sister be pleased to know you speak of her so familiarly." She noticed Korvich writing on his notepad. "Surely you can't possibly think that she—"

"I'm sure she'll check out just fine. Who else has a house key?"

"My children." Her two sons lived with their families: one in Needham, the other in Dover. Chief Korvich took down all the information.

"Is that it?"

"Yes." Then, after a brief pause, she looked at me with a puzzled expression and said, "'Do you still have your copy, Harold?"

"Me?" I'm sure I looked as surprised as Korvich looked.

"Don't you remember, dear? Franklin and I gave you a key shortly after you and your lovely wife moved to Concord."

"I don't think so."

She frowned slightly. "I guess I could be mistaken. It was long ago, at least ten years."

Korvich smiled, enjoying my discomfort. I wanted to tell him to go fuck himself, but then I'd probably have to perform cardiopulmonary resuscitation on Lorraine Peterson.

"Really, Mr. Korvich," she said, standing. "This has all been quite draining. Surely I can answer any other questions by telephone later in the day."

"Sure, sure. You positive about not wanting me to look for a loaner?"

"Come, Harold. I'll have Dottie prepare us a nice lunch when we get home." She headed for the door, and I trailed behind.

Korvich called after her. "Mrs. Peterson, I'd like you not to discuss this with anyone. I'll be checking with your handyman, and with that high-school student"—he checked his notepad—"Teddy Richardson. I'd like them to hear about this first from me, not from you."

"You don't want me to—how would you say it—'tip them off?' "

"That's right."

She stood by the door and stared at him. "Do you promise to leave my sister alone?"

"No."

"I see," she said. "Please take me home now, Harold."

Korvich said, "Stay for just a minute, okay, Doc? Mrs. Peterson, if you can wait for a couple of minutes in the reception area, I have something personal I need to discuss with Dr. Kline."

"I'm certain you do," she said. She closed the door as she exited.

"Well? What is it?"

"Relax, Doc. Just tell me—have you ever murdered someone?"

"Of course not."

"So I guess you didn't kill Charles Morris, is that right?"

"You've got to be joking."

He shrugged his shoulders. "Figured it wouldn't hurt to ask. You seem like a pretty honest fella, figured maybe if you did it you'd tell me now and save a lot of aggravation for both of us. So—where were you around five A.M. on March seventh?"

I couldn't believe what I was hearing. "What is this—a Grade-B movie script?"

"Oh, sure," he said. "Like 'We have ways of making you talk,' and 'Round up the usual bunch of suspects.' " He laughed. I didn't. "Seriously, though—do you remember where you were?"

"How the hell do I know? At that time of day I'm sure I must have been home. Asleep."

"You got someone who can vouch for you on that?" He knew I was a widower, but I had no reason to think he knew anything about Veronica.

Again I stifled the urge to suggest that he perform a sexual act upon himself. "Sure, that makes a lot of sense. I got up early that morning, drove over to Lorraine Peterson's house, let myself into her house with a nonexistent key she thinks she gave me ten years ago—"

"Nonexistent?"

"Come on, Chief. The woman's getting old, and she's upset by what happened today. Her memory is playing tricks on her."

"Funny—she seemed pretty alert to me. Maybe you got one of those drawers at home like I have, where you toss keys and other things you think you'll use one day, and by the time you get around to looking in the drawer, you forget where the keys came from."

"So I took this nonexistent key that you're sure I have, and I went inside her house, to a goddamn pegboard in a goddamn pantry that I've never been in, and I headed straight for the key to her car. I had this uncontrollable early-morning urge to go cruising in a 1985 Buick. And while I was satisfying that urge I clipped Charles Morris on Musketaquid Road, then I drove back, locked up, and went home. Am I missing anything?"

"Who said anything about 1985?"

"Excuse me?"

"How do you know the car is from 1985?"

"Mrs. Peterson said it was eight years old."

"Did she?"

"You know she did." He'd obviously heard her say so, just a few minutes earlier. His memory wasn't bad; he was just screwing around with me, trying to rile me. It was working. "I'll take Mrs. Peterson home now. She's had a difficult morning, in spite of your exemplary effort to treat her with deference and respect."

I turned to leave, but he spoke to me again. "So there I am, talking to you on the phone last week about your patient Michael Cafferty. Then all of a sudden, out of the clear blue, you start asking me questions about the investigation into the Morris hit-and-run. And now I gotta ask myself, 'Why was he so interested?' "

"I told you—Marjorie Morris is a friend of mine."

"Exactly right. That *is* what you told me over the phone last Wednesday. But when we talked at the inn over the weekend, when I reminded you of that, you downplayed it, said you were just acquaintances. Changed your story." He paused. "Anything else you want to change?"

I put my hand on the doorknob. He saw that and said, "There's one more thing you should think about."

"What's that?"

He rubbed a hand through his slicked-back hair. "It wasn't an accident."

"Excuse me?"

"The hit-and-run. It wasn't an accident. It was premeditated murder."

"What are you talking about?"

"We discovered a couple of things from the car, things that tell me whoever hit Charles Morris did it on purpose."

"What did you find?"

He smiled. He was silent for several seconds, then said, "Thanks for coming by, Doc. You've been a big help."

"Go screw yourself, Chief. And *I'm* completely sincere about that."

11: Alibi

"Do you think he'll show up?"

Bobby checked his watch. "Relax, pal of mine. He's only five minutes overdue."

We were sitting in my office, waiting for Frank Porter to arrive. "I hate it when people are late," I said. "It's so damn passive-aggressive."

"If you say so." Bobby yawned, leaned back in his chair, and rested his feet on the edge of my desk.

"How come it doesn't bother you?"

"Billable hours. Tick-tock, tick-tock. Your meter is running, too. That should take some of the sting out of waiting."

"Yeah, well, I still hate it."

"You're not your usual charming self. Korvich really has you steamed, doesn't he?"

"I didn't like the way he treated either of us this morning—Mrs. Peterson or me."

"I think Lorraine Peterson can take care of herself. And you should just blow it off. You know—don't worry, be happy."

"Didn't George Bush use that song in his reelection campaign?"

"I think his advisers talked him out of it," Bobby said. "Considering how things turned out, maybe he shouldn't have listened to them." He glanced over at me. "What are you holding?"

"It's a key I found after I spent an hour and a half looking through drawers and file cabinets. There's a tag attached to it with the name Peterson on it. I don't remember ever seeing it before."

"Are you going to tell Korvich you found it?"

"Do you think I should?"

"Are you asking me as your friend, or your attorney?"

"You're not a criminal lawyer anymore." Early in his career, Bobby was one of the best. But he wearied of representing the sort of people he would never otherwise choose to associate with.

He said, " 'Criminal lawyer.' That's an interesting label, don't you think? Sort of like 'child psychiatrist.' Anyway, as your lawyer, I'd say put it back where you found it and let Korvich get a search warrant. As your friend, I'd say toss it away."

"Am I hearing this from the guy who once called himself out at home?"

He shrugged. "What was it Walt Whitman wrote? 'Do I contradict myself? Very well, then—fuck it.' "

"He certainly had a way with words."

"One of our finest poets."

"Do you really think Korvich will get a search warrant for that key?" I asked.

"I wouldn't worry about it if I were you. Where were you at the time Charles Morris was killed, anyway?"

"I assume I was asleep."

"With Veronica?"

"Probably. She was spending just about every night here."

"She'd make a good alibi. A special agent of the FBI—that should satisfy Korvich. Besides, I'm sure he doesn't suspect you at all. He's just asking questions, which is what he's supposed to do. A cop on an investigation is like a sculptor. He starts with a block of marble, then keeps chipping away and chipping away at the material that doesn't belong. After all the chipping is done, what's left is the solution to the mystery."

Outside my open window, I heard the quiet hum of a BMW. Frank Porter shut the motor, got out of the car, and strolled leisurely to my office entrance, whistling as he walked.

He entered without knocking. "Sorry to be late, fellas. I had an emergency phone call from a client. 'Dr. Porter, I'm having a really rough day.' You know how it is with borderlines, Harry."

"What does 'borderline' mean?" asked Bobby.

"It's a diagnosis," I said. "Borderline personality disorder. Think of it as shorthand for someone who is unstable and prone to acting impulsively."

"Like Celeste Oberlin," added Porter, yawning. "Speaking of which—where do we stand, counselor?"

"Well, Harry has read the material that her parents produced."

Porter smiled at me, an unctuous little grin that made me want to slap him silly. "I'm sure Harry understands what I was trying to do with Celeste. Don't you, Harry?"

I couldn't stand his arrogant attitude toward the suit and his cavalier approach to the tragedy that befell his patient. I said, "Frankly, no, I don't."

His smile faded for just a moment. His lips curled, and there was a flicker of something sinister in his eyes. But it all happened in an instant, and then he was back to his smug, oleaginous self. He said to me, "Surely you must have heard of the term 'corrective emotional experience.' "

Bobby interrupted. "What is that?"

Porter said, "You encourage a client to regress to the point in time when she was traumatized. Then you help her relive the trauma safely, with you as her guide, so she can get through it and move beyond it. Isn't that right, Harry?"

"Not exactly," I said. "But surely *you* must have heard of the term 'iatrogenic illness.' "

"What the hell is *that*?" Bobby asked.

I kept eye contact with Porter as I replied to Bobby's

question. "It's an illness caused by a doctor's misguided effort to heal a lesser malady. It's the cure that kills. Isn't *that* right, Frank?"

"I resent that. I didn't do anything improper."

I said, "You encouraged a very vulnerable patient to develop a sick dependence on you. And you encouraged bizarre fantasies in someone who already had a hard time sticking to reality. Not exactly a textbook treatment plan, Frank."

Porter furrowed his brow and forced a pensive look onto his face. "Celeste was a very difficult client. There was nothing typical about her, so there couldn't be anything typical about the approach I took with her." Turning to Bobby, he asked, "What's the best way of handling this situation?"

"In a submissive position."

"What do you mean?"

"Use your imagination. You're going to get screwed. The best you can hope for is to get it over quickly."

Porter glared at his attorney. "You want me to admit that I'm somehow responsible for Celeste's suicide. I won't do that."

Bobby said, "Nobody's talking about admitting anything. We're talking about damage control. If you play things sensibly, you won't have to admit misfeasance, malfeasance, or any other kind of feasance. This is how it works. Both parties agree to leave the merits of the suit unadjudicated. Your insurance carrier pays a settlement, but you admit no wrongdoing. The Oberlins sign a binding pledge not to pursue the suit, now or ever. And they agree to keep the details of the settlement confidential, or else they forfeit the settlement. And since they don't go public with their allegations, you get to continue your practice as if nothing had happened."

Porter said, "Are you finished?"

Bobby shrugged. "I suppose I am."

"Good. Now, get this straight." He folded his arms

tightly across his chest; thus tensed, they appeared surprisingly muscular. "Celeste Oberlin was a suicide waiting to happen long before I began working with her. She'd already failed with half a dozen other therapists. When I look back on it, I'm amazed I managed to keep her alive as long as I did."

Bobby said, "You can believe all that and still allow the Oberlins to receive some compensation for their suffering. Jesus Christ, man—the money won't be coming out of your own pocket."

Porter leaned forward. "Not a single fucking nickel, I don't care whose fucking pocket it comes out of!"

I said, "Calm down, Frank."

"*You* calm down!"

"I *am* calm."

"I'm calm, too," he said, struggling to rein in his sudden flash of anger.

Porter and I stared at each other, each of us taking the measure of the other.

Bobby shifted in his seat, folded his hands, and sat quietly for a moment. Then he said, "You don't believe the Oberlins will go through with this suit, do you?"

"No."

"Why?"

Porter paused. "I know too much." He smiled. "If they don't realize that yet, then maybe it's time to throw a little scare into them."

"Tell me what you know."

Porter said, "It would mean revealing information told to me in confidence by Celeste Oberlin."

"You're allowed to tell *me*, Frank. You're *supposed* to tell me. I'm your lawyer, for chrissake."

"I know that! I'm not a moron." Porter gestured toward me. "What about him?"

"Harry is an expert witness for the defense, so the attorney-client confidentiality extends to cover anything you say in his presence."

Porter considered that for a little while. Then he reached

into his pocket and pulled out an audiocassette. "This is a recording from a therapy session with Celeste Oberlin."

I reached into a file cabinet and pulled out a portable tape player. I handed it to Porter. He snapped the cassette into place and turned the machine on. There were a few moments of high-pitched tape hiss. Then suddenly we were listening to a woman's muffled moans and sobs. The mournful sounds continued for several seconds, until she was able to force her tears down and her words out.

The woman—Celeste Oberlin—said. "The next time it happened was on Christmas Eve, just after my sixth birthday. We were spending the holiday at our vacation home in New Hampshire. Daddy came into my room and pulled my covers back, and he got into bed next to me."

Somehow, just knowing that she was later driven to death by her own demons lent a chilling immediacy to her words. The room suddenly seemed very still; the air temperature felt ten degrees cooler.

On the tape, Celeste Oberlin began to cry again. "This time . . . he didn't even pretend to be nice. When I felt him rub up against me, all hard and wet . . . it frightened me, and I pulled away. That's when he grabbed my ears and pinned my head to the pillow. And he leaned over me . . . with his legs pressing down on my arms . . . so that I couldn't move at all. I can still smell his sweat, and the alcohol on his breath."

The crying intensified, but she forced herself to talk through her tears. "He pushed himself against my mouth and told me to lick it. He never did that before. Until then it was just us touching each other. And I . . . just sort of froze up, really scared. He twisted my ears very hard, and when I opened my mouth to scream, he shoved himself into me. I thought I was suffocating."

She began to wail: a gut-wrenching noise that ended with the sound of someone struggling for breath. Then she fell silent. After perhaps half a minute Porter's voice said, "Did you send your mind somewhere else? Someplace where it wouldn't feel the pain?"

"Yes. I flew outside."

"Tell me how you did that, Celeste."

"I turned away so I wouldn't have to look at him while he was doing . . . that. I looked outside my window and saw a butterfly. And I just kept my focus on the butterfly, until I became the butterfly. And then it was okay, because I was floating above everything. I could float as far away as I wanted, but it didn't matter anymore because I couldn't feel anything."

After another long pause she continued. "The next thing I remember is eating breakfast on Christmas with my mother and father. I don't remember what happened after he forced my mouth open. I don't remember opening presents on Christmas morning. In fact, when we all sat there at breakfast, everything seemed so normal, I'm not even sure if I let myself remember then what had just happened the night before."

"But you remember now."

"Yes." There was a brief silence, punctured by a moan so primal that it sounded like a bleating animal. "Yes! I remember now!" She began to choke and gasp for air, like a person suffocating.

Frank Porter pressed a button on my portable tape player and brought the tape to a stop. "Warren Oberlin sexually abused Celeste from sometime before her third birthday until around the time of her first menstrual period—which, thankfully, came just before she turned twelve, a little earlier than most girls have it. She was so frightened that she completely blocked the memories out, even as they were forming. She kept them hidden, even from herself. The memories threatened to break through once she turned nineteen and began having intercourse with boyfriends. That's probably what the drugs and alcohol were all about—attempts to anesthetize herself, to keep the recollections buried inside. She began to remember, really remember, during her work with me."

Porter took the tape from the machine and handed it to Bobby. "This is tame compared to some of the other recordings I made. If you get a copy of this to her parents, pretty soon they'll be offering to pay *me* just to keep my mouth shut." He turned to me and smiled. "That's a joke, of course."

"Of course."

Porter stood. "I have clients to see. Tell Warren Oberlin I look forward to seeing him in court."

Bobby took a can of Coke from my refrigerator and sat at the kitchen table, across from me. He switched the small television on and turned to a twenty-four-hour cable sports channel. Pickings were slim on this Wednesday afternoon: a feature about synchronized swimming that he put on in the background with the volume muted.

He took a sip from the soda can. "If one synchronized swimmer drowns, do the rest have to drown, too?"

"I think that's one of the options they're given."

"Uh-huh." He watched the soundless array of swimmers for a moment, then turned to me. "I wonder why Porter calls his patients 'clients.' "

"A lot of psychologists do that," I replied. "Social workers do it, too."

"Why?"

I shrugged. "Just to be different from psychiatrists, I suppose. They say they're not working with sick people, just normal people who are having some problems in their lives."

"Which would certainly be an understatement in the case of Celeste Oberlin. What did you think about the tape Porter played for us?"

"I don't know. There's a lot of controversy in my profession about recovered memory syndrome. That's the psychiatric term for the phenomenon Porter described—the notion that you can forget a whole series of traumatic events for years, then recover the memories intact, with all of the vivid emotion of the original experiences. But there are two problems with that concept."

"What are they?"

"First of all, research indicates that the more traumatic an event is, the *less* likely it is that the person will forget it. It's one thing to forget that someone gave you a spare key to their house ten years ago. It's something else to forget a whole series of things that most people would consider . . . well, horribly unforgettable."

"Like traumatic war memories," he offered.

"Exactly. I've treated a lot of Vietnam veterans who suffered from post-traumatic stress disorder. Their problem isn't that the traumatic memories are repressed. Just the opposite—they can't get rid of their memories, even when they sleep."

"You said there are two problems with this recovered memory stuff. What's the second problem?"

"Well, it turns out that memories are more malleable than most people think. They change over the years, sometimes in remarkable ways. For example—did I ever tell you how I found out about Kennedy's assassination?"

"I don't think so."

"I was twelve years old. I was sitting at my desk in school. The principal's voice came over the loudspeaker. She was crying. It seemed like an eternity passed before she could make the announcement. My teacher had us bow our heads in a moment of silence, and then I heard someone screaming in the corridor. The screaming went on and on, and all the while we sat there with our heads bowed."

"What's your point?"

"Just before my parents sold their house and retired to Florida, I drove over to sort through things that had been sitting in the attic for years. I came across a journal I used to keep when I was a kid, and I read the entry for November twenty-second, 1963. It turns out I was home sick from school that day, and I was lying in bed watching TV when I saw a news bulletin about the assassination. All those years I'd been living with a memory that was entirely manufactured. Even after I read the journal, I had no recollection of staying home that day or learning the news by watching television. I still don't. Don't get me wrong—I'm sure the journal version is accurate. But when I think about the assassination, I still picture myself in that classroom, listening to the principal's sobs and the unidentified screaming in the hallway. My false memory is more real to me than the truth."

"How do you think that happened?"

"I'm not sure. Maybe I heard someone else talk about how the class learned the news, then somehow incorporated that version into my own recollections so I'd feel like part of the group."

"I didn't realize you were so suggestible."

"Everyone is suggestible."

Bobby smiled. "That's what makes lawyers and psychiatrists so dangerous."

"Exactly. On the tape, Frank Porter asks her if she sent her mind somewhere else, and the next thing we know, she's an insect flapping her wings outside her window. I once watched a colleague at the VA use hypnosis to help a patient remember the details of a terrible ambush by the Vietcong. It worked so well—his memories came pouring out so fast and so vivid—that I felt like I was right there in the jungle beside him, listening to mortar blasts and getting splattered by blood from the flying body parts of my comrades. But guess what?"

"What?"

"They were interviewing the wrong patient. This guy was in the army during the war, but the closest he ever got to Vietnam was Fort Lee, New Jersey. The hypnosis was supposed to recover memories. Instead, it created them."

"Holy shit."

"Yeah," I replied. "Holy shit."

Bobby thought for a moment. "There are a couple of other things to consider, too. She was talking about Christmas Eve at their vacation home."

"So?"

"You'd have to be one mean motherfucker of a butterfly to make it through to December in New Hampshire." He paused. "And how the hell did she turn to look out the window if her father nailed her head to the pillow the way she says he did?"

My phone rang shortly after Bobby left. The first words out of my caller's mouth were, "You have balls, I'll say that much about you. And I'm completely sincere about that."

Alfred Korvich didn't even identify himself, so possessed was he with his own importance that he assumed I would recognize his voice on my own. He was right.

"Yes, sir," he continued. "It definitely takes balls to tell your chief of police to go screw himself. Most people would think twice before saying something like that."

"I did think twice," I said.

"Oh." He wasn't certain what to make of that. "Well, I'm just calling to make sure Mrs. Peterson got home all right."

"I dropped her off hours ago."

"Yes, I guess you did. Say—about that key you say you don't remember getting from her. You want me to come out and help you look for it?"

"It's sweet of you to offer, but I couldn't impose on you like that."

"Well, you just let me know if you need any help. We're here to serve the citizenry. Of course, every once in a while, we turn to a member of the citizenry such as yourself to help us."

"And would this be one of those times?"

"Well, now that you ask—I have some questions I'd like you to ask Marjorie Morris when you talk to her."

A paranoid rush shot through me. I was already feeling guilty about making arrangements to meet Marjorie, and now the chief of police was talking about it.

"Who told you I would be talking with her?"

"Friends talk. And you said you're her friend. Or was it 'acquaintance'? When someone changes his story, sometimes I forget which version is in play at the moment."

"It's been nice talking with you, Chief."

"Okay, okay—I'll lay off, I just want you to talk to her about her father, see if she has any ideas about who might want to murder him."

"Isn't that a job for you fellows?"

"I called on her this afternoon. When I told her I thought the accident wasn't really an accident, she said that was impossible, and she pretty much talked around answering any of my questions."

"Maybe she just doesn't like you—hard though it may be to believe that."

"Nah, that's not it. It's just that nobody likes to hear that a family member was murdered. You tell them that Uncle Joe or Cousin Sally was killed on purpose, and it's like an insult. Because maybe it says something about Joe or Sally, that someone could hate them enough to kill them. I've seen survivors react that way before."

"Oh, sure. This happens in Concord all the time. We get lots of murders here."

"Save the sarcasm, Doc. I've been around and I've seen my share. I haven't spent my whole career in this town, you know."

I was willing to concede that it might be so. "Suppose I agree to talk to her for you. What do you want me to ask her?"

"Oh, things like—did her father seem upset or preoccupied before he was killed? Did she notice any other changes? Was he drinking more than usual? Drinking *less* than usual? Any business problems or other reversals she might know about? Any strangers calling the house or showing up, either before he died or after? Did he ever talk to her about being threatened by someone? You get the idea. You and me, we're not all that different, you know. We both have to cut through a lot of bullshit to get to the truth."

"Sort of like chipping away at a marble block, huh?"

"What are you talking about?"

"Nothing important."

"Well, will you do it?"

I thought for several seconds. "What's your evidence that Charles Morris's death was more than just an accident?" When Korvich didn't answer right away, I said, "I'll talk to Marjorie. I'll ask your questions for you—*if* you answer that question for me first."

"Why is that so important?"

"Because if you answer it for me, it means you're not going to bother me anymore about the key you think I have, or my alibi for March seventh. Because if you really think I might have anything at all to do with this, then you won't reveal the information to me."

"How do I know you won't tell your friend Marjorie? I don't like the details of a police investigation getting out until I'm ready to release them."

"That's easy. I'll promise not to tell her, and you'll decide you can trust me on that."

He pondered the challenge for a while. Finally, he said, "We found a map on the floor in Lorraine Peterson's Buick."

"So what? Lots of people have maps in their cars. Where else would you keep them?"

"I'm not talking Rand McNally here. This map was hand-drawn. A crude diagram of the roads in the Nashawtuc Hill part of town. With a line penciled in that matches Charles Morris's jogging route. And three crosses."

"Three crosses?"

"Three crosses marking important points of interest. A cross where the Morris house is. A cross where the car was stolen from Mrs. Peterson's house." He paused.

"That's two crosses," I said. "Where was the third?"

"On Musketaquid Road, at almost the exact spot where Charles Morris was hit."

It didn't require any particular genius to see what he was hinting at. The driver wouldn't have drawn the map *after* the hit-and-run. And if drawn before, then it could only be a blueprint for murder.

Korvich said, "One more thing. I told you this morning about the damaged headlight and the yellow fibers from the jogging suit. And I told you last week that there were tire impressions of a car stopping and making a U-turn. What I didn't tell you was this—the tire impressions matched up with Lorraine Peterson's Buick, and we found damage and fibers near *both* headlights."

I thought about this information, then said, "I don't get it."

"The driver struck Morris from behind—which is the direction you'd pick if you wanted to hit someone on purpose. Then he came to a quick halt, turned around, and went back to finish the job. He hit Morris a second time going in the other direction. Which is why both sides of the front of the car show signs of impact. Morris must still have been standing, or the second headlight wouldn't have picked up fibers."

"I see your point."

"I don't care if you see it. I only care that you keep it to yourself."

"I already gave you my word on that."

"What do you think I am—a fucking idiot? People break promises all the time. People lie all the time."

"Not all people," I said.

"All people—sooner or later. Here, I'll prove it to you. Did you look for the key Mrs. Peterson insisted she gave you?"

I hesitated. "Yes."

"Did you find it?"

"Yes."

He chuckled. "Well, now—you really *do* have balls." He paused for a moment. "Now all you need is an alibi for five in the morning on March seventh."

"I'm glad you called," I said, moving closer to the side of my bed so I could hold the phone more comfortably. "I've been worried."

"There's nothing to worry about," Veronica said. "It's not dangerous work."

"I wasn't worried about you. I was worried about us."

She didn't respond to that; I guess she, like me, feared making things worse by looking at them too directly. In my professional life, I encourage people to take risks and talk about what's bothering them. In my personal life, I can be as reluctant as anyone else to face problems head-on.

"Did Melissa and Mrs. Winnicot leave?" she asked.

"Yes. I talked to Melissa a little while ago. I think she's trying to convince herself she's not enjoying herself, because it wouldn't be cool to admit you're having fun with your grandparents." I paused. "Where are you?"

"I'm still in Pittsfield. Let me give you the phone number of the hotel I'm staying at."

I wrote the number on a pad next to the telephone. I didn't ask her if she'd been in Pittsfield since Monday. I didn't tell her I knew that she lied about getting a call from her boss on Monday morning, and I didn't tell her I'd seen a light on when I drove past her place the previous night. Neither one of us made mention of the fact that neither had tried calling or paging the other for two and a half days.

I asked her how things were progressing in the case of the man who tried to kidnap a young girl and who was now suspected of killing at least two children.

"It's going more slowly than I would like," she said. "Louis Laggone's real-estate attorney acts like he's the second coming of Clarence Darrow. He's already filed a million motions with the court, and he pontificates about them endlessly whenever he has the opportunity. I guess he realizes this is his moment in the sun. He even filed a motion to get the records of the little girl's school counselor. Somehow he learned that she has a learning disability, and I think he wants to build a case that she misremembers or distorts things. He also learned that her school performance has slipped since her parents separated last year, so he's looking for anything to suggest she's unstable or looking for attention. That's why he wants to go on a fishing expedition through the counselor's records."

"A judge wouldn't grant that kind of motion, would he?"

"This judge is a she, not a he. And she already has

granted it, after a fashion. She ordered the records turned over to herself. She'll review them privately to determine if they hold anything of relevance to the defense, and she'll release them if they do."

"Do you think you'll be able to tie him to the open murder cases?"

"I don't know. He and I spent some time today talking about his favorite vacation spots in northern New York State. I think he's trying to tell me that the bodies are there somewhere. It's like a novel with three subplots. I'm trying to get enough information to find the bodies. He's trying to reveal enough to be viewed as cooperative without revealing so much that he gets tied directly to the murders. Meanwhile the lawyer is trying to parlay his client's cooperativeness into a deal on the attempted-kidnapping charge they're holding him on."

"What sort of deal?"

"Andy tells me that Laggone's lawyer inquired about a plea bargain to something less than attempted kidnapping."

"Andy?"

"Andy Galloway, the district attorney. I mentioned him to you before."

I thought: Before it was "Andrew," not "Andy."

She continued. "The lawyer talked about a possible plea to simple assault. Andy said that it would have to be assault and battery, since the girl says Laggone grabbed her. Andy also wants to add assault with a dangerous weapon, because Laggone brandished a gun when he tried to abduct her."

"How do you think it will turn out?"

"I can't imagine Andy letting go of the assault-and-battery charge. As it is, he risks catching a lot of flak from the community if he drops the attempted-kidnapping case. As far as threatening the girl with a gun, there's a slight problem there."

"What's that?"

"They can't find a gun. Loony Louie has no record of gun ownership, and no one has ever seen him with one.

And the locals didn't find one with their search warrant—or bullets or any other implicating evidence."

"He disposed of it, obviously."

"I know. But I hate it when a case goes forward with gaps like that. I guess I still think like a prosecutor."

We talked a little while longer. I told her about the party at her father's house, without mentioning his concern about her unhappiness; the meeting with Bobby and his client, without mentioning Porter's name or any significant details; and the strangeness of being alone in my house, without mentioning directly that I missed her. I omitted references to the developments in the investigation into Charles Morris's death, since it was the chance meeting with Marjorie that triggered our argument on Sunday. And I sure as hell didn't inform her of my lunch plans with Marjorie for the next day.

I said, "If I ask you something, do you promise not to ask me why I'm asking you?"

"Am I allowed to ask why you don't want me to ask why you're asking what you want to ask?"

"Huh?"

"Just go ahead and ask me already," she said, chagrined. "If you want to keep something secret from me, I can't stop you."

I hesitated. "By any chance, do you remember what we did the night of March sixth?"

She paused for just a second or two, searching her steel-trap memory with the speed and accuracy of a computer. Then she spoke warmly, saying, "Yes, I do, sweetheart. Melissa slept at Ginny Conway's house, And you and I barely slept at all."

Of course, I thought. Melissa's friend had a birthday sleep-over party, and Veronica and I took every advantage of the privacy her absence afforded us. We cavorted until just before dawn, finally falling asleep in front of the fireplace. I remembered the red glow of the coals reflecting off her body, warming her soft skin.

She said, "That was a lovely night. It's so sweet of you to think of that now."

This was too good to be true. Not only did I have an alibi for the night of Charles Morris's murder—in the event that Alfred Korvich ever decided to press the point—but I'd also stumbled inadvertently into reminding Veronica of a very romantic interlude, impressing her with my sentimentality for having done so.

"Harry, why are you laughing?"

"Oh, I'm just remembering what a terrific night that was."

"Oh, Harry—I'm so glad you remember that."

"Of course I remember. How could I ever forget it?"

12: Waiting to Die

"I swear to God," said the plumber, angry as usual. "I don't know why I don't just leave her."

"You say that often," I replied.

He drummed his fingers on the armrest of his chair. "One night last week, I'm getting ready to go to bed, when my wife suddenly remembers to give me a phone message she took hours earlier. So now it's too late to return the call, and I'm pissed. But I don't say anything, because I don't want to start an argument. Then two days later I come home from work, and I ask her if anyone called while I was out. And now *she's* really pissed, and she says, 'Don't ever ask me that. I would have told you already if somebody called.' I mean, you just can't win with her."

"Is this really about winning and losing?"

"It's just a figure of speech," he said. "The other morning, I'm already in the shower when I realize I forgot to get a towel from the linen closet in the hallway. But then she comes in to get something, so I ask her to please get me a towel. 'I'm busy,' she says, 'I'll get it in a minute.' "

"Did she get it for you?"

"What do *you* think?" he asked, looking triumphant in a bitter, ironic way.

I resisted the invitation to choose sides. When I didn't respond, he continued. "The thing of it is, it only takes six and a half seconds to open the bathroom door, get a towel out of the linen closet, and bring it into the bathroom. And that's if you do it leisurely. If you rush, you can do it in three or four seconds."

"Six and a half seconds?"

"Exactly six-point-five," he said.

"How do you know that?"

"I timed it afterwards." He smiled, as if he'd proven a point. But then the smile faded and he sank back into the chair.

I said, "I know a young boy who used to weigh his dessert every night to prove his mother was giving more to his brother." I said nothing more, waiting to see if he would take the opening to cut through the anger and talk about how unloved he felt.

He was quiet for several seconds. There was a subtle change in his manner. His voice grew softer, his gestures less animated. Then, slowly and softly, he said, "I honestly can't remember the last time she said something nice to me."

"No wonder you feel so terrible."

He sighed deeply. "I used to feel like I was just hanging around, waiting for my life to begin. Somewhere along the way, things switched. Now I feel like I'm just waiting to die."

Concord Academy is a private high school with about three hundred students. It sits on a thirty-five-acre plot on the rim of the town's center, set between Main Street and the Sudbury River. The school has a larger endowment than many colleges, a fact proudly proclaimed in its publicity brochures. Costs rival those of an Ivy League college; the tab for the full four-year program runs into six figures.

I arrived shortly before noon on Thursday to meet Marjorie Morris for lunch. Students milled about on their way to the dining hall, the sons and daughters of wealthy families from around the country—indeed, from around the world.

I waited for Marjorie on a bench outside the performing

arts center. I was gazing across the river at the stately homes rising above Nashawtuc Hill, when my attention was drawn by the sound of loud voices coming from inside the building. I turned and saw Marjorie behind the glass door, in heated conversation with a tall, muscular man whose back was toward me. He had long hair, strikingly blond, swept back Adonis-like and held in place by its own massive abundance.

The building was twenty yards from my bench. I rose instinctively when I saw Marjorie arguing with her companion. I hesitated at first, caught between the urge to intercede and the thought that I should mind my own business. But when the man lunged forward and grabbed Marjorie's wrist, I headed swiftly toward the door.

Marjorie tried to pull free from his grip. As he held on to her his body spun around. His eyes met mine when I was about ten yards from the building. He had a full, square face with deep-set metallic blue eyes. Viewing him from the front, I realized he was probably young enough to be a student at the school. He looked familiar, but I couldn't connect his image with any specific memory. When he saw me reach for the door handle, he released his grip on Marjorie, then walked in the other direction, through an archway and down the corridor.

Marjorie muttered something underneath her breath and started massaging her wrist where he had grabbed her. When she saw me standing there she looked startled, then embarrassed.

"Are you all right?" I asked.

She nodded and stopped rubbing her wrist.

"What was that all about?"

"It's nothing, really. He's one of the students I coach. He got upset when I criticized his interpretation of a scene. I guess we theater people just tend to be a little emotional."

"Shouldn't you tell someone?" She looked at me with a quizzical expression. I said, "You know—the headmaster, or someone like that. The dean of students is a friend of mine. I could tell her what I saw."

"Thank you, really. But it's not a problem, certainly not anything worth getting him in trouble for."

I decided not to argue the point. My work had taught me how foolhardy it is to give advice when none is requested. I had a hundred and one answers for the plumber, but he was still too involved in his diatribe against his wife to ask for help. Marjorie wasn't asking, either.

We left the building and walked across the campus toward Main Street. A few students smiled and said hello to Marjorie, calling her by her first name.

I said, "I didn't realize things were so informal here."

"They're not, usually. But my situation is different. I just come here a few times each week to coach some of the drama students. It's an extracurricular activity, not a course they take for credit. I'm more like a big sister than a classroom teacher. If one of them called me by my last name, I'd probably turn around and look for my late mother's ghost."

We crossed Main Street and turned toward Thoreau Street, a short distance ahead of us. Marjorie wasn't in the mood for talking. She kept her eyes on the ground in front of her as she walked, furrowing her brow as if she were trying to memorize an algebraic proof. A man walked past us, then turned to catch an extra glimpse of her. She gave no indication whether she was aware of him.

The pizza shop a block down Thoreau Street was a no-frills take-out place with a few tables for people who preferred eating on the spot. Marjorie sat while I walked to the counter to order our food. When I returned to the table, she was staring out the window and absentmindedly tearing small pieces off a paper napkin.

"Earth to Marjorie," I said as I waved a hand slowly, back and forth. "Do you read me? Please acknowledge."

She smiled at that. Her green eyes seemed to sparkle for a moment, but then she waxed glum again. She took a deep breath and released it slowly. "I'm sorry, Harry. Maybe this wasn't such a good idea, after all."

"Why do you say that?"

"I have a lot on my mind. I'm not very good company. And I really wanted to make a good impression today, too. I was so nervous thinking about it this morning, I practically pulled my hair out trying to brush it into place. I still feel like a mess."

"Are you telling me it never ends?"

"What do you mean?"

"Every morning my daughter goes through the same thing. I was hoping she'd grow out of it, preferably within the next week. She reminds me of that old song by Rod Stewart—the one about combing his hair in a thousand different ways, but it always looks just the same."

"You enjoy talking about your daughter, don't you?"

"More than anything."

"It must be nice having a child."

"Except on bad hair days."

I walked to the vending machine and got two soft drinks. I placed the cans on the table and sat down again. "Anyway," I said, "I'm the one who should be worried about making a good impression, considering what a classy place I've brought you to for lunch."

"You always made a good impression on me, Harry. Even when I was a little girl."

I flipped the tab up to open my soda can, and I remembered that the police found a similar tab on the floor of the car that had been used to kill Marjorie's father. I doubted she knew that; from Korvich's description of their interaction the previous afternoon, the police chief had been more interested in getting information than giving it.

I said, "Alfred Korvich wants me to pump you for information about your father."

She was daydreaming again and turning another napkin into confetti. "Who? Oh, him. How did he know you were planning to see me?"

"He figured we'd be talking sooner or later, because he knows we're friends."

"How does he know that?"

"I told him. The day after you and I met in the cemetery,

I was talking to him about another matter, so I took the opportunity to ask him if any progress was being made in solving your father's case. He asked me why I was so interested. I think his exact words were, 'What the hell do you care, anyway?' So I told him I was an old friend."

"I'm flattered."

"Just because I said I was your friend?"

"No—I'm flattered that you were the one who initiated the conversation. It shows you were thinking about me. I know I was thinking about you."

They called the number of our order, which rescued me from having to respond to what she had said. I brought our food back to the table and started in on my pizza. Marjorie picked at her salad, barely eating a thing.

"I received a very upsetting visit from Mr. Korvich yesterday. The police think someone killed my father intentionally. He seemed quite certain about it."

"I know. He told me when he asked me to talk with you."

"I couldn't sleep at all last night. To think that he may have been murdered ... I find the thought most distressing."

"Of course."

"It was hard enough to accept him dying so suddenly when I thought someone killed him by accident. But to think it might have been intentional ..." Her voice trailed off. After a moment she said, "I guess I'm not hungry for my salad."

"Would you like a slice of my pizza? Pepperoni, with extra tomato sauce."

"No, thank you," she replied. "I keep wondering what it is that makes the police believe he was murdered. I guess that's easier than wondering why he might have been murdered. I asked the police chief why they believed that, but he told me it was too early to discuss the details. He just said it had something to do with physical evidence. I didn't ask him what he meant by that. I guess I was too shocked to ask much of anything."

I knew Korvich didn't want me to reveal what he told me about the hand-drawn map or the fact that Charles Morris had been struck two times by the same car. And I remembered him asking Mrs. Peterson not to mention anything about her Buick being identified as the car that was involved. What he had said to me in the taproom at the Colonial Inn was right on the money: *You don't like me, do you, Doc?* I didn't like the way he treated people, but I knew it wasn't my place to criticize the way he was handling his investigation. I decided not to tell Marjorie what I knew about the evidence.

"Why does he want you to get information from me?" she asked.

"He indicated that you and he didn't communicate very well with each other yesterday."

Her cheeks flushed. "The day my father died, just a few hours after Chief Korvich informed me about the accident, he came back to my house a second time. He asked me—I can't believe he actually asked me this—he asked me why I didn't cry earlier that day when I learned about my father. He was just as tactless yesterday when he told me my father was a murder victim. The only thing he wanted to talk about was my father's jogging outfits. I think the police chief is a wretched person—crude, insensitive, and stupid."

"He has that effect on people. I think he just likes to rattle people's cages, hoping something will shake loose that leads him somewhere."

"Why are you defending him?"

"I'm not," I replied. "I'm just explaining him to you so you don't take it personally. I think he realized he didn't handle himself well with you, and that's why he asked me to talk to you."

"What sorts of questions are you supposed to ask me?"

"He wants to know more about your father, especially any enemies he may have had, or any things he may have done that would make him a target for murder."

Marjorie pushed her salad plate away and used a straw to sip from her can of Diet Coke. She thought for several seconds, then said, "My father was not a loving or lovable man. You knew my mother, Harry—what a kind person she was. Anyone else would have left him years earlier. It wasn't just the drinking, or the affairs, or the occasional smack across the face. It was the way he wore her down mentally. Eventually her depression caught up with her. My freshman year at UCLA, she took an overdose of her antidepressant. I flew home to see her in the hospital. I blurted out something foolish, like, 'What are you doing here?' And she was really sedated, so I don't even know if she realized what she was saying when she answered me. . . ."

Tears began to trickle slowly down both cheeks. I offered her a napkin for her face and a hand to hold. She took both.

"What did she say?" I asked.

"She smiled at me and said—very calmly, as if we were sharing pleasantries over afternoon tea—she said, 'I'm just waiting to die, honey.' "

I thought about the plumber who said very much the same thing to me earlier that day. I wondered: Once you've peered into the blackness of the longing for death, do you ever pull yourself completely free from it?

Marjorie continued. "Fortunately, before he could drive her to suicide, he drove her to divorce. She ended her marriage and saved her life." She laughed softly. "Goodness, that sounds like something from the script of a B movie."

We sat quietly for quite a while, as my pizza grew cold and my soda got warm. I said, "Is there anything you can think of that I should pass on to Alfred Korvich?"

She shook her head. "My father's nastiness found a perfect outlet in his work. He was in the corporate-law division at Tilton, Prescott, and Goode. If I were Mr. Korvich, I would begin making inquiries there."

"I suppose he already has."

"Oh?"

"I agree with part of what you said earlier. Korvich is crude, and he's insensitive, too. But he's not stupid. Quite the opposite, I think. I suspect he's already making his presence felt at your father's firm. Anyway, I'll tell him you made that suggestion." I smiled at the image of Lower Case *b* cavorting with the button-down guys and well-coiffed gals in a high-rise on State Street in Boston.

We left the pizza shop and retraced our route up Thoreau Street. Marjorie hooked her hand inside the crook of my elbow, escort style, and we headed back toward Concord Academy. I said, "May I ask you a personal question?"

"Of course."

"You said your father was unloving and unlovable. Why did you come to live with him when you left California?"

"I bottomed out. I had nowhere else to go. And yes, I said he was unlovable, but I never said I didn't love him. For better or worse, I'm very much my mother's child."

"I'm sure she was very proud of you."

"I don't know. We were estranged the last couple of years she was alive. I used to think it was because she disapproved of the life I was leading. In the end, too late, I realized it was just another example of me pushing love away." She sighed. "But that's another story, for another time. I don't want you to be my therapist—I already have one of those. I want you to be my friend."

We crossed Main Street and walked past the clapboard houses that long ago had been converted into dormitories. Marjorie said, "Will there be another time?"

"Why wouldn't there be?"

She smiled. "You answered a question with a question—which, of course, isn't really an answer at all."

"I'm sorry. Sometimes my work habits spill over into my personal life."

"Your personal life—is that what this is?"

"I don't understand the question," I said.

She stopped walking. She pulled her hand away from my arm and turned to face me. "Harry Kline, when I was a little girl who hated herself for having no friends, you were always kind to me. I remembered your face across the years, but not your name. Then I saw you on a television program a few years ago, talking about a book you'd written, and I was so happy to finally have a name to link with the face. Not long after I moved to Concord, I saw you somewhere in town. I walked right in front of you, but you didn't recognize me, and I didn't feel sure enough of myself to say anything. I saw you again a couple of months later, walking with your lady friend. When I saw you sitting on the bench in the cemetery last week, I was determined to make some sort of contact. I told myself I'd give you a few minutes to recognize me, then walk away if you didn't. And you didn't recognize me, but I changed my mind about just walking away."

"I'm glad you did."

"So am I."

We stood there, neither one knowing quite what to say next. Then Marjorie broke the silence. "I'd like to see you again, Harry. I'd like that very much."

"I wouldn't be—"

She gently pressed her fingertips against my lips. "You don't have to say anything. I know you're with Veronica. I know there may not be room for me in your personal life, as you called it. But I wanted to say what I was thinking before I lost the courage to. All right?"

"All right."

"Good."

We walked across the campus until we came to the performing arts center. Students filled the pathways, moving toward the various classroom buildings. "Memory can play tricks on you," Marjorie said. "I don't remember my friends or me looking this young in high school. It doesn't exactly make me feel old, but it does seem strange."

"Imagine how it seems to me."

"How old are you, Harry?"

"I'm forty-two."

"Do you feel old?"

I shook my head. "Ted Williams was forty-two when he played his final game with the Red Sox. He hit a home run his very last time at bat. I was there that day. I was only nine, and my father and I played hooky together—me from school, him from work. I think I decided a long time ago that it was impossible to get old until you're at least forty-three."

She thought about that for a moment, then burst out laughing. She tossed her head back, and her long, red curls swung in the breeze. "I'm sorry for laughing, Harry, but I think that may be the silliest thing I ever heard." She checked her watch. "I still have a few minutes before I have to get back. Let me show you something."

Marjorie grabbed my hand and led me across the soccer field to the Sudbury River. It was narrow and flowed gently. She pointed to a bend in the river, about a quarter mile to our left. "Walk with me to that spot."

We reached the bend after a few minutes. She pointed across the river and to the left. "That's my home," she said.

It was a three-story clapboard house, yellow with dark brown shutters and trim. Its expansive, well-tended lawn sloped down to the wildflower tract that lined the river.

She said, "I swam home from here once. The water is only about thirty feet wide, and it just comes up to your waist. I guess it would be more accurate to say I waded home. The water was cold. I ran into the house, stripped off all my clothes, and lit a fire. It was all very silly, but fun. I remember thinking how nice it would be to do that with someone I loved."

A single canoe passed by left to right, heading upstream in the direction of North Bridge.

"I'd better get back now," she said.

We walked back to the soccer field, recrossed it, and stopped in front of her building. I said, "Thanks for inviting me."

She leaned toward me and kissed me on the cheek. Gazing past her, I saw the blue-eyed student with Adonis-like blond hair. He was leaning against a tree about thirty yards away, arms folded tightly across his chest, staring intently at us.

"Your student is watching us. The one you were having creative differences with before. He doesn't look happy."

She sighed, saying nothing.

"I don't know why," I said, "but he looks familiar to me."

"You've probably seen his father in the news. He's a state senator. They say he may be governor someday."

"Of *course*. Carter Ellington. His son looks just like him."

"He's Carter Ellington Junior," she said. "But he hates that name. Everyone calls him Junie."

13: Irregular Procedure

I checked my office answering machine as soon as I got home. In less than two hours, I'd received ten calls. The first nine were all hang-ups, with no messages recorded. That had never happened on my office line before.

I doubted nine people had called without leaving a message. More likely one person had called repeatedly. It wasn't a patient: A distressed patient would have called my answering service if he couldn't reach me, and the service would have paged me. It wasn't a friend, because a friend would have called on my unlisted home phone, not my office line.

Somebody definitely wanted to talk to me. He was persistent. Maybe he didn't leave a message because he didn't trust me to call back. Or maybe he wanted the element of surprise on his side when he finally got through.

The tenth call was from Marjorie—obviously recorded during the ten minutes between the time I left her and the time I returned home. "Thank you, Harry" was all she said.

I thought about Marjorie, and I thought about Carter Ellington Jr. When Michael Cafferty mentioned someone named Junie, I naturally assumed he was referring to a female. Now I understood why he laughed when I asked him if Junie was his girlfriend. The last thing Michael said as he left his therapy session two days earlier was *Junie's right. I'd probably be better off not coming here anymore.* The fact that Michael would discuss his therapy with Junie meant that their relationship held importance for him.

And Marjorie's relationship with Junie apparently held importance for her. The scene I'd witnessed between them suggested a connection that went beyond a casual student-teacher one, as did her refusal to invoke disciplinary proceedings against him.

I remembered what Alfred Korvich said to me about the state senator's son, whom he suspected of being the mastermind behind the burglary Michael Cafferty was charged with. *Carter Ellington Junior takes from other people just for the sake of taking. For the sheer joy of causing misery.*

While I contemplated all of this, my office phone rang, and as if on cue, Korvich's voice came booming through. "I love these banker's hours you keep," said the police chief. "Some of us have to work for a living. Well, what did you learn?"

"What are you talking about?"

"What am I talking about, he asks. What do you *think* I'm talking about? Marjorie Morris—what did she tell you?"

"How did you know I saw her today?"

"Call it a lucky guess."

"Yeah, right. What were you doing? Spying on me?"

"Relax, Doc. Jesus, do you always take things this personally? Talk to me, Doc. Tell me what she said."

"I'm surprised you didn't manage to get it on tape."

"We only do that on Tuesdays and Fridays, as a cost-saving measure to the taxpayers."

"I didn't learn anything. I didn't *expect* to learn anything. I have a hard enough time doing *my* job, Chief. I can't switch my head around to ask questions like a cop."

"What's the big deal? We both do the same sort of work. We both ask questions for a living. Hey—maybe we could switch jobs for a day, just for sport. What do you think?"

"It's not the same thing," I said, treating his remark with more seriousness than it deserved. "I ask 'how do you feel' questions. You wanted me to ask 'what do you know' questions."

"Sure, fine—I promise to think on that real hard when I get the chance someday. For now, just tell me what you learned."

That she thinks you're a jerk, I thought. "Not a hell of a lot. Marjorie thinks Charles Morris came up pretty short on the husband-and-father aspect of things. She thought you should ask around at his law firm."

"We've already begun doing that. Lawyers don't like to talk much about their own business. But I definitely got the idea from a couple of secretaries that grief did not consume the place after he died. So tell me, Doc—did you honor your promise not to tell her where the investigation stands?"

"What do you think?"

Korvich paused for barely a moment. "I don't think you told her."

It wasn't the reply I expected. "How do you come to that conclusion?"

"I figure someone who would tell me to go screw myself—I think if you revealed what I asked you not to reveal, you'd be more likely to brag about it than deny it."

He was sharper than I wanted to give him credit for being. "Are you still assuming it was a premeditated murder?"

"No reason to change my point of view that I know of. We can probably rule out one person, though. Teddy Richardson, the kid who was starting the Buick while Mrs. Peterson was out of town. The doors and steering wheel had no fingerprints at all on them."

"How does the absence of fingerprints rule him out?"

"It would be reasonable for his prints to be all over the driver's side," Korvich explained. "He would have a legitimate explanation if we found them there. Therefore, he wouldn't have any reason at all to go to the trouble of wiping them off. Of course, he did seem a little nervous when we questioned him about the car. But, hell—so was the

Widow Whitney, and chances are pretty goddamn slim she knows anything about this."

"You questioned her? Even after Mrs. Peterson asked you not to?"

"She asked me if I would promise to leave her alone. I didn't promise."

"Would it matter to you if you *had* promised?"

He thought for a second. "Hard to say, Doc. That's another thing I'll think on real hard when I get the chance. Let's stay in touch."

"I'll be counting the hours."

"And stay away from that extra tomato sauce at the pizza shop. It's a first-class ticket to heartburn."

I was just about to hang up when I heard him say, "Oh, by the way, we found something else. There was one partial fingerprint inside one of the rear doors. If there was someone sitting in the backseat, we may have three murderers."

"I don't follow you."

"If someone was in back, it means there was probably someone else sitting in the front passenger seat."

"All right—three people in the car. But only the driver would be charged with murder."

He chuckled. "Massachusetts has something called a felony murder law. If several people commit a crime as a joint venture—in this case, unauthorized use of a motor vehicle—and if someone is murdered during that crime, then everyone involved in the joint venture shares in the pleasure of being charged with the murder."

I recalled hearing about that law. A couple of years earlier it was used to convict a getaway driver of murder when his cohort killed a bank guard during a robbery.

Korvich said, "The partial print doesn't match up with anyone else who had a key to the car or the house. Let me know when you have a couple of minutes to give us your prints."

I would have told him to go screw himself again, but I didn't want the material to die from overuse. Instead I asked him how many times he called that afternoon without leaving a message.

"I didn't call before, Doc. Why?"

I told him about the hang-up calls the microchip in my answering machine logged in.

"Must be someone else, Doc. Wasn't me. It also doesn't sound like that big a deal."

Alfred Korvich was wrong: It was a very big deal. The phone rang again as soon as my conversation with him ended, and a voice on the other end said, "Dr. Kline?"

"Speaking."

"My name is Warren Oberlin. You're aware of my suit against Dr. Frank Porter. I know you're a consultant to his lawyer. I think it would be useful for us to meet."

His speech was careful and controlled, without expression. He had kept the element of surprise by not leaving me any messages. If he had left messages, I would've called Bobby immediately, who no doubt would've told me not to return the call.

He continued. "I want to speak with you about the tape recording."

"The tape recording?" I was stalling until I could figure out exactly what to do. It didn't take a lawyer to realize the plaintiff in a suit should never directly contact the defendant's attorney, let alone a potential witness hired by that attorney. I didn't know if there was a law against it, but I couldn't imagine that Oberlin's own attorney would have advised it.

He said, "Please don't pretend you don't know what I'm referring to. It's demeaning to you, and it insults my intelligence."

"I don't think it's advisable for me to speak with you, Mr. Oberlin. I'm sure Mr. Beck would object to our talking."

"Yes, Dr. Porter's lawyer would object. And my lawyer would object. Lawyers always object to something. It's an annoying trait of the breed. But a doctor's natural inclination is to heal. It makes doctors more disposed to considering all sides of an issue. And I want to speak with you about my side."

"Talk to your lawyer, Mr. Oberlin. I'll tell Mr. Beck you called me. Let them figure out what should occur next."

"What should occur next is a meeting between the two of us. I feel strongly about that. And when I feel strongly about something, people usually do what I request."

He was unyielding. His cool, measured words conveyed a sense of underlying menace. I knew instinctively that he was right—that most people probably did give him what he wanted. But I didn't think I could do that in this instance.

"I'm sorry, Mr. Oberlin. You'll just have to accept no as my answer."

Now his voice became louder and softer at the same time, as though he had placed the mouthpiece closer to his mouth to capture a harsh whisper. "Everybody has to accept no sometimes. But I work very hard to limit the number of occasions when *I* have to accept it. I'm afraid I can't allow this to be one of those occasions."

He assumed he would get what he requested from me. That assumption, with its vague implied threat, bothered me more than the request itself.

The standoff continued through two more rounds of request and refusal. I finally realized there was no way to get him to voluntarily halt the conversation he had begun with me.

I hung up.

The phone rang once again a few seconds later. I didn't respond. My answering machine picked up after four rings. I heard my outgoing message, and then. "You're obviously listening, Dr. Kline. Please pick up. Don't make this harder than it has to be."

I just stood there. After a few seconds Warren Oberlin hung up.

* * *

I'd never seen Bobby so angry. He clenched both fists and pressed them tightly against the kitchen table. "Who the hell does he think he is? If his attorney had anything to do with this, I'll have the judge slap sanctions on them so fast their balls will freeze in the wind."

"That certainly sounds uncomfortable," I said.

"Don't kid around, Harry. In a criminal trial, Oberlin would automatically be charged with intimidation of a witness, even if he was as cordial as could be. And it sounds like he was less than cordial."

"How would you feel if you just learned that your daughter's voice had returned from the grave to accuse you of sexually abusing her?"

"I'd feel like it was pretty damn important not to do anything without talking to my lawyer first. And no lawyer in the world would let him go through with the stunt he just pulled."

"That's what you would *think*."

"Huh?"

"I asked you how you would feel, and you told me what you would *think*."

"Don't play psychiatrist with me, Harry. And stop jerking me around. I forbid you to talk with him again."

"Hey—relax. I didn't talk with him this time. I hung up."

He took a few deep breaths to calm himself down. "I fucked up," he said. "When the case was given to me—when I reviewed the materials the Oberlins found in their daughter's possessions—I assumed Frank Porter would settle quickly. When he didn't, I let my sympathy for the Oberlins keep me from doing my job."

"What are you talking about?"

"My job is to defend Frank Porter, if that's what he wants, regardless of how I 'feel' or what I 'think' about him. And defense goes hand in hand with offense." A tight grin crossed his face. "It's time for me to find out more about Warren Oberlin."

14: The Plaintiff

When Michael Cafferty called to cancel his Friday-morning appointment, he tried just a little too hard to sound as sick as he said he was. His cough sounded too induced, the hoarse throat too forced. I was willing to bet the fever he mentioned was nonexistent.

"So I really don't think I should come to see you today. Okay?"

"Of course."

What else could I say? Maybe he really was ill. Or maybe he and a buddy had plans to ditch school for the day and wanted to get an early start. More likely he was just getting cold feet about being in therapy. Every new patient faces it early on: the eternal struggle between change, which is unknown and may be dangerous, and the status quo, which at least is familiar.

He said, "So I'll see you Tuesday afternoon?"

"Tuesday afternoon it is."

"Well, okay, then."

"I hope you're feeling better."

"Oh, I'm sure it's just some sort of twenty-four-hour kind of thing. I felt fine last night. If I stay in this morning, I'll probably feel better this afternoon."

It seemed to me that he was already beginning to sound better. We call it the flight into health: the sudden, temporary relief from distress a patient experiences when he

avoids—or abandons outright—the hard work of psychotherapy.

I walked over to the refurbished barn that served as Mrs.
Winnicot's apartment. I watered her plants and fed her
tropical fish, just as she'd asked me to do.

I felt uncomfortable being there. In my work, it's expected that I get to know the secret parts of the lives of my
patients. Psychotherapy is like a doorway to a patient's
soul: I step in, examine the contents that others seldom see,
rearrange a few things here and there, then step out—and it
seems so perfectly natural to do all that in the context of
the treatment relationship. But now, walking around in my
housekeeper's dwelling when she wasn't there, I felt like a
reluctant intruder, embarrassed and out of place.

The barn was one of the things that drew Janet and me
to the old farmhouse almost a dozen years earlier, just after
she became pregnant. We figured we could transform the
barn into an office for me, or a guest apartment for our parents and other visitors. But the pregnancy was difficult, and
we decided a live-in housekeeper was in order. We assumed
Mrs. Winnicot would remain with us until Melissa was
three or four years old, five at the most. We still had other
plans then for that reconverted barn—plans that didn't take
into account Janet's sudden illness when our daughter was
four.

Janet died. Mrs. Winnicot stayed. In all the time since
then, there had been no discussion of her leaving, until she
herself broached the subject a week earlier.

I looked around the apartment: a bedroom, sitting room,
and large kitchen. I didn't know what I would do with the
space if Mrs. Winnicot decided to move in with her son and
his family. I supposed I could rent it out. But I didn't need
the money, I didn't know if the zoning ordinances permitted
it, and I didn't think I'd like having a stranger in our midst.

I continued to ponder this as I walked over to Estabrook
Woods. I turned off Monument Street and headed toward
the narrow road that led to an entrance to the woods. As I
walked past the old Buttrick mansion, now the Park Service

visitor center, a large black van glided to a stop next to me. I realized afterward that it must have followed me when I exited my driveway on Monument Street.

The front passenger door opened. A mountainous, woolly man stepped out. He wore a dark, tight-fitting one-piece jumpsuit with a matching windbreaker. "Sir, if it would please for you to come here for a talk." He spoke in one of those Eastern European accents that can make a love song sound like a declaration of war. When I hesitated, he reached for the handle of the rear door on the passenger side, opened it, and said, "Please, if you will come into it for a talk, sir."

I peered inside the rear of the vehicle without approaching. Sitting behind the driver was a pale-faced man, older than me, with a military-style crew cut. He looked my way and opened his mouth to say something to me, but then his eyes opened wide in shock as he gazed at something past my shoulder. He shouted, "Isadore! No "

In the very next moment I a felt sudden pressure against the small of my back and my left shoulder. In an instant I was pinned against the side of the van by Isadore's hulking torso.

He was big and he was brutal, but he was sloppy in his work. I saw a way out and I took it. I bent my left leg underneath me and planted my foot flush against the van. I pushed off with as much power as I could muster. At the same time I flung my right arm back, elbow first, in a jabbing motion. I was aiming where I thought the bridge of his nose might be, but I didn't take his height into account; my elbow landed lower, directly on his Adam's apple. Then I came crashing backward into him, carrying both of us to the ground. He was on his back. I was on my back, too, stretched out on top of him.

He was big, but I had three advantages over him: the element of surprise, the top position, and a brain. I knew it was senseless to run. I also knew I had about one second before he reached up to pin my arms and immobilize me. I reached down and grabbed something I'd never grabbed

on another male outside of my urology rotation in medical
school. I squeezed as if my life were riding in the
balance—which, for all I knew, it was.

He tried to yelp, but the blow I'd landed on his Adam's
apple made it difficult to force the sound through. What
came out was a squelched, agonized noise that barely
sounded human.

I quickly rolled off of him, sprang to my feet, and kicked
at his knee with all my might. I hit the nerve; his leg jerked
reflexively, then fell limply to the ground.

I looked inside the van. The pale-faced man with the
crew cut was staring at me without expression. I glanced
back at Isadore. He had pulled himself into a sitting position; he glared at me with a dazed, crazed expression that
spoke of pain and anger. I knew that when the former subsided, he would pounce.

I turned again to the man in the backseat. Now I noticed
the wheelchair in the compartment behind him. There was
a small platform by the door that could be raised or lowered to let a handicapped person in and out of the van.

I heard Isadore struggling to his feet. The man in the van
yelled, "Isadore! Sit!" He pointed at a granite block, ten
yards away, that served as a historical marker. He kept
pointing until the man lumbered over and sat on it. "Good!
Stay!"

Isadore and I glowered at each other, then I turned my
attention to his master.

The man addressed me by name. "Please join me back
here, Dr. Kline. My driver will take us for a short ride. We
can leave Isadore here to contemplate his misbehavior."

"Wouldn't that sort of thing require him to have an attention span?"

"I see how upset you are. Otherwise you wouldn't be so
intentionally cruel." He was unnervingly calm. He patted
the seat next to his. "Please."

I looked at the front seat. The driver was an older
woman, at least sixty years old. I turned back to the man
and said, "Who the hell are you?"

"I'm Warren Oberlin. I thought you might have guessed."

I looked at Isadore, then at Warren Oberlin and his elderly driver. I reasoned that a wildebeest would be harder to outrun than a paraplegic and Grandma Moses. I stepped into the van.

A thick transparent partition separated the rear of the interior from the front. Oberlin pressed a button on a microphone that was mounted at the base of the partition. "This is a lovely area, Roberta. You may proceed as you see fit."

I glanced at the driver. A small pistol was strapped to the right side of her rib cage. These were strange people, indeed. She pulled away from the curb and headed toward Liberty Street, past the muster field where the colonials gathered just before the battle at North Bridge.

Oberlin said, "This is a pleasure for me, Dr. Kline. I read your book about the Vietnam veterans you worked with." He gestured toward his atrophied, immobile legs. "I have experience in that regard myself. Did you serve in country?"

I shook my head. "I was never in the military."

"You had a student deferment, I imagine."

"Briefly. Then I lucked out in Nixon's lottery."

In the middle of my freshman year at Tufts, President Nixon instituted the draft lottery. Birthdays were paired with numbers, from 1 to 365. The lower your number, the greater were your chances of being inducted into the armed forces. A government estimate at the time indicated that anyone with a number higher than 125 was unlikely ever to be drafted. My number was 344.

I said, "I drew Ted Williams's lifetime batting average."

"The lottery was a brilliant tactical move on Nixon's part," Oberlin said. "It defused the antiwar movement by letting people such as yourself know ahead of time that you were unlikely to be called. People are less likely to protest when they don't fear for their own lives—the ones who 'lucked out,' as you aptly put it."

The driver turned left at the end of Liberty Street, heading toward the center of town along Lowell Road.

Oberlin continued. "I had a student deferment when Johnson was in office. I gave it up in order to enlist. I suppose that puts me in a minority position." He pointed again at his legs. "And I suppose one could argue that I brought this upon myself."

"That would be a foolish argument."

"Yes, it would," he said. "Thank you." He looked out the window for a few moments. "I thought you may have been in the service when I saw how you handled Isadore. Please forgive him, Dr. Kline. I directed him to escort you into the van. Sometimes he takes my orders much too literally. I wanted someone who is fierce and loyal and bright. Isadore is only fierce and loyal. Such is life."

"You wanted an Airedale terrier, but you wound up with an Afghan hound."

He frowned. "That's not quite how I would choose to put it." He pointed to the rear compartment of the van. "I have a refrigerator back there, and a fully stocked bar. Can I offer you something to drink?"

"No, thank you. But I'd appreciate it if you would tell me why you kidnapped me."

"It wasn't my intention for you to feel as though you had been abducted. As I said, Isadore is difficult to control on occasion."

"Good help is hard to find."

"Exactly so," Warren Oberlin replied. "Perhaps you would do me the kindness of reaching a can of diet ginger ale for me."

I got a can out of the refrigerator and handed it to him. He opened it, took a swig, then looked closely at it. "I remember when opening one of these required a church key. You know—one of those bottle openers with a triangular pointed head. Are you old enough to remember that?"

"Vaguely."

"Then the manufacturers developed the zip tab—the one you pulled completely off the can to open it. But environmentalists complained about the litter, and consumer organizations complained that the tabs were causing too many injuries. So they finally developed the push tab we use today. It stays attached to the open can, unless you fidget with it or draw a defective one." He held the can up for inspection. "All in all, a metaphor for twentieth-century mankind's incremental journey toward perfection. Or just another example of the idiotic musings of a man with far too much time on his hands."

Oberlin finished his beverage, then held the empty can in front of him, his hand wrapped completely around it. He held it up for me to see. Suddenly he clenched his hand into a fist, squashing the can. Then he flipped it around quickly in his hand and squeezed once more, completely flattening it.

He said, "For someone in my situation, it becomes important to keep your arms and hands strong in order to compensate for the loss of power in your lower body. Isadore taught me how to do that to the soda can using just one hand."

"I would have guessed that flattening it against his forehead was more his style."

He smiled for the first time. "He offered to teach me that as well, but I told him I wasn't ready yet for advanced techniques."

"And he understood what that meant?"

He smiled again, then placed his crushed soda can in a litter bag on the floor. "You listened to the tape that Dr. Porter gave to Mr. Beck, is that correct?"

I nodded.

"Mr. Beck passed a copy along to my lawyer. He listened to it, but I haven't listened and have no plans to do so." He paused for a moment. "My lawyer told me he can probably get it excluded unless Dr. Porter proves my daughter gave permission to have her sessions recorded."

"I don't know anything about that."

"You can relax, Dr. Kline. I'm not trying to get information *from* you. I came to give information *to* you."

Our illustrious police chief had used almost the same words when he first called me to discuss Michael Cafferty. It seemed like everyone wanted me to be well informed about one thing or another.

"Dr. Porter believes that this tape will discourage me from pursuing my suit against him. He's wrong. The tape will benefit me far more than it benefits him."

He waited for a response. When none was forthcoming, he continued. "My daughter never spoke to her mother or me about her therapy with Dr. Porter. But I could tell she was getting sicker, and I certainly believed he was not helping her. After she died, we discovered the things he had written to her. We knew then that his therapy with her was hurtful. And now the tape recording makes me even more certain of that. I never knew she had accused me of doing those terrible things to her."

We drove through the town square, past the Colonial Inn and the rectory where Father John Fitzpatrick lived. Lowell Street became Lexington Street on the other side of the square, heading toward Merriam's Corner.

Warren Oberlin faced me directly. "How did Celeste sound on the tape?"

"I really shouldn't be talking about—"

"Please," he interrupted. "I just need to know how my daughter sounded."

I thought for a moment. "Confused, frightened. And very, very sad."

"Yes. Through it all, she always seemed so sad." He sighed, then looked out his window for a while. Then he turned to me and said, "Have you ever killed anyone?"

I was startled by the sudden jump in the conversation, so much so that I didn't respond.

He continued. "No, I don't suppose you have. I've done regrettable things, Dr. Kline. Beginning in Vietnam, then continuing in my business dealings. I've caused a number of people to endure hardship or damage. Many were completely innocent and suffered merely because they were in my way. But I hope you believe me when I tell you I could never have done the things to Celeste that Dr. Porter claims I did."

"What I believe is irrelevant. But I can tell you that almost everyone accused of something like that denies it, sometimes even in the face of overwhelming evidence."

"Evidence like that tape recording you heard."

"Porter says he has other tapes, too," I said.

"Oh?"

Immediately I regretted what I had said. I'd apparently revealed something new to him, something that I learned in the context of Frank Porter's confidential relationship with Bobby Beck. And Bobby was right: I had no business talking to Oberlin about the facts of this case.

Oberlin said, "One tape, five tapes, five hundred tapes— none of that matters. Would you be so kind as to pick up the manila envelope underneath your seat?"

I found the envelope, picked it up, and held it out for him to take.

He said, "I want you to have it."

"What is it?"

"A copy of my medical records."

"Why do you want me to have that?"

"In late 1967, I returned from Vietnam with a Purple Heart and a piece of shrapnel lodged near my spine. The shrapnel often caused great pain and occasionally made it difficult for me to walk. But the doctors advised against removing it. They said the operation was too risky. If I went forward with surgery I might lose use of my legs entirely. So I lived with my condition for two years. I got married. I came into some money, and I turned it into more money very quickly. Celeste was born. And then the pain and the immobility got worse, and I decided I would rather risk permanent paralysis than live that way any longer." He paused. "As you can see, one should always be careful about what one wishes for. I've been this way since 1969."

"Did you sue that doctor, too?"

He flinched as if in pain. "Of course not. It was my decision to take the risk. And I certainly didn't need the

money, then or now. I already have more money than my
children's children could ever spend." He looked away. "Of
course, I no longer have any children. That's the whole
point, isn't it?"

"Is this supposed to be a defense against your daughter's
allegations? That a man whose legs are crippled couldn't
possibly commit such acts?"

He gestured toward the envelope in my hands. "Not just
my legs, Dr. Kline. I went into the operating room with
pain, and legs that usually worked. I came out pain-free,
but with legs that were useless. Legs, and other things."

"Other things?"

"I'm impotent, Dr. Kline. My last erection was almost
twenty-five years ago, when Celeste was still in diapers."
He paused, perhaps embarrassed by his very personal revelation. "So you see why that tape recording supports my al-
legation of malpractice more than it helps Dr. Porter's
defense."

It took me a minute to grasp the connection he was making. Then I said, "I think I understand. If what you say about
your condition is true, then you couldn't have done those
things. Which means Porter's therapy somehow caused your
daughter to fantasize them. Which means the very fact that
he brought those memories out of her in therapy is more evidence of malpractice."

"Exactly so."

Oberlin directed his driver to turn around and head back
to the spot where we had left Isadore.

I quickly scanned the materials in the manila envelope:
reports from surgeons, neurologists, and urologists. There
was even a psychiatric consultation from one of my former
medical-school mentors. Everything appeared in order, or
so it seemed from my cursory review of the records. Warren Oberlin was telling the truth about his condition.

We sat quietly for a couple of minutes while I absorbed
what I had just learned. I said, "Why are you telling me all
of this? How did you even know I was involved with this
case?"

"Dr. Porter's lawyer told mine that you were reviewing the materials. Of course, I recognized your name immediately from your book. As to why I'm telling you—I think you can help me get what I want."

"How much money are you looking for?"

"How much . . ." He shook his head. "This isn't about dollars. I already told you—I have more than I could ever need. And money wouldn't bring Celeste back. More to the point, the money wouldn't even come out of Dr. Porter's pocket. His malpractice carrier will cover everything. He isn't even paying for his lawyer. A money settlement wouldn't damage him in the least. And my objective here is to damage him."

"This sounds like another job for Isadore," I said.

He pushed down against the car seat with both hands, lifting himself into a more upright position. He said, "What I propose is simple and direct. Dr. Porter writes a letter to the psychology licensing board. The letter says three things. First, without going into detail and without identifying my daughter by name, he reports that he has been guilty of gross negligence in the treatment of a disturbed patient. Second, he states that he has come to realize that he is not fit to continue to practice. Third, he resigns his license, effective immediately and forever. In return for that, I drop the suit and promise never to hold him up to public ridicule."

"What do you get out of it?"

"What do *I* get out of it?" He drew a deep breath and exhaled slowly. He repeated that two times. Then he said, "Are you a father, Dr. Kline?"

"Yes."

"Can you imagine what it would be like to lose a child?"

"I can imagine it. But anything I might imagine would certainly pale in comparison to the actual experience."

He looked out the window as he continued. "My daughter was a very unhappy young woman. By any standard objective measure, she was an utter failure in life. School, work, friends, family relationships—you name it, and she did poorly at it. In the final analysis, what killed her was her mistaken assessment that she didn't matter in this world, and the hatred she felt for herself as a result of that belief."

He turned to face me. "She was not especially bright. She had no particular talent. She was not attractive. She never learned to trust or love another person. As a consequence of all of those things, others did not love her. But her mother and I—well, we loved her dearly. The physical losses I have endured are nothing compared to losing her. And I would surrender everything I have if I could bring her back."

I thought about Michael Cafferty's father pledging half his fortune to the Catholic Church in return for his son's recovery from illness. If Warren Oberlin could have known ahead of time what lay in store for his daughter, I think he would have jumped to make a deal like that.

"You want to know what I get out of it if Dr. Porter agrees to my settlement proposal. Well, the loss of his license would be a direct hit on his pocketbook, and I admit it would give me satisfaction to see him suffer in that regard. But more than that, I could feel that Celeste's life and death had meaning. If I can stop Dr. Porter from ruining another young life, then a purpose has been served by Celeste's suffering."

"So this is a totally selfless act, then."

"No," he said. "I'm not that good a person. I would reap something from the arrangement I've outlined. By stopping Porter from harming others, I would have the opportunity to atone."

"Atone?"

"As I said—I've done regrettable things. In low moments of late I've wondered if Celeste's death may have been visited upon me as punishment for my sins. But I can't claim much expertise in theology, so I don't know if that notion comports with any current theories about the nature of God and His relationship to man."

The van pulled up alongside the Buttrick mansion.

Isadore was still sitting on the granite historical marker. Warren Oberlin was right: The man did take directions very literally.

Oberlin beckoned to Isadore. "Please apologize to Dr. Kline for upsetting him."

Like a robot in a 1950s science-fiction movie, the gargantuan man immediately did his master's bidding. He walked to the van and held out his hand which looked nearly twice the size of mine. "I am sorry to be hurting you." He grabbed my hand and clamped it tighter and longer than he needed to, staring at me the whole time with a dull, fixed expression.

Isadore took the front passenger seat. The driver headed back to Monument Street. When we reached my house, Isadore stepped out of the van and opened my door.

As I got out of the van Oberlin said, "Don't forget to take these medical records with you."

"If I take them with me, I have to turn them over to Mr. Beck."

"Of course."

"And then he'll probably give a copy to Dr. Porter," I said. "If I were you, I wouldn't want to have to reveal myself so nakedly to him. Maybe you should hold on to the records for now."

"Yes, perhaps so." He seemed surprised by my response. "Thank you." He wrote something on a scrap of paper and handed it to me. "This is my private telephone number. You can circumvent my secretary."

Isadore shut the rear door, then climbed into the front passenger seat. Just before closing his own door, he looked at me and said, "I will be pleased to be meeting you again, Dr. Kline."

"I'll count the days, Izzy," I replied, but the door was already closed.

15: False Memories

I called Bobby immediately and gave him a quick rundown of my encounter with Warren Oberlin.

"Son of a bitch," he muttered.

"Who—me or Oberlin?"

"Neither one of you, although I'm not exactly jumping for joy about your *ex parte* little tête-à-tête. I'm talking about Frank Porter. He's got some explaining to do. I want to set up a meeting with him for this afternoon. Are you free?"

"Anytime after two o'clock. Do you think he'll do it on such short notice?"

"He will—or he'll be looking for a new lawyer."

Bobby put me on hold while he called Porter on another phone. After a few minutes he came back on the line. "Four o'clock," he said. "And don't forget to bring the records Oberlin gave you."

"I didn't take them."

"You didn't *what*?"

"He offered them to me, but I didn't take them."

"And I'm sure you had an *excellent* reason for doing that."

I thought for a moment. "Well, no, not really. I just didn't feel comfortable taking them."

"You didn't feel *comfortable* taking them? I don't believe this. Listen, Harry—please, *please* don't ever decide to become a lawyer. With your consummate legal talent, you'd put the rest of us out of work in a month."

Bobby hung up before I could respond, saving me the aggravation of justifying my behavior.

The truth was, I liked Warren Oberlin. I didn't know anything about the suffering he said he had caused for innocent people. But this was a man capable of rising to the occasion to do what he believed was right rather than what was expedient. He was entitled to a student deferment during the Vietnam War, yet he surrendered it, placed himself in harm's way, and paid dearly for it. Later he accepted the consequences of his failed surgery without going after the doctor who—it could have been argued—bungled the operation.

Of course, I had no way of knowing if he had told me the truth about those events. But his description of them was consistent with the one playing out before me: his unorthodox but principled proposal for settling his suit against Frank Porter.

He wasn't looking for compensation. He wasn't looking for naked revenge. Warren Oberlin was looking for justice. I hoped he would find it.

Bobby and I met in the parking lot outside Frank Porter's office building in Lexington Center. He said, "I haven't told him yet about your run-in with Warren Oberlin, or Oberlin's settlement offer. I want to get some answers from him first."

We walked into the lobby. As we climbed up one flight of stairs I said, "Who do you think this building is named for—John Adams or Sam Adams?"

"What's the difference?"

"One is a dead president, the other is a dead beer."

"I mean, what's the difference who it's named after?"

"None, I suppose. I was just curious."

"You're a very curious guy, Harry. I've always said so."

"Thanks."

"Don't mention it."

We entered Porter's reception area. Almost immediately, the door to his office swung open; no doubt he'd been informed of our entrance by the indicator in his desk clock that he'd shown me on my previous visit.

Bobby said, "Thanks for finding the time to squeeze me in, Frank."

"My pleasure, counselor."

Sarcasm was evident on both sides. I knew that each of them would have been pleased if circumstances were different and they never had to deal with each other again. It was one of the major differences between Bobby's work and mine: If a therapist and his patient dislike each other, their chances of working successfully together are nil. But that need not be the case between lawyer and client. I wondered how it felt to be extending services to someone you couldn't stand.

Bobby said, "I'd really like to see if we can make this case go away, Frank. I want to get some more information from you, tell you about some things I've learned since our last meeting, then think about it over the weekend and decide how to get this over as fast as possible."

"Good," Porter said. "We're finally getting somewhere."

"This is all new to you, isn't it?"

Porter looked confused. "What do you mean?"

"You've never been sued before," Bobby said. "That's what you said on your application for malpractice coverage."

"No, I haven't."

"I just want to be certain I know of anything that Warren Oberlin could use to embarrass us in court if we have to go to trial—prior acts, or even prior allegations, that could be made to suggest a pattern of misconduct. Sometimes matters that might never be admissible in a criminal case are allowed into evidence in a civil suit, so I need to know about any allegations of impropriety. I like surprises on my birthday—not when I'm defending a tort action."

Porter didn't respond right away. He looked like he was mulling something over in his mind.

Bobby said, "You have to level with me, Frank."

Porter remained silent for several seconds, then said, "I was asked to take a year off during my graduate-school training at the University of Texas."

"Why?"

"I had a field placement at the school's counseling center. An undergraduate on my caseload claimed I made sexual advances toward her. Nothing ever came of it. She never sued. My faculty adviser suggested I take a leave of absence. I went along with it, even though I knew they could never prove anything. It would have come down to my word against hers." He thought for a moment. "She was pretty unstable. Celeste Oberlin reminded me a little of her, as a matter of fact."

Bobby asked, "Did you have sex with her, or try to have sex with her, or do anything that a reasonable person would interpret as trying to have sex with her?"

"Which one?" he responded. I thought that was an odd response.

"Either one," said Bobby.

"No," Porter said. "Neither one."

Bobby thought about Porter's answer for a moment. Then he said, "Tell me how Celeste Oberlin became your patient."

"A referral from a former client. Another incest survivor, someone I'd treated a couple of years earlier."

It's become part of the parlance of therapists who work with incest victims to refer to them as survivors. It's supposed to help create a sense of empowerment.

Bobby said, "So she came to you for help dealing with being sexually abused by her father?"

"No, as I explained a couple of days ago, she had no specific memories of that until we began working together. She'd already been hospitalized several times for typical borderline personality problems—overdosing on antidepressants, impulsive self-mutilation whenever she thought someone was rejecting her. A lot of the time she had no memory of hurting herself. That dissociation is what gave me my first clue about the cause of her problems."

Bobby turned to me for an explanation. I said, "Dissociation means casting experiences out of conscious awareness because they're too painful to contemplate."

"You mean, like amnesia?"

"No," I replied. "Amnesia is an after-the-fact forgetting. Dissociation refers to someone preventing himself from being aware of something as it's happening. In its most extreme form, you have multiple personalities, where the main personality doesn't even realize the subordinate ones exist."

"Like *Sybil*," said Bobby, "or *The Three Faces of Eve*."

"Right."

Porter said, "Incest survivors use dissociation to block out the experience of sexual abuse. The tape I played for you gives a perfect example, thanks to Celeste's recovery of the memory. You'll remember she said she focused on a butterfly until she actually became the butterfly."

"I remember," Bobby said. "I also remember that she didn't mention it until you specifically asked her if she had sent her mind somewhere else."

"I already knew that was her practice, from her description of earlier incidents."

"I also remember she said it was Christmas, which makes me wonder what kind of butterfly could survive a New England winter."

Porter hesitated for just a moment. "She may have had the sequence of events a little confused, but not the psychological reality of the event."

Bobby rubbed his chin and thought for a moment. "You said the molestation began before she turned three years old. Isn't that a little young to have reliable memories?"

"Not necessarily. With the proper techniques, you can bring someone fairly far back. It's called age regression. Sometimes you use guided imagery or hypnosis to facilitate it. It's all part of something called 'recovered memory therapy.' "

"On the other hand," Bobby said, "if my father was having sex with me for nine years, up until the point of puberty, I would remember that. I don't see how someone could lose those memories, then recover them a decade later. And if the person's mind is unstable enough to allow the memories to be lost, how can you be certain the memory is accurate when she finally 'remembers' it?"

Porter leaned back in his chair and folded his arms behind his head. "These things are difficult for a layman to understand. Sometimes it's easier to dismiss the accusation as the crazy fantasy of an unstable client. But the human mind is a flexible instrument. It will do anything to survive abuse—even if it means repressing whole chunks of experience and storing them in its recesses. Recovered memory therapy brings them out again."

Bobby said, "Tell me, Frank—do you think it's possible that Celeste Oberlin had just reached the point where she sincerely believed something that simply wasn't true?"

"No, I don't. I believed my client. I still do."

"Did you ever seek corroboration? Did you ever talk to either of her parents?"

Porter laughed—a scoffing, dismissive snicker. "Do you really believe they would have admitted it? Abusers almost always deny what they've done. So do the wives who sit by silently. Isn't that right, Harry?"

"Yes."

Porter grinned.

"Still," said Bobby, "you might have learned something that either would have confirmed or disconfirmed Celeste's belief—your belief—that she was an incest victim."

"Such as?"

"What do you know about Warren Oberlin?"

Porter shrugged. "He's some sort of investment specialist. I believe he's rich."

"He's incredibly rich," said Bobby. "I've done some investigating since our last meeting. It seems that once he made his first hundred thousand dollars, he had no difficulty turning it over severalfold in a relatively short period of time. The problem is—no one knows where that first money came from."

"What do you mean?"

"He was in the army in Vietnam. A half year after he returned he began making very large and, as it turned out, very shrewd investments. But the source of that original capital is unclear. There have been rumors of involvement in a Southeast Asian drug cartel, and that he laundered his money somehow with the help of a clever attorney. Since then, he's never looked back."

"Lucky him."

"It may have been more than luck," said Bobby. "He was involved in a huge commercial-land-purchasing enterprise in New Hampshire a number of years ago. It was a very controversial undertaking, stirred up a lot of local opposition. One state legislator who opposed the plan disappeared. Another one resigned suddenly. A third one changed his position inexplicably. Some people think Oberlin had something to do with each of those incidents."

"Am I supposed to be surprised by that? Someone who would do what Oberlin did to his daughter could be capable of any number of evil acts. Anyway, what's your point?"

"My point is, Warren Oberlin isn't someone you want to fuck with—not unless you're dead certain that you're right. But your problem is you start out so convinced that you're right, that you don't even entertain the possibility of alternative explanations." He leaned forward in his chair. "Did you know Warren Oberlin is a paraplegic?"

Porter said nothing, but the startled look that flashed briefly across his face spoke clearly to his ignorance of Oberlin's handicap.

Bobby continued. "He's been that way since Celeste was one year old. Hard to believe you'd be unaware of something so basic. Didn't Celeste ever mention that in her therapy? You know, something like—'He climbed out of his wheelchair to mount me'? Or, 'He repositioned himself so his colostomy bag wouldn't get in the way'?"

Porter didn't respond. He furrowed his brow as he contemplated the new information. He picked up the paper-weight from his desk—the insect fossilized inside a block of amber—and passed it nervously from hand to hand.

Bobby continued, "Warren Oberlin was the victim of botched surgery on an old war wound. And here's the kicker, Frank. The same operation that left him paralyzed also rendered him impotent. He's got the medical records to prove it. Harry has already inspected them."

Porter glanced at me. I nodded, confirming what Bobby had just reported. Porter thought things over for several seconds. Then he said, "You don't need to have an erection to shove your dick in a little girl's mouth."

I couldn't take it any longer. "Think about it, Frank," I said, exasperated in the face of his smug attitude. "The man can't move his legs, yet he struggles to pin his daughter down to her bed, just so he can force her to suck on a penis that is incapable of getting erect or even feeling any sensation. Hell, he wouldn't even feel if it she bit the damn thing off. Do you have any idea how ridiculous that sounds?"

Bobby pointed at me, gesturing me to be quiet. Turning to Porter, he said, "Oberlin has suggested a settlement."

"What sort of settlement?"

"He wants you to quit."

"Quit what?"

"Quit your profession. He says he's not in this for the money. His idea of victory is for you to resign your license. He seems to think he'll be doing some sort of public good if he forces you to do that."

"What do you think?"

"I'm not here to pass judgment on you, Frank."

"I mean—what do you think his chances are of going through with the suit?"

"He sounds like the sort of person who follows through when he makes a threat."

"Would he prevail if it went to trial?"

Bobby turned to me. "What's your professional assessment, Harry? Is this a case of malpractice?"

I nodded. "The letters and pictures you sent Celeste

Oberlin make it clear that your approach went well beyond the bounds of standard practice. And I think her memories of sexual abuse were actually caused by your therapy, not rooted in a preexisting reality. You were wise to purchase malpractice insurance."

"Thank you for that very *professional* assessment of my work," Porter said with evident disdain.

"I'm not finished," I said. "Warren Oberlin wants to put you out of business. Well, I think you might lose your license anyway if this case is opened to the sort of public scrutiny a trial would invite."

"Are you finished now?"

"I'm finished."

"Good." He turned to Bobby. "Do you see any way out of this, short of giving up my practice?"

"If this were a licensing board inquiry instead of a civil suit, I might be able to persuade the board to let you continue practicing with certain temporary restrictions—mandatory supervision, remedial instruction, limits on the sorts of patients you can see, things like that. But I doubt that Oberlin would settle for that. His aim is to ruin you, not to reform you."

Porter mulled over his attorney's assessment of the situation. "Let me see if I have this straight. If I accept the settlement offer, I *definitely* lose my license. And if I go to trial, I *may* lose my license later—but only if the licensing board decides to take the case up because of the negative publicity. Am I missing anything here?"

Bobby said, "There's also the financial aspect—compensatory and punitive damages running into the millions if there's no settlement."

"That's why I pay insurance premiums. But I don't care about losing the insurance company's money. Besides, I'm not the only one who has to worry about negative publicity here."

"What's that supposed to mean?" asked Bobby.

"Whether or not a jury believes Celeste's accusations, it won't be much fun for Warren Oberlin to have them aired publicly." He smiled. "And who knows what else I might be forced to reveal at a trial?"

Bobby said, "You realize that as an officer of the court, I cannot knowingly introduce falsified testimony or evidence."

"Relax, counselor. Who said anything about falsified testimony? Geez, an honest lawyer—talk about oxymorons."

I figured we could take turns: I could pin Porter's arms back while Bobby belted him, then we could switch places. It was an appealing fantasy.

Porter stood and walked to his window. He leaned on the sill with both hands and looked out at the paved bicycle path. "She killed herself a week too soon."

In unison, Bobby and I both exclaimed, "What?"

"We were talking about having a showdown with her parents. She was going to ask them to come with her to a therapy session. When they got here, she was going to confront them with her accusations, then break off her relationship with them. She was even considering suing them for the damage she suffered. She was going to take back control over her own life, and I was going to help her."

I slammed my fist against the armrest of my chair. "You arrogant, incompetent fuck! No wonder she fucking killed herself!"

Bobby and I repaired to the Yangtze River restaurant after our meeting: the same establishment I'd watched Porter and his patient enter eight days earlier. As I waited for the wonton soup to cool, I apologized for my outburst in Porter's office.

"Ah, don't worry about it. It'll give him something to think about while he makes up his mind what to do about Oberlin's proposal."

"How long does he have to decide?"

"We have discovery motions before the court in twelve days. I don't think Oberlin's attorney will force the settlement issue before then."

I cut a wonton in half with my spoon and swallowed a

piece. "I like my wonton soup with chicken broth, not this beef broth."

"Thanks for sharing that with me."

"I really hope you lose this case, Bobby."

"Gee, thanks again, pal of mine."

A heavyset couple and their extraordinarily heavyset son and daughter walked into the restaurant and stared intently at the buffet setup in the center of the room.

Bobby said, "What can you tell me about recovered memory therapy?"

The waiter cleared our soup bowls and brought our entrées to the table. Bobby had the Szechuan spiced beef; I had curried chicken with onions. The waiter placed a mound of white rice between us.

"It's a radical offshoot of feminist-inspired treatments," I said. "It has an explicit ideology. It assumes that sexual abuse is rampant, but that it's so painful that the child dissociates when it happens and forgets it. The memories are preserved intact in the brain and in other organs of the body—so these therapists believe—and they can be recovered intact with the proper techniques. Until they're recovered, they fester inside and cause all sorts of psychological turmoil."

Bobby took a large helping of rice and sprinkled soy sauce on it. "So the job of the recovered memory therapist is to bring the memories out."

"That's what they say they do," I said, mixing together on my plate a scoop of rice and a serving of the curried chicken. "The problem is, when you base a patient's therapy on an ideology, the ideology becomes more important than the individual patient. Therapists like Porter use very suggestive techniques. If a patient says she has a feeling she may have been abused, but no specific memories of it, the therapist may say something like, 'Imagine what might have happened, then write it down.' By working together, eventually the therapist and patient come up with a very clear description of things that may never have happened."

"I hope I don't have to take this case to trial. Listening

to testimony like that would bore my ass off. I'd probably dissociate."

The heavyset family had made its way to the buffet counter. They were elbowing one another out of the way, mixing and piling food high on their plates. Bobby said, "An hour later they'll still be fat."

I continued. "Manufacturing false memories isn't as hard as you might think. A lot us are unhappy. A lot of us are angry with our parents. And a lot of us tie those two things together, because it's always nice to have someone to blame for our troubles. With the right kinds of suggestive techniques, it's an easy jump from blaming your parents for metaphoric abuse to blaming them for physical or sexual abuse."

"Metaphoric abuse. I hear Emily Dickinson's children took her to court for that."

"Emily Dickinson never had children."

"Oh." He took a bite of beef.

"Do you know what the hippocampus is?"

"Hippo campus?" He thought for a moment. "A college for zookeepers?"

"When I encode an experience into my memory, each component gets stored in a different area of the brain. This meal, for example. The memory of how the food tastes goes to one brain region, the visual image to another, the sound of your voice to another, and the actual content of your scintillating conversation to yet another area. The hippocampus coordinates the process of breaking the experience into components. But with trillions of memories spread out like that in pieces, there's lots of room for error. Here—I'll show you. Give me your coffee."

"You don't like coffee," he said.

"I don't want to drink it. I want to demonstrate something."

He handed me his beverage. I placed it in front of me, alongside my water and my Coke. I reached over to the unoccupied table next to ours and retrieved an empty glass.

I said, "Think of this empty glass as my brain."

"No problem there."

I picked up my glass of water. "This represents the memory of the first time I went to the Boston Garden with my father to see the Celtics play." I poured some into the empty glass. "This Coke represents the memory of the first time I went to a Celtics game *without* my father." I poured again into the same glass, then reached for Bobby's coffee. "And this coffee represents the memory of the first *Bruins* game he took me to at the Garden." I poured a third time.

I swirled the glass in my hand until the liquid was a uniform color: a translucent light brown. I held the mixture aloft.

"What's your point?" he said. "That watching games at the Boston Garden can make you sick to your stomach?"

"Now, suppose I want to remember everything I can about that first Celtics game. The month, the year, where I sat, who won, what I ate for dinner before the game and what time I got home afterward." I swirled the glass again. "How the hell can I retrieve that memory, uncorrupted by fragments of other memories?"

I set the glass in front of him. The Heavysets passed us on their way from the buffet setup to their table. Bobby said, "The father looks thirsty. Maybe I should offer him this drink."

"You get my point," I said. "There's no scientific evidence that memories can be completely sealed off from consciousness for several years, then suddenly reemerge without significant distortion."

"I get your point. Pass the hot oil and vinegar."

Veronica called that evening to tell me she was in northern New York. Louis Laggone's grandmother owned property there. The old woman was in a nursing home, but the family still held the property, a couple of acres, as an investment.

Veronica said, "I think he may have buried the two missing children there."

"He told you that?"

"No. But he's been leading me to New York the whole time, talking all about the fishing spots his father used to take him to years ago before he abandoned the family. Then I learned about the grandmother's property. When I asked Laggone about it, he told me he was finished talking to me and not to come see him anymore."

"How long will you be there?"

"I don't know. We brought a forensic botanist with us. He came up from Georgia, one of the only people in the country to specialize in the field. He may be able to identify patterns in vegetation growth or land contouring that could isolate sites to dig at. It's a long shot, but it's worth trying. Otherwise, there's an awful lot of area to turn over."

"Who is 'we'?"

"Excuse me?"

"You said, 'We brought a forensic botanist with us.' "

She hesitated for just an instant. "Andrew Galloway, the Berkshire County district attorney."

During our previous phone conversation, I was a little suspicious when she began referring to him as "Andy." Now her decision to revert back to calling him by his full name made me even more uneasy: It was if she were covering her tracks.

She said, "He's been putting pressure on me to come up with something on the missing children. It makes me wonder if there's something wrong with the case against Laggone for the attempted kidnapping of that little girl from the Pittsfield area."

"What does Galloway say about it?"

"He won't talk about the kidnapping case. Maybe he's just trying to keep total jurisdiction over it. Or maybe there's something else going on. Whenever I raise the issue, he just cranks up the pressure on the missing-children cases. It's making things very hard between us."

I imagined myself asking her if there was anything else very hard between them, and I bit down on my lip to keep myself from saying that. I wondered how many times he'd suggested they fuck each other's brains out. I wondered how many times she'd declined.

I said, "Ever notice that all you have to do is change one letter, and the word 'decline' becomes 'recline'?"

"What are you talking about?"

"Nothing. Just a random thought."

"You've been doing too many crossword puzzles."

I wanted to ask her when she would be coming home, meaning my house. But I realized that issue—where was her home?—was a sore one between us. I said, "When will you be coming back?"

"I don't know right now."

"I miss you."

"Yes. We need to talk about things when I get back." That was all she said in reply. We colluded in making some innocuous end-of-conversation small talk, then hung up. I realized that she hadn't left the name or number of the place where she was staying.

As days went, this had been a reasonably unpleasant one: ambushed by Warren Oberlin's pet cossack, driven to homicidal fantasies by the most irresponsible therapist I'd ever known, and now left hanging by my . . . by my what? My girlfriend? My lover? My companion? I refused to even consider the euphemistic "significant other" option. I didn't know what she was to me anymore. And I didn't know what I was to her.

The Friday-night television pickings were slim. I sat in the den with the remote control, aimlessly clicking my way through the channels. Cher was talking about the wonders of a beauty treatment on an infomercial. On a home shopping channel, a former National League batting champion was pushing autographed baseball merchandise. He looked as though he were one or two sheets to the wind; he kept saying things like, "My balls are the real thing."

I dozed off for a short while, until I was awakened by the ringing of my telephone.

"Hello?"

"Hello, Harry. It's Rita."

Rita Jacobs was Janet's mother. After my wife died—not right away, but within a few months—I stopped calling her parents Mom and Dad. I'd never been entirely comfortable calling them those names, anyway; I wonder if any spouse ever is. In any event, it no longer seemed necessary or appropriate once Janet was gone. Before I got married, I'd always called them Mr. Jacobs and Mrs. Jacobs, but reverting to that formality seemed equally uncomfortable. Somehow, without ever talking about it, I had slipped into the pattern of calling them by their first names.

"Melissa is asleep," Rita said. "I just wanted to call and let you know how much we've enjoyed having her with us these past few days. She's getting to be so grown up. The time goes so fast." She paused. "I'm also calling to let you know that . . . well, I think I upset her today. I may have done something very foolish."

"What do you mean?"

"We took her to visit Mark Twain's house. It's funny—you can live somewhere for so long without going to a place that tourists might visit on their first trip. We've been in Hartford for twenty years, but I'd never been there before. So I really had no way of knowing. . . ."

Her voice trailed off. I waited for her to continue.

"The young woman who gave us our tour talked about Mark Twain's family. Did you know that he had four children, and he outlived three of them? I didn't know that. I started to feel a little shaky, and then the guide recited the words Twain placed on the tombstone of one of his daughters. 'Warm summer sun shine kindly here. Warm southern wind blow softly here. Green sod above lie light, lie light. Good night, dear heart, good night, good night.' And then I . . . It was just too much to bear, sneaking up on me without warning like that. And I began to cry, and so did Melissa, probably because she saw how upset I was. And poor Nathan—he just stood there with that blank expression of his, he didn't know what to say."

That didn't surprise me. Nathan Jacobs wouldn't know a tender feeling if it jumped up and bit him on the nose.

"I'm so sorry," Rita said. "What a terrible position to put Melissa in, seeing me like that. As if she didn't have enough to contend with, being without her mother."

I remembered what Melissa said before she left for Connecticut. *It makes me sad when they don't talk about her, because it makes me afraid to talk about her.*

I said, "Please don't worry about upsetting her. I think it's better for her to see you like that than for you to pretend for her sake Janet's death doesn't trouble you anymore."

"Does it still trouble you, Harry?"

"Yes."

"Do you still think about her?"

"Of course. Every day. I always will."

"Do you think you might get married again?"

I hesitated. "I don't know."

"I want you to know that Nathan and I would be very happy for you if you did."

I couldn't picture her husband being happy about anything regarding me, but I was willing to believe that Rita might. I appreciated the sentiment: Here was my former mother-in-law—made former by virtue of her daughter's premature death—giving her blessing to having another woman act as a parent to her only grandchild. I wondered if Melissa had said something to trigger this—something about my relationship with Veronica.

As we ended our conversation I asked that she pass along my regards to her husband. This was hypocritical politeness on my part; I had no particularly kind regards for him, nor he for me. But I suddenly realized that I needed something right then that he could probably give me, and I asked Rita to call him to the phone.

"Great little kid you have," Nathan Jacobs said when he came to the phone.

"Thank you."

"Hey—I said *she* was great. Why are *you* thanking me?"

Because I'd like to think I had something to do with it, I thought.

He began to laugh, so amused was he by what he perceived to be his own wit. "Rita says you have a question for me."

"Yes, sir. It's about college football."

"Well, you came to the right place."

"What can you tell me about someone named Andrew Galloway? I think he played for Oklahoma."

"I *know* he played for Oklahoma. Fullback. Galloping Galloway, that's what they called him. His junior year, he gave Earl Campbell a run for his money in the Heisman Trophy voting. Everyone figured he'd be a shoo-in for it in his senior year. And he probably would have been. If."

"If what?"

"If he hadn't tried to be a damn hero. Early his senior year, coming out of a restaurant one night, saw someone getting mugged, ran up to help, took a bullet in the leg. Shattered his kneecap, ended his college career, destroyed his chance to make the pros."

Now I remembered—not all of the details, but the essential parts of the story. He was from western Massachusetts, so there was a fair amount of Boston-area press about his misfortune when it occurred, fifteen years earlier. I recalled his movie-star good looks: accepting an award for heroism from President Carter at a Rose Garden ceremony, enduring countless media interviews with equanimity, refusing to bemoan the loss of a promising sports career.

He said, "That was an easy question. Give me another one."

"Excuse me?"

"Give me another one. See if you can stump me."

That's what it always seemed to come down to between us: a question of who was right and who was wrong, or who was better than the other at this thing or that. I don't remember exactly how we got started down that road, but

I doubted we'd ever get off. And as I realized the hopeless-
ness of it all, I felt a momentary, inexplicable twinge of pity
for both of us.

So there it was. Veronica was on an out-of-town adventure with a man closer to her own age than was I: an attractive star athlete, intelligent and articulate, with both
heroic and tragic dimensions.

It was a perfectly crappy ending to a perfectly crappy
day.

16: Assault

"Harry? It's Donald. I hope I didn't wake you up."

I glanced at my watch; it was nine-fifteen. "No problem. I've been up for hours."

"I wasn't sure," Veronica's father said. "I didn't know how late you'd be sleeping on a Saturday, especially with no one else around the house to disturb you."

"I haven't slept past nine since the Kennedy administration."

He laughed. "You're not old enough to remember the Kennedy administration."

"Sure I am."

"Veronica was born when he was in office. I used to say it was the only thing that happened during his term that I approved of. Of course, that was before the poor man was murdered."

I was in the middle: almost equidistant in age from Veronica on one end, and her father on the other. At times it felt odd to be dating someone whose only knowledge of certain events that profoundly affected my life had come from history books. Once she found a Beatles tape in my car and said—in jest, I think—"Oh, right. The group Paul McCartney was in before Wings."

Donald said, "When is Melissa returning home?"

"Tomorrow night. My housekeeper is picking her up in Hartford."

"Well, then. Would you like to come to the Red Sox game with me tomorrow afternoon?"

Donald's firm owned season seats, shared by the several partners. He'd just been offered the tickets to Sunday's game by a colleague who had a sudden change in plans. I accepted his invitation immediately, and we made arrangements to meet outside Fenway Park.

I decided to take the walk that I was forced to cancel the previous day when I was accosted by Warren Oberlin and his behemoth. The skies were gray; the wind was brisk. I slipped a sweatshirt on and walked swiftly toward Estabrook Woods.

The woods occupy an area of more than two thousand acres, almost four square miles. I don't know how many miles of trails cut through it. I followed a circular route through the woods that would return me to the entrance point without causing me to retrace the path I took coming in. The woods are never crowded, and on this blustery day I didn't see another person until I'd been hiking for almost an hour. Walking in the opposite direction, a thin, long-haired teenage boy with thick glasses avoided eye contact as we passed one another.

I wondered whether Donald Pace's unexpected invitation was motivated by his awareness of the strain between his daughter and me. He wanted Veronica to be happy, he thought that she could be happy with me, and he wanted to help set things right between us. Maybe he hoped that spending some time with me might help accomplish that.

Donald wasn't old enough to be my father, but I'd come to see him as something of a paternal figure. And I didn't resent his attempt—if it was an attempt—to influence the outcome of the problems Veronica and I were having, because his approach was gentle, and he respected our right to screw things up even while he tried to keep us from doing so.

Nathan Jacobs's efforts to influence his daughter's life had always been much more direct, intrusive, and overbearing. He was accustomed to issuing directives, and to having them carried out unquestioningly. He opposed our relationship from the beginning, perhaps because it was the first important decision Janet made without first seeking his approval. He expressed his antipathy toward me in a hundred ways over the years: some subtle, some obvious. Almost every major disagreement Janet and I ever had was related to something he did or said. Not even the birth of his first and only grandchild could mellow him.

Several months after Janet succumbed to cancer, her parents visited Melissa and me for a few days. One evening they were sitting in the den, unaware that I was just about to walk into the room. I overheard Nathan Jacobs say to his wife, "None of this would have happened if we'd kept Janet with us in Connecticut. There were plenty of boys there she could have been very happy with."

I appeared in the doorway just as he finished his words. Our eyes met for a moment.

Rita, whose back was toward me, didn't see me. She said, "Janet was very happy with Harry, dear."

I waited for him to say something to her in reply: an acknowledgment that his bitterness over Janet's death was being directed against me unfairly and irrationally. But his only words were: "I've said all I'm going to say on the matter."

It was a defining moment: Everything that preceded seemed crystallized in it, and it set the tone for all that followed. I would always think of him as the primary cause of whatever unhappiness Janet experienced in her too-brief life. And he would always view me as the carcinogenic agent responsible for that brevity.

Lost in those unpleasant thoughts, I didn't hear the footsteps until they were almost upon me. Coming from the rear, they were rapid-paced and they grew louder very quickly. Someone was running along the broad, groomed path—not an unusual occurrence—and he was about to breeze past me. I continued walking, but moved a step toward the side of the path to leave a wider passage for the runner.

Suddenly I was hit with the full force of the speeding jogger's body. He rammed me in the back—hurling me off the path, through the air, and toward a gully that ran alongside the trail. As I flew through the air my neck snapped backward in a whiplash reaction, then quickly rebounded forward until my chin hit my chest.

I smashed against a tree. The impact spun my body around. For an instant I could see the runner speeding away. Then I fell backward, crashing to the ground. The gully was muddy and soft, weakening the force of the jolt against the back of my head as it struck the earth.

I was too stunned to move. The blow knocked the breath out of me, and I was gasping for air. I pushed against the ground with one elbow and slowly rolled onto my side. My lungs filled again. I heard someone groan, and then I realized they were my groans. I began a slow inventory of my body, stretching and testing out my limbs one at a time. Everything hurt, but everything worked.

I raised my torso to a sitting position, facing the trail. I heard the runner's receding footsteps, and my adrenaline took over. I stood, faltered for a moment, then began chasing after him. My labored breathing seemed to echo in my ears. I felt the blood pulsing through the veins in my temple.

After about a minute the path forked. I stopped. I listened. I heard nothing. If I chose the left path, I would go deeper into the woods; the right path would lead me back to my starting point. I chose the right path and lumbered onward.

I spied a broad figure, slightly hunched and walking briskly away from me, fifty yards in the distance. I shouted after him; he didn't turn around or say anything, and he didn't change the rate of his movement. Moving as quickly as I could manage, I began to narrow the gap between us. It took me about a minute to reach a spot just a few yards behind him. I called, "Hey, you," several times as I closed the distance, but he didn't respond in word or action.

I lunged forward to cover the last few yards. "Hey,

you—asshole," I shouted. I grabbed the man's shoulder and whirled him around. Taken by surprise, he quickly dropped into a boxer's stance, raising clenched fists in front of his face in a defensive posture.

He was wearing Walkman headphones, which probably explained why he didn't hear me as I pursued him. His fists covered his face from view, but he could see me as he peered over them. A look of recognition flickered in his eyes, and he slowly lowered his hands and lifted himself out of his crouch.

"Well, now," said Father John Fitzpatrick. "I guess that would be *Father* Asshole, wouldn't it?" Then he looked more closely at me. "Dear Lord, man—what happened to you?"

My cheek felt wet and sticky. I wiped it with my hand. Then I looked down and saw that the hand was covered with blood. The sight and smell made me woozy.

The priest caught me just before I hit the ground.

17: "And When He Was in Affliction"

It took three stitches to close the wound over my right eye. A surgery resident at Emerson Hospital performed the procedure with relative ease and a few cubic centimeters of Novocaine.

Father John waited in the examination room while they took me into the hospital basement for X rays. When I returned, he was talking to Alfred Korvich. "I called the police," said the priest. "I hope you don't mind."

I shrugged. I didn't mind him calling the police, although I thought chances were slim of tracking down the runner who rammed me. But I wasn't particularly overjoyed that Korvich was the one who had responded.

I said, "Getting bored around the office? I'd hate to think our police chief has nothing better to do than go out on routine calls like this one."

"Father John calls, I give him my personal attention," Korvich said. "Besides, I've developed strong feelings for you these past couple of weeks." He grinned broadly. "And I'm completely sincere about that."

"I didn't know you cared."

Father John interrupted, "I feel like I've walked into a movie after it's already begun."

"You haven't missed much," I said.

Korvich sat on the edge of the examination bench. "Father John tells me this happened on one of the wide trails—eight, maybe ten feet across. Is that right?"

I nodded.

"Were you hogging the middle?"

"I pulled over to the side. He had enough room to pass me."

"And when he hit you, you fell to the side, not straight forward."

"Right."

He scratched the back of his head. "You go there often?"

"Yes."

"Well, based on what I'm hearing, including the angle he hit you from, it sounds like maybe he aimed for you on purpose. You been pissing anyone off lately, besides me?"

"I do my best."

"I'm serious. You have trouble with anyone recently? Someone who knows you well enough to know you might be in the woods today?"

I thought about Isadore, who certainly wouldn't count me among his cherished friends after our encounter the previous day. But the notion seemed ridiculous. Besides, I couldn't involve him without involving Warren Oberlin, and I saw no reason to do that. "I can't think of anyone," I said.

"How about we go back there, you show me where it happened. Maybe we'll find something worth pursuing."

My head was throbbing, and the rest of my body ached dully. "I don't think so. I just want to get some rest. Some asshole decided to clear a wider path for himself. Let's leave it at that."

He asked me if I were certain. I said I was. The surgery resident returned to tell me the X rays were negative. "Just a very mild concussion," he said. "Can you call someone to give you a lift?"

Father John offered to take me home. Perhaps Korvich would have offered if Father John hadn't said anything; he had, after all, developed strong feelings for me.

It was early afternoon when we pulled into my driveway. Father John gave me his arm for support and led me through the kitchen entrance and into the den. He went back to the kitchen, poured two glasses of cold water, and rejoined me in the den.

I said, "I nicked myself while I was shaving this morning, and then I almost burned my hand on the waffle iron. Maybe my biorhythms are off, because I sure seem accident-prone today."

"Chief Korvich thought that the incident in the woods might not be an accident."

"Chief Korvich needs a vacation. It was just a reckless bit of hit-and-run. Maybe I should say, run-and-hit. But it would have been nice if the jerk who hit me at least stopped to see if I was injured."

"Perhaps he was frightened," the priest said. "That would be a natural reaction to hurting another person." He glanced at his watch. "What time does your daughter come home from school?"

"It's spring vacation week. She's visiting her mother's parents in Connecticut."

"Ah, yes. I see." He sipped from his water glass. "I studied at Yale. What part of Connecticut are your in-laws from?" He glanced at me and paused. "What's wrong?"

"Nothing. I just don't like thinking of them as my in-laws anymore. We were never close, even when my wife was alive. And the one positive aspect of Janet's death was that I don't have to interact with her parents very often. I keep the relationship going because I don't want to deprive my daughter of her grandparents."

"Perhaps you don't want to deprive them of their granddaughter."

"Maybe. I don't know. I'm not sure I should get any credit for generosity when it comes to Janet's parents. Her father had a serious heart attack two years ago, hovered near death for a while, and the hardest part for me was pretending that I gave a damn."

He took another sip of water. "Perhaps you'd like to call your daughter. I'm sure the past couple of hours have left you feeling a little shaken."

"No sense worrying Melissa. She's coming home tomorrow night. I can talk with her then." I whisked my fingers lightly over my sutured head wound. "Maybe by then I won't look so much like Dr. Frankenstein's monster."

"It really doesn't look too bad. I've had similar injuries. I used to box when I was in the army."

"You fell pretty naturally into a fighter's stance when I grabbed you in the woods."

"I surprised myself when I did that. I guess it's like riding the proverbial bicycle. You never forget." He looked around the room, then gazed out the window at the field behind the house. "This is a very peaceful setting."

"It used to be a farm."

"How long have you lived here?"

"About twelve years. It's ironic, but I own it free and clear now, thanks to my ex-father-in-law."

"He bought it for you?"

"Not exactly. When we got married, Janet's father bought a million-dollar life-insurance policy for me. I should say 'on me,' because he did it without asking my permission. He said he wanted grandchildren, and he wanted them to have a nest egg if I died. He even purchased an annuity that would cover the premium for thirty years. And a rider that would pay off the mortgage on this place in the event that I ever died—buying the farm in case I ever bought the farm, so to speak. I resented his insinuation that I wasn't capable of planning for my own family's welfare. I also thought it was pretty hostile of him to give a wedding gift that could only be used if I dropped dead."

"What did your wife think about what her father had done?"

"She resented his implication that my life was more valuable than hers. So she insisted that she and I purchase a matching policy on her, including the rider for the mortgage buyout. That's the irony I was referring to a minute ago. We bought that policy as a direct response to her father's intrusiveness, and because of it I own this house free and clear. And between her insurance, and some other money she left, and some money I've saved . . . Well, you get the picture. Suffice it to say that I work because I want to, not because I have to."

"You're a fortunate man."

"In some ways. But I would just as soon have done without the experience of what I endured to get to this point."

"Ah, yes. Of course."

I shifted in my seat, and when I did, my head began to pound. "Sorry for going on like that. I don't often have the chance to talk about Janet."

"Perhaps you should find a way of talking about her more often. Maybe you could seek someone out."

"You mean a therapist?"

"Actually, I meant a clergyman. Are you Jewish?"

"Yes."

"Do you go to temple?"

"I haven't been to one in several years."

"I see. Do you pray?"

"I wouldn't call it that. Sometimes I talk to my wife. I used to do it more often than I do now. But I'm not sure I ever really thought it meant anything."

The priest studied my face for several seconds. "We Catholics believe in everlasting life," he said. "For those baptized in Christ, or baptized by desire, a place with the heavenly Father at the end of time, throughout all eternity."

"How can there be an eternity, if there's an end of time?"

He smiled. "It's complicated."

"Everlasting life in heaven." I shrugged. "It's a nice thought."

"It's more than a thought. It's the truth."

"I wish I shared your certainty. But I don't. I can't. I think God forgot me somewhere along the way. I know I forgot him."

"I believe that you're not certain, Harry. But I don't believe you can't be. And I don't believe God has forgotten you." He paused. "Tell me—what would it mean for you if there really is a communion of all souls, if everything is revealed at the end of the world?"

I chuckled. "I'm sorry, Father, but my first thought was, 'I could finally find out if there was a second gunman on the grassy knoll.' "

He smiled. "You should go to temple, Harry. If you don't want to do that, then you should drop in on one of our Masses. The important thing is to bring yourself into God's presence."

"I never really get anything out of going to services."

"Then you have to approach it with a more prayerful attitude. When one of my parishioners tells me he doesn't get anything *from* the liturgy, I always ask. 'What are you bringing *to* the liturgy?' "

" 'Ask not what your liturgy can do for you, ask what you can do for your liturgy.' " We both laughed at my poor imitation of President Kennedy. "I think it's too late for me to get religion. It doesn't make sense to me intellectually, and I'm too much of a cynic to take it on faith."

"Then the answer is really quite simple," he said.

"Oh?"

"You should pray for faith."

"But if I found faith that way, it wouldn't be real. It would just be a self-fulfilling prophecy, something I talked myself into."

"I don't know you well, Harry, but you don't impress me as the sort of fellow who could fool himself so easily."

"No, you don't know me, Father. If you did, you'd realize what a fool I am."

He leaned forward in his chair. "Do you have any pretzels?"

I began to stand.

"No," he said. "Don't get up. Just tell me where they are."

I directed him to one of the kitchen cupboards. He returned to the den a minute or two later with several pretzels in a small bowl. He placed the bowl on the table between us.

He reached for one and began to munch. "Someone far wiser than I am advised me to pray for faith when I was a young man. At the time I thought it was nonsense, too. But eventually it played a part in my decision to answer the call."

"The call?"

"The call to become a priest."

"I'd be interested in hearing that story."

He grabbed another pretzel, but he didn't eat it. He poked a finger through one of the loops and twirled the pretzel around and around, all the while gazing down as if he were thinking about something and trying to decide how much to reveal about it.

He said, "I don't suppose you've ever killed anyone, have you?" He looked up. "Why are you grinning?"

"I'm sorry, Father. It's just that this is the third time in four days that someone has asked me that question. I'm beginning to think I should hang a sign around my neck. 'I am not a murderer.' "

He winced when I said that, and I knew I'd trodden on sensitive ground. He said, "I had no particular skills when I entered the army. I had no particular skills when I came out. Except for boxing. I represented my unit in some tournaments, and I won them all. I was an angry young man. I used to enjoy hurting my opponents. I liked the sight of their blood. I liked the sound my gloves made when I pounded on their bodies." He paused. "Shall I go on?"

"Please."

"I was a middleweight, and people who knew about such things said I showed potential. An army friend helped me get hooked up with a gym and a manager in South Boston after I was discharged. Just a couple of months out of the service, I killed my sparring partner. He was younger than me, a kid who dropped out of school and was just looking for something he could do to make ends meet. I used to hit him hard, much harder than most fellows hit their sparring partners. I told myself I was helping him to toughen up, but I think I always knew I was just trying to make myself feel important and powerful at his expense. Then one day I hit him much too hard, he fell much too fast, and he never got up."

Father John placed his water glass on the table and sighed. He said, "I can't really say how that affected me at first, because I spent every waking moment of the next two weeks drunk. When I stopped drinking, I was consumed by self-loathing, and so I began drinking again This went on for quite some time. Finally, my mother persuaded me to visit her priest. I hadn't been inside a church for years, and I was prepared to give the old fellow a very hard time. But he was a good and gentle man, and he managed to defuse my anger while we were together. He asked me if I had lost my faith. I told him I didn't think I had lost it, because I didn't think I ever had faith to begin with. He told me, 'In that case, you must begin by praying for faith.' And my re-action was much like yours was just a few minutes ago, Harry. But I resolved to follow his advice, and each day I prayed for faith. And things began to change for me."

"How?"

He smiled. "They got even worse. Every day I prayed for faith, and every day I failed to find faith. And one morning I awoke to a crystal-clear recognition of what I had become—a sinful, selfish, loathing, loathsome drunk. And I resolved to kill myself." He looked at me. "You're a little pale, Harry. Perhaps you should lie down. I can fin-ish the story some other time."

"No—I'd really like to hear the rest."

"I bought a handgun from someone who used to peddle them illegally in one of the seedy bars I frequented. I was drunk when I bought it, but I wanted to be sober when I used it, because I didn't want to aim poorly in a drunken haze and take the chance of living on as a cripple or a vegetable. So I began to walk around the neighborhood to sober up. The more sober I got, the stronger I became in my resolve to kill myself. And then I found myself next to a church, and I was filled with hatred toward myself and toward God. And I spoke to God. I said, 'All right, you son of a bitch, I'll give you just one more chance to do right by me.' I went inside and found a Bible. I decided to close my eyes, open to a page at random, pick a random point on the random page, and read whatever passage I picked. 'Show me a sign,' I said, 'and make it a goddamn very clear sign, or I will go home and fire a bullet into my brain.' "

Father John reached into his pocket, got his wallet, and pulled out a tattered card with a handwritten passage. He said, "This is what I saw in that Bible when I opened my eyes."

I read the card: a verse labeled "II Chronicles 33:12."

> *And when he was in affliction*
> *he besought the Lord his God*
> *and humbled himself greatly*
> *before the God of his fathers.*

He said, "I had asked God to show me a sign, and what He showed me was myself. He pointed me to a passage that described exactly who I was and exactly what I was doing at that very moment. It was as if I'd opened the Bible to find a photograph of myself looking at that very Bible. For the first time in my life I felt the presence of the Lord. And I cried—a long, cleansing cry."

His eyes watered over as he spoke, and a chill ran through me.

"The next thing I knew, a priest was standing next to me. He asked me what was troubling me. I told him about my sparring partner and the illegal handgun and the passage I had found when I opened the Bible to a random page. He read it, and he said, 'The key word for you in this verse is "humbled." You said you would give God just one more chance. But how many chances do you suppose He has given you?'"

I handed the Bible passage to him. He cradled it in his hand. He said, "Five years later I was ordained. And the rest, as they say, is history. I consider myself blessed by the Lord's grace."

We sat quietly for a minute or two. He said, "You look surprised, Harry."

"I'm surprised that you would reveal something so personal to me. I assumed priests keep their private lives to themselves."

"I guess you've never had a priest as a friend."

"No, I haven't."

Father John Fitzpatrick smiled. "Well, you do now." He handed the card with the Bible passage to me once again. "Keep this, Harry. My first gift to you as a friend. And if you'll allow me to, *I'll* pray that you receive faith. That will be my second gift to you."

I stretched out on the sofa in my den after Father John left. Exhausted, I quickly fell into a deep and dreamless sleep.

When I awoke a few hours later, I was acutely aware of the silence in the house and, then, the loneliness in my heart. I was genuinely touched by Father John's story. My own life seemed petty and inconsequential in comparison.

I wandered aimlessly through the house. I realized how scant were the reminders of Veronica's presence: a few items of clothing in a closet and a dresser drawer, a couple of books on a night table, some food items that neither Melissa nor I would eat. How could someone who seemed so present in my life just a week earlier have left such a faint trace of that presence?

Melissa's room was decorated with artifacts and totems of her own preadolescent culture: icons of a young life that was growing further from my own with each passing day. Together we'd lived through the most devastating loss imaginable. For a long time afterward she seemed totally focused on me: desperate to please me, worried whenever I seemed unhappy, fearful of any deviation from our familiar daily routines. When Veronica came into our lives, Melissa was able to detach from me a little bit, and she'd grown more confident and self-sufficient as a result. And though I knew it was natural and healthy for her to pull away from me, still there were moments when I wished I could freeze time to stop that from happening. In not too many years she'd be gone from my home. What would I have left?

I climbed up to the attic, a place I seldom went. In the far corner were cartons filled with Janet's belongings and the souvenirs from our years together. I always told myself that at some point I'd weed through them and discard everything except the things I wanted to pass on to my daughter. When would I reach that point?

I returned downstairs and tried to call Melissa at her grandparents' house. I tried to call Bobby. There was no answer at either place. I didn't know where Veronica was staying in New York, so I called the Pittsfield hotel where she stayed earlier in the week on the chance she had returned there. She hadn't. I called her beeper number, but she didn't respond, and I didn't know if she was even in range.

I had to get away from my house—from the too few reminders of Veronica, and the too many reminders of Janet. I got into my car and drove, no particular destination in mind. For the next couple of hours I crisscrossed the greater Boston area in a series of drive-by visitations to the scenes of my past: the Tufts dorms and Somerville apartments I lived in during my college years, my childhood home in Newton, McLean Hospital in Belmont, and the V.A. Medical Center in Bedford.

At around six-thirty in the evening I found myself parked in front of the Cambridge apartment Janet and I shared early in our marriage, when I was in my residency training at McLean. I stepped out of my car and stood before the triple-decker, gazing at the third-floor windows and remembering the happy times we shared when everything was new and so much seemed to lie ahead of us. I wondered what we might have done differently if we'd known then that we would only have another six years together. Would we have had a child? I banished that question from my mind, afraid of where it might lead me.

I was reminded of the epilogue in *Mutiny on the Bounty*. The narrator returns to Tahiti more than twenty years after he was forced to leave. He learns that his Tahitian lover died shortly after he was taken from the island in chains to face a court-martial in England. And he learns that his daughter, whom he last saw as an infant, is still alive. At book's end he meets her, but he does not reveal who he is, for he fears that to embrace her and speak with her of her

mother would be more than he could bear. And as he aches
for what he has lost, he ends his story with these words:

*A chill night breeze came whispering down from the
depths of the valley, and suddenly the place was full of
ghosts—shadows of men alive and dead—my own among
them.*

I circled through Watertown on my way back to Concord.
The lights were off in Veronica's second-story condominium.
A lamp had been on when I passed by four days earlier. Had
she returned at some point during the week without telling
me? More likely the light was on a timer; I'd driven by
much later on Tuesday, so maybe it wasn't set to click on for
another hour or two. Or maybe it had burned out between
Tuesday and Saturday. Hell, I could drive myself crazy trying to figure out what was happening between us.

I drove into Concord via Lexington Road, heading past
Merriam's Corner and into the center of town. It was a little
after seven o'clock. Instead of continuing straight through the
town square toward my home, I turned left onto Main Street,
postponing my return to my empty, ghost-filled house.

As I headed west the last red rays of the setting sun
washed over me. I was very hungry—I hadn't eaten since
breakfast—but I couldn't bear the idea of stopping somewhere to eat alone. I drove beyond Concord Academy and
the town library, past Nashawtuc Road, and across the river.
I took the next right-hand turn.

I hadn't set out intentionally to wind up on Simon
Willard Road, yet there I was: cruising slowly past a three-
story house with yellow clapboards and dark brown shutters. I couldn't see the rear of the property, but I knew the
artfully landscaped lawn sloped gently down to the wildflower tract that lined the Sudbury River. I knew this because I had viewed that side of the property two days
earlier, when Marjorie Morris pointed her house out from
the opposite bank of the narrow stream.

I parked across the street from her house. I told myself I should leave, then I told myself I should stop telling myself I should leave. After a few minutes of this back-and-forth internal dialogue, I noticed a woman peering at me through the window of the house I was parked in front of. I turned my attention back to Marjorie's place. A short while later I glanced back at the house I was parked near; the peering woman had been joined by a man, and he was looking at me, too.

If I stayed parked there any longer, I ran the risk of having to answer a police officer's questions about what I was doing in that quiet residential neighborhood. But if I drove away now, I would draw at least as much suspicion upon myself: Why had I parked there if I hadn't intended to get out? No doubt the couple in the window had noted my license number, which they would dutifully report to the police if I suddenly pulled away. This left me with one option. I stepped out of my car, crossed the street, and walked up the front walkway to Marjorie Morris's house. I rang the doorbell and waited.

After several seconds the door opened slowly; I heard the piercing guitars and incoherent vocal shrieks of a rock band that sounded like something my daughter would listen to. Then the door was completely open, and Marjorie stood there in cutoff jeans and a paint-splattered T-shirt, a paint-brush in her hand and a look of astonishment on her face.

"Harry! What are you doing here?" She spoke loudly, making herself heard above the din of the music.

"I'm starving," I replied. The words were as spontaneous as they were idiotic. It was all I could think of to say.

"Would you like to come in?"

I followed her into a hallway area. She left for a moment to turn the music off. When she returned, we stood there awkwardly for a few seconds, neither of us knowing quite what to say.

Marjorie spoke. "I'm painting the display case for my father's gun collection, sprucing it up so I can sell it. I hate having guns in the house." She glanced down at her hands. "I must look like a mess."

"No, you don't. You look beautiful."

"Thank you for pretending. It's just that when I pictured this moment coming to pass—and I did picture it—I always imagined Debussy or Chopin, with me in a diaphanous gown."

"I guess I should have called first."

"You should have called long ago."

"Am I too late?"

She smiled. "No. But I can only answer for me. I can't speak for you."

She led me to a sunroom in the rear of the house. Wide windows, all of them open, let in a breeze that seemed to roll up the hill from the river. The direct sunlight was gone, and a faint pink glow reflected off the water, making the stream appear luminescent.

I sat on a sofa and looked out at the river. Marjorie remained standing. "My goodness, Harry. What happened to your head?"

I gave her a brief synopsis of the incident in the woods. She sat next to me and lightly touched my cheek, an inch or so from my wound. She said, "It must be very painful."

"I feel too miserable to let a little pain bother me."

"And why do you feel so miserable?"

I shook my head. "I don't know how to put it into words. That's pretty pathetic for a psychiatrist, isn't it? I think it has something to do with not knowing what to believe in. Or not knowing how to know what to believe in. Or not knowing *how* to believe, even if I were to know *what* to believe in. Hell, I have no idea what I'm even talking about."

"Then don't talk. We can just sit here together and watch the night fall on the river. Did you know Thoreau used to swim there?"

"No."

"He wrote about it in *Cape Cod*. He compared it rather

unfavorably to swimming in the ocean. Still, it's quite lovely, especially at this time of day."

We sat silently for a minute or two. Then she said, "Would you like me to fix something for you to eat?"

"No. I don't want you to leave."

"All right. I won't leave."

Marjorie held a hand out to me. I grabbed it and clasped it to my chest. She leaned across me and folded herself into my arms, and we held each other for what felt like half an eternity.

She said, "You can let me know what you want."

"I don't know what I want."

"I know what I want," she replied. She slid her hands inside my shirt, warming me. She brought her lips to my face and began kissing me: my forehead, cheeks, and lips—light and lingering, over and over again. "Please don't tell me to stop."

I didn't.

Afterward I started to drift off to sleep, my head cradled in her lap. "What is that?" I asked.

"What is what?"

"That song you're humming. I've heard it somewhere."

"I don't remember the name," she said, "but I always liked the words." She sang:

> *"In the darkness of the night*
> *I am waiting for a light*
> *To shine on down for me*
>
> *And I fall along the way*
> *And I never learned to pray*
> *But have some faith in me."*

18: A Willing Participant

Marjorie woke me a little later and we went upstairs to her bedroom. Three more times I drifted off to sleep, and each time I was awakened by the soft chafing of her skin against mine. When she finally lifted herself off of me for the last time, shortly before dawn, I murmured, "You're insatiable."

"No, I'm not," she replied. "Remember—you're sleeping with the daughter of an English professor. Insatiable means 'incapable of being satisfied.' And with you I am very, very satisfied."

She kissed me, and we fell asleep entwined in each other's arms.

The sun was well above the horizon when I awoke. I was alone in Marjorie's queen-sized bed. I heard running water and smelled coffee brewing in another part of the house.

My shoulder, side, and head hurt—a carryover from the incident in the woods. Other parts ached, too, but it was a good ache—a by-product of the night just passed.

Marjorie entered the room with a breakfast tray. "Oh, good," she said. "You *are* here. It wasn't just a dream. I hope you like French toast. And I brought the newspaper, too." She set the food tray on a glass-top ornamental table by the window, tossed the Sunday *Globe* onto the bed, let her robe fall to the floor, and crawled under the covers.

I said, "How am I supposed to concentrate on food with you lying next to me like that?" In the bright light of the midmorning sun, I could see clearly something I'd missed in the darkness: On the side of her left breast, nestled just below the midline, was a tattoo of a red butterfly. I touched it and said, "So it's real after all."

"Of course, silly. Both of them are real."

"I'm talking about the tattoo. I saw it in your movie, and I wondered if it was genuine."

"You saw *Blood Beach*?"

"Yes, on video."

"When?"

"The day after we met in the cemetery. You told me about it, remember?"

"I remember. I didn't realize you'd go right out and rent it. I'm flattered. And a little embarrassed. Did you like it?"

"I liked the part I watched. I turned it off after you got killed."

"How did you like my performance?"

"I thought you were good," I said.

She nestled against me. "Do you still think I'm good?"

"Definitely. It's just a little strange."

"How so?"

I shrugged. "I'm not used to this sort of thing. I've only been with three women in about twenty years—Janet, Veronica, and now you."

"You were faithful to Janet the whole time you were married?"

"Yes. And before we got married, too."

"How long have you known Veronica?"

"About a year."

She did the single-digit calculation in her head. "You said your wife died six years ago. If you met Veronica just a year ago, that means you went five years without—"

"Five years without."

"Wow! I didn't know that was possible. I'm sorry—I'm afraid I've embarrassed you."

"A little, but that's all right."

"And I'm afraid I've added a complication to your life."

"I was a willing participant, remember? You didn't do anything I didn't want done."

She laughed. " 'You didn't do anything I didn't want done.' You could get work writing lyrics for country-and-western songs. Goodness—five years without. You know, I went without for a while—my last year in California before I came back to Massachusetts last summer."

"And since then?"

She turned away, embarrassed. "One relationship, which was a terrible mistake, and which I finally managed to put an end to recently. There's no one else in my life right now."

Marjorie draped her arm across me and lightly traced circles on my chest with her fingertips. I said, "Aren't you worried the French toast will get cold?"

"I do have a microwave," she said. "Breakfast should reheat easily enough. Of course, by the time I'm finished with you, it may almost be time for lunch."

I glanced at the clock on her night table. It was a little after ten. "I was joking with a friend yesterday. I told him I haven't slept past nine since the Kennedy administration."

"Goodness, Harry—I wasn't even born then."

I sat up quickly.

She said, "What is it? Did I say something wrong?"

"No, of course not. But I just remembered—I'm going to the Red Sox game with that friend this afternoon. I need to get moving. By the time I get home, shower, and change, I'll have just enough time to get there."

"Can't you be a little late?"

"Unfortunately, no. He's holding my ticket. I'm meeting him on Landsdowne Street, outside the ballpark."

"You could shower here and wear my father's clothes. That would give us a little more time together."

I shook my head. "Call me strange, or call me homophobic—but the thought of wearing another man's underwear gives me the creeps." Especially a dead man's underwear, I thought.

She laughed. "You could wear mine, but we'd have to let it out a little bit in the front." She reached under the covers. "Or maybe more than a little bit."

"Hey—let go, or I'll never get out of here." Reluctantly, I threw off the covers and got out of bed.

"Your clothes are on the chair over there," she said. "I folded them for you. You left them strewn around—in the sunroom, on the stairs, in the hallway. Didn't your mother ever teach you how to take care of your things?"

I reached for my clothes. "My mother never covered this particular situation."

"*Wow!* You get dressed almost as quickly as you get undressed."

"I have many talents." I smiled and cast a lascivious look in her direction. "And so do you."

"Thank you, kind sir. Perhaps I can put them on my résumé."

Her doorknob didn't budge. "You keep your bedroom door locked?"

"Force of habit," Marjorie said. "It's strange. I leave the house unlocked all the time when I'm in it, but I always lock my bedroom door. I've done it since I was a little girl. Here, let me unlock it."

Marjorie walked me downstairs to the front door. We stood there, each one of us suddenly realizing that we had no idea what would come to pass in the wake of the night we'd just spent together.

She said, "Are you going to tell Veronica about this?"

"I don't know." I hadn't contemplated the etiquette of infidelity since my undergraduate days, when I had slept with my girlfriend's roommate. I revealed my indiscretion in the interest, I thought, of complete disclosure. My girlfriend lost her roommate, and I lost her.

Marjorie said, "Are you seeing her later today?"

I shook my head. "She's out of town on business. I'm

not sure when she's coming back, and I'm not sure when I'll see her. We're in what you might call a period of reassessment."

She smiled slightly. "I'm sorry for grinning, but I guess I'm not the magnanimous type. I want you to be happy, but I especially want you to be happy with me." She opened the door. "Can I see you later, Harry?"

"Melissa is coming home this evening from a visit with her grandparents. I'll call you."

I realized I hadn't answered Marjorie's question directly.

The passageways behind the stands at Fenway Park have always smelled of popcorn and cigar smoke, as far back as I can remember. Donald and I made our way to the box-seat entrance between home plate and first base.

He said, "Did your father bring you here when you were a boy?"

"Yes."

"Mine, too."

"And have you ever brought Melissa?"

"Sure. She loves it."

"I always imagined how much I would enjoy bringing my own child here. But I guess you know Veronica really doesn't enjoy the game."

"I know."

"It's one of her greatest faults, I'm afraid. I want you to know it has nothing to do with her upbringing."

We emerged into the sunlight, and Donald led me to seats just a few rows behind the Red Sox dugout. When I told him I'd never sat so close before, he beamed with pride. "I'm glad you like it, son," he said. At least I think he called me "son"; the noise made it hard to tell for sure.

We sat down just in time to stand again for the playing of the national anthem. Then Frank Viola took his warm-up pitches from the mound, and Donald asked me how my week had gone.

I thought: Just terrific. Since I saw you on Monday, I called a priest "asshole," told the town's police chief to screw himself, was asked three times if I'm a murderer, got attacked by an East European cretin, and was blindsided in the woods by an unknown assailant. My housekeeper is thinking of retiring. My daughter hates her hair. To top it off, your daughter walked out on me, hasn't come back, may stay away, and is probably banging the Berkshire County district attorney. And who the hell am I to talk, considering how I spent last night?

"I'm not trying to stump you," Donald said, smiling. "It's a relatively straightforward question. How was your week?"

"Uneventful," I said. "How about yours?"

A foul ball bounced off the dugout roof and whizzed past us, almost close enough for us to see the stitches and the signature of the American League president.

He said, "I spent my week negotiating the sale of a pet-food company to a Japanese-owned restaurant chain. I shudder to think what our Asian friends may have in mind. The world of corporate law is not a pretty one."

"Speaking of corporate law, did you know Charles Morris? He was in corporate law at another Boston firm."

"I knew him. He was at Tilton, Prescott, and Goode. He was killed in an accident recently. Why do you ask?"

I shrugged. "I knew his wife. She taught me in college. I was just wondering what you thought of him."

He pondered my question for a few seconds, then said, "Charles Morris was a Class-A son of a bitch. I don't know anyone who grieves his passing. And I know one or two people who probably wish they were driving the car that killed him." He paused. "Once upon a time I may have had that wish myself."

With two out, the Tigers' third batter drew a walk, bringing Cecil Fielder up to bat. I said, "Rather ironic that a designated hitter would be named 'Fielder,' isn't it? Why did you dislike Charles Morris so much?"

Donald turned to face me. "About twenty years ago my firm represented an international conglomerate in acquisition negotiations. Tilton, Prescott, and Goode represented the other company. I was lead attorney for our side, the first time I'd been entrusted with that responsibility. I wasn't a partner yet. Charles Morris was lead attorney for the other side. He was more experienced than I was, a partner in his firm, and he had a reputation for being somewhat ruthless."

Cecil Fielder struck out to end the top half of the first inning. Frank Viola slapped his glove against his thigh as he returned to the Red Sox dugout.

Donald continued his story. "In one of the early negotiating sessions, Charles Morris was being particularly stubborn about the wording of one paragraph that had been drafted by a young lawyer on my team. The young lawyer said something mildly antagonistic in return. I jumped in and smoothed the waters, and we moved on from there. I doubt I would even have remembered the incident if it hadn't been for what happened the following week."

Donald told me about a final negotiating session, during which the two teams of lawyers reached an agreement in principle on all the major points. As Donald left the conference room Charles Morris pulled him aside.

"What is it, Charles?"

"That skinny lawyer on your side. The one with the funny name. Humper."

"Humpholtz."

"Whatever," said Morris. "He's out."

"What do you mean, 'he's out'?"

"I didn't appreciate his remarks last week. He disrespected me."

"Don't you think you're overreacting? I'm sure he didn't mean anything by it, Charles."

"He's out. If Putnam and Blaine wants to seal this merger, then you'll get rid of him. Otherwise, I'll make sure the deal dies. And I can do it, believe me."

"I believe you're able to do it. But why would you *want* to do it? What good would that do for anyone?"

"No good at all. That's why I'm sure you'll see the wisdom of doing exactly what I'm asking you to do. If you want this deal to go through, fire Humper."

"Humpholtz."

"Whatever."

The Red Sox had loaded the bases with two outs while Donald and I were speaking. Mike Greenwell was up at bat.

I said, "Did you slug him then and there, or did you hire someone to wait for him in a dark alley?"

Donald averted his eyes from mine, and I knew immediately that I'd picked the wrong time for being flippant. "We gave Morris what he wanted," he said. "Of course, I didn't have the authority to terminate poor Humpholtz. What I could have done—what I *should* have done—was call his bluff. Instead, I brought the matter to the partners' attention, and they gave Humpholtz his walking papers. I told myself that I bore no responsibility. That, of course, was total bullshit." He paused. "What's wrong—you've never heard that word before?"

"I've never heard it from you."

"Take it as a measure of how much that incident has haunted me over the years. It was a cruel, abusive use of power. I was cowed by it, and someone else suffered for my actions. I'd like to think old Humpholtz learned why he was let go, plotted his revenge for twenty years, then ran Charles Morris down and got away with it." He smiled. "If they catch him and charge him with murder, I know a good lawyer."

Greenwell tapped a slow roller past the pitcher. The Detroit second baseman charged the ball and flipped it underhand to the first baseman, just in time to beat the runner to the bag. The Red Sox took the field to a smattering of boos after loading the bases and failing to score.

I said, "You say there were people who probably wish they were driving the car that killed Charles Morris. It almost sounds like you think someone set out to murder him."

"I was just blowing off steam," Donald responded. "Criminal defense attorneys sometimes get targeted by unhappy clients. Divorce attorneys may need to worry about clients or spouses of clients. But corporate-law specialists don't have to worry about that. Our work doesn't trigger that level of passion. Besides, there certainly must be more efficient ways of killing someone, if that were someone's intention. But we're outside my area of expertise now. My daughter knows more about that."

His mention of Veronica was an unintended but effective conversation stopper for a minute or two. We watched Frank Viola walk two of the first three batters he faced in the top of the second inning, sandwiched around a strike-out.

He said, "I haven't heard from Veronica since she left my house Monday morning. Have you?"

"We spoke on the phone a couple of times."

"Is she still in Pittsfield?"

"She's still working on that case, at least she was as of Friday. But when she called Friday night she was in northern New York, looking for evidence."

"Well, it's not uncommon for a week to pass without me hearing from her. That's something you'll probably have to get used to with Melissa someday. But isn't it unusual for Veronica and you to talk only two times in six days?"

"Yes."

He pondered that for a moment as we watched the Red Sox infield turn a double play to end the Tigers' second inning.

Donald said, "May I ask you a personal question?"

"Of course."

"What attracted you to my daughter?"

Scenes from my year with Veronica flashed through my mind, like a movie trailer condensing the high points of an entire film into one montage. Her intelligence, her intensity, her ability to be tough when she needed to be and soft when she didn't—all of this and more could have accounted for my attraction to her. But in the final analysis, I realized, it came down mostly to one thing.

I said, "What attracted me most to her was the fact that she seemed attracted to me."

He was quiet for a minute or two, and then he said, "I know I asked you this at my house, but is there anything I can do to help?"

"I don't think so. But thanks for the thought."

"If you and Veronica don't stay together, I'd be sorry if it meant I didn't see you anymore."

"Me, too."

"And Shana and I would both be very sorry if we couldn't see Melissa. I hope we can work something out about visiting with her."

"I'm sure we can."

"Good. It's possible, unfortunately, for a child to have too few people who love her. But it's definitely *not* possible to have too many."

Melissa and Mrs. Winnicot arrived home around nine o'clock. Melissa dashed inside first and ran to the den.

"Well, Dad—how do you like it?"

She stood in the doorway sporting her oddest coiffure yet. Her long hair was pulled back into five asymetrically spaced braided clumps, each clump held in place by a twist tie. Each twist tie had its own color. She looked like a cross between Buckwheat and a multicolored rag mop. She smiled broadly; she clearly liked the way she looked and was hoping I would share her enthusiasm for the hairstyle from hell.

"Wow," I said.

She bounded into my arms and kissed my cheek. "I'm *so* glad you like it."

"I do, sweetheart. I really do." And I did like it: not because it flattered her—which it definitely did not—but because it made her feel so pleased with the way she looked.

"Grandmom did it for me. I really love it."

Mrs. Winnicot came into the den. "I told her she's on her own with this one. I'll never figure out how to replicate it after it's combed out."

Looking more closely, I realized each braid had its own

distinct texture, as if her head were a testing ground for a Boy Scout who had gone berserk trying for his knot-tying merit badge.

"Grandmom said Veronica can call her and she'll tell her how to do it."

So Melissa had told my former mother-in-law about Veronica, after all. Placed in that context, Rita Jacobs's words two nights earlier made more sense now. *Do you think you might get married again? I want you to know that Nathan and I would be very happy for you if you did.*

"Is Veronica here?"

"No, she's still out of town."

"Oh. I wanted her to see my hair."

"She will, sweetheart."

She went upstairs to shower and get ready for bed.

Mrs. Winnicot said, "I believe she's worried that you and Veronica may be having difficulties."

"We are."

"I'm sorry." She paused. "Melissa had a good visit with her grandparents. When I picked her up in Hartford, all three of them seemed like they were having a hard time saying good-bye."

"How was your visit with your son and his family?"

She smiled. "Someday you'll know how delightful grandchildren are. Watching your child enjoy his own children is unlike any other pleasure in the world."

After a few seconds of silence I said, "I'm glad you had a good time. I guess I'm hoping that now you're going to say, 'But I can only take so much of that at a time. I don't think it would be a good idea to move in with them.' "

"I know," she said. "I'm sorry."

"Did you tell Melissa?"

"No. I thought you would want to determine how to inform her."

"Thank you."

"I told my son I would move there after the school year ends, perhaps the first week in July. That would be about two and a half months from now. I wanted Melissa to have time to adjust to the idea."

"I appreciate that. We can tell her tomorrow, after she comes home from school."

I went upstairs a few minutes later. Melissa had showered and changed into her robe. She was unpacking her suitcase when I came into her room.

"I'm glad you're home," I said.

"Me, too."

"I missed you."

"Uh-huh."

"How are Grandmom and Grandpop?"

"I saw him cry."

"I know. She told me when I spoke with her on Friday night. She was worried she may have upset you."

"Not Grand*mom*. Grand*pop*. I saw *him* cry."

"Oh?"

"I got hungry after I went to bed last night. I ate a piece of cake and then I went into the den to see what was on TV. Grandpop was sitting there, looking at their old picture albums. The ones with Mommy when she was a little girl. He didn't see me at first. I could tell he had tears in his eyes. Then he looked up and saw me. I felt bad about surprising him like that."

"What did he say?"

"Nothing."

"What did you say?"

"I didn't know what to say. I felt funny being there, and I wanted to leave. But, Daddy—he looked so sad sitting there. So I walked over to him and hugged him. He held on to me tight, and then he started to cry real hard. I could feel his whole body shaking."

The thought of that lonely, bitter man breaking down in front of my daughter made me ache. I felt ashamed of the things I'd said about him to Father John the previous day. Nathan Jacobs had lost his only child. How could I possibly understand what that was like? Could anyone ever bear a heavier burden? And who was I to judge the way he bore it?

Melissa said, "He apologized for crying."

"What did you say?"

"I told him I don't think people should have to apologize for crying. Then I told him I loved him. And then he said he loved me, too. Geez, now why are *you* crying?"

I brushed a tear off my cheek. "Because I have such a wonderful child. You'll understand when you get older and have children of your own."

"I *hate* it when you say that."

I laughed. "I know you do, sweetheart, I know you do. Now, get some sleep. Tomorrow is a school day."

"Ugh. I hate it when you say that, too."

I came downstairs and lay on the couch in the den to watch the Sunday-night sports summary on CNN. But I dozed off, and I fell into a frightful dream.

It was set in my ex-in-laws' den in Connecticut. Warren Oberlin sat in his wheelchair, alone in the room, crying over the death of his daughter. Marjorie Morris came into the room to console him. But it wasn't Marjorie as she was now; it was the little girl I'd known twenty years earlier. She went to him and hugged him. Oberlin put his arms around her. He held her tightly, too tightly, and Marjorie began struggling to be free. Oberlin pushed himself out of the wheelchair, still clutching Marjorie. He fell onto the floor, pinning her underneath him. He placed one hand over her mouth to muffle her screams, and with his other hand he began ripping open her jeans.

I awoke suddenly, startled and chilled. I reached for the telephone; and then I realized that although I knew every inch of Marjorie's body, I didn't know her phone number. I looked it up and dialed.

"I just had a very strange dream, and you were in terrible danger in it."

"And you called to see if I'm all right?"

"No. I mean, of course you're all right. That is, it was just a dream. I'm sure it didn't mean anything."

"Such talk could jeopardize your psychiatry license." She laughed. "Of course, Harry. It was just a dream. But I'm glad you called, just the same. I watched part of the baseball game this afternoon. And I never watch baseball, so I realized I was probably doing it because I knew you were there."

We made small talk for a few minutes. She asked me about Melissa's return home. I asked her if she finished painting her father's firearms case. It was the last thing in the world I had any interest in, and I sounded ridiculous asking about it, but I couldn't think of anything else to say.

After an awkward moment of silence I said, "It's six minutes from your house to mine. I timed it on my way home this morning."

"Then it would only take you six minutes to come back here."

It took me ten minutes: I told Mrs. Winnicot I was going to a late movie, asked her to stay in the guest room in the house in case Melissa woke up, then gathered up a change of clothes. I took my travel alarm, because I wanted to be certain I was back home by the time Melissa awoke.

On the drive to Marjorie's house, I tried to understand why I was going there and why I felt so drawn to her. Though I'd known her for half my life, in truth I knew her hardly at all. I knew she grew up with a father who was, in her words, neither loving nor lovable. I knew she had pushed her mother's love away, and that she ran out of time to reconcile with her.

I knew she felt bruised by her past—a past I knew very little about—and confused about her future.

I knew she was exquisitely beautiful, and that she took my breath away when she made love to me. But what I knew most of all was that she wanted me to be with her. In the end, that seemed more important than the other facts and details. *What attracted me most to her was the fact that she seemed attracted to me.*

I reached for the doorbell, but Marjorie opened the door before I could ring it. As I stepped inside I heard the peaceful strains of Debussy. " 'Clair de Lune,' " she said, closing the door behind us.

Her long red curls tumbled over her shoulders, full and loose. In the dimly lit entryway, the candle she was carrying threw a pattern of flickering light and shadows across her body, accentuating the curves and grooves that were visible through the folds of her diaphanous gown.

19: More Than a Complication

"I have a terrible headache," I said.

Marjorie lifted her head from its resting place on my chest and gave me a playful punch in the arm. "In the afterglow of love, one should never be hungry, need to go to the bathroom, or develop a headache."

"That may very well be, but I have to get up in five hours. If I don't take care of this headache, I may as well give up any ideas about sleeping."

"That sounds delicious to me."

"Sleeping—or anything else," I said.

"Very well," Marjorie said, pretending to pout. "I have some aspirin in the medicine cabinet. I'll get it for you."

"No, don't get up. I'll find it. I have to go to the bathroom anyway."

She laughed. "He has a headache *and* he has to go to the bathroom. Two out of three. Don't you dare ask me to go downstairs to make you a sandwich."

I flipped the light switch in her bathroom. The sudden flash of bright light forced me to squint, which in turn made it difficult for me to find the aspirin right away. Looking for it, I fumbled with the various vials and tubes.

One of the vials had a prescription label. It was for a month's worth of Elavil: an antidepressant that, though still widely prescribed, had in recent years taken a backseat to other, newer medicines. I questioned whether the relatively low dosage—twenty-five milligrams per tablet, three tablets per day—was sufficient to produce a therapeutic effect. In any event, the tiny yellow pills likely weren't having any effect on Marjorie: The prescription was two months old, but the vial looked full. Unlike tranquilizers, antidepressants need to be taken every day to be effective. Just popping one or two when you're feeling under the weather has no effect whatsoever.

I recognized the name of the prescribing psychiatrist. He was an older man, semiretired, who no longer had a psychotherapy practice. He saw a limited number of patients, referred to him by nonmedical psychotherapists—social workers and psychologists—for the sole purpose of prescribing medication. Marjorie had mentioned that she was seeing a therapist; her therapist was apparently using this doctor for psychiatric backup. And the psychiatrist had prescribed a dosage commonly used twenty years earlier, when its lack of consistent effect led some people to conclude, wrongly, that Elavil was not terribly effective.

I found the aspirin bottle and swallowed two pills. When I returned to her bed, Marjorie had pulled the covers off and was lying on her back, exposed to the dim glow of the moon that was shining through the window. Her long tresses covered her breasts, like an artist's rendition of Lady Godiva.

I had come to her these two nights feeling needy and unwanted, knowing that she wanted me. Perhaps because I'd grown so comfortable with her so quickly, I was struck by how little I knew about her. I opened my mouth to speak, but she placed her fingers over my lips. She slipped one of them inside my mouth, swirling it around, over and under my tongue.

With her other hand, she took one of my hands and guided it underneath her curls, resting it on her breast. She held my fingers in hers, moving them like pincers on the tip of her hardened nipple. Then she took her finger out of my mouth and moved her hand slowly down my body, the wetness wiping against my chest and stomach, sending a chill through me.

She wrapped both hands around my back, pulling me toward her. As we brushed against each other our bodies slowly spun, reversing position. On top of me now, she lowered herself onto me, a shudder pulsing through both of us as she did so.

Her body had a fullness I'd never experienced with anyone else. It was a tactile and visual delight: the undulating ripples in her flesh each time I thrust into her, the latticework of tiny folds underneath her heavy breasts as she writhed above me, the beads of sweat on the small of her back as I pressed her down on me.

"I would do anything for you," she breathed, soft and sultry. "Anything in the world."

No one had ever said that to me.

"Anything," she repeated. "Just make a wish."

"I don't have any wishes."

"I do," she said. "I wish I could make this moment last forever."

Marjorie leaned forward slightly, skimming her breasts across my lips as she picked up the rhythm of her rocking ever so slightly. She said, "I changed my mind about what I said a few minutes ago." She leaned closer. "You're allowed to be hungry now."

Before the alarm went off, I was awakened by Marjorie's thrashing. Still asleep, she mumbled something unintelligible and thrashed again. Then she bolted into an upright position, her eyes wide-open, her breathing shallow and rapid, a cold sweat on her forehead.

I reached for her hand. "What is it?"

It took a couple of seconds to switch her focus from her internal images to me. Her breathing slowed and her body relaxed. "A nightmare," she said. "I was dreaming about my father. I have them all the time now."

She looked down at her hand in my hand. My eyes followed her gaze. At the base of her wrist I noticed crisscross scar tissue, the telltale sign of an attempt to end her life.

Aware that I'd seen the marks, Marjorie tried to yank her hand away. I held on to it. She yanked again, harder this time, and pulled away from my grasp. She paused for a moment; then, recognizing the futility of pretending nothing had happened, she slowly held her wrist out for me to inspect.

"California," she said. "A long time ago." She leaned toward me, and I opened my arms to her. She nestled her head against my chest. "I've been trying so hard to appear normal and happy when I'm with you. I figured it was my only chance."

We sat there for a few minutes, me holding her, neither of us speaking.

I said, "I don't want to leave here. But I have to. I want to be home when my daughter wakes up."

"I understand. You don't want to make things more complicated for yourself than they already are."

"Yes."

"Well, I suppose I can take some comfort in knowing that I mean enough to you to represent a complication in your life."

"You're more than just a complication."

She smiled softly, but said nothing.

I took a quick shower and threw on my change of clothing. We went downstairs together and walked to the front door.

Marjorie said, "Are you still reassessing?"

"Reassessing what?"

"Yesterday you said that you and Veronica were in a period of reassessment."

"I haven't spoken to her since then."

"I'll try not to ask again. I'm just trying to figure things out for myself—what I'm getting myself into, and what I'm letting myself in for."

We kissed lightly, and then I left.

The sky was filled with dark clouds. Midway through the

six-minute ride to my house, just as I approached the town square, a heavy rain began to fall. By the time I circled around the grassy ellipse and turned onto Monument Street, the rain had covered the ground.

It was just after six o'clock. Melissa's alarm would sound in about an hour. My daughter would no doubt go through her usual morning routine: She would sleep through her alarm, or pretend to do so. I would go upstairs a few minutes later to roust her from bed. She would dawdle for the better part of an hour, concluding with the obligatory screeching about her hair in front of her bathroom mirror. Finally, she would dash downstairs just in time to eat half her breakfast, gather up her books and lunch, and hightail it down the driveway to meet the school bus. More often than not, this routine drove me to distraction. But I had found myself missing it during the previous week. It would feel good to get back to normal.

I turned off of Monument Street and drove up the long gravel incline to my house.

I pulled around the side of the house to park near the kitchen entrance. That's when I saw the blue Honda parked next to the house.

It was Veronica's car.

20: The Only Mistake I Made

I thought: What she doesn't know won't hurt me. The rain splattered on me as I stood outside the kitchen entrance, pondering the possibilities. . . .

If Veronica arrived and went to sleep at an hour when it was reasonable for me still to be out—say, at a late movie—and if she were still asleep, I could try to bluster my way through the dilemma: I could say I got home late and didn't want to wake her.

If she had just arrived, shortly before me—an unlikely occurrence at that early hour—I could say I went for an early drive. She might not believe me, but she wouldn't be able to prove that I was lying.

But if she had been there for several hours, and if she was awake now to see me come in, then I was screwed.

The downstairs was still: no obvious sounds of wakeful human activity. I walked noiselessly toward the stairwell. Veronica was a sound sleeper; I stood a fifty-fifty chance of slipping into bed next to her and then convincing her that I'd been there for several hours (back to the "late movie" plan).

It was when I passed the entryway to the den on my way to the stairs that I saw her: Veronica was stretched out on the sofa, lying on her stomach with her eyes closed, breathing in the slow, rhythmic manner of deep sleep. That was the good news.

The bad news was that she had gotten a pillow and extra sheet from the linen closet, and had changed into a night-gown. She hadn't drifted off to sleep while waiting for me to come home; she had intentionally avoided our bed—my bed, to be more accurate. *We're going through a period of reassessment.* Indeed we were.

I went upstairs as quickly and quietly as I could. I peeled off my wet clothes and placed them in the hamper. I slipped on my bathrobe. I glanced in the mirror. I noticed that my hair was wet; I would tell her that I just showered (which, in fact, I had). I headed into the hallway to go downstairs, then realized that my bed was still made. I zipped back into my room, engaged in some creative rearranging of the sheets, pillows, and blanket, then headed downstairs again.

Veronica was still sleeping. She had rolled onto her side and her breathing had changed. I figured she would proba-bly awaken soon.

I began making breakfast. A few minutes later I heard Veronica stirring, then walking into the kitchen. I pretended not to hear her at first, then feigned surprise when I turned around.

I said, "She breathes. She walks. She lives." I walked over and planted a light kiss on her cheek.

She had no particular reaction to the kiss that I could dis-cern, either welcoming or avoidant. She looked at the rain hitting the window and said, "What a lousy way to begin the workweek."

"It just started a few minutes ago. I think it'll let up soon."

Veronica looked at me and noticed the stitched gash over my eye. "What happened to you?"

I spent a few minutes describing the incident in the woods. I didn't tell her that afterward I felt so forlorn that I took a sentimental driving tour through my past. And I certainly had no intention of telling her where I wound up seeking solace.

I said, "You were already asleep when I got in last night.

I figured you were probably pretty tired, so I decided not to wake you up. What time did you get here?"

"Around ten-thirty." She yawned and stretched. "Where were you?"

"I went to a late movie. Got in around midnight."

"What did you see?"

"Indecent Proposal." I knew she didn't plan to see the film, so I wasn't likely to have to answer detailed questions about it.

"Did you enjoy it?"

"Redford had a couple of good scenes. Otherwise, it sucked. You were smart not to put it on your list."

She sat at the table and yawned again. "Where did you go to see it?"

The closest theater was in the next town. "Acton," I said. I had no idea if that particular film was playing there. I changed the subject. "You look tired."

"You're *so* observant."

"Are you back?"

"Obviously." She paused. "Sorry. I've had a couple of shitty days. I shouldn't take it out on you."

There was a Band-Aid on her hand. I remembered the gauze pad I had placed there, and the argument that precipitated her exodus eight days earlier.

I said, "What happened with your case?"

"You haven't seen the news?"

"I didn't watch TV last night, and I haven't read the paper yet. Did you have any luck in New York?"

I realized, as I had on many occasions, what a strange world Veronica worked in: where having luck meant unearthing the rotting bodies of two slaughtered children.

The water began to boil. Veronica walked to the cupboard and got a mug, poured herself some black instant coffee, and sat down again. "No," she said. "We didn't find any bodies."

"The forensic botanist couldn't help you?"

"To quote Galloway, 'He was as useful as a second asshole.' "

First it was Andrew, then Andy, then Andrew again. Now it was Galloway. I wasn't certain, but I thought that was a good sign.

"We turned up an awful lot of dirt. We didn't find a thing. And at this point I don't even know if Louis Laggone had anything to do with the missing children."

"Why do you say that?"

"Because he didn't have anything to do with the attempted kidnapping of the little girl near Pittsfield." She stood up. "Turn on the TV, or go outside and get the newspaper. You'll find out everything you want to know about this case. I'm tired of thinking about it. I'm going to wash up."

Veronica was right; the details were plastered across the front page of the *Globe*, with several sidebar articles in the second section. The little girl—the one whose report about the attempted kidnapping first brought Laggone to the attention of the police—had admitted that the whole thing was a hoax. Two weeks earlier Laggone apparently had caught her sneaking into the movie theater that employed him as an usher. She now said she made up the kidnapping story just to get him in trouble. She confided the truth in her school counselor, who persuaded her to reveal it to the police.

Veronica returned to the kitchen. She said, "I talked to the school counselor after the story broke. I asked her what she would have done if the little girl refused to retract her accusation. She said she didn't know."

"Confidentiality," I said.

"Right."

"I don't get it. If Laggone knew the kidnapping charge was bogus, why did he imply he knew something about the missing children?"

"Who the hell knows?" she said, clearly irritated. "I think there's some sort of genetic failing among people in that part of the state. Too much inbreeding. Maybe it was his idea of a joke. Or maybe he really *was* involved in the earlier cases. I don't expect to know, ever."

I buttered a slice of toast and set it in front of her.

She said, "I should have realized something was wrong when they couldn't find any evidence that Laggone ever owned a gun, or even used one. I should have insisted that they let me interview the girl. And I should have insisted that they let me question Laggone about the kidnapping case. If I had talked to either one of them, I probably would have realized it didn't add up."

"This isn't your fault."

She snickered. "Tell that to Galloway. Did the paper print the remarks he made at his press conference?"

"I didn't get that far in the story yet."

She gestured toward the newspaper. I finished reading the coverage of the case. The following statement was attributed to Berkshire County District Attorney Andrew Galloway: "Things got out of control after the FBI got involved. They insisted on trying to connect this case to the other cases, without any evidence whatsoever, and they led us on a wild-goose chase. Fortunately, the local police never let go of this matter. They deserve the full credit for bringing us to where we are today. Next time we'll know better."

Veronica said, "First of all, we didn't get involved until the locals asked us to. Second, *they're* the ones who connected this case to the earlier ones, which is why they decided to involve us in the first place. Third, it was sheer luck that the case broke. The police had nothing to do with the little girl changing her story."

"Would you like more coffee?"

"Yes. Thanks."

I refilled her cup and set it on the table

"Here's the most upsetting part to me," she continued. "It turns out the girl went to the police and recanted her story on Friday. Galloway kept a lid on it as long as he legally could, forty-eight hours, hoping I would turn up something on the missing-children cases. So the son of a bitch knew it for almost two days and didn't even tell *me*. He just kept pressuring me to come up with something. The bastard used me—totally, completely used me—and then he tried to make me look like shit."

I thought: I take it this means you're not planning to bear his love-child? I said, "Well, it's all over now."

"Yes. If I ever suggest we take a pleasure trip to the Berkshires, please shoot me first." She leaned back in her chair, closed her eyes, and ran her hands through her hair. "God, I'm so tired." Then she looked at me and said, "Maybe we should."

"Maybe we should what?"

"Take a pleasure trip somewhere. We've never done that."

The overture came out of the blue. I was unprepared for it. "That might be nice."

" 'That *might* be nice.' Don't get *too* excited, Harry. Your enthusiasm is underwhelming." She sighed deeply, then sipped her coffee. "I'm sorry. That was uncalled for. I'm furious with him, and I'm taking it out on you." She paused. "You're not like him."

It was a compliment I felt I didn't deserve. I was more like Galloway than she realized. At that moment I came close to telling her about Marjorie Morris. Then the moment passed. I realized that confessing my sins would likely not be the most sensible way of trying to effect a reconciliation.

But there was another reason for my silence: If I revealed what had happened—and if Veronica didn't assault me or walk out again after hearing what I had to say—I would have to end my recitation by saying, "But it's all over now."

I didn't want to do that.

Melissa was ecstatic when she saw Veronica sitting in her bathrobe when she came downstairs. As usual, though, she'd left herself very little time for breakfast. She took two sips of juice and grabbed a piece of toast. Her bus was due in four minutes, and it would take her a minute or two to walk down the long driveway to Monument Street.

"How was your trip, honey?" asked Veronica.

"It was okay. Will you be here later?"

Veronica glanced toward me, then back at Melissa. "I don't know. I just got back into town last night. I've got a lot to do. We'll see how the day shapes up."

Melissa's disappointment registered clearly.

Veronica said, "Do you think the fashion police will arrest me if I walk you down to catch your bus?"

"They wouldn't dare. You're a special agent of the FBI."

Veronica stood and walked briskly toward the door, tightening the belt around her bathrobe as she moved. She grabbed an umbrella—it was still drizzling lightly—then took Melissa's hand. They disappeared out the door and down the driveway.

I breathed a sigh of relief. A potentially disastrous situation had worked out reasonably well. Veronica hadn't arrived so late the previous evening that my absence was unusual. She hadn't awakened so early that my continued absence was suspicious. As far as she knew, I got home shortly after she fell asleep, then awoke shortly before she awoke. I imagined I'd feel like a heel later on, but right now I just felt thankful for the reprieve.

I stood, cleared the table, and started loading the dishwasher.

Veronica came back a few minutes later. She was wringing her hands, and I thought I noticed tears in her eyes. I asked her if anything was wrong.

She said, "I've been to too many crime scenes. I'm too good at my job—too good for my own good."

"What are you talking about?"

She sighed deeply. "I wish I could just pretend I didn't see it, or pretend it doesn't matter. But I did, and it does. I want to show you something."

Veronica led me outside. She pointed at our cars and said, "You probably don't notice it. Most people wouldn't. I saw it right away, even though I wasn't looking for it."

"What?"

"Look at the cars. Do you notice anything unusual?"

I stood there in the drizzling rain and looked at her Honda, then my Toyota. Nothing appeared out of the ordinary. "I don't know. Are you concerned that we're both contributing to the foreign trade deficit?"

"This isn't funny, Harry."

"What isn't funny? Give me a hint."

"Look at the driveway underneath the cars. You don't have to bend down. You can see it from here."

"I still don't see anything. Come on—I'm getting wet. Tell me what you're talking about."

She pointed at the driveway underneath her car. "I parked here at ten-thirty last night. The skies were clear. The driveway under my car is still dry. Do you see?"

"Yes."

"Now look under your car. The driveway is wet."

"I'm getting confused."

She grabbed my shoulder and slowly turned me around. "If you parked it here at midnight, and if it started raining at six, then why is it wet underneath your car?"

She backed away from me. I expected to see anger in her eyes, hear hatred in her voice—the way she had been when talking about Galloway an hour earlier. Instead, there were the look and sound of utter despair.

I thought I heard her voice quiver as she said, "I wanted to prove myself wrong. I wanted to believe it had something to do with the angle of the ground, water seeping underneath your car after you parked it, something like that. So I looked at your windshield. If you look closely, you can tell that your wipers were used recently. I guess you don't want me to show you what I mean, do you?"

"No."

She winced. "And it doesn't matter whether *Indecent Proposal* is really playing in Acton or not, because you didn't really go there last night, did you?"

"No."

She looked downward, then closed her eyes. "Think of something, Harry, please. Say something to convince me I shouldn't be thinking what I'm thinking."

All I could think of were the words: "I'm sorry."

"Yes, I actually believe you are. I'm sorry, too."

"Look—we've both made mistakes this week, and—"

She interrupted me. "I think the only mistake I made was coming back here."

21: The One with a Guilty Conscience

After Melissa left for school and Veronica walked out on me again, Michael Cafferty called and asked if he could see me as soon as possible. I usually don't see patients on Mondays, but he sounded worried.

He arrived at my office within the hour. Immediately he started to complain at length about a teacher who had given him a grade slightly lower than the one he thought he deserved. The problem seemed small, his distress appeared minor, and he didn't pose any questions to me or seem interested in any of my comments.

He talked in a similar vein about a squabble with his sister, then his jealousy of a cousin who was dating Miss Teen Pennsylvania, and then his uncertainty about what colleges he would apply to when he became a senior the following year. None of these problems seemed particularly pressing. None was identified by him as the source of his request for an extra session, one day before his next regularly scheduled one.

I wondered whether it was merely the second part of a two-part test, one he may not have been aware he was conducting. Sometimes new patients cancel sessions at the last minute, as Michael had done three days earlier. And sometimes they request extra sessions for no clearly discernible reason. Both actions can represent a testing of the limits of the new relationship: How much will you endure for my sake? How flawed can I be and still have your acceptance?

After filling nearly three quarters of his session with matters of little apparent consequence, he said, "I went home this weekend, which means I had to go to church. My father makes all of us go—me, my mother, my sister. I never get anything out of going to Mass, so I don't go unless I have to."

I spared him my imitation of President Kennedy: *Ask not what your liturgy can do for you.* . . . I said, "It sounds like attending church is important to your father."

Michael snickered. "He's a hypocrite. He goes to Mass on Sunday, and then he goes right back to screwing people on Monday. But I'll tell you this about my father—*he* would know exactly what to do if he was in my situation, and then he'd go out and do it."

"What situation are we talking about?"

He thought for several seconds. "I don't know how much I should say. It involves other people, too."

Most things do, I thought.

I briefly reprised the remarks about confidentiality I made during his first session. Then I said, "It's not like going to confession. There are some legal limitations, in theory. But those situations almost never come up in actual practice."

He breathed deeply. "A friend of mine did something terrible. Don't ask me what, because I can't say. Another friend is blaming himself for what happened, even though it wasn't his fault. I'm really worried about him."

"Which friend are you worried about? The one who did something terrible, or the one with the guilty conscience?"

"Both, I guess. But especially the one who didn't really do anything. He's so depressed, I don't know what he's going to do."

"Do you think he might try to hurt himself?"

He thought about that at length, then said, "I think he's probably just blowing off steam."

"What does he say?"

"He says things like, 'The only good part about getting older is you don't have as much time to live.' But I guess lots of people think about it sometimes. It doesn't mean you're actually going to do it, right?"

"That's right." I knew the "it" was suicide. "Is it something *you* think about?"

He sat up, surprised by the question. "Who, me? Hey, man—no way. I haven't even gotten laid yet." He laughed. "Sorry. It just sort of slipped out. I guess what I'm trying to say is, I haven't even done anything yet. There's too much I want to do before it's time for me to hang it up."

We psychiatrists call that attitude "future orientation," and you earn several points on the nonsuicidal scale when you evidence it. And given his age and his hormones, Michael's eager anticipation of yet-to-be-realized adventures with his genitalia was more convincing to me than a yearning to complete medical school and discover a cure for cancer.

"If you're not really worried about your friend hurting himself, I wonder why you wanted to come here today?"

"This thing that I said was terrible, I can't tell you the details. But it involves me, too, sort of. And I need to figure out how to do the right thing."

"Do you mean you have to decide what the right thing is? Or do you mean you know what it is, but you don't know how to go about doing it?"

"I know what I *should* do. That doesn't require a rocket scientist. But doing the right thing might involve hurting a friend."

I remembered the phone call I received from Alfred Korvich the day after Michael's first therapy session. I wondered whether Michael was referring to the unsolved robberies that Korvich thought he and two other Concord Academy students were responsible for. Perhaps my patient was trying to decide whether to implicate his friends.

And I wondered about something else. "The second time we met," I said, "you asked if there's a test for determining

whether someone is heterosexual or homosexual. Is that related to what we're talking about today?"

"In a way. I was wondering about these two friends.
They're roommates. I think they may be more than that.
Much more, if you see what I mean."

Now I wondered if the "something terrible" referred to a
homosexual seduction by one friend of the other. I said,
"When you asked me that question, I wondered if you
might have some questions about your own sexuality."

He laughed long and hard, then looked at me as though
I were an idiot. "I may be a virgin, but I'm hoping that's
a curable condition. Believe me, I know I like girls." He
glanced at his watch. "I need to get back to school."

"Tell me your friends' first names. That way, if you want
to talk more about this, we don't have to keep referring to
them as 'the one with a guilty conscience' and 'the one
who did a terrible thing.' "

"The first one—the one I'm worried about—is Theo.
The one who did something terrible is his roommate. I
mentioned him to you before, but you thought he was a
girl, I guess because of his name. His name is Junie."

Mrs. Winnicot and I sat in the den with Melissa after she
returned home from school. We told her about Mrs.
Winnicot's decision to join her family in New Jersey. It
went better than I expected. Melissa already knew how
much Mrs. Winnicot missed seeing her grandchildren since
they moved a few months earlier. And she seemed to sense
our housekeeper's uneasiness at breaking the news. She accepted the news sadly, but without trying to make Mrs.
Winnicot feel guilty about her decision.

Melissa went to sit on the sunporch while Mrs. Winnicot
prepared dinner. I let her have a couple of minutes to herself, then joined her. She was sitting on the glider, gently
rocking, gazing out at the field next to the house and the
conservation land beyond.

I sat next to her. "You were very nice to Mrs. Winnicot."

"She's always very nice to me."

"You won't be seeing her very often after she moves, but you'll still be part of each other's lives."

"I know. She told me there's a train that goes from Boston to Princeton." She stopped rocking. Still looking at the field, she asked, "Is Veronica coming here after work?"

"No, sweetheart."

"When is she coming back?"

I pondered the question for a few moments. "She may not come back."

She turned away from me and stayed silent for what seemed like a very long time. When she turned back to face me, I saw the tears that had filled her eyes. "What did you *do* to her?"

"I . . . disappointed her. It's very, very complicated."

"I don't think so."

"What do you mean?"

"I don't think it's very complicated," Melissa replied. "I think you just don't want to tell me."

"Do you want the truth?"

"I always want the truth."

I said, "The truth is, it *is* very complicated. And the truth is, you're right—I don't want to tell you about it. It's between Veronica and me. It has nothing to do with you."

"Of *course* it has something to do with me. If I can't be with her again, that's very much something to do with me. Can't you see that?"

I reached out to touch her shoulder, but she pulled away from me. She said, "If she was married to you, and the two of you broke up, you'd still have to let me see her."

"If Veronica and I break up, I'm sure she'll still want to be your friend."

"Will you let me see her?"

"Of course."

"If she wanted to keep me overnight on a visit, would you let her?"

"Yes."

"Really?"

"Really," I said. "Okay?"

She nodded and sniffled at the same time. But I knew that things were very definitely not okay.

Bobby sat across the table in the Colonial Inn taproom. I told him the whole story: the original conflict with Veronica about whether and where we would live together; her suspiciousness about Marjorie Morris even before I realized there was anything to be suspicious about; the fight eight days earlier that resulted in her walking out; my suspiciousness regarding her and Andrew Galloway; and, finally, the affair with Marjorie that justified all of Veronica's suspiciousness.

"And then there's Melissa," I said. "She absorbed a double hit this afternoon. First the news about Mrs. Winnicot, and then Veronica. I'm worried about how this is going to affect her."

Bobby swirled his empty glass, then set it down on the table and looked at me with a blank expression on his face.

"Well?" I said. "Say something. Do you have any advice?"

He shrugged. "Sure. Stop thinking with your penis."

"My penis?"

"Your penis. Or that thing hanging between your legs that passes for one. Penises are for peeing and occasional screwing. I'm told that in some cultures they make excellent paperweights and pincushions. But they're not for thinking."

"I'm not thinking with my penis."

"Come on now," he replied, clearly exasperated. "You had something good going with Veronica, and you risked it for a roll with someone you hardly know. What is it about her, anyway? What is it about Marjorie that makes you think she's worth the problems she's causing?"

"She's not causing the problems. I am."

"Well, that's true enough."

Bobby ordered another drink. I sipped my sparkling water. I said, "There's a passion there that I've never felt with anyone else."

"Oh, give me a break."

"There is."

"Yeah, well, take a cold shower."

"Easy for you to say."

"It's *not* easy for me to say. I've been married for seventeen years, faithful the whole time. I'm well acquainted with cold showers. It's all part of the bargain."

"You don't have to sound so pissed off."

"I *am* pissed off," he said. "You're acting like a jerk."

"It has nothing to do with you," I said, and then remembered I had spoken the very same words to Melissa a few hours earlier.

"Then why did you drag me out here to talk about it?"

"All right. Forget it. Sorry for the imposition." I tossed a couple of dollars on the table and walked away.

As I headed toward the exit I heard him say, "Now, *that's* mature."

"I can't stay long," I said. "Can we talk for a little while?"

"Of course," Marjorie replied. "Come in."

We sat on the couch in the sunroom. It was well past sunset. I could see distant headlights on the cars passing on Elm Street where the road crosses over the river.

"Veronica knows about us," I said.

She looked surprised. "I probably shouldn't say this, but I was prepared to go on secretly as long as you wanted to. I didn't know if you were going to tell her. I certainly didn't expect you to tell her so soon." She placed a hand on my arm and stroked it lightly.

I was sorely tempted to take credit for the behavior she was crediting me for. But instead I said, "I didn't tell her. In fact, I did my best to hide it from her. But she figured it out."

I recounted the events of the morning: my lie about spending the night at home, and Veronica's discovery of the truth. I wondered to myself where I would be right now if the weather had been different that day, if the telltale pattern of rain on the ground hadn't given me away.

"What did you tell her about you and me?"

"I didn't have to say anything. She already knew. We had an argument about you a week ago Sunday, after we saw you at Merriam's Corner. She said she could tell that you were interested in me. I told her she was imagining things."

"But she was right."

"She also said she could tell I was interested in you."

"Were you?"

"Yes, but I was trying hard not to admit it to myself. This morning, after it became clear that I had lied about being home all night, she just filled in the missing blanks with the obvious answers. And then she left."

She considered this for a minute or two, then said, "Are you sorry it turned out this way?"

"I'm not sorry I came here. I *am* sorry for the hurt I caused for Veronica. And Melissa." I looked at her. "I don't know how this is going to turn out. I don't even know how I *want* it to turn out. I can't promise anything to you."

"I'll take the chance, Harry. I've been hurt before."

When she said that, I remembered the crisscross scar on her wrist. Without thinking, I glanced down at it.

Marjorie saw me looking at her wrist. She said, "I was married once. I think I mentioned that when I saw you in the cemetery. I was very young, right out of college. Too much fighting. Too much cocaine. And when he finally left me, too much pain." Marjorie raised her wrist so I could get a better view. "This was supposed to be my way out. I failed."

"I'm glad."

"So am I. I haven't always been glad. And it wasn't the last time I thought about wanting to die. But I never tried to hurt myself again. And I am glad now."

She leaned against my shoulder. I wrapped my arm around her and we watched the cars on the overpass in the distance.

She said, "I feel like I should tell you this. I'm not sure why. I did something extremely stupid a few months ago. I got involved with someone at the school. But it's all over now. I just wanted you to know that."

My beeper sounded. We both tensed. I checked the read-out and saw my own home phone number. "My daughter or my housekeeper is trying to find me." I checked my watch; it was nine-fifteen.

I went into the kitchen and called home. Mrs. Winnicot answered. "A woman named Roslyn Maxwell called. She says you know her."

"I do." She was dean of students at Concord Academy, the person who referred Michael Cafferty to me.

I dialed the number Mrs. Winnicot gave me. Roslyn Maxwell answered on the first ring. "Harry, can you come over to the school right away?"

"Sure. What's wrong?"

"We have a student named Theo Richardson. He just killed himself. And Michael Cafferty has barricaded himself in his room."

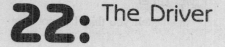

22: The Driver

The three-story dormitory looked like an old Colonial home, and probably had once been one. I arrived there less than five minutes after speaking with Dean Roslyn Maxwell. Two police cruisers and an ambulance were parked outside.

Roslyn greeted me at the door. About fifteen teenagers were milling around in the common area on the first floor. "The police wanted the students to vacate the second and third floors," Roslyn said. She introduced me as a doctor to the police officer stationed at the base of the stairwell, then led me to the second floor.

Through an open doorway, I saw two paramedics tending a stretcher. A human form lay completely still upon it, covered with a drab-green blanket. A uniformed police officer was taking pictures of the room. On the floor in the middle of the room was a knotted sheet, crumpled into a ball. It was directly under the light fixture.

"He hanged himself," Roslyn informed me. She directed me to the next dorm room. The door was closed. "This is Michael Cafferty's room. He ran in there when the police evacuated the floor, a half hour ago, and he won't come out." She knocked. "Michael, it's Dean Maxwell again. I have Dr. Kline with me."

"I know," he answered. "I heard you talking to him. For

what it costs to go to school here, you should be able to afford thicker doors."

A sense of humor, even a macabre one, is generally in-
compatible with actively suicidal behavior. When I heard
Michael's snide remark, I breathed a little easier.

I said, "Michael, I'd like to speak with you."

"Okay."

After a few seconds I said, "Well, may I speak with
you?"

"I said okay. Go ahead. I can hear you."

"Can I come in?"

"Not now. I want to be alone."

"Are you all right?"

"Oh, sure. I feel great. How do *you* feel?"

It was a barbed remark. He'd come to me that morning
because he was worried about his friend. Now his friend
was dead. Who could blame him for feeling bitter?

I said, "This is an awful thing. I'd really like to come in
and talk to you."

"I just want to be alone. Maybe a little later."

Just then a familiar form lumbered up the stairs, potbelly
first. He stood in the doorway of the dead boy's room, just
a few yards away. "Well, well," said Alfred Korvich. "Run
into any trees lately? What brings you here?"

"I asked him to come," Roslyn said. "One of our students is very upset by what has happened here tonight."

"The Cafferty kid?"

"How did you know?" she asked.

He smiled. "Ol' Uncle Al knows everything." He beckoned me to step into the open room with him. He pulled
back the blanket as far as the corpse's shoulders. "Know
him?"

He was tall, with long, straight hair. He did look familiar,
though I knew we'd never met. "No," I said.

"You do know his name, though."

"Dean Maxwell said his name was Theo Richardson."

"And you've heard his name before, of course."

Sure, I thought. The one with the guilty conscience. But Korvich would have no way of knowing that. I said, "No."

He said, "Theodore Richardson. The one who started up Lorraine Peterson's Buick while she was in Palm Beach."

Mrs. Peterson had called him Teddy Richardson. And Michael Cafferty had referred to him only as Theo, with no last name. No wonder I hadn't made the connection.

He's a nice boy, very . . . delicate. That's how Mrs. Peterson had described the dead boy. Michael implied that Theo and his roommate might be gay lovers. The dead boy's roommate was named Junie. Alfred Korvich thought Junie was a sociopath who was responsible for a string of local burglaries and had asked me to persuade Michael Cafferty to give testimony against him. I witnessed Junie lunging after Marjorie Morris. Marjorie refused to let me report the matter to Dean Roslyn Maxwell. Dean Maxwell was the one who referred Michael Cafferty to me.

What the hell did all of this mean? It gave me a headache thinking about it.

Alfred Korvich asked Roslyn, "Did you tell him about the letter?"

"No."

Korvich opened a small notebook. "The boy left a letter on his desk, right next to his glasses. I sealed it up for now, but I wrote down what it said."

Roslyn said, "If you'll excuse me, I need to see if the headmaster has been able to make contact with the Richardson family. I'll be in the dorm manager's apartment if you need me." She went downstairs.

Korvich read from the notebook. " 'To the family of Charles Morris. I had no idea. I'm sorry. May God forgive me.' "

The paramedics carried the stretcher downstairs and outside to the waiting ambulance.

Korvich and I were alone in the room. He said, "This sounds like a confession to me."

"What do you think he meant when he said, 'I had no idea'?"

He shrugged. "Who knows? 'I had no idea I'd have to hit him twice to kill him?' 'I had no idea he was such a bleeder?' Got me."

I walked into the hallway and over to Michael Cafferty's door. I knocked and asked him if I could enter. He said he wanted to be alone. I tried the doorknob anyway; it was still locked.

Alfred Korvich overheard us. He come over, pounded hard on the door, and bellowed, "Michael Cafferty, this is the chief of police for the town of Concord. We're sealing off the entire second floor until the morning. You can open the door, or you can stand back while I break the damn thing down. Your choice. I'll count to ten."

He got as far as the number three, and then the door opened slowly from the inside.

"Smart choice, kid. They'd probably just tack the repair bill onto your tuition bill. Go ahead, Doc." He held open the door for me, then shut it after I entered the room.

Michael offered me a chair. I sat down and looked at the wall decorations: a poster from a rock band called the Red Hot Chili Peppers; a bulletin board with pictures of nubile, bikini-clad women from *Baywatch*; a retouched photo depicting a handshake between a goofily grinning Alfred E. Neuman and an equally goofily grinning Dan Quayle.

There were three dead potted plants on a shelf above one of the beds. "My roommate's," he said. "He calls it his low-upkeep shelf. He has a strange sense of humor."

Michael sat on his bed with his back against the wall. He picked up a soft-drink can from his end table and took a sip. "Theo is dead," he said.

"I know."

"This is my fault. I knew he was upset. I should have done something."

"You did do something. You came to see me. I listened to what you said and didn't take it seriously enough. You exercised good judgment. You can take yourself off the hook."

He thought about that for a while as he twiddled something in his hand.

I said, "The police have a suicide note from Theo. He implicated himself in a hit-and-run accident on Musketaquid Road last month. Is that the terrible thing that you were referring to this morning?"

He nodded.

"I don't understand. You told me Junie was the one who did something terrible. You said Theo was blaming himself, but that it really wasn't his fault."

"It *wasn't* his fault. Junie knew Theo had a key to that car up on Nashawtuc Hill. It was Junie's idea to go for a little joyride. Theo didn't want to, but Junie had, like, this weird power over him. So Theo passed the key over to him. Junie was the one driving. Theo was just a passenger. The only thing Theo did wrong was let him drive the car—and then keep quiet about it after he hit that man."

"Is that what Theo told you?"

Michael considered the question for several seconds. "No."

"You mean, Junie told you he was the driver?"

"No."

I was puzzled for a few seconds, and then the obvious dawned on me. In my office that morning he said: *It involves me, too.*

"You were in the car, weren't you, Michael?"

He nodded. "I was in the backseat. You've got to believe me, Dr. Kline—nobody wanted anything like this to happen. Afterwards I wanted to tell someone, but I didn't want Theo or Junie to get in trouble. And Theo was too frightened to tell anyone. And Junie said if we just kept quiet, no one would ever know. But I knew. And Theo knew."

He thought it was an accidental killing. He probably assumed Junie rammed Charles Morris the second time because he was in a panic to get away from the accident scene. He obviously didn't know about the hand-drawn map. Michael Cafferty didn't realize he had witnessed a premeditated murder.

I remembered Korvich telling me that they found a partial fingerprint in the backseat area. They also discovered a soft-drink tab in the otherwise pristine interior; they found it on the floor near the rear seat.

I looked at Michael's soda can. The tab had been pulled off. I said, "What's that you're twiddling in your hand?"

"Huh? Oh, this. It's just the top piece from my can of Coke. Nervous habit. I pull them off all the time. Don't worry—I'm not thinking of cutting my wrists." He looked at me and said, "What am I supposed to do now?"

"I want to see you in my office first thing tomorrow morning. In the meantime I'm going to ask Dean Maxwell to have you housed in the infirmary tonight."

"The infirmary?"

"Yes. You've had a shock. I'd like to have you in the infirmary in case you have any problems during the night."

He looked confused, but he agreed to go along with my recommendation.

"Stay here," I said. "I'm going to find Dean Maxwell to tell her what I want to happen."

I shut the door behind me and headed downstairs. I wasn't really worried that Michael might face a medical or psychiatric emergency during the night. I wanted him in the infirmary because it was the easiest way of placing him under observation in a protected environment. He didn't know it, but he was the only living witness to a cold-blooded killing. But I knew it. And Junie knew it.

Roslyn was talking to the dorm manager downstairs. I asked the manager to excuse himself and he obliged. I turned to Roslyn and said, "Do you trust me?"

"Of course I do."

"I want you to have Michael Cafferty placed in the infirmary overnight, in a room by himself. An interior room with no windows. I want you to have a campus security guard seated outside his door at all times—and I mean *all* times. If anything unusual happens, call me immediately. And don't let him leave. Tell security that they should restrain him if he tries to go anywhere. Call me as soon as he wakes up, and then have someone drive him to my office."

She looked at me intently. "What's wrong, Harry?"

"I can't tell you. That's why I asked if you trust me."

She considered this for a moment or two. "I'll make sure it all happens the way you've described. And I'll drive him to your office myself."

We walked upstairs to get Michael. Roslyn called the infirmary and then the campus security office. A security guard arrived a few minutes later to take Michael to the infirmary.

Alfred Korvich walked into Michael's room just as he was being escorted out. "Your name is Michael Cafferty, correct?"

"Yes, sir."

"I'd like to ask you some questions about what happened here tonight."

I said, "He's in a state of exhaustion, Chief. I've made arrangements for him to be placed under medical observation. Can you wait until tomorrow?"

Korvich stared at me for several seconds. Finally, he said, "All right. It'll wait until tomorrow."

As Michael walked toward the door he turned to me and said, "You can take this." He handed me the ring tab. "Like I said, I'm not going to cut my wrists." All of this happened under the police chief's watchful eye.

Korvich spied the open Coke can sitting on the end table across the room from him. He scratched his head, rubbed his chin, and then began to walk toward it.

Just then there was a commotion outside the room. Someone shouted, "Hey, you can't go up there," and then I heard footsteps bounding up the stairs.

Korvich turned toward the door and walked quickly into the hallway. I grabbed the Coke can and emptied its remaining liquid into the soil of one of the dead plants. I was just about to crush it—probably not as expertly as I'd seen Warren Oberlin do it, but well enough to be able to fit it into my pocket—when I realized that doing so would make the can's importance obvious to Korvich. Instead I held it in plain view as if it were my soft drink, and left the room.

A muscular young man with thick blond hair finished loping to the top of the stairwell just as I came into the hallway. He almost knocked me over as he dashed toward the room where the suicide took place. He stopped in his tracks inches away from me. Our eyes locked on each other. He glared at me: a cold look that spoke of absolute maliciousness, abject terror, or both.

I didn't know if he recognized me from our indirect encounter four days earlier. But I certainly recognized Junie.

He brushed past me and headed toward Theo's room—his room. Alfred Korvich jumped into the doorway, blocking Junie's access.

"Get out of my way!" Junie tried to push his way into the room, but Korvich stood his ground and the young man bounced off of him. "Who the fuck are you?"

"I'm your local police chief, worm."

"I want to get into my room."

"No way, fella. Police investigation going on."

By now the uniformed officer from the foot of the stairs had made his way to the second floor.

Junie pointed at Korvich. "Do you know who I am? I'm Carter Ellington Junior. The senator's son."

"I don't care if you're *Duke* Ellington. Go downstairs with the others. You'll all be sleeping elsewhere tonight. And you'll be sleeping in police lockup if you're still here when I reach the number ten."

He began counting. I half expected him to say: *Go ahead. Make my day.* Junie stood there with his hands on his hips until Korvich reached the number eight, then turned away and walked down the stairwell.

Korvich looked at me and gave a little nod. I nodded back. Then he noticed the Coke can in my hand. I raised it to my lips and pretended to drink from the now empty can. I nodded again, but he didn't return it.

"You're a strange guy, Doc."

"Getting stranger all the time, Chief."

He turned in the doorway and surveyed the scene. "I always hate it when a kid dies, especially this way. At least he succeeded. I knew another case, kid hanged himself, but instead of dying he just suffered permanent brain damage. He's still living, nothing but a vegetable."

"Then he didn't hang himself," I said.

"Of course he did. I just told you."

"To hang means to execute by suspension. If you don't die, then it's an attempted hanging, not a hanging. You can look it up in the dictionary."

He wheeled around and snarled at me. "Yeah? Well, *you* look it up. And while you're at it, look up 'condescending' and 'asshole.' "

I left him standing there. I walked downstairs, through the milling crowd, and out to my car I tossed Michael Cafferty's soda can in my litter bag and leaned back in my car seat.

I recalled my first session with him, almost two weeks earlier. He asked me a series of questions, all of which seemed to represent an attempt to understand what the limits of confidentiality were. I assumed all of the questions dealt with hypothetical situations.

Perhaps I should have listened more closely to one question in particular: *Suppose I wanted to talk to you about a murder?*

23: The Right Thing

On Monday morning, Michael Cafferty had told me: *I know what I should do. That doesn't require a rocket scientist. But doing the right thing might involve hurting a friend.*

By Monday night, his friend was dead. And though Michael probably didn't realize it, the police were likely honing in on him as an accessory in the hit-and-run murder of Charles Morris.

Actually, there was no reason why Michael *would* think the police might come for him. As far as he knew, Charles Morris's death was an accident. He had no cause to believe that he would even be charged with leaving the scene of an accident, since he wasn't the driver.

I knew better. I recalled the felony murder law Alfred Korvich told me about: All participants in a joint-venture crime could be charged with murder if someone was killed. The three students had stolen a car. For reasons I couldn't even begin to guess at, Junie had committed a premeditated murder. I knew that if Michael didn't go to the police on his own, then by the end of the day he might be arrested on a charge that could put him in prison forever.

I assumed it wouldn't take Korvich very long to tie Michael to the hit-and-run. The police had recovered a partial fingerprint—Michael's print—from the murder vehicle. All they needed to do was match it against Michael's finger-prints.

I made my first phone call at six-thirty on Tuesday morning. "I'm sorry to bother you so early. In fact. I'm sorry to bother you at all. But I have an emergency with a patient who may be charged in a murder case. I need some information, and I couldn't think of any other way to get it so early in the day."

Veronica said, "That would be a pretty ridiculous story to make up if all you were doing was looking for an excuse to call me."

"Yes, it would."

"So I guess you're not making it up."

"I'm not making it up."

Veronica considered that for a few seconds. "What do you want to know?"

"How useful is a partial fingerprint to the police?"

"Not useful at all if they're trying to get a computer match with an unknown suspect. Very useful if they have prints from a known suspect to compare with the partial."

"When the police arrest a juvenile, do they subject him to the same booking procedure they use on adults? Do they take his fingerprints?"

"Each case is different," Veronica said "What charge are we talking about?"

"Attempted breaking and entering, I suppose. My patient was caught after he tried to break into someone's house."

"Any prior criminal history?"

"No."

"Did the arrest occur in Concord?"

"Yes."

"Are you sure he's younger than seventeen? Because in this state, once you reach that age you get arraigned in adult court."

"He's younger than seventeen," I replied.

"Well, then. You have a minor delinquency charge, a small town with very little serious crime, and a defendant

who has no previous problems with the law. I'd be surprised if they would take fingerprints in a juvenile case like
that, unless your patient had a totally incompetent lawyer.
Some court-appointed attorneys just go through the motions."

"The kid's father is a multimillionaire. I suspect he had
a good lawyer."

"Then you can be pretty sure they never took his fingerprints."

That probably gave me a couple of hours to work with.
If the police already had his prints to match against the partial print, then they were probably already readying an arrest warrant. But if they didn't, they'd have to find and lift
fingerprints from Michael's room.

Veronica said, "Is there anything else you wanted?"

"No. Wait—yes. If I promise to stay out of the way,
would you be willing to visit Melissa this evening? Maybe
you could take her out to dinner. She misses you."

"You would really let me do that?"

"Of course."

"Tell her I'll be there at six. Tell her I miss her, too."

I hung up, then immediately dialed Bobby. I said,
"Number one, I'm really sorry for last night. Number two,
where will you be in a couple of hours?"

He replied, "Number one, don't worry about it. Number
two, I'm taking the day off. Thanks for waking me, by the
way. Why do you ask?"

"I'm seeing a patient who may decide he needs a criminal attorney immediately."

"You know I don't do that sort of work anymore."

"Just to handle the arrest proceedings, which could happen in a few hours. He doesn't even know he might be
arrested today, so I doubt he's made contingency plans."

"If he doesn't know, how do you know?"

"It's a long story."

He sighed. "What's the charge?"

"It's a homicide case."

"Shit."

"Is that a legal term?"

"Sometimes. Look, I don't want to do it, but I'll do it if you want me to."

"If my patient wants you to, then I want you to."

He yawned. "I hate thinking about work so early in the morning. All right—if he wants you to want me to do it, call me. Did that sentence make any sense?"

"Yes. Thanks. Good-bye."

I wondered how much progress Alfred Korvich was making piecing things together. What if Veronica was wrong about the fingerprints? Perhaps the police had made a special point of taking his prints after he refused to tell them who his accomplices were. I could almost hear Korvich saying, "If he wants to act like a criminal, we'll treat him like one."

I decided not to take any chances. I called Roslyn Maxwell at her apartment on the grounds of Concord Academy. I asked her to have Michael Cafferty rousted from bed immediately, and to bring him to my office as soon as possible.

"Yesterday you told me you already knew what the right thing is. What do you think that is?"

"To go to the police, obviously. Maybe if I had, Theo would still be alive."

We didn't have time right then to go down that track. I said, "Are you still considering it?"

"I don't know. I mean, it was an accident. That old guy never should have run on such a dark road so early in the morning. I looked it up in the library last week. You can get as much as fifteen years for motor-vehicle homicide. That's a long time. I mean, the guy is dead. Why ruin Junie's life, too, if he can get away with it?"

"Is there a downside to keeping Junie's secret?"

He sighed. "I know Theo's parents. They seem pretty nice. I guess it would make things a little easier for them if they knew he wasn't the driver."

"Anything else?"

He thought about that for a few seconds. "Well, the victim's daughter teaches at my school. I don't know her, but she seems nice enough, too. Junie knows her, though. I don't know how he can look her in the eye."

"Anything else?"

He pondered my question for quite a while. "I don't think so."

"Are you prepared to live with the lie of not telling?"

"The lie of not telling versus ruining a friend's life. Seems like a toss-up to me."

"Why did you get so angry with me last week when I asked you about Junie? You said, 'That's a closed subject.'"

"I didn't like the way he was blowing the whole thing off, while Theo—who didn't do anything nearly as bad—was suffering inside."

I was struggling for a way not to tell him what I knew: that it was a case of intentional murder, and that he could well be charged with some sort of accessory role. I wanted him to do the right thing on his own.

I said, "Yesterday you told me your father would know what to do if he was in your situation. What do you suppose that would be?"

He laughed. "I don't know. Probably pay someone to do whatever was necessary to make the problem go away."

"I doubt that."

"Why? Too hard to pull off?"

"You obviously have a conscience, considering how hard you are on him and on yourself. And conscience doesn't grow on trees. It's usually passed down from parent to child. Perhaps there's more of him in you than you realize."

He sat there silently for several minutes. I had a fantasy of cruisers surrounding my office, and Alfred Korvich standing outside with a bullhorn. *We know you're in there, Cafferty. Come out with your hands up.*

Finally, he turned to me: confused, adrift, searching. "Please tell me, Dr. Kline. What should I do?"

I had heard that question from my patients thousands of

times over the years. And almost invariably, I sidestepped their requests that I take the responsibility for making their decisions. When you make a decision for a patient, you damage the sense of confidence and independence that you should be helping him build.

I thought, I can't tell him what to do. I could help him weigh the pros and cons of his various options I could help him explore his thoughts and his feelings about Theo, Junie, and himself. I could help him focus on the reasons behind his reluctance to decide for himself. But I couldn't make his decision for him. I told myself I had no choice but to look him directly in the eye and tell him that only he could choose his course of action.

I looked him directly in the eye. I said, "You *must* go to the police immediately."

He breathed deeply; I couldn't tell whether my answer had brought him relief or more anxiety. "You mean, like, just go over there right now?"

"It may be wise to talk with a lawyer first. After all, you'll be putting yourself right in the middle of a criminal investigation."

He thought about that, then said, "I can call the lawyer my father hired for the breaking-and-entering case. His office is in Wellesley."

It was almost nine o'clock. Waiting for his lawyer could waste precious time. I said, "The sooner you take care of this, the better you'll feel."

"What do you think I should do?"

I'd already given him one direct suggestion. Like most things, the second time is easier. "I know a lawyer here in Concord who may be able to help you. I'll give him a call."

I let Bobby use my office to meet with his new client. I went to the kitchen and toasted a bagel for myself, my first food of the day. On the table was a note that Melissa had somehow found time to write before she left for school. It read: *Veronica is taking me to Papa Gino's for dinner. Thank you. I LOVE YOU.*

I scanned the morning *Globe*. There was nothing about Theo Richardson. I guess a teenager's suicide isn't unusual enough anymore to make the Boston headlines. I figured the weekly *Concord Journal* would have an article on Thursday.

After about twenty minutes Bobby walked into my kitchen and poured himself a glass of orange juice. "I'm taking the kid back to his dorm room. He wants to shower and get some fresh clothes. They rushed him over here for some reason and he didn't get a chance to do that stuff before he came. Then we're going over to the police station."

"The dean of students rushed him over here because I asked her to. Just like you should rush him over to the police station. Hell, you shouldn't even wait that long. I think you should try to reach Alfred Korvich by phone right now."

"What are you worried about?"

"This isn't just a vehicular-homicide case, Bobby. He doesn't realize it, but he might get charged with first-degree murder."

"What in the world are you talking about?"

I told him about the hand-drawn map, the soda-can tab, and the partial fingerprint. "Korvich is building a murder case," I said, "and anyone who was in that car could get caught in it."

"How do you know this?"

"From Korvich."

"I had no idea that you and Lower Case *b* had grown so close."

"He's developed strong feelings for me. He told me himself."

"Gosh. Is my job in jeopardy?"

"What job?"

"My job as your best friend."

"Nah, no one else would be crazy enough to take it."

Bobby drained his juice glass and placed it in the kitchen sink. "Your patient thinks his witness statement is going to get his friend locked up for a few years. Now it looks like he could send a state senator's son to prison for the rest of his life. I need to review this with him before he makes a final decision."

"What will you advise him?"

"The same as you would. Run, don't walk to the nearest police station. Do not pass 'Go.' Do not collect two hundred dollars."

"Just don't tell him you learned all this from me."

"Why?"

"Korvich gave me this information in confidence, as a favor to me, before he had any idea who was involved. I'd rather not have a patient know I can't be trusted with a secret."

24: Nightmare

Bobby and Michael left my office a little after ten o'clock. I knew Alfred Korvich would waste no time getting an arrest warrant for Junie after taking Michael's statement. The arrest of a popular state senator's son for first-degree murder would trigger a media feeding frenzy. And then Marjorie would be beset by journalists—perhaps as early as noon—looking for her reaction.

I didn't want her to learn the news that way. I called Marjorie and told her I was taking her on a picnic. We picked up sandwiches at a shop in town, and by eleven we were sitting on a blanket in the shade of a maple tree by Buttrick mansion, atop the hill that sloped gently down to North Bridge.

She said, "The emergency with one of your patients last night—did everything turn out okay?"

"My patient is all right."

"I'm glad." She yawned. "You must get nervous every time your beeper goes off."

"Yes, I usually do."

She yawned again. "I couldn't fall asleep after you rushed out. And when I finally did, I began having nightmares about my father again."

"Nightmares about the accident?"

"No. My dreams started long before then. They started when I moved into his house last year. I think I used to

270

have them when I was a child, but I'm not certain. There's so much I can't remember from back then, no matter how hard I try."

"Is it always the same dream?"

"I'm not sure. I don't remember much of the content, just the feeling. I'm always afraid of suffocating in the dream. My father is there, but he thinks it's funny. He knows I'm frightened, but he just grins. And then I realize it's him I'm afraid of, and I wake up terrified."

"Sometimes dreams can be as frightening as something real."

"My therapist thinks they probably *are* real." She hesitated for a few seconds. "I told him about the dreams, and about how frightened I felt in the middle of the night. The next thing I knew, I was telling him about how I've always locked my bedroom door, ever since I was a little girl, even when I was living alone." She lay back on the blanket and closed her eyes. "My therapist thinks I may be a survivor of childhood sexual abuse."

"What do you think?"

"It would help explain a lot of the unhappiness in my life." She ran a hand through her curls, over and over. "I don't know anymore. I started seeing him because I was depressed and couldn't sleep. When he said I was an incest victim, the idea seemed ridiculous to me. Then he said I was probably repressing the memories, but that they were still there, somewhere inside me, frozen in time. Like this fossil he has on his desk. An insect preserved intact inside a piece of amber. He said he could help me get in touch with the memories, and that it would help me feel better. Every week he tries exercises with me to try to free up my memories. And sometimes I start remembering. But the memories don't feel any more solid than the dreams, and I'm still depressed a lot of the time. My therapist says it will take a while. I don't know. I'm thinking of stopping therapy, anyway. I canceled it last Thursday so I could have lunch with you."

From the moment she mentioned the fossilized insect, I had no doubt who her therapist was. I felt a sickening sense of dread in my stomach: like seeing an accident unfold before me in slow motion, forced to watch, unable to stop it from happening.

It gets tricky when you try to warn someone about a destructive therapist. What I already planned to tell her was going to be enough of a shock for one day; I pushed my worry about Marjorie's therapy with Frank Porter aside for the moment.

I said, "I have something important to tell you."

She bolted into an upright sitting position. "Oh, no."

"What's wrong?"

"That solemn look on your face," she replied. "Are you going to tell me we can't see each other anymore?"

"No. This has nothing to do with us. It's about your father's death." I thought I saw her pull a couple of inches farther away from me. I said, "The police are going to make an arrest today, probably within the next couple of hours."

Her eyes widened. "How do you know that?"

"That's a long story, and a lot of it is confidential information from a patient. When you and I had lunch at the pizza shop last week, you said you didn't believe that your father was murdered intentionally. But he was."

She sat quietly, waiting for me to continue.

"On March seventh, three teenagers stole a car on Nashawtuc Hill, not far from your house. They drove down the hill, turned right on Musketaquid Road, and struck your father." I saw her lower lip tremble almost imperceptibly. "Would you like me to stop?"

"No. If I have to hear this from someone, I want it to be you."

"They pulled to a stop and turned around. Your father was still standing, or he had fallen but struggled back to his feet. They hit him a second time."

Tears filled her eyes. "They said he died instantly."

"Regrettably, no. I'm sorry to have to tell you that."

She turned away from me and shifted her gaze down the hill toward the bridge. "But it could still be an accident.

The driver could have panicked after he hit my father, then driven away so fast he hit him again without meaning to."

I shook my head. "There's something else. The police found a hand-drawn map of the Nashawtuc Hill area inside the car. Your father's jogging route was marked on it. Your house and the spot where he was killed were marked on it as well. That's not something the driver would have done afterward."

She sat there silently for several seconds with her hands folded in her lap, then said, "My God."

"One of the teenagers committed suicide last night. That was the emergency I rushed out to deal with. He was a student at Concord Academy. His name was Theodore Richardson. Some people called him Teddy. I think most people at the school called him Theo."

"I'm not sure. . . . A skinny boy? Long hair and glasses?"

"Yes."

"I think I met him once. I don't understand. Why on earth would Theo Richardson set out to kill my father?"

"He didn't. He just helped steal the car. The driver was someone else. Someone you know." I paused, letting her prepare herself for what was coming. "Carter Ellington Junior murdered your father."

Marjorie had no reaction at first: just a blank, uncomprehending stare. Then she brought her hands up to her face, as if covering herself from view could somehow hide the awful truth from finding her. She bit down on her hand, hard, muffling a scream.

She stood, unsteady on her feet. Her eyes darted in all directions, as if she were a penned animal looking for any point of escape. And then she ran down the hill toward the river: arms flailing wildly like tattered sails in a strong wind.

I jumped up and ran after her. Just before I caught up with her she dropped to her knees. She clutched her stomach and began to gasp for air. I placed my hands on her shoulders, trying to steady her. She looked at me: a wild, panicked look. Her face was flushed, and her breathing cycled rapidly and out of control. She tried to say something, but the words were choked behind the fast-paced cycle of inhaled and expelled air.

I lifted her in my arms. She felt light and insubstantial. I carried her back to the blanket. I placed her down in a seated position, supported her weight against my body, and reached for the paper bag that had held our sandwiches. I placed the bag over her mouth. She resisted, like someone who feared suffocation. I thought about her recurring nightmare.

"Breathe into the bag," I said. "It will calm you down."

The air mixture rich in carbon dioxide soon had its intended effect. Her hyperventilation attack abated. Her body went limp, and I slowly let her slide onto her back. Now the tears flowed as she lay there. They welled up in her eyes, then spilled out across her face. I dabbed them with a napkin and stroked her forehead.

After a while her tears subsided. She sat up and faced me. "I told you that I did something very stupid, that I got involved in a relationship that I had a hard time getting out of." She hesitated. "The person I got involved with was Junie. Dear Jesus, what have I done?"

We drove around for a while, neither one of us speaking. We crossed over into the wooded countryside of Carlisle, then circled back toward Concord through Acton.

Marjorie said, "You're thirteen years older than me. It's been that way my entire life. Until I came home from California, I don't think I ever made love to anyone who was less than five years older than me."

"How old is your ex-husband?"

"Almost your age."

"One foot in the grave." My feeble attempt at humor fell flat.

She said, "Last fall, I told my therapist that I'd only been with older men. He said it was because I never got beyond my relationship with my father. He said I was replicating it over and over again, getting involved in unstable relationships with older men who used me and hurt me. He called it repetition compulsion."

We passed the small shopping centers and fast-food restaurants that dot Acton's main road: establishments that Concord's town fathers would never allow to sprout up in our town.

"My therapist was already convinced that I was molested by my father when I was a girl. He took my attraction to older men as a final proof."

"What did you think of that?"

"I didn't like him trying to convince me that something I didn't really remember was definitely true. I guess I was looking for some way to prove him wrong. So I told him about someone who *wasn't* older than me. I told him about this student at the school I was attracted to."

"Junie?"

She nodded. "Frank—that's my therapist's name, he goes by his first name with his clients—Frank asked me what was stopping me from having a relationship with Junie. I said I didn't think it would be wise to start something up with a high-school student. Frank started in again on my father and this repetition-compulsion thing. We got into an argument, and then he said if I was so sure I was right, why didn't I initiate something with Junie?"

"Jesus," I muttered.

She hesitated for a few seconds. "Two days later I seduced him."

"I think you need a different therapist."

"I think I need a different life." She paused. "You must hate me."

"I don't hate you."

"You may not hate me, but you're going to leave me. No—please don't say anything. I've known all along my chances were slim." She sighed deeply. "I'm tired, Harry. I'm just so tired. When will it all end?"

Just before we crossed over the town line into Concord, we passed the Acton Cinema.

"I'll be damned," I said. "*Indecent Proposal* actually *is* playing here."

"Is that supposed to be some sort of sick joke?"

"No. I was just thinking about a conversation I had with a friend."

I turned onto Elm Street, heading toward Simon Willard Road. "Do you have any idea why Junie killed your father?"

"Probably because I broke off our relationship. I began sleeping with him last November. I ended it in January. He couldn't take no for an answer. You saw a little of that last week, when you came to school to pick me up for lunch."

"But why would he kill your father?"

Marjorie shrugged. "People do strange things when they can't get what they want. Maybe he was trying to hurt me by killing him. For all I know, maybe he was trying to kill me."

"I don't understand."

"I used to go jogging along the same route. I think I told you that once before. Sometimes I went with my father, and sometimes I ran a little earlier. Junie knew that, because he went running with me once when my father was out of town. Maybe he thought it was me on Musketaquid Road that morning, not my father. After all, it was still dark outside."

At about one o'clock, I turned left onto Simon Willard Road and pulled over to the curb in front of her house. We sat there for a minute or two. She said, "It was a colossal mistake on my part. Terrible, terrible judgment."

I didn't ask to stay. She didn't invite me in. We kissed each other lightly on the cheek, and then she stepped out of the car and disappeared through her front door.

As I pulled away from the curb another car glided to a stop in front of Marjorie's house. A young woman with a notepad emerged from the driver's side; out of the other door stepped a young man carrying a video camera.

I thought: The first of a descending horde.

25: Confession

Within the space of a few hours Carter Ellington Jr. was arrested, booked, arraigned, and released on bail. It's a wonder how quickly things move when your father is the chairman of the state senate's judiciary committee.

The newscasts that night and the papers the next morning were rife with speculation regarding the effect Junie's arrest might have on his father's career. The Republican governor was up for reelection the following year. Senator Ellington was often mentioned as a likely candidate for the Democratic nomination. The governor wasted no time at all telling anyone with a microphone, camera, or notepad that he wasn't interested in commenting on, drawing attention to, or taking advantage of "the good senator's personal problems." His comments were dutifully reported by all the major news organs.

The Middlesex County district attorney, who was also on most pundits' lists of potential Democratic gubernatorial candidates, took the unusual step of handling the arraignment and bail hearing himself. Afterward he, too, wasted little time seeking out anyone who would listen to tell them that he had no comment on "my friend Carter's unfortunate burden."

No one was able to obtain comments from the murdered man's daughter. But who cared? The story in this trial would be the defendant, not the deceased. But I assumed word of Marjorie's affair with Junie would surface in the months to come as the case moved forward to trial. And Marjorie probably assumed the same thing. At least her mother was no longer alive to witness what promised to be an excruciatingly painful public humiliation.

Alfred Korvich called me midmorning. I said, "Do you have something against Wednesdays?"

"What are you talking about?"

"I don't see patients on Wednesdays. I like to relax. Last Wednesday you called me down to the station so I could watch you torment Mrs. Peterson. What's on your mind today?"

"A thank-you, and a request for a personal audience. A little irritable today, aren't you? Look—I really need to talk privately. Can you come to my office?"

A half hour later I was back in the Naugahyde palace on the second floor of the police station. Korvich said, "Thanks for persuading the Cafferty kid to come forward."

"I didn't have anything to do with it."

"That's not what I hear."

"You can't believe everything you hear."

"Yeah, sure. I just want to let you know I'll do what I can to see that he gets a fair deal. Coffee?"

"No, thanks. I'm curious—did you figure out who the partial fingerprint in the backseat came from?"

"Of course. The Cafferty kid gave us a full set of prints yesterday. We were getting ready to work on lifting prints from his room when he came in and saved us the trouble."

"You didn't take his prints when he was arrested for the attempted burglary?"

He shook his head. "We tend not to do that in low-profile juvenile matters."

"How much of an ordeal is he in for? Is this likely to turn into a case of his word against Ellington's?"

Korvich set his coffee down. He sat in a swivel chair, leaned back, and raised his feet onto his desk. "The handwriting on the map seems to match up pretty well with Ellington's. And the map was written on paper that's identical to some paper we found in his room." He yawned, stretched, and drummed his fingers on his armrest. "Oh, yeah—and then there's the little matter of the fingerprints."

"*What* fingerprints?"

He smiled broadly. "Ellington's prints. They're a perfect match to the crystal-clear, nearly complete set we were able to lift from the map right after we found it last week."

"You never told me about those prints."

"Shit, Doc—I wouldn't even tell my *own* psychiatrist everything."

"So you think chances are good for getting a conviction?"

"I don't even think it'll come to trial. I think both sides will try for a plea bargain, maybe second-degree murder. Second-degree murderers can be released on parole after fifteen years. Carter Ellington the younger would get out in his thirties. Better than doing a natural-life sentence on a first-degree murder conviction. In fact, the senator's son has already demonstrated what you might call, oh, a cooperative attitude."

"How so?"

"He gave us a complete statement."

"How complete?"

"There's no such thing as 'how complete,' Doc. Something is either complete or it's not complete. You can look it up in the dictionary."

"Touché."

He nodded. "How's that cut above your eye doing?"

"I'll live. Why do you ask?"

"Because that was part of the defendant's complete statement."

"I don't get it."

"He and Theo followed you into the woods last Friday from a distance. They split up. Whoever found you first was supposed to run into you as hard as he could. Theo passed you, but he chickened out. Ellington is the one who attacked you."

I remembered passing a thin, long-haired teenage boy

with thick glasses on my walk in the woods. No wonder
Theo's corpse looked familiar to me in his dorm room
Monday night.

"Why did he do it?"

"He said he thought you were nosing around in his business. He just wanted to shake you up a little, maybe put
you out of action for a little while. I suspect that if we
hadn't caught up with him he might have tried it again—
that, or something more serious."

I pondered that for a few moments. "How was I nosing
around in his business?"

"He was afraid the Cafferty kid would spill the beans to
you. Which, of course, he eventually did, right?"

"No comment."

"Of course." He brought his feet off his desk and leaned
forward. "There was also the matter of Marjorie Morris. He
thought you were getting too close to her." He waited a few
seconds for a response, then said, "Did you know he was
screwing her?"

"Is that really important?"

"It's not important whether you knew. It *is* important that
he was screwing her. According to his statement, that was
part of the motive." Korvich picked up a manila envelope
from his desktop. "Come with me to the conference room
down the hall."

In the room were an eight-foot table and a half-dozen uncomfortable hard-plastic chairs. Perched on one end of the
table was a television set that was hooked up to a videocassette recorder.

"Have a seat at the other end of the table, Doc. I already
fast-forwarded to the part I want you to see."

He started the tape, then paused it immediately. Junie's
frozen image came onto the screen. He was seated at that
very conference table, at the same end now occupied by the
monitor. At the time the taping was conducted, he was
looking straight ahead at the space I now occupied. The effect was startling: almost as if he were in the room at that

very moment, his face bordered by a rectangular picture frame, looking directly at me.

The previous day's date and the time of taping were displayed as a constant readout at the bottom right of the screen.

Korvich said, "The pair of hands on the right belong to his attorney. The voice asking questions is mine. I was sitting where you are now." He released the pause button and the tape began to roll.

Junie said, "It started the week before Thanksgiving. Marjorie told me I needed to do extra preparation for a play the drama club was rehearsing. She was directing it. I was the male lead. It was just her and me in the building. There was a scene where I'm supposed to sit on a couch and kiss the female lead. Marjorie told me I wasn't holding my arms and hands the right way, and she wanted to coach me through it.

"We sat on a couch, and she was showing me how to position myself. She kept rubbing up against me and I realized she wasn't wearing a bra, and I could feel, uh, feel her, you know, nipples. And I started to get excited, and I think she could tell. Because after a while she excuses herself to go to the bathroom, and when she comes back she's let her hair down and I think she unbuttoned an extra button on her blouse.

"She stood in front of me and said, 'Do you think about me sometimes?' And I don't know what to say to that. She says, 'Because I think about you all the time. I want to be your friend.' And I say, 'We *are* friends.' And she says, 'No, I mean I want to be your *friend*.'

"Then she sat next to me again and asked me if I wanted to touch her." Junie smiled, a nervous smile. "And I guess I didn't need too much convincing. So she unbuttons her blouse completely and lets it fall to the floor. I noticed this small tattoo of a butterfly on her left, uh, left breast. I couldn't take my eyes off of it. After a while she said, 'Are you just going to sit there all night?' And that's when she, uh . . . you know."

Korvich said, "She seduced you."

Junie nodded. "It was the first time I went all the way with someone."

But it wasn't the last. Under Korvich's careful questioning, Junie detailed a series of clandestine couplings, most of them at Marjorie's house when her father was at work or out of town.

"She played it so cool when other people were around. And she played it so hot when it was just the two of us. I didn't know if I was coming or going." His lawyer cleared his throat. Junie said, "Maybe I should find some other way to put that."

Korvich said, "When did things start to change?"

"In January her father caught us, walked right in on us while we were doing it on the floor in front of the fireplace. She told me later that he was supposed to be in New York on business and his meeting was canceled. But you know, sometimes when I look back on it, I wonder if maybe she knew he would be coming home, and maybe she set the whole thing up for him to catch us.

"Anyway, her old man picked me up and slammed me against the wall. He was one mean dude, and pretty strong for an old guy. He asked me if I was one of Marjorie's students, and I said I was. He demanded to know my name. When I told him, he knew immediately who my father is. He said if he ever caught me hanging around his daughter again, he'd see to it that I got expelled and he would make trouble for my father, too.

"Marjorie and I didn't see each other for the next couple of weeks, except in class. It was driving me crazy. I pulled her aside one day and told her I thought I was in love with her. And she said she wanted to be with me, but that it couldn't happen unless we did something about her father. I didn't know what she meant by that when she first said it, but over the next week or two she got more specific.

"She told me her father used to molest her when she was a little girl. She said she hated him. She said she also hated him for standing between us. She asked me to kill him."

Junie went on for several self-serving minutes detailing his attempts over the next several days to dissuade Marjorie: first by joking about her request; then by trying to suggest alternative options, like moving into her own place; then by refusing outright to do as she bid.

"Finally, she said, 'If you won't do it just for love, maybe you'll do it for love and money.' She gave me four thousand dollars. Half up front, half after I . . . after I did what she wanted me to do."

He was silent for a long time. He buried his face in his hands and cried.

Korvich said to him, "You killed Charles Morris for four thousand dollars?"

Junie looked up, weeping. "I killed him because I loved Marjorie. I don't know why I took the money. I don't know why I did anything. It was like she had this hold on me. I couldn't bear to live without her."

According to Junie, Marjorie detailed the jogging route she and her father often followed together. She described the outfits they wore. They settled on a date, and Marjorie said she would be certain her father ran without her that morning.

"I was supposed to use this credit card and driver's license I stole to rent a car under a false name. That part worried me a little. Then I remembered Theo had a key to this car that wasn't being used, that was owned by someone who was out of town."

Korvich addressed him. "Let me see if I have this straight. You were worried about using the stolen ID to rent a car, but you were willing to commit murder."

Junie looked downward. He said nothing.

After several seconds of silence, Korvich continued. "Did you split the money with Theo and Michael?"

Junie shook his head. "They didn't know it was intentional. They thought I hit some guy by accident."

"Why did you take them with you?"

"Theo had the key to the car. He insisted he had to come

along if I went for a ride so he could make sure the car got back okay."

"And Michael Cafferty?"

Junie laughed, a derisive laugh. "He was always tagging along after me, like some goddamn puppy dog. But I knew if I didn't do it that day, I might never have the courage to do it again. Besides, he was drunk. They both were. They managed to get a couple of six-packs somehow. I don't think Michael even realized I hit anyone, not until Theo began yelling."

Marjorie kept her distance from him after the murder. Junie said she told him they couldn't afford to draw attention to themselves. She said they had to wait until the school year was over.

And she gave him more money.

Alfred Korvich stopped the tape. "I don't know about the sex abuse as a motive. I do know Charles Morris had a large estate, and his daughter stands to inherit all of it." He pressed the rewind button. "So—what do you think, Doc? Did Ellington do it for the money, or did he do it for the honey?"

"I think it's a crock of shit," I said. "Totally self-serving bullshit."

He shook his head. "I gotta tell you, Doc. Something didn't sit right with me from the very beginning. She just took the whole thing too calmly when the medical examiner and I went to talk with her. Even when I checked back with her later that day, thinking maybe she had a delayed reaction, she was unusually calm."

"Different people grieve in different ways. But even if she wasn't upset that her father was killed, it doesn't mean she had any role in it."

He reached into the manila envelope and pulled out two snapshots. "We found these in Ellington's room, right where he told us they would be."

He passed them to me. The photos showed Marjorie, naked, posing provocatively on her bed. He said, "Pretty nice, huh? No wonder that kid let himself be led around by his dick."

"He could have stolen these."

"From who?"

I shrugged. "Good point."

"Unfortunately, you can't tell from that angle if she has a butterfly tattoo on her left breast. Come to think of it, though, that may be a good thing."

"Why?"

"When the time comes, we can compel a body examination. If she has that tattoo, I'd say Ellington's credibility rating goes up several notches, wouldn't you? I mean, if it's not in the pictures, but it is on her body, then how else would he know about it?"

She could always argue that Junie had seen the tattoo in *Blood Beach*. But if Korvich didn't know about that film, I didn't see any reason to mention it to him at this point.

I said, "Let's assume, for the sake of argument, that they were having an affair. That doesn't mean she wanted her father killed or that she played any role in Ellington's actions."

"You got an alternative hypothesis?"

I thought for just a couple of seconds. "Sure. They have a brief affair. She comes to her senses and breaks it off. He can't take no for an answer, the old 'if I can't have you, nobody can' routine. He knows she goes jogging along Musketaquid Road. He runs down the wrong person, thinking that he's killing her."

Korvich rubbed his chin. "Not bad." He reached into the manila envelope. "But we got these things from Bay Bank with a judge's order an hour ago. One of them was written less than three weeks ago."

He passed me photocopies of two checks: one written in February, the other in early April. Both were made out by Marjorie Morris. Both were made out to Carter Ellington Jr. And both were in the amount of two thousand dollars.

Korvich said, "You got an alternative hypothesis about *them*?"

I gave the photocopies back to him. "Why did you ask me to come here? Why the hell are you giving all this information about the case to *me*?"

He placed the materials in the manila envelope. "You seem to be pretty good about getting people to come forward. If she's involved, and if she wants to help herself, this is a good time for her to talk with me. Because once the story starts to break—and these stories always break—it will be too late."

"What makes you think I have that much influence with her?"

He paused. "Do you know the Bromleys on Simon Willard Road? Cornelius and Gertrude?"

"No."

"Last Saturday evening they called us to complain about a suspicious car parked in front of their house. They said the man inside the car was just sitting there and didn't appear to have any business being in the neighborhood. We sent an officer to check things out. They told him that right after they made the complaint, the man got out of the car and went into the Morris residence. I guess I don't have to tell you who we traced the car to, do I?"

"No."

"And I guess I don't have to tell you that the car was still parked in the same spot the next morning."

I considered this for a few moments. "Let's assume that she and I are lovers. Aren't you worried the information you've given me will piss me off so much that I'll just let her hang?"

Alfred Korvich smiled at me. For the first time the smile appeared genuinely friendly. He said, "I think you care about her. I think that's what wins out in the end. I guess I'm an incurable romantic, Doc—and I'm completely sincere about that."

26: The Hour of Our Death

Psychiatrists can't read minds.

We study the chemistry of the brain we give medications to alter it.

We listen to our patients' words; we classify them.

We observe our patients' behaviors; we codify them.

We match their complaints and impairments against esoteric theories of psychological development, and we come up with diagnoses and labels that fool us into thinking we understand that which is, ultimately, incomprehensible by man: the human spirit.

There are no foolproof truth serums. There are no undeniably accurate lie detectors. There are no sure-fire techniques for plumbing the depths of a person's soul and extracting absolute. essential, objective truth.

Was Marjorie Morris guilty of conspiracy to commit murder? I didn't presume to have any special power to divine her secret hopes and fears, or her true nature. And I hadn't followed Father John's advice to pray for faith. But I couldn't and didn't believe she was guilty, and for now I was willing to take *that* on faith.

The only evidence Korvich had was Junie's statement and the canceled checks. But Junie had every reason in the world to fabricate a story that implicated Marjorie; it could mean the difference between a life sentence and a verdict that carried the possibility of eventual parole.

As for the checks, there had to be some other explanation—one that only Marjorie could provide. I tried calling her as soon as I returned home, but she didn't pick up. I left a message on her answering machine.

Korvich was right about one thing: I had to tell Marjorie what he had revealed to me. Because if I was wrong—if she *was* involved in the murder of her father—she would have a much easier time if she came forward on her own. And if I was right, she needed to be warned as soon as possible about Junie's lies.

It was around noontime, and I was dead tired. I went upstairs to my bedroom to lie down. I realized something was out of place, but it took me a few minutes to realize what that was. The books on one of the night tables—Veronica's books—were gone. I checked the closet and the dresser drawer she used; the few items of clothing she had left behind were gone, too.

By design, I wasn't home when Veronica arrived the previous evening to take Melissa to dinner. I thought she would want it that way. I went to see *Indecent Proposal* instead. When I returned from the movie, Veronica had already brought Melissa home and gone back to Watertown. Now I realized that with her she took the few things she'd left behind as reminders of her presence; I hadn't noticed their absence the night before.

I lay there for a while, thinking about the power that objects have to evoke memories. After a while my musings led me to climb into the attic and survey the boxes in the corner: the inanimate remnants of my departed wife's presence.

It had been ages since I'd opened the boxes. I discovered that they were better organized than I recalled. They were divided into four piles. The first pile contained the memorabilia that I wanted Melissa to have one day: the photos, scrapbooks, and personal materials that might somehow help her absorb a sense of her mother. There were toys from Janet's childhood, poems she wrote in high school, college papers, her wedding dress—the things that Melissa was already beginning to come up to the attic to look at.

The second pile—its cartons sealed to protect them from Melissa's rummaging—contained personal souvenirs of my relationship with Janet: birthday and anniversary cards; love letters written during my second year in medical school, when Janet spent her junior year studying in France; other scribblings and miscellaneous items that were too personal to give to Melissa, and of no value to anyone else.

A third pile contained boxes of clothing and other items that I had intended to sell or give away. Somewhere along the line, I lost sight of that intention.

In the fourth pile were the remainders: things that had no manifest personal meaning, would be of no use to anyone, and that didn't fall into the category of things that Melissa would want to keep as totems or treasures. These were the mundane articles and minutiae of daily living that held no particular sentimental or functional value: underwear, outdated college textbooks, half-empty perfume bottles. More than the other piles, the continued presence of this one spoke to my reluctance to let Janet go.

Sooner or later everything except the first pile would have to be disposed of. I wondered what the hell I was waiting for. And in that very moment I knew that I had to begin the task of ridding myself of them, or run the risk of being stuck in time forevermore, like the bug in Frank Porter's chunk of amber.

The pile of reusable clothing and items seemed like the easiest place to start. I borrowed Mrs. Winnicot's station wagon. It took a half hour to carry the cartons outside and load them into the car. I forced myself to keep moving, for any delay could spell an end to the project. I drove to a Goodwill trailer in the parking lot of the local Stop & Shop and left everything with the elderly man in charge.

It was two o'clock when I returned home. I was determined to take the effort as far as I could. I loaded the cartons that held the unusable items of no clear sentimental value. And then I forced myself to cram in the sealed

cartons that held the personal reminders of my first and
most enduring love.

The town dump is directly across Route 126 from Walden Pond. If he were still alive, Thoreau would either hang
himself or laugh himself to death. The guard at the gate
told me the dump was closed to the public at that hour;
only commercial trash collectors were allowed in.

"Look—I really have to get in there."

"Sorry, buddy. No can do. I make an exception for you,
I gotta make an exception for everybody."

" 'Exceptions.' "

"Huh?"

"You said, 'exception for everybody.' It should be 'exceptions.' "

He grinned unpleasantly, and I noticed that he still had a
few teeth. "You really know how to win friends, don't you,
buddy?"

"I'm sorry. I'm at the end of my rope. In the past week
two people have beaten on me, I had to view a suicide victim, and a friend is about to be arrested for a murder she
didn't commit. My wife is dead, my girlfriend walked out
on me, and my daughter thinks I've ruined her life. And if
I don't get into the dump today, I'll never throw this stuff
away. And if I don't throw this stuff away . . . Ah, shit."

Maybe he pitied me. Maybe he thought he owed me
something for the comic relief I had provided. Or maybe he
thought I was so fucked up that the next disappointment
would trigger a string of random murders, with him as the
first victim. For whatever reason, he let me pass.

I made my way to a huge pile of trash in a corner section
of the dump. An earth-moving machine was churning over
the bags and cartons that had been unloaded there that day.

First I threw the cartons with the nonpersonal items onto
the pile. The perfume bottles broke. One carton split apart,
and three bras were lifted by a strong wind, like three pairs
of skullcaps with wings attached.

After a few minutes of unloading and tossing, only the
sealed cartons with personal items remained. I took the first

and flung it as far as I could into the huge trash pile, directly in the path of the earth-moving machine.

I turned back to the station wagon for another sealed carton. But the sound of the approaching machine triggered something in me—an instinctive need to protect something I loved from sure destruction. I wheeled around and ran into the knee-deep pile of refuse. I reached my carton just as the driver of the machine stopped short to avoid hitting me.

He jumped down from the cabin. "Jesus Christ! Are you out of your fucking mind?"

"I believe I am," I replied. "They're putting it to a vote at town meeting next month."

"Yeah, well, you're a fucking moron. Give me a heart attack, why don't you?" He climbed back to his perch and revved the engine, loud and long.

I drove out of the dump and back toward the center of town, half a load lighter than when I started.

I left a second message on Marjorie's answering machine around dinnertime, but she never called back. I tried her number again at around nine-thirty, and this time she picked up after four rings.

I said, "I need to talk with you. Can I come over?"

"I'm getting ready for bed," she replied, sounding very subdued. "Give me half an hour. I'll leave the front door unlocked for you."

I turned onto Simon Willard Road thirty minutes later. Two cars were parked in front of Marjorie's house. One looked like the car that pulled up as I was leaving the previous day. The second one bore the logo of one of the local television stations. I assumed a few members of the press were camping out there, hoping for a comment about the high-profile arrest in the death of Marjorie's father. When word of her alleged complicity leaked out, no doubt twenty times as many reporters would be there.

Parked nearby was a police cruiser. A lone officer was

leaning against the vehicle, drinking from a can. I assumed it was nonalcoholic. I assumed the push tab was still attached. And I assumed that Cornelius and Gertrude Bromley were irritated no end by the unwelcome intrusion into their peaceful upscale neighborhood.

I parked my car a couple of houses down from Marjorie's place and headed toward her front door. The police officer eyed me as I walked past him. I introduced myself.

"Yeah," he said. "I thought you looked familiar. You were down at the station with the chief earlier today."

"That's right. You must be working a double shift."

"Yeah. A pretty easy one. The chief just wants somebody out here in case the reporters bother anyone in the vicinity. Quiet neighborhood. Not much happens here."

"There was the hit-and-run, of course."

"Yeah. Ironic, isn't it? Senator Ellington introduces a death penalty bill every year. I bet he's glad now he hasn't been able to get it passed."

I let myself in the front door, then turned the deadbolt lock behind me. The first floor was dark and quiet. The hallway light on the second floor cast a dim glow on the stairwell, giving me enough illumination to see my way upstairs.

Marjorie was seated at the glass-top ornamental table by her bedroom window, gazing at the darkness outside. Her bathrobe was loosely tied, revealing most of her body from the waist up. Her hands were in her lap, cupped together, holding a small notepad. She appeared lost in thought; she didn't register my presence until I said hello. Then she turned to face me, slowly. Her eyes scanned my face in haphazard fashion, as if she were having difficulty focusing. She appeared calm, almost too calm. Still there was no clear acknowledgment of my presence.

The notepad dropped from her hands and fell under the table. "I'll get it," I said. I walked toward her to pick it up. When I kneeled down, I saw the note she had written:

Dearest Harry,

I told you that day in the cemetery: I bring trouble with me wherever I go. Time now to break that cycle. When a limb turns to decay, you sacrifice it to stop the rot from spreading.

I'm sorry for my father. I'm sorry for Junie. I'm sorry for complicating your life. May God forgive me. If there is an existence beyond this one, I know I will be thinking of you.

I noticed now that her pupils were dilated. Her breathing was shallow. A blue-gray tinge was overtaking her natural skin coloring, especially on her lips and her nipples.

I looked at the table. There I saw her vial of Elavil: on its side, cap off, empty. The vial had been full two days earlier, with enough medication in it to last a month. Even at her low dosage, the vial had contained more than two thousand milligrams of the drug—enough for a substantial overdose. I was observing typical symptoms: confusion, impaired concentration, and drowsiness.

She had asked me to wait half an hour—long enough for the overdose to begin working. If her stomach didn't get emptied very soon, she had enough medication in her to cause congestive heart failure.

I moved quickly to the nightstand on the other side of the room. I picked up the telephone receiver and pressed it to my ear. The line was dead. I tried to get a dial tone, over and over, to no avail.

Behind me, a trembling male voice said, "I took the kitchen phone off the hook so you wouldn't be able to use it."

I placed the receiver back in its cradle and turned around. Carter Ellington Jr. was standing in the middle of the room, directly between Marjorie and me. Marjorie turned her head slightly in our direction, but she didn't appear to comprehend what was happening.

I stood. "I'm going downstairs to hang the phone up, and then call an ambulance."

His eyes were red, as if he had been crying. "I don't think so."

He wiggled his arm at his side, drawing my attention to the blue-steel revolver he was holding.

I said, "She'll die if we don't get help."

"I know."

Now I noticed the latex gloves he wore. I thought: No fingerprints. "Is that one of her father's guns?"

He nodded, then began slowly raising the gun into firing position.

Just then, behind him, Marjorie's body jerked violently. Then she slumped forward, her head crashing into the glass top of the ornamental table.

The sudden noise diverted his attention for a brief moment. He twisted halfway around to see what was happening. In the instant he was turned, I charged toward him. He whirled back to face me a split second before I plunged into him. He pulled the trigger, but he was out of position; he fired wildly in my general direction. The sound echoed off the walls and windows.

I crashed into him, full force. The gun flew out of his hand; I heard it hit the floor several feet away.

My momentum carried both of us to the wall. The back of Junie's head struck against it, dazing him for a few seconds.

I felt an odd sensation—a burning wetness, just below my left shoulder—and I knew I'd been shot. In the distance, I heard someone pounding against the deadbolt-locked front door.

Inside my blood-soaked shirtsleeve, I felt no sensation in my left arm. I tried to keep Junie pinned against the wall with the weight of my body, but he was too strong for me. He threw me off as though I were an insect. I fell onto my back, sprawled out across the floor.

I pulled myself to a seated position. I scanned the room, looking for the gun I had knocked from Junie's hand. Both of us saw it at the same instant. It had slid partway underneath the oak dresser near the foot of the bed; only its barrel was visible. Junie was closer to it than I was. He moved toward the dresser. I thought, My daughter will be an orphan.

I rose into a crouched position. I tucked my chin against my chest. I pulled my right arm tightly across my chest. I sprang forward, leading with my right shoulder, launching myself toward him with all my remaining might. I rammed him in the small of his back. He smashed into the dresser.

First his head snapped back, and then it propelled forward in a whiplash motion. It smacked hard against the protruding edge of the oak dresser. In a flash, his entire body went limp. He slid down the side of the dresser until he was on his knees. His face was still pressed against the sharp edge. Blood began to leak from one of his ears.

I heard glass shattering downstairs, the sound of someone hurling his body through one of the windows. Then I heard people running toward and up the stairs.

I struggled to my feet and moved woozily toward Marjorie. She was wedged awkwardly between her chair and the table, precariously placed, looking as if she were about to tumble onto the floor. I kneeled next to her, grabbed her hand, and searched frantically for a pulse, a reflex, any sign of life. I found none.

The police officer from outside appeared in the doorway of the room, his gun drawn. Immediately after him came three reporters, one of whom aimed a video camera at me as I looked in vain for Marjorie's pulse. Then the cameraman panned across the room, focusing on Junie's inert form where it leaned against the dresser.

The police officer whistled, an exclamation of surprise and dismay. He faced the reporters. "Okay, all of you. This is a crime scene. I want everyone downstairs, now."

There were murmurs of protest, but the reporters complied with his direction. As he ushered them from the room I noticed the notepad with the suicide note on the floor near Marjorie. Her message was personal, directed only to me; I didn't want to share it with anyone. I picked up the notepad and placed it in my pocket.

The police officer turned back to face the carnage. I lowered Marjorie's hand gently into her lap. "She's dead," I said. "I don't know about him."

We both gazed at Junie. His body was silent and still. He was still on his knees: face pressed forward against the sharp edge of the dresser, arms hanging limply at his sides. His head was cocked at a slight angle, and the blood flowing from his ear dripped onto the plush carpet, which absorbed the liquid like a sponge.

I was sickened by the sight of his crumpled figure. I was doubly sickened to know that I was responsible for causing it. I stumbled into the bathroom and vomited in the toilet.

I stood up, felt light-headed, and held on to the towel rack to steady myself. My upper left arm felt hot near the bullet wound; my lower arm was numb. My skin was clammy, I felt chilled, and I knew I was beginning to go into shock.

I returned to the bedroom. The police officer was kneeling next to Junie.

I pulled a pillowcase from one of the pillows on the bed and began to fashion a crude tourniquet for myself.

The police officer stood up and looked at me, noticing for the first time that I had been wounded. He said, "They need a clergyman. You need a doctor." He gestured with his hands at the death scene in front of him. "And maybe you also need a lawyer."

A paramedic tended to me in the second-floor study while the medical examiner surveyed the situation in Marjorie's bedroom. The paramedic cleansed and bandaged a flesh wound on the posterior side of my left upper arm. Several times each minute the hallway was bathed in the pale blue reflected light from the police photographer's flash camera.

Bobby arrived as the paramedic finished with me. He waited until she left, then closed the door and sat down next to me. "Are you okay?"

"I've been better."

"That's quite a scene in the other room."

"Yes." I was light-headed, and my voice sounded far away. "I can't believe I killed him. I didn't have to hit him that hard."

"Listen to me, my legal genius. When you give your statement to the police, don't lead off with that particular revelation." A look of consternation crossed his face. "You didn't talk to them yet, did you?"

I shook my head. "I thought I should wait for you. And for my bleeding to stop."

"Good judgment on your part. You were pretty agitated when you called. Tell me exactly what happened here tonight."

There were two reasons I had waited for Bobby to arrive before I spoke to the police. It obviously made sense to have a lawyer present when answering questions about killing someone. And I wanted to audition my version of events for him before I gave it to the police. In the fifteen minutes it took for Bobby to get to Simon Willard Road, I had time to put together a narrative that was a blend of fact, inference, and fabrication. I intended to present that version as fact to the police; if it could pass muster with Bobby, it likely would satisfy them.

I told him about the affair between Marjorie and Junie. I described Junie's videotaped confession, and his claim that Marjorie was complicit in the murder of her father. I told him that I came to Marjorie's home that night to warn her about Junie's accusation.

I said, "Alfred Korvich showed me the tape because he hoped I would persuade her to surrender herself. But I didn't believe she was involved when he showed me that tape, and now I know she wasn't involved."

"How do you know that?"

"Because Junie told me she wasn't," I lied. "Right before he tried to kill me."

"Whoa. Back up. What happened when you got here?"

I told him about Marjorie's overdose. "Junie got here before me. He must've circled around to the river side of the house to avoid being seen. Marjorie wasn't very good about locking her doors. He came here to kill her, but she beat him to it."

"How do you know that's why he came here?"

"He told me so. He wore latex gloves, and he took a gun from Charles Morris's collection. He intended to shoot her and make it look like she killed herself."

"Why?"

"If the police believed she killed herself, they might think she did it because she knew Junie's arrest was certain to result in her own arrest. And she would only know that if she actually was guilty. So by staging her suicide, Junie would make them believe he told the truth in his confession. He was angling for a plea bargain by implicating Marjorie."

"If she didn't put him up to killing her father, why did he do it?"

"He was trying to kill *her*. He was angry at her for breaking off their affair, and he knew she often ran on Musketaquid Road before sunrise."

"This is getting pretty convoluted," Bobby said. He found a pen and some paper on a desk in the corner of the room. "I'd better start making some notes."

"Marjorie saved him the trouble of killing her. But when I showed up, he had to change his strategy fast. In the new plan, I became the distraught lover who kills himself after finding his girlfriend's body."

"Like *Romeo and Juliet*. Or *West Side Story*."

"Maria doesn't die," I said.

"Come again?"

"In *West Side Story*, Maria doesn't die. And Tony doesn't kill himself. Chino shoots him."

"Thanks for sharing that with me." Bobby sighed deeply. "Let me see if I have this straight. These are the things he admitted to you. One—he wanted to kill Marjorie Morris in the first place, not her father. Two—he lied in his confession, meaning Marjorie was innocent of any role in her father's murder. Three—he planned to kill her tonight to cover his tracks. And four—Plan B called for him to kill you instead." Bobby raised an eyebrow and scratched his head. "What I can't figure out is, why the hell would he tell all these things to *you*?"

I shrugged. "I kept asking questions, stalling for time. And he was pretty nervous. I think he liked having a chance to think everything through out loud. I guess he figured it didn't matter what he told me, since he was going to kill me."

Bobby took a minute to consider everything I had told him. Then he asked, "If Marjorie was innocent, why did she kill herself?"

"She tried to do it before. Who knows why anyone ever commits suicide? She had an unhappy life. She was being medicated for depression. Her father's death started her final slide. Learning that he was killed by her former lover probably took her over the edge."

I remembered Marjorie's words the day before: *I think I need a different life. I'm just so tired. When will it all end?* Perhaps I hadn't listened closely enough.

Since Monday night, I'd wondered if being more attentive to Michael Cafferty's concerns about Theo Richardson might have prevented a suicide. Now I was wondering the same thing about Marjorie.

I said, "I think it may be time for me to retire from psychiatry."

"Why?"

" 'No one who, like me, conjures up the most evil of those half-tamed demons that inhabit the human breast, and seeks to wrestle with them, can expect to come through the struggle unscathed.' "

"What are we—back to Shakespeare again?"

"It's something Freud wrote in one of his case studies."

"What does it mean?"

"Shit, Bobby—what does any of it mean?"

Bobby pondered my story for a couple of minutes. "So Junie was screwing her," he said. "Jesus, things sure have changed since I was in high school."

There was one more part to my version, one final embellishment to try on my best friend before reporting it to the police. I said, "Her shame about their relationship may have contributed to her suicide. She probably knew Junie would reveal it. He was already blackmailing her."

"What do you mean?"

"He demanded money from her, said he would tell school officials about their affair if she didn't pay him. She'd already paid him four thousand dollars."

"Marjorie told you that?"

"Junie told me that."

"Is there anything else he told you that I should know before you give a statement to the police?"

"No. That's it."

"How did you escape?"

I told him about Marjorie's final collapse and how it diverted Junie's attention long enough for me to lunge at him. Then I described the struggle that ended with his death.

"I still can't believe I killed him," I said.

"What do you think you were supposed to do? Talk him into handing you the gun? You're not that good a therapist."

The door to the room swung open. Alfred Korvich was standing in the hallway.

Bobby said, "Come in, Chief. Don't feel as though you have to knock."

Korvich ignored Bobby's sarcasm. He looked at me, gestured toward Marjorie's bedroom and the carnage there, and said, "You live an interesting life, don't you, Doc?"

He waited for my reaction. When there was none, he called down the hall for a detective he had brought with him. The two of them took seats in the study with us, and I repeated the narrative I'd just delivered to Bobby.

He pondered all of this for a minute or two, then said, "My officer tells me you were only here for a few minutes before he heard the gunshot. Ellington seems to have crammed a lot of information into those minutes. I guess that's because you're such a terrific listener."

With a gesture of his hand, Bobby cautioned me not to respond to Korvich's goading.

Korvich rubbed his chin, which was sporting something well beyond five o'clock shadow. "How do I know you're not the one who came here with a gun?"

"You won't find my prints on it."

"Maybe you wore latex gloves."

"Perhaps you'd like to search me. Or maybe you think I ate them."

Bobby said, "Come on, Chief. Carter Ellington Junior was the one wearing latex gloves. Do you think he came here to do a rectal exam?"

Korvich's detective laughed at that remark. Korvich scowled at him, then sighed. "Ah, what the hell. Only two people know the whole story, and the medical examiner tells me their talking days are over."

27: Raise the Dead, Heal the Living

"I just saw you on the Channel Five early-morning news," Veronica said. "Are you all right?"

Her call had awakened me. "Is it in the newspaper, too?"

"No. The story must have broken too late to get in. Are you all right?"

"I don't know. Let me see."

I pulled myself into a sitting position in bed. Sharp pains coursed through my left upper arm. My neck was stiff from ramming into Junie.

I said, "I'll live, if you can call this living."

She paused. "I'm sorry about your friend."

"Thank you."

She paused again. "Did you love her?"

"I don't know how to answer that."

"Did you *tell* her that you loved her?"

"No."

"Did she tell *you*?"

"Not in so many words."

Veronica thought about that for a moment.

I said, "I'd really like to see you."

She hesitated. "I'm sorry, Harry. I don't think that would be a very good idea."

We said good-bye.

Did you love her?

I hadn't thought of that word in connection with Marjorie

while she was alive. Yet hearing Veronica pose the question, I didn't recoil in repudiation of it.

I didn't have an answer now. Perhaps one day I would. For if Janet's passing taught me one thing, it was this: Relationships continue beyond death. They live on in your mind after the lost one is gone. You examine new experiences in the context of that old relationship. And at the same time—and this was the lesson—you reexamine and re-form the old relationship in the context of those new experiences.

It would take some time to figure out how I felt about Marjorie Morris.

My telephone rang again. It was Father John Fitzpatrick. He, too, had seen the morning news and was calling to inquire about my well-being.

I asked, "My physical well-being, or my spiritual well-being?"

"Both."

"The physical is adequate. The spiritual is terrible."

"Why, Harry?"

"Because a friend is dead. Because I killed someone. Because I'm a liar and a sinner, and I don't know what to do about it."

He thought for a moment. "You can pray for the soul of your friend. You can ask forgiveness for the killing and the sinning. All of this is easy to say. It's not always easy to do."

"That's for sure. I've never been much for praying."

"Would you like me to pray for those things?"

"I guess it couldn't hurt."

He chuckled. "I'll take that as a yes. And as for the lying, you can resolve to be truthful. This, too, is sometimes easier said than done."

Before he hung up, he told me I could call him if I wanted to talk about anything. I thanked him but I knew I probably wouldn't take him up on that.

You can resolve to be truthful. I walked down the hallway to my daughter's room. She didn't respond when I knocked. I entered her room and gently shook her until she began to stir.

"*Dad-dee!* My alarm didn't go off yet. It's not time for me to get up."

"I'm sorry, sweetheart, but I have to talk to you about something very serious." I sat on the edge of her bed.

"Uh-oh. What is it?"

"You asked me why Veronica left, and I told you it was very complicated."

"I know. I hate it when you say that."

"Well, I've been thinking about it, and it's actually very simple. She left because she knew I was seeing another woman."

A look of palpable dismay crossed Melissa's face. "Who?"

"Marjorie Morris. The woman who said hello to us at Merriam's Corner a week ago Sunday."

She thought about that for a minute. Then she tightened her hand into a fist and smacked it against her mattress. "No *wonder* Veronica is so sad. How could you *do* that to her?"

"These are complicated things for someone your age to understand."

She smacked her palm against her forehead. "There you go again. Please go away. I want you to leave me alone."

"There's more I have to tell you. Because you have a right to know, and because you're going to be hearing about it when you go to school today."

Her eyes widened. "You mean, *everybody* knows about you and her?"

"She committed suicide last night, Melissa. I was there when she died, but I was too late to save her. Someone else was there, too, and he tried to kill me. He shot me."

"He *shot* you?" she screeched.

I rolled the sleeve of my bathrobe up to show her the bandage. "I wasn't hurt badly."

Her jaw dropped open. Her face lost its color. She was

silent for several seconds, and then said, "Daddy, this is making me so scared."

I pulled my sleeve back down. "It's all over now. But I was afraid, too."

"Were you scared of dying?"

"I was afraid of never seeing you again."

I touched her cheek with my fingertips. She placed her hand on them, pressing them to her face. "What would happen to me if you died?"

"I'm not going to die, sweetheart."

"But what would happen?"

"There's nothing to worry about. I promise. Honest."

She was old enough to realize that only a fool makes promises about things he can't control. She was inviting a discussion about my mortality and her fears of being parentless—something I had never done with my own parents even as an adult. I wished I had a more satisfactory reply for her, but I was treading on the border of the land of my greatest ignorance.

Melissa said, "Is the man who tried to kill you in jail?"

"No."

"Dad-*dee*!" she cried, obviously frightened.

"It's all right. He can't hurt me again." I hesitated. "He's dead."

"I don't understand."

"I killed him, Melissa."

"You shot *him*?" She was incredulous.

"No. I killed him without a weapon."

She cocked her head to one side, trying to figure out what to make of this new information.

"Are you in trouble for doing that?"

"No."

She thought for a moment, then said, "I'm glad you killed him."

"Well, I'm not."

"Why not? *He* was trying to kill *you*."

I sighed. "It's complicated."

" 'Complicated.' That's what you always say when you don't want to talk about something with me."

I smiled. "Maybe we can talk about it later, but now it's time to get up and get ready for school."

She let herself fall back against her pillows, covered her eyes with her hands, and said, "I don't want to go to school today. Don't make me. *Please.*"

"Why?"

"I want to be with you."

I thought for a few seconds, then said, "All right."

She removed her hands from her face. "Really?"

I shrugged. "Sure." The truth was, I wanted her with me, too.

As I was heading out her door she called after me. "But if I stay home from school, can I still go to my ballet class this afternoon?"

"Of course."

She smiled. "Good. I need a check for next month's tuition."

"I'll write one when I go downstairs." I turned to leave again, and she called after me once more.

"Dad?"

"Yes."

"Why can't I have a normal life?"

"Sweetheart, nobody has a normal life."

"Some are more normal than others."

"Well, I suppose that's true." I paused. "When you were younger, I could answer all your questions. Things get more complicated the older we get."

" 'Complicated.' Ugh. There's that word again."

I kissed her cheek and returned to my room.

I'm glad you killed him. The next time I was asked if I had ever killed anyone, I would have to answer, "Yes." Of course, I could lie about it. Hell, lying seemed to be the order of the day. I had lied the previous night—fluently and convincingly—to the police, and to my best friend. I asked myself why I had done that.

Junie never told me he went there to kill Marjorie. But

a person's character counts for something, and by his own admission he had the character of a murderer. Whomever he had intended to run down on Musketaquid Road—Charles Morris, as Junie said in his videotaped confession, or Marjorie Morris, as she herself suggested and as I claimed in my version—he had executed a premeditated, cold-blooded murder.

And there was more. He had attempted another premeditated murder: mine. He told me, *I took the kitchen phone off the hook so you wouldn't be able to use it.* He knew I was coming. He could have left the house before I arrived. Instead, he prepared for my arrival and planned my murder.

Besides, there was the matter of the latex gloves. As Bobby said, Junie didn't go there to do a rectal exam. Yes, I lied when I said he admitted going there to kill Marjorie. But I truly believed that I had accurately reported his intentions.

Junie didn't tell me he lied in his videotaped confession. He said nothing to exonerate Marjorie, nothing to deny his claim that she conspired to have her father killed. And he never admitted blackmailing her by threatening to tell school officials about their affair.

And maybe Junie had told the truth about that money Marjorie gave him: Maybe it really was a bounty for killing her father, rather than payment to an extortionist. The facts could fit either version. I had picked the version that suited me best. I did that because relationships *do* continue beyond death. I cared deeply about Marjorie, and having failed to save her in life, I wanted to protect her now.

No one would ever be able to tie Marjorie Morris to the hit-and-run killing. It was Junie's word against mine. One of us was an admitted murderer; the other's sins were less apparent. I would never know the truth for sure, but I couldn't believe—I wouldn't believe—that someone I had come to care for could have set out to murder her own father.

I went downstairs to start breakfast. While the coffee was brewing I went into the den to write a check for Melissa's

ballet class. I opened my desk, took my checkbook out, and
flipped it open. And then it hit me: *Marjorie paid Junie by
check.*

If I were paying someone to commit murder, I would use
cash. I wouldn't want to create a paper trail—the sort of
trail Junie used to his advantage when he gave his statement to Alfred Korvich.

But if I were giving money to an extortionist, I would
want proof of the transaction, in case I decided later to go
to the police. If I were making blackmail payments ... I
would pay by check.

I went over it a few times in my mind. The reality was:
I still could never be certain what the truth was. I remembered what Korvich said the night before—that only the
two dead people knew the whole story.

And then I realized he might be wrong.

I was waiting in the corridor outside his office when
Frank Porter arrived for work that morning. He grudgingly
invited me in. We sat across the desk from one another.

"Well, what do you want, Harry? I only have a few minutes before my first client." He pointed at the gash above
my eye and laughed. "Did one of *your* clients finally get
wise to you?"

"Fuck you, Frank. They're patients. Not clients. Not consumers. Not dinner companions at the Chinese restaurant.
You're supposed to be their doctor, not their business partner."

"Geez, calm down."

"Junie did this to my eye. He attacked me last Saturday."

"Who's Junie?"

"Don't pretend to be even dumber than you are, Frank.
Marjorie Morris told me she was coming here for some of
your world-class treatment. I'm sure you know who Junie
is."

He considered this for a few seconds. "I didn't know that
you knew her."

That much was probably true; she hadn't seen Porter in

at least two weeks, and before then she probably had no cause to bring my name up in a therapy session.

Porter said, "I just heard they arrested him for killing Marjorie's father."

"That happened two days ago, Frank."

He shrugged. "I'm a busy guy. I don't always keep up."

"Did you watch the news on television this morning? Read the paper?"

"No. Why?"

"Marjorie is dead."

"Marjorie is *dead*?"

I nodded. "She committed suicide last night."

His eyes widened. "She committed suicide last night?"

"That's what I said. And Junie is dead, too."

"How did that happen?"

"I killed him."

He looked astonished. "You *killed* him?"

"That's what I said."

"Why?"

"Because he tried to kill me."

"He tried to kill—"

"What are you, Frank—a fucking echo? He tried to kill me. I beat him to it."

"How did you kill him?"

"With my bare hands."

He bit his lip and stroked his close-cropped beard. I was willing to believe that this was the first he'd heard of the previous night's events. He thought about all of this for several seconds. "Why did you come here?"

"After his arrest, Junie told the police that Marjorie masterminded the murder of her father. I want to know if Junie was telling the truth."

"I never met him."

"You met *her*, damn it. Did she ever talk about a plan to kill her father?"

"Wait a minute, wait a minute—let me see if I'm getting this straight. Harold Kline, that great ethical psychiatrist, wants me to reveal what my client told me in confidence."

"She's dead. It doesn't matter to her anymore."

"The life is over, but the confidence lingers on." He smiled. "Hey—that sounds a little like an old song, doesn't it?"

"Don't fuck with me, Frank. Tell me what you know."

"What if I don't? Are you going to kill me, too?"

"They say it gets a little easier each time."

"I'm younger, faster, and in better shape than you, Harry."

"So was Junie. And he had a gun."

"All right," Porter said, "let's see what my choices are here. If Marjorie told me about a plan to kill her father *before* the murder took place, then I had a legal duty under the licensing law to notify the police. Right?"

"Right."

"And if I didn't notify them, that means I committed an ethical violation. You could get me in trouble with the licensing board. Which is something you'd no doubt take great pleasure from."

I didn't respond.

He continued. "And if she told me about her involvement in a murder plan *after* he was killed, my ethical obligation is to keep her statement in confidence. Right?"

"Right."

"So you want me to either admit to a past ethical violation, or commit one right now. Am I missing anything?"

"Yes. You could just say, 'That's the craziest thing I ever heard. She never discussed planning her father's murder, either before or after he was killed.' That wouldn't be much of an ethical violation, would it?"

"Yeah, well, you can forget it. Figure out what you need to know some other way. Why are you so hopped up about it, anyway?" He paused, and then a broad smile flashed across his face. "Wait a minute—I get it. You were fucking her. That's it, isn't it? And now you want to know whether she was the person you thought she was when you were fucking her."

"You're a real prize, you know that, Frank? People come

to you for help, and you convince them they have problems they never really had. You make them get sicker, and then they kill themselves. It's a wonder one of them hasn't killed *you.*"

He leaned back in his chair. "I'll be damned. You *were* fucking her. You're a stud, Harry. A hell of a stud." He laughed so long and so hard that he almost fell out of his chair.

I couldn't take it anymore. I jumped to my feet and leaned over his desk. I saw utter fear in his eyes at that moment, and it felt good. I remembered what Father John said about his boxing opponents: *I liked the sight of their blood.*

I reached out and grabbed the paperweight off his desk: the block of amber with the fossilized insect. I juggled it in my hand for a few seconds and said, "This is what it all comes down to, Frank."

I flung the amber against the wall with all my might. It shattered into hundreds of pieces, spraying shards and slivers across the room. Then I turned and walked away. When I last saw him, Frank Porter was cowering behind his desk.

Maybe it wasn't rational, but I blamed Frank Porter for Marjorie s suicide. I'd seen his handiwork in Celeste Oberlin's case; I knew how capable he was of shattering the life of someone who turned to him in need.

I thought Marjorie would still be alive if she had never become involved with Carter Ellington Jr. And it was Porter who pushed her into that relationship. He had no business being in a position that gave him the power to cause such destruction in people's lives.

I passed a pay phone on the way to my car. I stepped inside and dialed a number I had on a piece of paper in my wallet. The call went directly to him, bypassing his secretary, just as he said it would.

Warren Oberlin answered the phone with the words, "I'm listening."

"It's Harry Kline."

"Dr. Kline—I'm glad you called. I've been hearing about

you on the news all morning. I thought about calling you
to see how you are, but I thought you might take offense."

"I wouldn't."

"Good. I shall remember that in the future. What brings
you to call me today?"

"You didn't hear this from me."

"As you wish."

I said, "Frank Porter got his doctorate from the University
of Texas. He received training at the counseling center.
He was forced to take a leave of absence after a student he
was counseling accused him of trying to have sex with her.
The whole thing was hushed up. I hope you can use this information to your advantage."

"I'm certain that I can. Is there anything I can do for you
in return?"

I pondered the question. Resolve my unanswered question about Marjorie. Bring Veronica back. Ease my daughter's anger and sorrow. Forgive me for my sins. Raise the
dead and heal the living.

I said, "No, I don't think so."

"I'm curious, Dr. Kline. Why did you decide to give me
this information?"

Maybe I was doing it on professional principle: the desire to save others from Frank Porter's lethal incompetence.
Maybe my motivation was more base: revenge for Marjorie's death and the havoc in my life. Most likely, it was a
combination of both.

I said, "I'm telling you because it suits my purpose to
tell you. And it suits your purpose to know."

"We have an overlapping interest, then. Such a conflu-
ence often leads to a happy conclusion."

"Let's hope so."

"Indeed," he said. "In the meantime I am in your debt.
Remember that. I can be helpful in many ways to those
who help me."

I didn't doubt that for a second.

* * *

The weekly local paper arrived in the mail shortly after I returned home. I turned to the police log: the record of all calls received by the police department since the previous issue. The paper never printed anyone's name in the log, even those who had been arrested and charged with a crime. I don't know whether this was a reflection of the paper's practice or the police department's policy.

I read an entry that had been logged in at seven-fifteen on Sunday evening.

A Simon Willard Road resident notified police regarding a suspicious-looking vehicle parked outside her home. Upon investigation, it was determined that the vehicle belonged to a town resident who was visiting another home on that street.

I cut the item out and put it in a locked file cabinet for safekeeping. I placed it in a file with another item, one I had put there the night before: a small, inexpensive spiral notepad emblazoned with the logo of CVS, a local drugstore chain. I read Marjorie's last words one more time.

I wouldn't need any cartons for her: The clipping from the *Concord Journal* and the notepad with her suicide note were the only tangible things I had to remind me of Marjorie Morris.

28: An Act of Faith

The following Monday, May 3, there was a small memorial service for Marjorie Morris at the Dee & Son Funeral Home. I was there, as were a few students and faculty members from Concord Academy, two relatives whose names I didn't catch, and Alfred Korvich. The smallness and impersonality of the occasion made me weep.

That same day Bobby brought me the news that Frank Porter had quietly resigned his license to practice psychology in the commonwealth of Massachusetts. "The Oberlins' lawyer did some digging and learned about Porter's trouble at the University of Texas. They persuaded the young woman to come forward. They were going to fly her out here to depose her. I don't know if it would have been allowed into evidence, but Frank decided to cut his losses."

"Just as well," I said.

"I agree. He's a shining exemplar of the Equine Paradox."

"What's that?"

Bobby smiled. "The Equine Paradox goes like this. 'There are more horses' asses in the world than there are horses.' "

Later that week Michael Cafferty pleaded guilty to one count of unauthorized use of a motor vehicle. Under a plea-bargain arrangement, he was sentenced to continue his period of probation from the earlier charge, and to perform fifty hours of community service. Since the proceeding was held in juvenile court, it was closed to the public. I was there at his request to lend moral support.

Michael's father was there, too. James Cafferty didn't look like the imposing character I had imagined. He was old and frail, with a cane and a hearing aid. Juvenile-court proceedings are informal, and when Michael's father asked to address the court he was allowed to do so. He said, "Your Honor, I haven't always been a good father. But Michael has always been a good son. I just want you to know how proud of him I am for doing the right thing."

Alfred Korvich was waiting outside the courtroom when I exited. He asked me to walk next door with him to the police station. He led me once again to the conference room. "I have another tape I'd like you to see, Doc." While we were waiting for it to rewind he said, "That night at Marjorie Morris's house, did you touch her medication vial?"

I tried to remember. "Not that I recall."

"I was wondering then—why did we find your fingerprints on it?"

I thought for a moment. "I picked it up and examined it a few days earlier. I found it while I was looking through her medicine cabinet for some aspirin."

"Pretty rude, isn't it, Doc? Poking around like that?"

"Well, sometimes you . . . Hey—how do you know they were my prints? Where did you get a set to compare them with?"

He smiled. "Never underestimate ol' Uncle Al." The tape finished rewinding. "I want you to see the raw footage the Channel Five cameraman shot the night Marjorie Morris died."

The scene started outside on the front lawn. The halogen streetlight provided enough illumination to allow me to follow the action. The Concord police officer rammed into the front door with his shoulder but couldn't budge it. He ran to the living-room picture window, shielded his face with his forearms, and crashed sideways through the glass.

The video image began to jump wildly; the cameraman apparently let the camera dangle at his side as he and the other reporters followed the officer through the window. Then he steadied the camera, although the image continued to bounce as he ran up the stairs and down the hallway to Marjorie's bedroom.

Suddenly the screen was filled with the images of Marjorie and me. She was perched at an awkward angle on her chair, leaning into the ornamental table. I was kneeling at her side looking for a pulse. After several seconds the camera began to pan slowly across the room, away from us and toward the body of Carter Ellington Jr.

"There it is," Korvich said, rewinding the image for a couple of seconds. He picked the action up again just as the camera began to pan away from Marjorie and me. He froze the image on the screen. "Do you see it?"

"See what?"

"Here, right underneath the table." He pointed at a small, flat rectangular object. "It looks like one of those notepads they give away at CVS when they're having a sale."

I hesitated for just an instant. "Good eyes, Chief. That's exactly what it is."

"We didn't recover it at the scene. Any idea what happened to it?"

"Of course. I picked it up. It's mine. It fell out of my pocket while I was kneeling next to the table."

"You always carry CVS notepads around?"

I shrugged. "Sometimes."

"You wouldn't happen to have one on you now, would you?"

I made a show of checking my pockets. "Nope. Thought I might, but I don't."

"Do you think you have that pad at your home now?"

"Probably. I bet I have a half dozen of them lying around. Don't you?"

He frowned. "I'm not too pleased about you picking it up, even if it was yours. Crime scenes should be left intact."

"I guess I just wasn't thinking, Chief. Sorry."

"You're sure it was yours."

"Of course."

He looked at me for a long time, then said, "Never, ever underestimate me."

"I wouldn't think of it," I said. "And I'm completely sincere about that."

That Saturday, the day before Mother's Day, my daughter and I walked to Sleepy Hollow Cemetery and placed flowers on Janet's grave. When we went there six years earlier, on the first Mother's Day after Janet's death, there were dozens of other people making similar pilgrimages. "Let's come early the next time," my then-four-year-old daughter said that day. "Mommy needs quiet to hear us from down in the ground." We'd been coming a day early ever since.

We stood together by the gravesite, lost in private thoughts. After a few minutes, Melissa turned to me and asked, "Do you think Mommy would have liked Veronica?"

"Yes. Your mother always looked for the good in people. She would have found a lot of good in Veronica."

She considered that for a moment, then asked, "Do you think Veronica would have liked Mommy?"

"Well, that's a little trickier. Veronica has definite likes and dislikes. It's not always easy to know what she's going to think or how she's going to feel about something. But I think she would have liked her, even if only because she was your mother. She would want to like your mother, because she cares so much about you."

"I miss her."

"I do, too."

She said, "I'm talking about Veronica."

"Oh. Well, you still get to see her." She called Veronica every few days, and Veronica had come out a second time to take Melissa to dinner. I had asked again to see Veronica, and again had been turned away.

"It's not the same."

"I know."

She looked at me with tear-filled eyes. "You have to do something about this."

Early Sunday morning, Mother's Day, we called my parents in Florida. Then Melissa decided to call Janet's parents. She spoke to them for a few minutes. She was just about to hang up when I said, "Wait. Give me the phone, please." Rita Jacobs was on the line. I said hello, then asked to speak with her husband. It was hard to know who was more surprised by that: Rita or me.

"Hello, Nathan."

"Harry. Do you have another football question for me?"

"No."

"Oh."

"I just wanted to thank you for letting Melissa visit with you last month. I don't think I had a chance to tell you how much she enjoyed it."

"Oh."

"Actually, I guess I've had plenty of chances. I just haven't taken any."

"Oh."

That was it. I guess some things never change. "Well, I'll be talking to you."

"Sure thing, Harry. Take care of that kid of yours. You never know. You just never know."

Melissa went upstairs to get dressed. A few minutes later I picked up the phone to dial the weather report. I heard Melissa's voice on the line.

"I'm using the phone, Dad," she said from the upstairs extension.

"Hello, Harry," said Veronica.

"Sorry," I said. "Let me know when you're finished."

I was just about to hang up when Veronica said, "Melissa wants me to come out today for a visit. Is that all right with you?"

I sighed. "Sure. Maybe I'll go bike riding or something."

"Or you could spend the day with us," she said. "That is, of course, only if you want to."

"I'd like that."

"Well, then. That's settled."

"Yes," I said.

"Yippee," Melissa chimed in.

Thanks to a cancellation, I was able to make a reservation for Mother's Day lunch at the Colonial Inn. The three of us walked down Monument Street into the town square. The conversation was animated and friendly when all three of us were walking together; it was sparse and strained when Melissa ran ahead of us.

We got to the restaurant a little early, so we decided to walk around in the center of town for a few minutes. In front of St. Bernard's, we ran into Father John as he was heading inside for the eleven-thirty Mass.

"Harry, it's good to see you. And Melissa—do you remember me?"

"Sure." She blushed and turned away.

Father John laughed good-naturedly. He held his hand out to Veronica and introduced himself. Then he turned to me. "I can't tell you how happy I am that you've decided to come to our service today."

"Well, actually . . ."

Veronica dug her fingernails into my arm. She said, "Actually, he's been talking about coming for quite some time, haven't you, Harry?"

Father John turned to welcome some of his parishioners. Veronica said to me, "I can't believe you were about to brush that nice man off like that."

"I'm hungry. And I'm not a Catholic."

"Neither am I."

"You're a Christian."

"I'm an Episcopalian. That's different from being a Catholic."

"I'm ignorant about these things."

"And so proud of it."

Melissa covered her ears with her hands. "Stop it, stop it, stop it! I don't want it to be like this!"

I said, "All right, Melissa. You get to break the tie vote. Do we go into this church that we don't belong in, where we won't understand a single thing that they're doing, or do we eat lunch?"

Veronica said, "Nice way to load the question, Harry."

"Stop it!" shrieked my daughter. She turned away from us and walked into the church.

"Shit," I said. "I guess that settles that."

"Watch your language here, Harry. I'm deadly serious about that."

We followed Melissa to the seats she had chosen, which I thought were uncomfortably close to the altar.

After the opening processional Father John said, "May almighty God have mercy on us, forgive us our sins, and lead us to everlasting life."

It may have been my imagination, but I thought he was looking directly at me. Forgive us our sins, I thought. Easier said than done.

I hadn't been inside a house of worship since Janet died. Whatever faith I once may have had, it seemed to evaporate in the wake of her death. I didn't think it would ever come back, however I might long for it.

Lost in thought, I missed the first part of Father John's sermon. Toward the end I heard him say, "God calls on us to love people we don't like, absolutely and completely. He calls on us to forgive people who have hurt us, absolutely and completely. When He walked the earth, the Lord showed us perfect love and the forgiveness of sins. To live with Him in eternity, we must strive to follow His example in this life."

They were admirable sentiments. But I had a hard enough time loving the people I loved. And I was having a hell of a time liking or forgiving myself.

He continued. "Today we honor our mothers, whether they be on earth or in heaven. In the year I have been with you in this beautiful town of Concord, a number of you have lost your mothers. I know your names. I have shared your tears. I see you here today. But the Lord brings us good news—that whosoever follows Him shall dwell with Him forever in the kingdom of heaven

"For those whose mothers are among us still, let us offer a prayer of thanks. And for those whose mothers have left this world, let us pray that they be in the house of the Lord, where one day we will join them—where time is eternal and souls dwell in communion with God, and with one another."

I turned to my left, wondering what effect the priest's words were having on my daughter. Melissa was holding Veronica's hand, squeezing it tightly, as Veronica wept silently and profusely.

Outside the church, Father John shook my hand and thanked us for coming. Then he put an arm around my shoulder and whispered in my ear. "I know you think you don't believe in anything, Harry, and that you have no faith. But just remember—even *wanting* to believe is an act of faith."

"You cast a pretty wide net with that statement."

"I know. That's the whole idea."

As we walked away Veronica asked me, "Do you know where Mount Auburn Cemetery is?"

"Sure. On Mount Auburn Street, interestingly enough."

"Take me there, please. I want to visit my mother's grave."

Melissa and I stayed a respectful distance from Veronica as she approached her mother's grave for the first time in more than twenty years. She carried the flowers we bought on our way to the cemetery. After a while she waved, beckoning us to join her.

The tombstone was set beneath blooming cherry trees on the Cambridge hillside. Veronica touched it and said, "My mother's name was Rachel. It means 'like a lamb.' "

"It's a beautiful name," I said.

Melissa stared at the dates on the stone. "She was only

thirty when she died. That's even younger than my mother was."

"I've never visited her grave before, not since the funeral when I was nine years old."

"I know," I said.

"How did you know that?"

"Your father told me. I think he was hoping I'd persuade you to come here."

She smiled. "You have my permission to take full credit for it."

Melissa said, "Veronica, can I ask you a question?"

"Of course, honey."

"How did your mother die?"

Veronica glanced at me, asking without words for permission to answer my daughter's question. I nodded.

"She was killed by a man who broke into our house to rob us. My father wasn't home. She died trying to protect me."

A look of utter despair flashed across Melissa's face. "You were there?"

"Yes."

"And you saw it happen?"

"Yes."

"Oh, no!" Melissa began to wail, loud enough to draw attention from visitors at other gravesites. "That is so awful!" She fell into Veronica's arms and cried.

"It's okay, honey," Veronica said. "It's okay now."

Melissa stepped back. "Did they put the man in jail?"

"No, honey. They never caught him."

"But they *have* to catch him! *You* have to catch him! Can't you get the FBI to help you? *I'll* help you if you want." She paused. "I didn't mean to make you cry."

"That's okay, honey. These are good tears. I'm crying because you're such a sweet, wonderful girl, and because I love you so very much."

We stepped out of my car and stood between the house and the barn. Veronica spoke to my daughter. "I need to discuss something with your father for a few minutes. If you wait for me in the field, we can go for a walk afterward."

Veronica waited until Melissa was sitting on the grass, about thirty yards away. "When is Mrs. Winnicot moving?"

"July first, give or take."

"Have you decided what to do with the space after she's gone?"

"No."

"I know someone who might want to live there."

"Oh? Who?"

"Me."

"You're *kidding*."

"Think about it, Harry. It wouldn't be so bad. I could help you with Melissa. She needs a woman around her." She paused, then cast her eyes downward. "And I need her around me."

"I don't even know if the zoning laws would permit me to have a tenant."

"Mrs. Winnicot is a tenant."

"She's an employee. I think the rules are different. Anyway, even if the town would let me have a tenant, I wouldn't feel right charging you rent or signing a lease or anything like that."

"Excuses, Harry. Just excuses. Don't let them get in the way."

I thought about it for a few minutes. "I suppose if it isn't working out, you can always go back to your place in Watertown."

"No. If we're going to do this, we're going to do this right. I'll sell my condominium."

"Is that smart? If you sell it without buying another place, won't you take a beating on the capital-gains tax?"

She smacked her palm against her forehead. "Come *on*, Harry. I'm trying to get this deal done. Work with me on this."

My daughter was watching our every move, trying to

ascertain from our body language what was happening. I said, "Did you already mention this to Melissa?"

"Of course not. It's not my place to do that."

"What about us? Would I be allowed to visit?"

"The landlord always has a right to inspect the premises." She smiled. "If he plays his cards properly, he may even have the right to inspect the premisee."

"There's no such word."

"There is now. Come on, Harry. I believe we could make it work. What do you think?"

I felt a wave of energy pass through me, as if a great weight were being lifted from my shoulders. I said, "I think that even wanting to believe is an act of faith."

She laughed and said, "I have absolutely no idea what you're talking about. But it sounds like we have a deal."

"What do we do now? Do we shake hands on it?"

"We could." She moved closer to me. "Or we could seal it with a kiss."

Veronica fell into my arms and we held on to each other tightly. I said, "I wish I didn't have to let go of you."

"You don't."

Off in the distance, my daughter leaped as high as she could, her arms outstretched toward the heavens.

Here's a sneak preview of Philip Lubers next harrowing tale, **PRAY FOR US SINNERS**. Coming next year from Fawcett Books.

I let myself into the barn and climbed the stairs to Veronica's apartment. I walked through the living room and into the bedroom.

Veronica was sitting on the edge of the bed, toweling herself dry from her shower. She watched me set the folder with the murder materials on her dresser. "Put it in the safe," she said. "Melissa may come over in the morning. It's not a healthy thing for an eleven-year-old to see."

I thought: *It's not a healthy thing for anyone to see.* I opened the small safe that doubled as a nightstand. I placed the folder on top of Veronica's service revolver. Then I shut the door and spun the dial.

"Are you staying here tonight?"

"Yes," I replied.

"Did you remember to leave a note for Melissa?"

"She was still awake a few minutes ago. She knows I'm here."

She nodded toward the bed. "I don't think I feel like . . . you know, doing anything."

"Me neither." I kicked off my shoes and began to get undressed.

She asked, "What did you think of the materials?"

I hesitated. "It's sad beyond words."

She sighed. "I couldn't bring myself to look at the pictures. I had a hard enough time just reading the reports." She looked at the floor for several seconds. "What do you think I should do, Harry?"

I didn't know what to say. "Let me take a shower first. Then we can talk about it." I grabbed a towel, walked into the bathroom, and turned the water on full force.

I was worried about her. Her depression had ripened for several weeks. I knew it was related to the murder I had spent the previous hour reading about.

I couldn't bring myself to look at the pictures. Over the years Veronica had visited dozens of murder scenes. Before she moved over to the FBI, she prosecuted homicide cases. So she was no stranger to scenes of utter depravity: She walked in them, studied them, sifted through the evidence . . . all in the name of justice, and all without blinking an eye.

But Rachel Pace's murder was different. And Veronica couldn't bring herself to look at the pictures.

I crawled into bed and made sure the covers on my side were tucked firmly in place, lest Veronica pull them off me during the night. *You always thrash around when you sleep.* I moved toward her. Her back was facing me; I placed an arm around her waist and kissed her lightly on the neck. The fire glow reflected off her cheek.

She said, "I've never had a fireplace in my bedroom before. It soothes me."

"It was Janet's idea. She thought that when Melissa grew up we would give the house to her, and we'd move over here. She had it all planned out. I guess things have a way of not working out like we plan them."

"I know." She brushed her dark curls off her face. "It still bothers me sometimes when you talk about your wife. Maybe someday it won't." She turned around. "Harry, please tell me. What do you think I should do?"

I knew she was talking about Rachel's murder again. "Any reasonable person in your situation would have a hard time deciding."

"Don't talk to me like I'm one of your patients. I need to know what's on your mind. What do you think I should do?"

I held her in my arms and said, "I think you should let it be."

She pressed her cheek hard against my chest and wrapped her arms tightly around me. "I guess I should," she said. "But I can't." She trembled silently, and I felt her tears dropping onto me. In our year and a half together, I had seldom seen her cry.

Veronica turned away again and stared at the fading fire.

She said, "When I was in school I read a play about a man whose spirit was forced to wander in limbo until the person who killed him was brought to justice. And that's how I think of her. She's out there, somewhere ... wandering ... and I have to do something to help her rest in peace."

Nothing is worse than having to watch helplessly while someone you love suffers. I went through it with Janet when the cancer devoured her. I had done it with Melissa countless times, over sorrows large and small. When the only thing you can do is love someone, love never seems enough.

I rested my hand on Veronica's side. "Whatever you decide to do, I'll help you any way I can."

She clasped her hand over mine: tightly at first, then more weakly as she drifted off to sleep. She said. "Her last words to me were, 'We'll always have each other.' "

And as the flames died and the embers cooled, just before she fell into a fitful slumber, Veronica Pace murmured, "I have to know.... Who killed my mother?"

Published by Fawcett Books.
Coming in 1998 to a bookstore near you.

PRAY FOR US SINNERS
by Philip Luber

MURDER ON THE INTERNET

Ballantine mysteries are on the Web!

Read about your favorite Ballantine authors and upcoming books in our monthly electronic newsletter MURDER ON THE INTERNET, at **www.randomhouse.com/BB/MOTI**.

Including:
- What's new in the stores
- Previews of upcoming books for the next three months
- In-depth interviews with mystery authors and publishers
- Calendars of signings and readings for Ballantine mystery authors
- Bibliographies of mystery authors
- Excerpts from new mysteries

To subscribe to MURDER ON THE INTERNET, send an E-mail to **srandol@randomhouse.com** asking to be added to the subscription list. You will receive the next issue as soon as it's available.

Find out more about whodunit! For sample chapters from current and upcoming Ballantine mysteries, visit us at **www.randomhouse.com/BB/mystery**.